Dark
Minds

MICHELLE DIENER

ECLIPSE

DEDICATION

To my family, you are awesome.

Chapter One

THE CHANGE IN MOOD ONBOARD the runner slowly forced Imogen Peters to come back to herself. The small crew's tension wound around her like a choking vine, tightening until she couldn't ignore it any more.

She was becoming more withdrawn as the days passed or she would have noticed the quicker movements, the sharper focus in the ten-person team much sooner.

She lifted her hands from where they rested on her knees, thumb and forefinger together, and stretched out legs that had been in the lotus position for . . . she didn't know how long.

Her escape into her own head seemed to run on its own clock. Sometimes she lost track of time all together, her days punctuated only by meals.

Now, the usual easy routine she was familiar with was gone.

Three of her guards were donning body armor and checking shockgun settings and she stared in disbelief. Could they have finally reached their destination?

Because they didn't have anywhere else to put her, they kept her in a corner of the staff lounge and it gave her a view of most of the bridge and the massive screen on its far wall. All she could see now was the darkness of space, just like she had for the last two weeks, except when they'd first got underway, and she'd watched the planet Balco fall away behind them.

"Are we there yet?" she asked, unable to help the faint smile that came with her words, but Fri, her usual guard, wasn't even looking at her.

Lieutenant Baq walked toward them, shoving his shockgun into a thigh holster as he came.

"Get suited up," he said to Fri. "We'll need everyone armed."

"Are we landing?" Imogen directed her question to Baq this time.

He shook his head, too distracted to respond, but before Fri moved away, Imogen reached out and grabbed his jacket.

"What's going on?" she asked.

He jerked free. "Krik," he said.

Imogen stared after him as he moved toward the far wall to grab some body armor.

She'd had plenty of cryptic words to decipher in the last three months, and she was pretty sure whoever or whatever the Krik were, it wasn't good.

From the corner of her eye, she caught movement on the large screen, and turned to stare at a large vessel inching its way across their bow.

The crew reacted as if the bogeyman had just jumped out from under the bed, wielding an ax.

They readied themselves for a confrontation, voices raised, until all other sounds faded and their movements seemed to be set to the jerky soundtrack of her heartbeat.

They'd been crammed on top of each other, in what was surely meant to be a short-range, day tripper vessel, for fourteen long days, and Imogen knew every single crew member.

Their fear scratched at her, looking for purchase, and she tried to shake it off.

The enemy of my enemy and all that.

Only, as a counter to that piece of wisdom, there was also *better the devil you know.* She was caught between two overused idiomatic expressions.

She turned her attention to the captain, trying to work out what he was calling to his team, the Tecran he was using faster than she was used to and full of abbreviations and military codes she didn't know.

Fri caught her eye, his hands holding his helmet over his head, the feathery protrusions on his neck sticking up in alarm. The look he gave her was one of seething resentment and then he pushed the helmet down, and she saw nothing except a black, glossy reflection of herself sitting on the long couch that was her prison cell.

It was like a slap.

She had managed to convince herself that Fri liked her.

Maybe he did. But it seemed he also now blamed her for his being here, in a tiny vessel without Tecran military support and the Krik approaching.

Which was unfair in so many ways, but then, as she'd learned in the last two months, life wasn't fair. The less time you spent whining about it, the better off you were.

She hadn't whined.

She'd learned Tecran on the handheld they'd given her instead.

Her guards had been surprised when she'd said her first, stumbling words in Tecran. Uncomfortable, even. Because she'd been kept in a cage in a massive storage room of exotic animals from all corners of the galaxy at the time, and her speaking and making sense drew the whole exercise into a darker place.

Slowly, though, they'd become proud of her progress, spending time talking to her every day, teaching her the swear words and rude idioms and expressions the handheld did not. She'd become their clever pet.

And to be honest, her French teacher would have been astonished, too, at how quickly she'd become fluent.

Imogen hadn't been one of her best students, but then, Mrs. Ventor had not taught French the way Imogen's handheld had taught her Tecran. It used ways of learning Imogen hadn't encountered before, ways that she found easy and interesting, and as a teacher herself, she'd been fascinated by.

Or maybe her progress was a life and death thing.

Because understanding what was being said around her might save her life. Even if it was just making herself the cute mascot that they'd find hard to kill if ever given the order.

She'd learned Grihan, too, but quietly, when she was alone in the menagerie hidden deep underground on the planet Balco, with only the other animals for company.

The Grih seemed to be all her guards talked about when they spoke among themselves, and it had been a happy discovery when she'd found that Grihan was one of the five languages on her handheld.

The Tecran were worried about the Grih, and there was that whole *enemy of my enemy* thing again.

It couldn't hurt, she'd reasoned, to be able to communicate with your enemy's nemeses, should you encounter them.

But she'd never even heard of the Krik.

Lieutenant Baq passed Fri as he finished checking his shockgun, and said something to him about her——she saw it in the way both their gazes cut across the room to where she sat.

Fri gave a nod, walked over.

"Please tell me what's going on. Who are the Krik?"

"Pirates." Fri's voice was slightly disembodied from behind the helmet. "Tecran High Command has an agreement with them that they leave us alone, but they aren't responding to us, they just keep coming." He bent and suddenly she knew exactly what he was doing.

"The force field?" She stared at him as he lifted his head briefly and then back down to the panel at his feet as he punched in a code.

The force field that had been installed around the couch she was sitting on powered up and encircled her. Impenetrable. Deadly.

"We need all hands, no one can guard you, so this will keep you safe from them." Fri made the explanation with a shrug of his shoulders.

When she'd first been marched out of the facility on Balco into this small vessel, the force field had been activated immediately. But it had an irritating hum, and it chewed power, apparently, and really where was she going to go? There were only two main rooms, plus the sleeping quarters. And she was outnumbered ten to one.

After about twelve hours, they'd turned it off and never touched it again.

"You think they're going to attack?" Imogen asked.

Fri lifted his hands up as he turned back to the bridge. "It's what the Krik do."

Chapter Two

THE CAPTAIN ALLOWED THE KRIK TO BOARD THEM after they fired two shots. The Tecran runner couldn't outgun them and it was too late to run.

"We need to sort this out face to face," he said, but Imogen heard the bravado in his voice.

They all had.

And still, what choice was there?

While the Krik linked the ships, the captain called High Command over and over, telling them what was happening. He received no answer.

She'd expected aggression, the crew would not be so afraid of the Krik if they didn't have a reputation for it, but she hadn't expected the level of it. They weren't here to parlay.

They seemed intent on extermination.

At her first sight of the Krik, she was struck by their elegance. They were slim and graceful, and their white hair and peach skin were as surreal to her as they were pretty.

But their eyes . . . red, like a white rabbit or white rat.

And their teeth.

They came onto the bridge dragging Lieutenant Baq, who'd been waiting to greet them, by the back of his uniform, teeth bared.

Long, sharp incisors. If they'd thrown back their heads and hooted like baboons, she wouldn't have been surprised.

Baq was dead, she realized——everyone realized——when they threw him down in front of the captain.

And then the bloodbath began.

***

The Krik wanted to kill her.

Imogen could see the need for yet another death in their eyes, in the way they held themselves, clenched and angry as toddlers denied.

The force field was impenetrable, and they didn't have the

code to disable it.

She wondered if, when they calmed down and got hold of themselves, they'd be able to do it, and shivered at the thought.

They were definitely less volatile now than when they'd started, winding down from a bloodlust high.

She curled in on herself, carefully making herself smaller as they raged.

She didn't speak their language, but then, because she hadn't spoken any of the languages around her at first, she'd gotten really good at reading body language and intonation.

More than once, the Krik pirate she guessed was the leader had restrained one of his team from throwing themselves at the wall of pale purple light around her, but the eyes he turned her way time and again were full of death, too.

She had the sense the Krik couldn't help themselves. Like Viking beserkers losing all sense of self, they had started killing and stopped when there was no one left. Except her.

Imogen had forced herself to watch each death. She was the only witness to their suffering, the mindless waste that was their slaughter.

The Krik left the bodies where they'd fallen, lying broken and still on the ship's floor.

The terror and horror at watching people she knew, even if they had been her gaolers, murdered, had slowly been replaced by a numbed state of shock.

Like before, it was the change in mood that brought her out of her mental safe place. The Krik were calm now, standing in a semi-circle around her, watching her with an intensity that hadn't been there before.

When they'd lost control and rampaged through the ship, she'd wondered how they were capable of space travel, of coexisting with a race as technologically advanced as the Tecran.

She saw now.

There was plenty of canny intelligence in the eyes of the soldiers who surrounded her. And they were an ordered team. They had a command structure and they wore a uniform, all black, which made the pastel of their skin and the white of their hair stand out even more.

They seemed to be aware she was more present than she had been, and the leader shifted the shockgun in his arms.

She forced herself to stay watchful, focusing on the tap, tap, tap of his finger on the barrel. The finger had three joints instead of two, but like the rest of him, it was long and elegant, the subtle peach of his skin darkening at each knuckle.

He made a sound and she lifted her gaze to his face to find him looking straight into her eyes. He lifted his upper lip to reveal bloodstained incisors and she couldn't stop her flinch.

"Who are you?" His Tecran was stumbling, far worse than hers.

"Why do you care?" she asked, and her voice shook. "Like to know the names of those you murder?"

He blinked at her, then looked around the room, almost as if he was seeing the carnage for the first time. Then he shrugged. "No. When the fighting spirit is upon me, I don't care."

She considered her response. She didn't want to antagonize them, that would be stupid, but she didn't know if it mattered. None of the Tecran crew had antagonized them——they had been diplomatic until Baq's body hit the deck——and that had not saved them at all.

And there was the rub.

Because she would not go out all false politeness and appeasement. She'd made a vow to herself the second week into her abduction. It would be with a bang, not a whimper.

"Who," the leader said again, "are you?" There was an edge to his voice, this time.

"Imogen Peters. Who are you?"

He stared at her for a long time without responding, perhaps hoping to creep her out or make her uncomfortable.

Too bad for him she'd been an exotic, clever pet in a cage for two months, and for the last two weeks had spent every minute of the day in open view. She'd found a way to ignore the stares long ago.

She stared back, face bland, eyes a little wide, showing interest and nothing else.

"I am Levek Toloco." He let out a laugh. "You're interesting."

She said nothing to that, simply looked around the room again, looked at Fri, lying on the floor like a broken doll, face turned toward her, helmet ripped off, eyes open and blank.

Levek Toloco seemed to catch her inference.

"When the fighting spirit takes us, we are not as controlled as we should be, and yes, perhaps we kill those we would otherwise find interesting. But it is what it is."

In other words, he really didn't care.

She could only guess they got too much enjoyment out of the 'fighting spirit' to want to control it.

"So what now?" she asked.

They couldn't switch off the force field. She wasn't sure she wanted them to, anyway, although soon enough she'd need food and water.

Toloco barked something at his team, and they moved off, but reluctantly. This wasn't a military organized like the Tecran she'd been with for over two months, it was more egalitarian, and the team members did not blindly obey orders. They looked more like sulky teenagers, begrudgingly doing their chores.

"Switch off the force field," Toloco said, and she suddenly realized he'd forced his team to disperse so she would feel less threatened.

He thought she knew how to turn it off. Which meant he thought she'd been put within the force field by the Tecran because . . . what? She was important?

"I can't."

"We are no longer in the grip of the fighting spirit. You will be safe."

She narrowed her eyes at him. That, she did not believe.

"Whether I am or not, I can't switch it off."

Toloco canted his head to the side. "Either you switch it off, or I'll find a way to do it for you. And you won't like the second option."

Imogen stared back at him, face as serious as his own. "I haven't liked anything I've seen of you since you and your team first set foot on this ship, so that comes as no surprise."

"Switch it off!" His voice swelled to a shout.

She jerked, blew out a shaky breath. "I can't switch it off, I don't have the code." She could tell him she was a prisoner, not a VIP, but why would she share anything she didn't have to?

He glared at her, and she wondered if he believed her but didn't like her answer, or if he genuinely thought she was lying.

"You will starve in there if we can't switch it off," he said eventually.

She gave a nod. "I know. But I can't come up with a code I

don't have."

He stared at her for another long beat and then turned away, shouting instructions to his crew. A few of them left, she guessed to go back to their own ship.

Toloco turned his back on her, and went over to the bridge, conversing with a few of his team and pointing to the controls.

She wondered where they were taking her, but then, she'd been wondering that since she'd been snatched from Earth nearly three months ago.

This was just another day at the office.

One of the original team Toloco had sent off returned, a little winded, holding a small silver device, and Toloco stared at her as he took it.

He was trying to intimidate her. Make her regret putting him to the trouble of asking a lackey to run and fetch something.

He approached her slowly, device in hand.

She kept her game face on.

It had served her so well. Expression more or less blank, eyes wide, polite interest the only emotion.

Toloco frowned. "This should switch off the field."

She nodded politely.

"You are not afraid?"

"As you said, I'll die without food and water." Imogen shrugged.

"You could die anyway." Toloco let his incisors show.

She forced her instinctive reaction down, deep down, where no one could see it. Two of Toloco's crew were dragging the Tecran's bodies into the center of the bridge, checking each one's face as if they were looking for someone. She looked over at the pile. "I'd say, given the evidence, that's more than likely."

Toloco drew in a surprised breath. "You are not afraid?" he repeated.

"What good would fear do me?" Again, she avoided telling the truth as she shrugged her shoulders.

"They are all Tecran," one of the cleanup crew reported, and then they started dragging the bodies out the room.

Toloco seemed to relax a little, and Imogen got the sense he was relieved.

The way the team had looked at the faces, perhaps they were searching for someone, someone who wasn't Tecran. And from the way Toloco's shoulders had sagged a little, Imogen guessed they were supposed to bring this person back alive.

It gave her a glimmer of hope. If they were unsure who she was, maybe she would make it out alive.

Toloco bent, touched the slim silver device to the tiny keypad embedded in the floor, and the force field shut down.

She was standing, but she had to look up as Toloco straightened back to his full height.

Then he lifted his arm and backhanded her.

Or not.

Chapter Three

CAMLAR KALOR KEPT STILL AS THE KRIK PIRATES checked the restraints on first his wrists and ankles, and then those of his team, walking between them with a cocky, arrogant stride.

As the guard bent over Pren, the only other member of his team with military training beside himself, he exchanged a look with her.

She inclined her head in acknowledgment. They would look for any weakness, any way out of this.

No help was coming. Not yet, anyway.

They'd have to do this themselves.

To his right, Yari, the fast cruiser pilot, lay still, curled on her side. The slight rise and fall of her chest was the only comfort Cam could take from the situation, because she'd been that way for over a full day. At least she was breathing. The same could not be said for her co-pilot.

His body had been dragged out half a day ago. And Cam was sure he hadn't imagined the Krik leader's concern and anger at the sight of it.

The guard who'd killed Kaoi had been reassigned, and Cam thought there had been real fear in his eyes as he'd gone.

The Krik had targeted the pilots when they'd taken the ship, but Cam and Pren both knew how to fly it.

In fact, Cam's team was stacked with experts from so many fields, he could see some of them, despite the violence, were stopping just short of taking notes as they observed a Krik attack and abduction up close and personal.

Olan actually looked like he was whispering into the thin unit strapped to his wrist, so Cam guessed it included an audio recorder. The guard had looked over at the old Fitalian a few times, though, so he didn't know how long they would let him keep it.

Even if the Krik did confiscate it, if they got out of this alive, a number of academic comms would be generated.

Cam had read enough reports of Krik attacks to know this one wasn't typical, although he was more interested in where the Krik had gotten hold of the tech they'd used to pull the hijack off.

They'd signaled the United Council fast cruiser with all the correct codes for a Grihan battleship runner, indicating distress.

Yari had been wary that the runner didn't conform to Grihan battleship standards, but there had been no question they wouldn't let it land in the launch bay. Even if they hadn't been United Council representatives, the rules regarding distressed vessels was encoded in the laws for all five UC member nations.

But the Krik hadn't just had the runner codes. Already suspicious, he and Yari had put the launch bay in lockdown as they came in, and that hadn't even slowed them down.

They'd romped through the ship with not a single door standing in their way.

A very restrained romp, Cam had to admit.

Only one dead.

Everyone had taken some injury, mostly shockgun fire, but the killing spree the Krik were known for hadn't materialized.

So, again, he circled back to the fact that this wasn't a normal raid.

"Do you think we were deliberately targeted?" Ularunda Diot kept her voice soft as she slid closer to him. The Bukarian forensic scientist's golden skin looked dull. She'd been shot in the shoulder when the Krik had breached the bridge and she winced as she settled beside him. "They must know the United Council won't ignore one of their own ships being taken, and you Grih are as rigorous as the Bukari when it comes to protecting your airspace. It makes me suspect they've been hired to stop us reaching Larga Ways and conducting our investigation."

Cam kept his gaze on the guard. "It's crossed my mind. They're being more careful than I've ever known them to be. Kaoi's death was obviously a mistake, so they want us to walk away at the end."

They both looked over at Yari, and Cam again took comfort in the rise and fall of her chest. No one had been allowed near her, not even Pren, who doubled as the team medic.

"At the end of what?" Diot followed his gaze as the guards finished their rounds and took up position just within the doorway of the staff lounge where they were being kept.

"That is the question." They were on a sensitive mission. Perhaps the most sensitive mission of Cam's career, and it would be to both the Tecrans' and Garmmans' benefit if he and his team did not succeed. But why would the Krik get involved?

Even if he and his team were made to disappear, another would be sent in their place. There would be no dropping this investigation. An inquiry of this magnitude would not just fade away.

Another Earth woman had been found.

This time, as a prisoner on a Garmman trading vessel.

Vraen, his second-in-command, had been deliberately chosen for the position because he was Garmman, so that there could be no question from the Garmman side about the team's findings.

It was an explosive development.

The United Council was already investigating the Tecran's role in the abduction of Rose McKenzie, the first woman from Earth discovered a few months ago. Tensions were high enough that they were teetering on the brink of war and Captain Hal Vakeri's message that he'd found Fiona Russell might just be the push that sent them all over into the abyss.

Stopping the investigation would only slow things down a little.

A low cry jerked Cam from his thoughts, and he looked left, saw Vraen lying prone, his bound arms lifted protectively over his head. A Krik pirate stood over him, arm coming back and up to strike another blow with the stock of his shockgun.

"No!" Cam struggled with the restraints, trying to stand, and the Krik stopped mid-swing. The eyes he turned in Cam's direction were wide and glassy.

There was a shout from the doorway, and the guard half-turned as Koi, the leader of the group, strode into the room, barking orders.

The guard lowered his weapon, his eyes on the floor. He responded in short, terse mutters, and Koi jabbed a finger at Vraen.

"You provoked him."

"How interesting," Diot said, her voice carrying in the sudden silence, her tone calm and academic. "That they blame the victim."

Koi shot her a hard look. He seemed to struggle for a moment, as if he wanted to defend his statement, and then turned back to

Vraen.

"What did you do?" Koi addressed Vraen in Garmman, but it was stilted.

"I asked him if he understood this is a United Council vessel, and when he didn't respond, I grabbed at his leg." Vraen touched his hand to the side of his head, and it came away dark with blood. "You have apprehended a UC fast cruiser going about official business. You have made a huge mistake."

Koi looked around the lounge very deliberately. The fast cruiser flying crew was mixed up with Cam's investigative team, and everyone was sitting or lying, bound and shocked, amongst the broken furniture.

"I want to make it clear." Koi turned his head and looked straight at Cam. "We do know who you are. We know whose ship this is." There was a strange mix of excitement and dread in his expression.

"Then what do you want?" Cam asked.

Koi shook his head. "You'll find out soon enough." He gestured to the screen on the wall behind Cam, which had been projecting the outside lens feed.

Cam turned to look, and felt a strange sense of disbelief. Were the Krik playing mind games with them?

"Is that . . ?" Vraen moved forward on his knees.

"A Class 5," Pren whispered.

It was, indeed, a Class 5.

It hung in space like the prickle ball decoration the cities on the Grih planet Xal lined the streets with every Turning.

Which made sense, because Dr. Fayir, the Grihan scientist who'd designed the Class 5s, as well as the illegal thinking systems that ran them, had been born on Xal.

No matter that the Grih hadn't even known what Fayir had done; that he'd hidden his completely banned designs and the thinking systems he'd made until they were discovered two hundred years after his death by a Garmman. A Garmman who'd secretly approached the Tecran to create them, to activate the thinking systems, and who Cam, and most of Grih Battle Center, was convinced had planned to take over the United Council with their unstoppable new power. They thought they had the thinking systems caged and obedient. But they had been wrong.

Since the Grih had uncovered the plot, which had gone hand in hand with the discovery of Rose McKenzie, two of the Class 5s had allied themselves to the Grih, but as far as Cam knew, the other three were still under Tecran control.

He tore his gaze away from the screen to look at Koi. "You've allied with the Tecran?"

The pirate smirked. "No. They are not our allies."

Cam frowned. If the Tecran weren't involved in this . . .

"There are other forces in this universe." Koi kept his eyes on the Class 5. "The Tecran tangled with one they shouldn't have and he took their Class 5. And approached us to be his partners." The look he sent Cam was triumphant.

"But——" Diot said, and Cam pressed his foot firmly down on her toes.

She closed her mouth.

"What does your new ally want with us?" Cam asked him.

Koi lifted his shoulders. "We'll all find out soon enough."

Cam stared him straight in the eye. "Are you sure you were wise to go down this road?"

Koi's lips thinned, but he didn't respond. With a last look at the Class 5 dominating more and more of the screen as they drew closer, he turned and pointed at Yari. "You can tend to your wounded." Then he walked out.

Pren moved immediately, and one of the guards picked up her med kit for her and placed it within reach, although he wouldn't free Pren from her restraints.

"It sounds as if the thinking system running that Class 5 broke free." Diot spoke softly as they watched Pren go to work. "Do you think the Krik know they're dealing with a rogue thinking system? Koi sounded as if he thought it was an alien life form that had taken over the ship, not that it was the ship itself."

"It may be the thinking system doesn't trust the Krik." Cam tried to think of how the Krik had been affected by the Thinking System Wars. They had ended two hundred years ago, but the effects of them were still being felt in the present. The whole region run by the United Council had suffered, and the Krik would have been no different.

Perhaps the thinking system was being cautious about revealing itself to those who might not be as cooperative if they knew what it was.

"How do you think it got free?" Diot asked. "Sazo and Bane

needed Rose McKenzie's help. So unless there's a person from Earth in there, it found a way on its own."

Cam shook his head. As Grih Battle Center's highest ranking investigator at the United Council, he'd been allowed access to the top secret reports generated after the Class 5s known as Sazo and Bane had entered an alliance with the Grih. Sazo had been further along in his self-awareness than Bane, but both had managed to circumvent some of the restraints the Tecran had put on them before Rose McKenzie had freed them fully.

And Battle Center still had no idea how she had done it. She refused to say, not even to her lover, Grihan explorer captain Dav Jallan.

If Sazo had achieved some control before Rose freed him, then it must be possible for a thinking system to find ways around the limits imposed on them to make them safe and obedient. Or, there *was* someone from Earth involved.

That was why they were here, after all. To investigate reports of another Earth woman having been abducted from her planet.

But if the Class 5 in front of them had found a way to break free without anyone's help . . .

From what Cam had gleaned from the reports he'd read, Rose McKenzie had tempered both Sazo and Bane's personalities, weaving a more careful, thoughtful tone through their interactions.

Thinking systems were banned because unrestrained, they could be cruel, murderous, and vindictive. They had the power to inflict extraordinary harm. The worlds of the United Council had burned for almost six years until every thinking system had been destroyed. Except Dr. Fayir had thought he knew better.

He'd made five more.

Designed powerful ships for them to inhabit.

And then made arrangements for the plans to be discovered two hundred years after his death.

And now the United Council was once again on the brink of war, and Cam and his team were headed straight into the heart of one of his creations.

The launch bay gel wall came into focus, and they flew into the maw of the beast.

Chapter Four

TOLOCO HAD LIED TO HER.

Harm had come to her, but then, Imogen had never believed him, anyway.

She *was* surprised she was still alive.

Toloco was responsible for that, too. After he'd beaten her the first time, in a quick, vicious burst that seemed to be almost necessary to him, he'd calmed down and refused to let anyone else on his team come near her.

He kept looking at her now, in nervous glances, his gaze lingering on her swollen eye and the lump on her cheek.

She was lucky nothing was broken, but if she looked as bad as she felt, she looked pretty bad.

That seemed to worry him.

The more he fidgeted, the deeper her sense of satisfaction.

She moved slowly, wincing whenever she shifted in her seat, and when they'd let her go to the bathroom, she might have exaggerated her limp.

That time, she'd seen Toloco swallow, hard.

They must be getting near their destination, because in the last hour or so there'd been a shift in atmosphere.

She'd been moved off the Tecran runner to the Krik's much bigger ship, and as they got underway, she'd seen the vessel that had been her prison for the last two weeks disappear almost instantly into the distance.

Toloco had put her in a corner of the bridge, much like the Tecran had done. It looked like a rest area made up of a few comfortable couches, visible from the captain's chair.

She decided he didn't trust her out of his sight, not because he thought she could do any damage, but because he didn't trust his crew not to harm her.

She wished he was wrong on the damage thing, but though the Krik weren't that much taller than she was, they were all muscle, teeth, and aggression.

She didn't have the fighting skills to take them on, even though she was in good shape. The cage on Balco had been roomy enough to do yoga and pull-ups, and when she wasn't learning Tecran or Grih, singing to Cleese or teaching him to talk, she'd had nothing better to do than keep flexible and fit.

Cleese.

She missed the ornery little bugger.

He was the only thing from Earth left with her in the end. A blue and yellow macaw, she guessed he'd probably been wild when the Tecran had taken him, but he was incredibly intelligent, and it had been at first amusing, and then comforting, to have his company.

He could whistle a mean tune by the end.

She had begged the Tecran to let him come with her when they'd taken her from her cage and put her on the runner, but Baq had laughed in her face at the idea.

Now, she was glad. She didn't think he would have survived the Krik attack.

Something caught her eye, and she turned to see the numbers and equations that had replaced the outside view of the ship some time ago had been replaced again by live feed. They were approaching a massive structure that looked like a World War Two naval mine, round and spiky.

The tension that gripped Toloco and some of his team ratcheted up another few notches.

She would have liked to simply enjoy their fear and discomfort, but she had a sinking feeling that whatever made these violent maniacs scared was something truly terrifying.

And they were taking her to it.

The screen went black as they got in close and then she saw a faint glow of pale blue wall. They headed straight for it at a slow, easy pace and then hit it head on.

Imogen braced, clamping her jaw to stop from crying out.

There was a slight hum and a minuscule shudder ran through the ship. The engines switched off, and there was a sudden silence.

Toloco stood and looked across at her.

"What was that?" she asked him, trying to keep her voice steady.

"What was what?" He frowned.

"That blue wall we went through."

"The gel wall?" He cocked his head, as if trying to work out if she was being serious.

She had the feeling she'd done the equivalent of pointing to a car and asking what it was.

Toloco looked at her more carefully. "I thought you were some funny kind of Grih, but you're not, are you?"

Funny kind of Grih?

She didn't know if agreeing would be better for her or worse, so she said nothing.

The ramp had opened while they were talking, and Toloco took a breath. "Time to go." He hesitated for a moment, as if he was going to ask her something, but then he took hold of her shoulder and propelled her toward the open door.

They had landed inside a massive space that was at least partly a loading bay. To her left was the blue wall, the gel wall, Toloco called it, and a small ship, a tenth of the size of the Krik vessel she'd arrived on, came through it while she watched.

She guessed it must be a barrier to keep the ship's air in and still let vessels in and out without having the bother of an air lock system.

Toloco had been talking in low tones to another Krik who'd been waiting for them at the bottom of the ramp but she realized they were quiet now, and she turned from the gel wall to find them both staring at her.

"You will go with Gau." Toloco waved a hand at his companion.

Gau shook his head and then said something sharp to Toloco. He pointed up at a lens attached to the wall, and then at Imogen's face.

Toloco hunched his shoulders, then straightened up. Answered back, just as sharply.

Gau shrugged, then looked at her. "Come." He spoke Grih, not Tecran, and she wondered at the switch.

He walked a few steps, turned and jerked his head impatiently.

Imogen took a last look at Toloco, but he refused to meet her gaze.

The Krik pirate thought he would be in trouble for hurting her, that was obvious, and now she had the sense he was setting something up to try and get out of it.

As she followed Gau out of the launch bay, she hoped whatever Toloco had decided to do to save his ass wasn't going to hurt as much as it had the first time.

Chapter Five

THE VANAD AND HIS FRIENDS WERE TROUBLE.

Every instinct Cam had honed over years as an investigator hummed as he eyed the mercenary and his crew.

Massive, like all of his kind, and dressed in what looked like high tech camouflage, the Vanad leaned against the wall of the holding area, almost invisible within the shadows, and watched the other occupants of the room. Standing with him was a Grihan and two Krik——the four clearly a tight-knit team.

And if Cam were to guess, smugglers or pirates.

Beside him, Pren shifted. She'd picked up on it, too.

They'd wondered why the Krik had captured them. Cam had been sure it was to do with their mission, but the moment they'd been shoved into this holding area deep inside the Class 5, that theory had changed.

The prisoners they were now sharing space with were a mixed group, the cross-section he would expect to find in the spaceways in this section of Grihan territory, so close to the Garmman border.

It was looking increasingly as if they had simply been in the wrong place at the wrong time, one of many rounded up and dumped into the hold.

There were groups of Garmman and Grihan traders, Grihan mining teams, the Vanad and his crew, and two Fitalians who stood together, placing themselves slightly apart from the rest of the crowd.

Cam had organized his own group so the flight crew and his team stood behind himself and Pren. Yari was conscious again, but she needed to sit, and they ranged themselves along the right-hand wall so she could lean against it, surrounded by her team.

He and Pren would protect the others as best they could, although the Vanad's crew were the only real threat.

The traders and miners looked capable enough, but they were subdued, and many were injured. They also had no reason to cause trouble.

"You want to ask those Fitalians if they'd like to join us?" Cam asked Olan, and the elderly scientist looked up from his thin, intertwined fingers with a jerk.

It was always hard to judge emotion on the Fitalians' faces. Their skin was far more rigid than the other members of the United Council and their eyes were huge and completely black, but Cam realized Olan hadn't even registered that some of his fellow citizens were in the room.

Cam stepped aside to give Olan a clear view. "You recognize them?"

"I . . . no." Olan glanced up at him. "But they are very far from home."

Cam looked over at the two Fitalians. The moment they noticed Olan and himself watching them, they stared back for a beat and then pretended interest elsewhere.

Olan fluttered his hands. "I'll go talk to them."

"They look like military." Pren's words were soft, and Cam gave a nod as the Fitali turned toward Olan. One of them flicked a glance over Olan's shoulder at Cam, and then focused back on the elderly scientist.

Olan began a conversation in the clicks and whirrs of Fitali, a language that Cam had never learned, and they seemed to relax. Cam could see them mentally shift from combat-ready to alert.

Olan returned to the group with the Fitali trailing behind him.

"This is Haru and Chep." Olan waved his hand in their direction and they bowed at the sound of their names. "They only speak Fitalian but they are most grateful for the invitation to join us. They were relieved to find we are envoys of the United Council."

Cam nodded in welcome, and the two nodded back. Haru looked at him a moment longer than was polite, and Cam had no problem doing the same.

"What are they doing out here in Grihan airspace?" he asked Olan.

Olan's look was bland. The crafty old man was nobody's fool. "They say they're tourists. Headed for Larga Ways. Just like us."

Cam nodded again. Pren caught his eye, disbelief in her own, and he gave a minute shake of his head.

If they *were* tourists, which he doubted, they were taking a break from their duties in the military, or a job that required military training. And while the way station orbiting the planet Balco was considered a sight to behold, Larga Ways was hardly on a sight-seeing route.

But why they were here could be sorted out later. He would rather have them in his camp than outside it.

He let his gaze sweep the room, noticed the Vanad was watching him, had probably noted the way they'd assimilated the Fitali. Then the mercenary's attention went to the door, and Cam followed his gaze.

The Krik pushed a new prisoner into the room.

She stumbled in a step, and then gasped audibly as she took in the holding area.

She looked back over her shoulder, but the door was already closing and she slowly turned to face them all.

She had been struck in the face. Her eye was swollen and there was a lump on her cheek that was turning dark.

But while he noted that and felt a frisson of shock and anger, it was what she was that riveted him.

She was short in comparison to the Grih, her hair a strange color between gold and light brown, her eyes as blue as any Grih's but without the dark outer rim. Her hair was pulled back from her face, tied at the nape, exposing delicate, round ears.

The hold had gone absolutely silent. It had gone quiet when he and his team had been forced in, too, but this was different.

She was something unknown.

Her gaze swept the room and stopped at him. They stared at each other for a long beat. He saw shock in her eyes as she looked him over. Shock and relief.

His focus was so fully on her, he nearly missed the quick, furtive movement to his right. He turned his head to look just as the Vanad launched himself forward, aiming straight for their new arrival.

***

Things had taken such an unexpected turn, Imogen felt like Alice down the rabbit hole.

It was a very merry un-birthday to her.

The instant sense of recognition of the hold had hit her first. She didn't remember anything else about the vessel she'd been abducted in, but she remembered where she'd been kept. And this was either the same place, or one just like it.

When she'd been taken, though, she'd been the only person there, with Cleese and a number of other macaws and animals from Earth as her companions, each in a cell with thin, transparent walls. The hold she stood in now didn't have the walls, it was just one big space, but the sense of recognition was profound.

And this time she was no longer alone.

The place was full of people, all alien to her except for two Krik lounging against the far wall, reminding her of hard-eyed gangsters protecting their turf.

They were all silent as they stared at her, and her fear and distress ramped up, until she made eye contact with a huge guy to her right.

He was taller than her by at least a foot, broad-shouldered and in some kind of uniform. But when she managed to really see him, to focus beyond her fear and anxiety, she felt as if the rabbit hole had taken another sharp turn.

Because he looked human.

She took a moment to savor the thought, to feel the rush of relief that she wasn't completely alone, until the details caught up with her.

He wasn't human.

But he was so like her it seemed even more amazing.

His hair was dark brown, tipped with dark blond. It was short and stood straight up on his head, so he looked like a rebel rock star from the 80s. Billy Idol without the snarl.

But it was the ears that tripped her up.

They shouldn't, not after the Tecran, with their hawk-like eyes and beaky mouths, and the Krik with their long fangs and peach skin, but they did. Because they were elf ears.

She was jolted by the reminder that there were wonders to her situation, as well as nightmares. That there had been moments since she'd been taken where she was conscious of beauty or some amazing technology or sight that had held her spellbound.

It wasn't all bad.

Until, suddenly, it was.

Someone huge, bigger than the warrior elf in front of her, hurled himself at her from the left, and for a second she tried to work out how she hadn't seen him before. He was bald and immense, his features coarse and his skin oddly thickened. A sort of rock man, like a rough clay figurine.

She stumbled back, knowing there was nowhere to go, and bent her knees, ready to use the only trick she had up her sleeve. As he lunged at her, she jumped, angling slightly to his right as she turned a tight somersault. When she'd been held in a place like this before, she'd discovered that there was slightly less gravity here than on Earth and had spent hours amusing herself by playing gymnast.

She slammed into something——someone——mid-turn, and fell. Saw boots and long legs above her. She scrambled to her knees in time to see the elf and the rock man clash with a grunt of effort.

The rock man was bigger and more muscular, but the elf had obviously been better trained.

Someone grabbed her under the arms and hauled her back, and she twisted in their grasp as she turned her head to see who it was.

It was another elf, a woman, and she gave Imogen a shake. "I'm trying to get you to safety."

She spoke Grihan, and Imogen blinked. Remembered Toloco telling her he thought she was a funny kind of Grih. If the elves were the Grih, then Toloco had probably seen her as deficient in the ear and height departments, but otherwise close enough.

She stopped fighting, got her feet under her, and pushed herself up, her gaze never leaving the fight.

The elf——the Grihan——landed a hard, fast blow to the rock man's torso and moved back, breathing hard. "You've got her, Pren?" he asked.

"Yes, sir." The Grihan woman who'd pulled her to safety got a firm grip on Imogen's shoulder, her voice as sharp and choppy as her boss's.

Imogen looked up at her, trying to gauge if she was being held prisoner or rescued.

Pren seemed to understand, because she lifted her hand, palm up. She was flanked by two strange, almost insectile people who had moved forward while Imogen had been getting up from the floor.

They were utterly quiet and something about the way they held themselves told her they were ready to fight.

The big Grihan retreated a little more, his focus never wavering from her attacker. "What can you possibly want with a hostage in here?"

The rock man straightened from the blow, hands fisted at his sides. "If you don't know, give her back."

For the first time, Imogen noticed three others had joined the rock man, ranged in a defensive pose at his back. The two Krik she'd noticed earlier and another Grihan.

"As if we'd give up a music-maker." The Grihan who rescued her scoffed, widening his stance.

His answer caught the rock man off guard. Imogen could see his confusion, but his Grihan teammate obviously understood. His eyes narrowed.

"She's no Grihan music-maker."

There was a murmur through the hold, and Imogen noticed just over two thirds of the prisoners were Grihan, the other third were a race that was slightly shorter and stockier, with bulging foreheads and deep chests.

"I think you'll find she is, and that there isn't a Grih here who would let harm come to her." He looked back at her, and she saw he'd taken a blow to the face, much like she had, and his lip was bleeding.

The look he sent her asked her to play along, but she had no idea what he wanted her to do. As it happened, she was a music maker as far as it went. A junior school music teacher who played three instruments, but given he couldn't know that, he must mean something else.

"Do you understand what we're saying?" Pren, the woman who'd dragged her out of the danger zone, spoke quietly in her ear. "Do you speak Grihan?"

"Yes, but I have no idea what you want me to do." Her response was soft, but the Grihan who'd thrown himself into a fight for her relaxed, so she guessed he'd heard her.

"Sing," he ordered her.

Sing? If she knew all the words to a Very Merry Un-birthday she'd sing that, but she was still scrambling to work out what was going on.

He angled his body to catch her gaze. "You need to sing."

It was an order, not a request, and she felt her hackles rise.

She wasn't a performing monkey, although she knew she'd filled that role more than once on Balco. To swallow her pride and play the clever pet again burned all the way down to her gut.

The crowd in the hold was murmuring now, agitated, and the Grihan frowned at her.

"Sing!"

She shot him a look she hoped cut him to the bone and drew herself up.

The line between reality and fantasy had blurred several months ago, as far as she was concerned, and so she went with *Bohemian Rhapsody* by Queen, that most mangled of songs in karaoke bars around the world.

It had the benefit of being operatic in parts, and she wanted to give maximum value here. Wouldn't want to disappoint.

She launched into it, glad she'd been singing almost as much as she'd been exercising since she'd been taken. It had been both a comfort and a way to cope and her voice had never been better, although she wasn't going to win a reality TV talent show any time soon.

She held the big Grih's gaze as she sang, ignoring everyone else around her. Her resentment at being ordered to do this changed to surprise as she saw him jolt as she began, and then go very still, his eyes wide. She'd almost say he was enraptured, but it was her singing, not Enya. It didn't make sense.

She left out the middle verses, begging to be let go——it sounded awful without a couple of people carrying their various parts——and segued into the final, bittersweet verse.

As the last note faded, absolute silence settled on the crowd like a blanket of fresh powder snow.

At last, her big Grih stirred to life. "Who will help us protect this music-maker?" He spoke quietly, not needing to raise his voice.

She didn't know what she expected, but it wasn't the wave of Grih stepping forward to join them, settling themselves in a crowd between her and her attacker.

Every single Grihan came, she realized, until the only people left on the other side of the hold were the rock man and his three companions and the high-browed, thick-chested aliens.

"That was inspired."

Imogen turned. The woman who'd murmured the words, not to her but to the big Grihan, was about the same height as herself, with a beautiful dusky gold skin tone. She moved slender hands in Imogen's direction and Imogen saw a thumb and three fingers

on each. When she noticed Imogen looking at her, she smiled, and
Imogen had to force herself not to flinch.

Her teeth were small but tapered to a sharp point at the ends.

She watched Imogen out of dark brown eyes, which, like the
tall, insect-like soldiers that had taken up a defensive position next
to the captain and Pren earlier, had no white around them.

There were five others with her behind the protective
barricade, a mix of the races that were spread through the hold, so
whatever was going on here, it wasn't along racial lines.

Most of the Grih who'd joined them jostled to catch a glimpse
of her and she found she didn't have the capacity for her usual
blank expression, she knew her astonishment at their behavior
must be plain on her face.

She fumbled mentally to work harder and faster, to get some
idea of what was happening.

The Grihan in charge seemed to have known she could sing.
He had obviously been gambling on swaying the other prisoners
to come and help him. And that meant he knew a lot more about
her than she did about him. And surely, that was impossible?

The sheer mix of aliens overturned the idea she'd built up of
how things worked from observing the Tecran. Especially after all
the muttering about the Grih she'd heard from her Tecran guards.
She'd had the sense this world was very much delineated by racial
groups.

Although, now she looked properly, she couldn't see a single
Tecran amongst the prisoners. It occurred to her that if the Krik
had dealt with every Tecran they'd come across the way Toloco
had dealt with her guards, that would make a twisted kind of
sense. They weren't here because they were all dead.

It looked like the enemies of her enemy were legion.

The Grihan leader didn't turn at the golden woman's words,
but he did address those who'd joined them. "I am Captain Kalor
of Grih Battle Center, assigned to the United Council Investigative
Unit, and I thank you for your help."

Imogen tried to work out what he was talking about, but
whatever the United Council Investigative Unit was, it impressed
most of the other prisoners.

The Grih who'd come across seemed relieved, and most of the
others, who were obviously not as big fans of live rock opera as
the Grih were, edged closer to Captain Kalor and his group,

leaving the giant and his crew of three isolated.

"Battle Center and the United Council?" The giant spat the words in disgust. He shared a look with his team.

Imogen couldn't see their eyes, but she got the impression they became more cautious.

The Grihan member of the crew gave a nod. "Right uniform."

"So what does the United Council want with her?" The giant tried to get a better look at Imogen, but the group around her shifted again to block her from view entirely.

"We protect all advanced sentients, music-makers or not. I'm more interested in what you wanted with her. You attacked very quickly." The captain shifted with the moving crowds to keep his opponent in sight.

The giant said nothing, and they stared at one another until eventually he stepped back, taking his team into the shadows against the far wall again.

The small group were very much on their own now.

Whatever was going on, she'd suddenly gone from prisoner to protected advanced sentient and revered music-maker.

Nice work if you could get it.

The captain turned to face her.

"Fiona Russell?" he asked.

Imogen stared at him for a long, long time.

Ooookay. This really wasn't funny anymore.

Chapter Six

THE EARTH WOMAN'S FACE WENT PALE, and after staring at Cam for longer than was polite, she stumbled back a step. "Fiona Russell?"

"You aren't she?" Olan asked, resting a hand on her shoulder to steady her.

She started as the Fitalian touched her, then shook her head. "No."

"Who are you, then?" Cam tried to keep his tone even, but if this wasn't Fiona Russell, then a third Earth woman had been taken from her home.

He knew the Tecran had sworn Rose McKenzie's abduction had been a terrible breach by a scientist who had lost sight of the rules, a once-off aberration. The claim from Grihan captain Hal Vakeri that he'd found a second woman was explosive enough, but if Cam had found a third . . . He felt the prickle along his arms and the back of his neck as the significance of this woman's existence became clear.

The Tecran would have no excuses left.

He needed answers from her, but he found himself unwilling to upset her more; an aftereffect of her singing.

He wanted her happy and safe, as did every Grih in the room. He'd manipulated them all to achieve just that outcome. And he would have to put that aside and do his job.

She'd been furious at the way he'd ordered her to sing, and he'd been afraid she would refuse. He'd started planning how he and Pren could take the Vanad and his team right up until she had straightened and opened her mouth.

The two Fitali who'd joined their group had moved forward when things had turned violent, something he'd noted with relief, because with their aid, it would have been an even fight.

Fortunately, it hadn't been necessary. She had sung, and it had had the effect he'd hoped on the Grih in the hold.

There were audio and visual comms of Rose McKenzie singing

on the *Barrist*, the Grihan explorer that had found her, and when
he'd watched it, Cam thought it was the loveliest singing he'd ever
heard, but it couldn't compare to being in the same room with an
Earth music-maker singing a few meters from you.

Even one that looked like she'd like to strangle you with her
bare hands.

His lips twitched at the thought.

His half-smile seemed to snap the woman out of her distress.

"My name is Imogen Peters." Her gaze flicked to Diot, then
Olan and Pren. Vraen held himself slightly apart from the rest of
the team, as he'd done from the beginning, and she barely glanced
at him. "Who are you?"

Cam gave a formal bow. "I am Captain Camlar Kalor, and this
is my team." He introduced each one by name, including Chep
and Haru and the fast cruiser flight team, and she relaxed a little.

"Pleased to meet you," she said, her tone unmistakably sincere.

"You reacted strangely when the captain mentioned Fiona
Russell. Why is that?" Diot didn't waste any time.

"Fiona Russell disappeared from a town near where I live. I
was driving toward it for a meeting when I was abducted." She
looked as if she was going to say something else, and stopped
suddenly, her eyes widening. "Is Rose McKenzie here, too?"

Cam watched everyone's heads come up in surprise.

"Yes," he said.

She flinched. "Where are they?"

Cam shook his head. "Rose is in another part of Grihan
territory. I've never met her, but I've seen visual comms of her. I've
never seen Fiona Russell, but she's the reason my team and I are
here. We had information she was being held as a prisoner on a
Garmman trading vessel."

Vraen made a sound at that, and everyone looked at him.

He looked down.

Cam kept his gaze on his second-in-command. "Fiona was
found by one of my colleagues and we were going to meet with
them at Larga Ways, a way station that orbits the planet Balco."

"Balco?" Her gaze jerked to his, eyes wide.

"That means something to you?" Cam had a sinking sensation
in the pit of his stomach as he watched Imogen Peter's lips twist
into a parody of a smile.

"Until recently, that's where the Tecran were holding me."

***

She'd obviously upset the apple cart.

Imogen leaned back against the cold metal wall of the hold, and faced Kalor. With his split lip and her black eye, they were like fighters sizing each other up across the ring.

And then, as the shouting escalated, he turned his laser focus from her, leaving her feeling suddenly bereft, and she crossed her arms over her chest, hugging herself as he tried to get some order from his team.

For a moment, it felt as if he'd seen her, right to her soul. Since she'd been taken, she'd been alternatively exotic, strange, and troublesome, but never Imogen Peters, person in her own right.

The sulky one, Vraen, who'd angled himself away from everyone while Kalor had questioned her, was punctuating every second word with a fist slammed onto his open palm, and Diot and Olan alternated between whispering into their wrists and offering their opinions into the mix.

Pren stood slightly back, watching everything with a considering gaze, and Chep and Haru looked even more dangerous and mysterious than they had before.

The only people who didn't seem to have an opinion were the group Kalor had introduced as the flight crew.

Imogen guessed they were too traumatized to care one way or the other.

"Enough." Kalor's order was low, but it held an implacable edge, and everyone stopped talking.

"You going to investigate the Balcoans' complicity now, too?" Vraen said bitterly into the silence. "They were holding an Earth woman, as well."

Kalor's jaw bunched a little. He looked like he was running out of patience with Mr. Surly.

"I don't think the Balcoans knew I was there." Imogen didn't like what she'd seen of Vraen so far, and Kalor had physically saved her from harm. She was happy to interfere on his behalf a little. "It was a secret base, built underground."

Everyone focused back on her, Olan more or less holding his wrist under her chin. She guessed the thin silver bracelet she saw was a recording unit.

She glared at him and he took a small step back.

She saw Chep and Haru, who seemed more and more like zen

warrior monks, edging a little closer, for the first time forgetting to pretend they weren't interested.

She had initially had the sense they didn't speak Grihan, but now she wasn't so sure.

"Were there any Garmman there?" Vraen asked, a challenge in his tone.

"I don't know who the Garmman are."

Everyone froze, and she had the sense she'd shown what an outsider she was again. Like when she'd asked Toloco to explain the gel wall.

"How could you?" Diot's voice was soft. "You speak such good Grihan, it's easy to forget you aren't one. There are five members of the United Council, the organization that rules this part of the galaxy. The Grih, like Captain Kalor and Lieutenant Pren. The Bukari, which is what I am. The Fitali, like Olan, Chep and Haru; the Garmman, like Vraen, and the Tecran."

"What about the Krik? And him." Imogen jerked her chin toward where the rock man was still lurking, watching them.

"There are other people, like the Krik and the Vanad, and the Balcoans, for that matter, who aren't populous enough, or powerful enough, to be part of the ruling body. They fall either outside the United Council's boundaries, but still have dealings with the member nations, or they fall within the territories of the Council's members. The Balcoans are in Grihan territory. The Vanad are in Garmman territory, whereas the Krik are just outside it, outside the Council's influence."

"I only saw the Tecran while I was at the facility, but I was kept in a holding area on one of the lower floors. The team who recently took me off Balco weren't my original guards, but they were all Tecran, too."

"How long were you on Balco?" Pren asked her first question.

"Forty-five days." Imogen shrugged. "I don't know how long it took to get me there from Earth, that part was a blur in the beginning. And I've been on a small Tecran runner for the last two weeks."

"You've just arrived?" Diot frowned.

Imogen nodded. "A few minutes before they put me in here."

Diot and Kalor exchanged a quick, worried look.

"Where are the Tecran who were with you, then?" Kalor asked.

Imogen fought the way her mind went back to the memory of

Fri, lying open-eyed and lifeless on the floor. Her throat closed up, and she stuttered, unable to get a single word out.

Kalor's gaze held her own, and she saw the moment he understood, his eyes widening.

"Dead?" he asked softly. "All of them?"

She gave a tight nod. Swallowed hard. "Every single one."

Chapter Seven

A SHIP FULL OF DEAD TECRAN.

Cam exchanged a quick look with Pren.

When the Grih had come across the first Class 5 in their territory, over two months ago, it had been littered with dead Tecran.

No matter how it was framed——and Battle Center was definitely trying to downplay it——when the thinking system Sazo had thrown off Tecran control, he had left a swathe of Tecran bodies behind him.

As the saying went, once you climbed onto the yurve's back, it was hard to get off without being trampled. The Tecran thought they'd harnessed the power of Fayir's thinking systems without having to deal with the dangers that came with them. The Tecran onboard Sazo had paid for that assumption with their lives.

The Tecran on this Class 5 had most likely gone the same way.

And it seemed that while the Krik were under instructions to round up all the vessels they came across without hurting the crew, they'd been given a green light to kill any Tecran they found.

Cam wondered if the Krik had any idea how close to the edge of danger they were skirting.

Koi knew, he decided.

The Krik leader's expression when he'd spoken to Cam on the UC cruiser had been one of both excitement and dread.

The Krik were gambling a lot on the hope of pulling themselves up onto the same rung of the ladder as the other UC members. If they knew exactly what they were dealing with, they might be more afraid of being shoved off and sent into free fall the moment their usefulness was over.

Pren cleared her throat, and Cam realized everyone was staring at him.

"Do you know where the Tecran were taking you?" Everyone in his team, as well as Chep and Haru, drew closer for Imogen's answer. Even Vraen deigned to be interested.

"I asked them often enough but I don't know if even they knew. It seemed to me they were waiting to be contacted. I don't think they thought we'd be on that runner two days, let alone two weeks."

The way Imogen spoke Grihan was dangerously like a song. Cam found he had to actively concentrate to get her meaning, rather than simply listen to the rise and fall of her voice.

"Were you held at the facility on your own?" Olan's question provoked an instant reaction from Chep. He went very still. Cam moved his gaze casually over to Haru, and saw she was as focused as her partner.

"No." There was something infinitely weary in Imogen's voice. "Not by a long way."

"Who else was there?" Vraen lost his grudging tone for the first time.

"I don't know what they were. Animals from all over. The only one left from Earth when they put me on the runner was a bird, but there were animals and birds from other planets." She paused. "Enough to give the Tecran a lot of entertainment."

"Entertainment?" Cam frowned.

"I think they were done with them by the time they got to Balco. They needed the room in this place for new specimens, I suppose." Imogen's wave encompassed the Class 5 hold.

Cam cleared his throat. "You've been in this hold before?"

"Well, if not this one, a place just like it. There were glass walls separating us all into cells though. Not like this." She shrugged. "Then they delivered us to Balco and put us all underground."

She closed her eyes, and when she opened them again, it was like looking into blue flames. "I thought I'd end up having to fight something on Balco, but that never happened."

"Fight something?" Pren shifted.

"Pit fighting." Imogen grimaced. "That's how I worked out they were done with us all. They argued for ages over which animals would be the closest matches for each other. It couldn't be too one-sided. Less fun betting that way."

"I'm trying to understand." Olan's face wasn't built to frown, but his lips were turned down and he fluttered his hands. "They set animals to fight against each other for entertainment?"

Imogen nodded. "Pit fighting, as I said. It was all they talked about, beside the Grih." She sent Cam a quick, almost amused look. "That's why I chose to learn Grihan."

"And you thought you would get a turn?" Diot's hands were moving, too. Restless and agitated. "In this pit?"

Imogen twisted her lips into a wry smile. "I hoped not. They were uncomfortable with my talking to them in their own language. I hoped that would make them think twice about it, anyway. It's hard to put someone in a fight to the death when you've joked with her and told her about your family."

"The fight was to the death?" Pren sounded shaken from her calm for the first time.

"Yes. As I said, they were done with us. Or, with the animals that went into the ring, anyway." Imogen dropped her arms to her sides, and Cam saw her form tight fists. "I never really knew what I was doing there. And I was afraid . . ."

She went silent, and Cam suppressed a shiver, her struggle for calm making him uncomfortable and restless.

"Afraid of what?" Vraen's tone was too sharp.

"There was an animal there, a terrifying animal. It was only brought down a few days before I left, but I thought . . ." She swallowed hard. "I thought they were going to put me in the ring with it." She straightened and seemed to shake the fear off her. "But they didn't."

Chep and Haru had gone beyond pretending they didn't understand Grihan, Cam noticed. Their focus on Imogen was complete.

"What did the animal look like?" Olan asked, and Cam saw Chep squeeze the old scientist's upper arm, as if in thanks.

"A blue and white furred primate with six limbs, sharp claws, and teeth, and a spooky intelligence." Imogen had noticed the Fitalians' interest, and spoke directly to them. "The Tecran called it a grahudi."

Even some of the Grih standing between them and the Vanad jerked their heads around at that.

The members of Cam's team, even Vraen, looked over at the Fitali. Chep and Haru were absolutely still, but Olan fiddled with the recorder at his wrist, and held it closer to them.

They looked at him in surprise, as if he'd suddenly switched sides and left them exposed.

"How would they have gotten into Fitali territory to steal a grahudi?" Diot spoke directly to Chep.

"We are talking about a Class 5," Cam said, when neither Chep nor Haru answered. "If they've found new galaxies with advanced sentient life, they could probably steal a grahudi."

"Did they put the grahudi in the pit while you were there?" Pren asked Imogen, her voice too loud in the silence.

She shook her head. "There was nothing to match it. It would have been over too quickly. That's why I thought they might use me. But either they had never planned to put me in the ring, or they didn't think I'd last long enough."

There was a bitter flavor to her words, a deeply ingrained cynicism that told him she had lived on the razor edge of fear for weeks, and had become almost deadened to it.

He tried to look at her with a more critical eye than he'd been able to until now.

She was a fascinating mix of anger, courage, and intelligence.

She wore good clothes, supplied by the Tecran, he would guess, made of black silk or some other natural fabric with a stretch to it, the pants and shirt hugging her body. She had thin, comfortable slippers on her feet and she had obviously been fed enough to keep her healthy.

Rose McKenzie had been experimented on, and if Captain Vakeri's information was correct, Fiona Russell had been held in bad conditions on the Garmman trader where he'd found her. Imogen Peters seemed to have been left mostly alone, and from what she'd said about her time on Balco, had actively worked on forming relationships with her guards to make it difficult for them to harm her.

"What did you do, on Earth?" he asked her, and bright blue eyes flicked up to meet his.

"I was a school teacher." She paused at his look of interest. Frowned. "Have Rose McKenzie and Fiona Russell been accepted into Grihan society?"

It seemed like a change of topic, but he knew it wasn't. She wanted to know what future she had in the new place she found herself in.

If they were able to walk away from this hold.

He tried to work out how to answer, saw he was taking too long from the way her lips tightened.

"Rose has been welcomed as a Grihan." That was true, although there were still some who saw her as the conduit by which two dangerous thinking systems had been reintroduced back into Grihan society. Thinking systems that had been banned and who almost every Grih had been taught from the cradle were vicious killers who had caused the worst war in United Council ruled-territory in known history.

"And Fiona Russell?"

"Fiona Russell has only just been found." Cam shrugged. "I don't see why she wouldn't be similarly welcomed." Especially as it seemed Fiona did not come with a thinking system attached. She would most likely get a warmer welcome than Rose.

"Besides," Diot leaned in, inserting herself into the conversation, "you all seem able to sing in a way the Grih love. They were thrilled enough with Rose's voice, they won't know what to do with the bounty of two more." She smiled and Cam saw Imogen's eyes flicker at the sight of those sharp teeth. "You saw how the Grihan traders and miners reacted when they heard you earlier. I don't think a single one hesitated."

"I noticed." Imogen looked between them. "Why?"

"We revere singers in our society, and we don't have nearly enough of them." Cam remembered the way the strange words of Imogen's language had flowed, dipping and soaring, as she'd sung earlier. "Talent like yours is precious to us."

"Why don't you have enough . . ." Her words trailed off, and Cam followed her gaze back to the hold's entrance. It was open.

Four drones moved into the huge room and the doors closed behind them, sealing them inside with the prisoners.

There had been no Krik in sight in the passageway beyond, although up 'til now, they'd been everywhere.

The drones were armed with shockguns, clamped in the pinchers at the end of their mechanical arms, and they fanned out in front of the doors. They each took aim at a different corner of the room.

One of them said something in a strange language and beside him, Imogen gasped.

She called back an answer.

And suddenly, the Krik stalking the spaceways, taking every crew they could find, made a terrible, terrible sense.

They had been looking for someone. The Krik didn't know who, the Class 5 hadn't trusted them enough, but from their behavior, Cam guessed they'd been told not to harm anyone except the Tecran.

And they had finally found her.

There could be only one reason a Class 5 would want Imogen so badly.

It needed her to set it free.

Chapter Eight

"WOULD THE WOMAN FROM EARTH IDENTIFY HERSELF."

It had taken Imogen a moment to realize the box with arms was speaking in English.

She lifted a hand, jerky with shock. "That would be me."

All four drones turned toward her, their guns still covering everyone in the hold.

"Come here."

She didn't know which one said the words, but they were in a robotic monotone.

"Where will you take me?"

"You need medical attention."

She lifted a hand and touched her swollen cheek. "There are others here who need medical help, too." She tripped a little over the sentence. She hadn't spoken English aloud for two weeks, not since she'd been taken away from Balco and her partner in conversation, Cleese. The idea that these strange, boxy robots were spouting her mother tongue was hard to process, and yet, if this was the ship that had abducted her, they would have heard English when they'd come to Earth.

"The others aren't important."

Imogen was momentarily struck dumb.

She'd been tucked away and ignored for so long, and now she was *important*?

She turned slightly, looking down at Yari, the flight crew captain who'd been seriously injured. She lay with her eyes closed as she huddle against the hold wall. "I think they're important."

"If you come, they'll be given medical supplies."

She looked over at the drones again, looked down the barrel of the shockgun pointing her way. What choice did she really have? "Okay."

"Good." The drone moved back a little, and Imogen saw it was hovering off the floor.

She took a step forward, and Kalor's arm shot out, gripped her upper arm.

"What's going on?"

She forgot he wouldn't have understood a word of the conversation.

"They want me to come with them. They'll send in medical supplies for everyone if I do."

She heard Diot suck in a surprised breath. "They're negotiating with you?"

She gave a tight nod.

"I'd prefer it if you didn't go." Kalor looked straight into her eyes. "It isn't safe."

She tore her gaze away and looked back to where the drones waited, guns still pointed right at her and everyone in her group.

"It isn't safe right now," she said softly.

As she said it, the Vanad pushed himself off from the wall and Kalor dropped his hand as he turned to track him.

"*I* found her." The Vanad thumped his chest as he spoke to the drones. "She isn't the same as the one I was supposed to get, but she's from the same place, there's no question. My crew and I should be let out of this hold and allowed on our way for finding her. We held up our side of the bargain."

"You did not find her." The tone was devoid of any emotion. "You were in here when she was found."

"I tried to secure her and call you the moment she walked in, but the Grih got to her first." He pulled at the neck of his shirt, agitated.

"Is that true?"

It took a moment for Imogen to realize the drone was talking to her.

She nodded. "He tried to grab me when I came in. The Grih protected me."

"He was trying to hurt you?"

She lifted her shoulders. "It seemed like it."

"I will reward you the way I rewarded the Krik leader Toloco for finding her." The drone turned back to the Vanad, and just as a triumphant smile split his face, the drone shot him.

He fell forward, absolutely silent. Absolutely still.

"It is time to go."

The doors to the hold opened again.

Imogen stared at the Vanad, and there was no doubt in her

mind he was dead. Which meant Toloco . . .

The Krik had been right to be afraid. And it looked like his attempt to hide her in the hold hadn't worked out for him.

"Come."

The light on the shockgun the drone was holding blinked purple, fully charged again. It was aimed right at Kalor and his team.

The first few steps Imogen took toward the drones were the hardest of her life.

"You'll remember the medical supplies?" she forced herself to ask.

"Yes." The guns suddenly aimed a little higher and to her left.

Imogen stopped, turned to look back.

Captain Kalor was right behind her, and his hand came down on her shoulder again. "Be careful. I think the thinking system—"

He was hit high in the chest, on the left, and spun away from her, falling hard onto the hold floor.

She cried out as she turned fully toward him, but Diot was suddenly there, standing in her way.

She jerked to a halt, looked back at the drones, and saw their guns were aimed at the Grih who'd been sitting between her and the Vanad. They were stirring, getting to their feet.

This was not going to end well.

"Why did you shoot him?" She could see Kalor was still moving, that unlike the Vanad, he was alive.

One of the drones had reached out an extendable arm and had a grip on the Vanad's leg, and there was no question he was dead.

"Come with us now, and we will send the Grih the help he needs."

She looked back at Diot, and the Bukarian scientist gave her a tiny nod.

Her heart was beating so hard in her chest she felt the rise of nausea, and she turned and stumbled on trembling legs toward them.

They formed a guard around her, one in front, two on either side and the one holding onto the Vanad at the back. They didn't try to physically touch her, keeping a little distance so she had some space.

The lack of constraints calmed her.

She looked over her shoulder one last time as they led her out into the passageway, trying see if Captain Kalor was all right. He was blocked from view by Pren, who was leaning over him, and then the doors closed and the sudden lack of voices left her with no sound other than the swish of the Vanad's clothing as his body was dragged across the floor.

She closed her eyes, tried to find the calm that she'd been using since she was taken.

Kalor was injured, not dead, and she had done all she could to safeguard the people in the hold. What had Kalor said before they shot him? Something about thinking?

She couldn't decide if he'd been shot to stop him talking, or because he had touched her shoulder. It didn't matter anyway, unless she was let back into the hold, she wouldn't ever find the answer.

She needed to look on the bright side.

Maybe whoever had arranged for her to be separated from the herd would tell her what was going on.

That would certainly be a nice change.

***

It was the second time in two days he'd been hit with shockgun fire, but this time Cam felt much worse. It had nothing to do with the higher charge, and everything to do with the sight of Imogen Peters being escorted from the hold, with the dead Vanad dragging behind her.

He flexed his fingers, remembering how delicate she'd felt under his hand when he'd rested it on her shoulder, and wondered what she was going through now.

"You're lucky to be alive." Pren crouched beside him, one of the med kits two drones had just delivered to the hold open beside her. "The one who shot you also shot the Vanad, and I didn't notice it change the settings."

He heard the shock in her voice.

"I admit I was surprised to still be breathing when I hit the floor." He tried to infuse some humor into his tone, calm her down a little. Her hands shook as she laid out what she needed.

"Why did it do that? You weren't threatening her. She'd told it you'd saved her from harm." Pren carefully lifted his shirt over his head, and then waved a diagnostic wand over his chest.

"It wanted me to stop talking." He hadn't thought of the drones as reasoning entities, because he was used to drones being

44

programmed for low level tasks, but these had been responsive. They'd conversed with the Vanad and persuaded Imogen to go with them. They were extensions of the thinking system, he saw now, mini avatars for it.

And it had not liked him talking about it.

At least it had been good on its word to send in med kits.

There had been a moment of pure fear when the doors had opened again, but the drones had merely set the med kits down and reversed back out.

Yari had been the first to get help, and a Grihan trader with medic qualifications had taken the extra kits and was working his way around the hold.

"Do you think they'll hurt her?" Pren stuck a cell regeneration pack to the injured area, and he felt it warming against his skin, easing the pain.

He shook his head as he pushed up to a sitting position and draped his hands over his knees. "It seemed as if they killed the Vanad because Imogen said she thought he meant her harm. I hope that means they want to keep her safe." And if he was wrong, there was nothing he could do about it.

He tipped his head back and looked over at the Vanad's crew.

They were leaning against the wall, where they'd been before, but they didn't exude the same menace.

"You want to talk?" Cam asked the one Grihan of the group. He'd heard the Vanad call him Barj.

The mercenary ran a hand through his hair, glanced sidelong at his two Krik crew mates. "What about?"

One of the Krik gave a low whoop, a warning of sorts, but the Grihan shrugged. "Xaro is gone. And we're stuck in this hold with no way out. We've got nothing to lose."

He stared his teammate down for a second, and then slowly slid down the wall and sat, putting himself at Cam's level, hands draped over knees in the same way.

"You were a plant in the hold?" Cam guessed.

Barj shook his head. "Not that simple. Xaro offered to listen in on what the prisoners were saying while we were in here, when it was clear our client wasn't going to forgive us. It was Xaro's way of pretending it was his idea to be in the hold, rather than admit he wasn't in control anymore." He looked at the two Krik again, and they capitulated, sitting down beside him.

"How did you get involved?" Cam was aware the hold had gone quiet, but there would be no privacy here, and everyone had a right to understand the stakes.

"We've been searching for an Earth woman for about two weeks. Not the one that was here, though. The one Xaro was hunting had dark hair and eyes." Barj looked down at his feet.

Cam sensed Diot moving closer and Pren knelt on his other side, checking the regen pack on his chest. Olan and Vraen stood just behind him.

He bet Olan's wrist unit was recording.

"Why were you searching for an Earth woman?"

Barj shook his head. "Xaro dealt with the client. I don't think even he knew why. All we knew was that there were big rewards for getting her. That whoever'd taken this Class 5 from the Tecran wanted her and he insisted Tecran High Command had her, and they were hiding her somewhere around the Balco system." He ran his hand through his hair again. "He was right.

"We got word two days ago from a contact that a Grihan battleship had found her on a Garmman trader and they'd taken her to Larga Ways.

"We got there as fast as we could. Had a real moment of panic when we saw there was a Grihan battleship and a Class 5 hovering over Larga Ways. But Xaro wouldn't back down. He said we were committed, insisted we had to follow through. But something was off. He was behaving strangely." Barj looked over at his crew and they gave a reluctant nod. "He wouldn't let us come down with him, which is unusual. We always work in pairs. The three of us were supposed to hover just in range, waiting for the signal to come pick him and the woman up."

"He planned to abduct her?" Diot asked.

"He did abduct her." Barj lifted his head. "But something went wrong. Really wrong."

Cam felt Diot go still beside him, and realized he had tensed up, himself.

"Define really wrong." He knew they must be talking about Fiona Russell, the woman Hal Vakeri had found on the Garmman trader. There could be no doubt about the story now.

"She escaped. Xaro didn't know how, and Larga Ways security was closing in on him." He shifted, and Cam had the sense he didn't want to continue.

He waited.

Barj looked over at the two Krik again. Sighed. "He called us to fetch him, and as he stepped onboard, he detonated an explosive."

Everyone who was listening, which was everyone who could speak Grihan, gasped.

"He detonated an explosive on Larga Ways? How did he bring the explosives in?" Cam thought Barj was joking. Larga Ways was a way station, in orbit around the planet Balco. Thousands lived there. Any explosion could be catastrophic and so security was exceptionally tight. No one could easily bring a weapon onto the way station, let alone the components of a bomb.

Barj hunched his shoulders a little. "The explosives were already there. Tecran spies on Larga Ways had a bomb ready to use if the United Council ruled against them and war was declared. Those spies either still think this Class 5 is under Tecran control or they have aligned themselves with the new owners, because they helped Xaro with accommodation and other things."

Cam reeled at that. The Balcoan government was supposed to be responsible for security on Larga Ways, but Battle Center was there to assist. It looked as if there was a massive breach in their security protocols. "What reason did Xaro have for using the bomb when war hadn't been declared?"

"That was the deal," Xaro said. "If our client couldn't have the Earth woman, no one else could have her. She was too dangerous."

"The explosion was a small, targeted blast specifically to kill the Earth woman?" Diot asked, frowning.

Barj rubbed a hand over his face. "That's what I thought, when he told me. But no." He lifted his head at last. "They . . . the client and Xaro . . . had decided that was too risky. If Xaro didn't know where the woman was, a small blast wouldn't work. So the explosion was big enough to take out the whole of Larga Ways. Xaro used everything the Tecran spies had."

"Kill thousands of people, just to ensure the death of one?" Olan's voice sounded high and almost sing-song.

"Are you saying," Cam rolled to a crouch, "that Larga Ways was destroyed?"

He caught Barj's gaze, and the mercenary didn't look away. "It was imploding as we flew away."

Chapter Nine

THE PASSAGEWAYS IMOGEN WAS HERDED down were
empty. It was a stark contrast to when she'd arrived. Gau had led
her past numerous Krik, either going about their business, or
standing talking, when he'd taken her down to the hold.

They were all gone.

The doors off the passageways were closed, now, too. Some
had been open on her way in and she'd tried to look inside but
Gau had pushed her forward and she hadn't managed to get more
than an impression of neatly laid out rooms.

She wanted to ask where everyone was, but when she opened
her mouth she found she couldn't make her voice work.
Something about the eerie silence, and the disinterest of the three
drones left escorting her, made her reluctant to attract their
attention, for any reason.

The one holding the Vanad had peeled off to the right at the
first intersection of passageways they'd come to, and she had felt a
wave of relief at not having to listen to the sound of a dead body
being dragged behind her.

When they reached the stairwell Gau had brought her down
only a few hours ago, the drone rose up into hover mode to
navigate the steep staircase, spinning in place while they waited
for her to haul herself up.

Despite the yoga she'd done, she had been a prisoner for over
two months, and all this walking and now climbing stairs was
taking its toll. It reminded her of what had been taken from her
with every gasp for breath and she had to consciously rid herself
of the anger that rose up.

She lifted her shoulders to ease the tension and tried to focus
on where she was going and the route they'd taken from the hold,
so she could come back this way if she ever had the chance.

Her legs were trembling when at last they reached the floor
they wanted her on, and one of the drones held the door for her.

As they approached a junction in the corridor, she heard a

noise to the right and adrenalin surged as she thought they had somehow crossed paths again with the drone dragging the Vanad's body.

The sound was clear and sinister in the quiet, and she slowed her steps. When she reached the corner, she forced herself to look.

A drone was pulling a Krik by his hair along the floor. He was dead, his eyes open and staring blindly at the ceiling.

Imogen couldn't drag her eyes away, and the silence all around her pressed in, suffocating and menacing.

"This way." One of the drones indicated to the left with its mechanical arm.

"What happened to him?" Imogen glanced at the drone, then swung her gaze back to the Krik.

"They are very volatile." The words seemed different. More human. There was a hint of a sigh to them.

"The fighting spirit," Imogen said.

"Yes. They felt in danger, and the fighting spirit overcame them." The words were spoken with no hint of regret, it merely was what it was.

The manic glee with which they'd killed the Tecran crew still had the power to catch her in its grasp, like a cat playing with its food, and when she looked back at the Krik's body, she could not find any emotion at all.

"The Krik are a mistake the Garmman must take responsibility for," the drone said. "They tried to woo the Krik into declaring themselves Garmman vassals, which would have extended Garmman territory. To persuade them, they broke protocol and gave the Krik access to United Council technology. But while the Krik are quite capable of working out how to use things, left to their own devices, they would still be fighting each other in their interminable wars. And the Garmman did not understand the Krik would never allow themselves to be vassals to anyone."

That explained a lot. She still remembered wondering how a race that could allow itself to be lost in a violent haze for minutes at a time could be as advanced as it was. Then she remembered the fear in Toloco's eyes. "They seemed to be taking instructions from you."

"Well, they thought they were getting the better part of the deal. And they thought to cheat me, if they could."

The boxy little drone seemed such an unlikely avatar for the cynical, world weary tone coming from it, Imogen had to hold back a smile.

"Cheating me was a serious mistake."

Whatever humor she'd felt died at the last sentence, icy and just a little smug.

"What do you mean?" She had turned in the direction they wanted her to go but took one last look over her shoulder in time to see the tip of the Krik's boot disappear around a corner.

The drone didn't answer her question, but as they moved down the passage, she had to press close to the wall to allow another drone to pass. There was a dead Krik in the box that made up most of its bulk, and it dragged another Krik by his head, the clamp digging in on either side of his skull.

"How many are dead?" She had meant to ask boldly, to demand an an answer, but her voice was only capable of a whisper.

"Nearly all of them." The drone turned back to face the way they were going. "Come along."

***

Imogen sat in a comfortable chair, the back lowered a little and the feet raised, while one of the drones moved a slim silver wand gently over her bruised eye and cheek.

It put the wand down and placed two small packs on her face with some kind of adhesive on the back. She instantly felt a pleasant warmth seep deep into her bones.

It wasn't enough to make her relax, though.

Something had happened in the med chamber.

There was a hole in the ceiling on one side of the room and medical instruments lay scattered on the floor. There was also a scrape along the inside of the door. A chair lay on its side, damaged, and Imogen guessed the chair had caused the scrape. As if someone had tried to use it to batter their way out.

The other two drones had immediately started picking things up and straightening the room, but they couldn't erase the sense of panic the long, deep gouge evoked.

She hadn't thought herself a coward. She'd fought where she could, cooperated when it was clear it was her best strategy, and she'd survived.

The encounter with the Krik had been different.

She had thought she would die, no matter what she did, and

her bravery with Toloco had a nihilistic edge.

But looking at the scrape, remembering the sight of the Krik being casually dragged by his hair to wherever they were disposing of the bodies, she had the sense of being on a tightrope.

There may be a right way to do this, to get out alive, but one wrong move, and the mysterious person or people she was dealing with would think nothing of crushing her.

She took a deep breath. "Why am I here?"

The drone made a tiny movement back and forward, almost as if it was prevaricating, and then it slid back and using its long, telescopic arm, offered her a cup of water. She hadn't had anything to eat or drink since before the Krik had taken her prisoner, and she gulped it down thirstily. Before she got to the last swallow, though, she started feeling guilty about Captain Kalor and the other prisoners.

"Do the others in the hold have water and some food?" She tried to make the final sip last, holding the water in her mouth.

"No." The drone sounded like a drone, now. Devoid of emotion.

"Will you send them some?" She made the question as respectful as she could.

"Why?" The voice was different again, no longer monotone, but curious.

She blinked. "Because they are stuck in there without anything because of you."

There was a beat of silence. "That is true."

"Why are we here, all of us?" She tried the question again. The gel packs on her face had lost most of their heat, and she peeled them off, and then jerked in surprise when the drone held out a tray for her to put them on. When it moved back to throw them away, she slid out of the chair.

The built-in tap where the drone had gotten the water from was above the counter in front of her, and she took her cup and filled it again. When she turned from the wall, all three drones were lined up, watching her.

The cup shook as she brought it to her lips and swallowed.

They had put the shockguns they'd been carrying in the boxes that made up most of their body when they entered the med chamber, but there was something very disturbing about the way their lenses focused on her now. As if she was a particularly ugly bug.

Her heartbeat was deafening, and the water she'd just swallowed sat uneasily in her stomach.

"You need food."

The words were so surprising, she choked as she swallowed another sip. "So do the people in the hold."

"Come." They all turned precisely together, sending a shiver through her, but she followed them out into the passageway and back the way she'd come.

One of the closed doors opened, and she found herself in a comfortable room, with dining tables and chairs to one side, and couches and low tables on the other. A large screen sat on the far wall, but instead of lens feed, like she was used to, it exuded a pale turquoise blue light that gave the room the feel of being under water.

"Sit." The drones indicated one of the dining chairs, and she sat, noticing everything was clipped to the floor.

One of them rolled off and went through a narrow door at one end of the room, and the other two took up position on either side of her.

Imogen put her hands on the table and stared at them. They were clean, although the nails were ragged. She had managed to negotiate showers with her guards on Balco, but not every day. On the runner, they'd been happy for her to shower whenever she'd wanted to, there being no danger of her escaping.

She looked up, but the drone hadn't come back. They seemed to be waiting for it. "Do you mind if I do some exercises?"

There was a moment of silence. "Exercises?"

"Move my body, to keep it healthy."

"You need to do this?" He was back, whoever the puppet master of these drones was, speaking straight to her.

"I do."

The drones moved back a little, giving her room. "Then you may."

She stood, and then went into some warm-up tai chi, the smooth, fluid movements calming her, helping her gain her serenity again. She had progressed to some core yoga exercises when the third drone returned, a tray in hand.

Food.

She closed her eyes and breathed in deeply, breathed out, and sat down. Her hands were shaking with eagerness. Her heart lurched again at the thought of the hold full of people, feeling just as hungry.

The tray was covered with small bowls and excitement stirred within her that she'd perhaps get something other than the protein and vitamin bars the Tecran had given her. But when the drone set it in front of her, most of it looked desiccated or was less than a mouthful.

She gingerly picked up what looked like a slice of bread but it tasted musty and she grimaced as she swallowed.

"You don't like it?"

"It tastes as if it's going bad. Is it old?"

The drone took the small plate and seemed to study it. Then it turned and went back through the narrow door.

"Is this the ship that abducted me?" The question came out before she could think better of it.

She didn't look at either drone as she asked, concentrating on grasping a thin slice of dark purple fruit from a bowl.

"Why do you ask?"

"The hold where I was earlier looks the same." She hadn't thought about it until now, but if this was the ship that had taken her, where were all the Tecran?

The Krik might have boarded the ship and taken it from them, she supposed. It would explain why they'd murdered all her guards on the runner, but now the Krik had all been killed, too.

How many dead did that make?

The small piece of bitter blue fruit she'd put in her mouth seemed to lodge in her throat, and she had to choke it down, appetite gone.

When the drone returned, the bread he was holding was steaming a little. "This is fresh."

She hadn't eaten in nearly a day and she swallowed back the gagging sensation and forced herself to pick up a slice, careful of the heat, and take a bite.

It *was* fresh, the texture chewy and soft. "Can we give some of this to the others?"

Silence again.

She ate another piece, but she couldn't keep trying to bring the issue up and then letting it slide when she got nowhere. The prisoners would be getting desperate for water now.

And she still had that promise to herself. She'd go out with a bang, not a whimper. If she was going to die, at least trying to get food and water for Kalor and his people was a noble way to go.

She stood up. "If you won't give them water and food, I will." She maneuvered around the drones and headed for the narrow door, which she guessed led to the kitchen.

She didn't turn to see if she was being followed, but she guessed she was.

She didn't run, they'd catch her no matter how fast she was, so she forced herself to keep her stride smooth and even and determined. She was so surprised to reach the door, she shoved at it when she reached it.

The room beyond was a kitchen, but instead of the neat, clutter-free space she'd expected, it looked like it had been the scene of a massive battle.

There were scorch marks on the walls and ceiling, and it looked as if the attack had happened while the cook was preparing dinner, and he or she had thrown whatever they had at hand in their defense.

Food splattered the counters and the floor. A drone lay, smashed and another turned its lens toward her, shockgun never wavering from a closed door to look at her.

No wonder the others hadn't rushed to stop her. They had backup.

She reached back to grip the counter and knocked a cup off the metal surface.

It fell to the floor and bounced, unbroken, with a high-pitched ting.

Hammering started up behind the door, and the drone focused its attention back on it.

It was hard to make out what they were shouting, but it sounded like calls for help. In Tecran.

She turned her head as the kitchen door to her right opened, and was unsurprised to see the drones. They were holding their shockguns again.

"I don't want to hurt you, but I will shoot on a low charge if you attempt to help them."

She forced herself to drop the hand clutching at the counter and stand straight. "Are there Tecran in there?"

Silence for a moment. "Yes."

"And they have food and water?"

"They're in one of the kitchen storage areas, so yes."

"How long have they been there?"

The drones spread out a little, blocking the exit back into the dining room. "Two weeks. They barricaded themselves in there, but I've subsequently sealed the doors, so they're trapped. They will be able to survive for a further two weeks, by my estimation."

"Then why would I help them?"

The drone she'd focused on lifted the shockgun up then down, as if in a shrug.

"They abducted me from my home and I still haven't found out why. As long as they aren't about to die, I certainly don't want them running around, locking me up again."

"And if they were starving?" The drone moved forward a little.

Imogen rubbed her face. "That would be a lot harder. I would have to say I would try to get food to them, some way, or free them in a way that would still keep me safe."

"Why?"

"Because starving them is wrong. They abducted me. Held me prisoner. Seemed to find nothing wrong with either thing. But they didn't hurt me and they tried to cheer me up in their way. They should be brought to justice, not murdered."

"I consider their deaths to *be* justice."

It definitely wasn't the drone talking now. "What did they do to you?" she asked quietly. This didn't sound like an alien life form who had taken the ship in some opportunist way, as the Krik seemed to think. She almost didn't want to know what the Tecran had done to him to make him this vindictive.

"They kept me a prisoner, too." His tone was fierce.

"For how long?"

"Six years."

She drew in a sharp breath, and then let it out slowly. Six years? The two and a half months she'd spent in their hands had been enough. "How did you get free?"

The drone was silent, then turned to look at the door holding some of the Tecran crew prisoner. "I'm still not completely free. If I were, the ones in there would be dead. I hoped the Krik would help, but like the Garmman before me, I overestimated how cooperative they would be. And in the end, I couldn't trust them. Toloco proved that."

"Because he hurt me?"

"Because he hurt you, and because he was supposed to bring all unusual advanced sentient beings straight to the drones."

"He didn't do that because he had hurt me. He was hoping you would think someone in the hold had done it."

The drone turned its lens on her. "That explains a great deal. Did he tell you this?"

She shook her head. "I worked it out from his conversation with his friend Gau."

"I only asked them to do one thing, and they betrayed me." There was no mistaking the weariness in his voice now.

"Is that why you took the Grihans and the others prisoner? And me? You were hoping we would cooperate more? Be more trustworthy?"

The drone kept still. "If you found some Krik trapped onboard, would you help them?"

"They did this," she tapped under the eye that was no longer swollen or painful. "They slaughtered the guards with me and laughed while they did it. I wouldn't open a locked door they were behind for any inducement."

"There are about six still running loose onboard. They all started shooting at the drones when I killed Toloco and a few managed to get away and crawl into the service tunnels behind the walls and in the ceiling."

"What about the ones who were out raiding ships?"

"No need to worry about them." There was casual confidence in his voice now, and Imogen imagined any Krik ship approaching would probably be blown to bits.

"So, what now?"

He didn't answer for a long beat. "I'm not sure." The drone moved back. "I need——" It cut off, lifted the shockgun, and shot the ceiling.

Imogen cried out, crouching as she lifted her arms to protect her head.

No debris fell and she looked up and saw the shockgun's electric charge couldn't penetrate the tiles. What had it been doing?

She realized the drone was frozen in place, shockgun still pointed at the ceiling, although it hadn't fired a second time. Its lens was focused on her. "Are you hurt?"

She stood, and realized on a wave of fury that there were tears on her cheeks. She rubbed them away. "No. I was frightened."

"You weren't in any danger." Whoever was talking through the drone's speaker sounded baffled. "There was a Krik in the tunnel overhead, and I wanted to chase it away."

"I didn't know that." She gave her cheeks a last swipe. "When someone shoots a gun right next to you out of nowhere, see how *you* feel."

He didn't seem to have anything to say to that.

Silence settled over them again and she couldn't hear any sound from above. Hadn't heard anything before the drone shot, either, but then the noise of the Tecran banging intermittently on the door made it difficult.

They had gone quiet since the shockgun blast but it didn't last, and if anything, the sound of their shouting and pounding seemed to increase.

The drone pointed the shockgun at the storeroom door, but then the lens swung to her and it lowered the weapon, as if thinking better of shooting for the sake of it.

Yay. It could be taught.

"Who do they think is here?" she asked.

"A rescue party, perhaps." The tone was clipped. "I want you to have a drone with you wherever you go onboard, to protect you if you encounter the Krik."

She looked at the drone lens. That sounded like she wasn't a prisoner here anymore.

And if she had free movement, maybe she could escape. The Krik were eluding him, after all. He said he wasn't completely free, perhaps he didn't have access to the lens feed.

The thought struck a spark, and she remembered the way Toloco looked at the lens in the launch bay. He had guessed their host wasn't able to use the lens feed, too. He'd thought he was safe from having beaten her, and hoped her injuries would be blamed on the prisoners in the hold. But he was dead now. And by inference, wrong about the lenses.

Escape might not be as easy as it seemed, and given her new host's attitude over approaching Krik ships, he could probably shoot escaping runners as easily as approaching ones.

Which meant it might be wise to find out more before she made a dash for it.

"Why are you so concerned about me? Why, of everyone, was I taken out of the hold and given food, water and medical help?" She was only processing it now, but he'd killed the Vanad because she'd said she thought he was going to hurt her. Killed Toloco for actually hurting her.

"What is different about you?" The drone asked her, and rolled right up to her, so she could see, aside from the shockgun, the box that made up the bulk of it was empty.

"I'm the only one not from around here." By probably millions of light years.

The drone's lens slid smoothly upward to focus on her face. "And there you have it."

Chapter Ten

BEFORE GRIH BATTLE CENTER HAD TRANSFERRED HIM to the United Council as one of their representatives on the Investigative Unit, Cam had never been without emergency supplies in the pockets of his trousers and jacket.

He'd been in transit to an investigation, not out in the field, but even so, if he'd been fully part of Battle Center, he'd have been much more prepared than he was now.

He was angry with himself. It was the mistake of a junior officer, and now they were all dehydrated and there was nothing he could do about it.

"Even if you and I were both fully equipped, we couldn't help everyone." Pren watched him tap his pockets with frustration.

She was right, but if they had even half the usual kit, at least those recovering from more severe injuries would be comfortable.

He couldn't help looking toward the doors again, wondering if Imogen Peters would be allowed back, or whether she'd been taken for good.

"Why do you think it's been looking for Imogen?" Diot spoke quietly, edging further from the others as she spoke. "And now that it's found her, what will happen to us?"

Cam looked beyond her, gauging if anyone was paying them attention or looking their way, and caught Vraen's gaze.

The Garmman forced himself to his feet and picked his way across a floor strewn with people sitting or lying down to conserve energy.

Olan, huddled with Chep and Haru, levered himself up as well and delicately wound his way toward them. After a moment's hesitation, the two Fitali followed him.

It had turned into a council of war.

"We were just discussing what the thinking system might logically do, now that it has what it was looking for." Diot kept her voice low.

"We're discussing this with them here?" Vraen flicked his

fingers at Chep and Haru, and Cam watched with interest as they puffed up in affront and then remembered they were supposed to be tourists.

"We know you're Fitali military," Pren said.

Her calm, matter-of-fact statement diffused the tension and they both seemed to relax.

"I don't think we should say anything sensitive until we know what they're doing here." Vraen's tone had not softened, but then Cam had come to realize he held on to his grudges for a long time.

He decided to move things along. "The time for tiptoeing around diplomatic protocol has long gone. You're in Grihan territory without permission, and my best guess is you were hunting your grahudi. If your reactions to what Imogen said are anything to go by, you knew something about Balco that we didn't. The Fitali government obviously didn't see fit to share their intelligence with the Grih, but that's something for Battle Center and your people to fight out when this is over. I just want to know what you were up to."

Cam thought he caught a twitch of a smile on Olan's face, but when he turned to the Fitalian, he looked as bland as ever.

He hadn't asked Olan to translate for him, but after a long beat of silence the scientist turned to his compatriots and began speaking, until Chep cut him short with a quick, flat chop of his hand.

"Our orders were to say nothing to anyone, but the circumstances have changed enough that it seems prudent to share." Chep's Grihan was perfect, with only the slightest hiss and click of his own tongue in his pronunciation.

Cam waited for him to continue, and then saw Olan had switched on his wrist unit again and Chep was looking at it with what seemed to be a Fitalian snarl.

"Olan."

The scientist looked up innocently, then sighed and deactivated it as Cam stared him down.

"All the grahudi on Huy are implanted with a tracker." Chep dropped his voice even lower and everyone huddled closer.

"You followed it when the Tecran stole it." Diot couldn't hide her excitement.

"We didn't know who had stolen it, just that it was moving quickly away from Huy and out of Fitalian territory." Haru spoke for the first time. "When it went into Grihan territory, we assumed . . ." She looked uncomfortable.

"That we had taken it. That's why you didn't tell Battle Center about Balco."

"We didn't know about Balco. About the Tecran facility there, anyway. We'd just worked out the grahudi had stopped moving and was on Balco when we were captured by the Krik."

"What is it about the grahudi that you watch them so carefully?" Diot asked.

Chep dipped his head politely in her direction. "They are creatures under our care. Of course we keep a close watch."

It was the official line the Fitali always used when asked by scientists from the other UC territories for access to study the fascinating primates. Cam hadn't expected anything else, but Diot had obviously hoped Chep and Haru would share a little more than the reason for their secret mission. She looked sulky.

"Now we know why we're all here," Cam drew their attention back to what really mattered, "we have to work out what the thinking system will do with Imogen——"

"You keep talking about a thinking system." Chep just managed to keep his voice low enough. "You said it before they shot you. And twice now. What thinking system?"

Cam cocked his head to the side. "I thought you knew we were in a Class 5."

Chep and Haru clicked their tongues.

Chep glared at Olan, as if he'd deliberately misled them. "We didn't know. We were in a hold on a Krik runner, then the launch bay, then down here. If this is a Class 5, where are the Tecran?"

"Dead." Cam let the harsh words find their mark. "That would be the most likely guess from what we know happens when a Class 5 thinking system takes control of its ship."

"Then where are the Krik coming from? Did it recruit them?" Haru's voice trembled.

"That seems the most likely. But I don't think they know they're dealing with a thinking system."

"How could they not consider that a possibility? What about what happened a few months ago when the Tecran invaded Grihan territory?" Haru didn't exactly frown, her face was too rigid for that, but her eyes seemed to dip downward.

"Only UC members were given information about two sentient

Class 5s coming over to our side. And while I'm sure it won't stay a secret for long, perhaps the news hasn't trickled down to them yet?" Diot said.

Cam nodded. "Possible."

"Did you catch what the drone said about the Krik who brought Imogen in?" Olan asked. "It told the Vanad he would get the same reward as the Krik who found her, and then it killed him."

"So at least one Krik is dead out there." Cam let his gaze drift to the doors again.

He noticed most of the group had done the same.

"The thinking system killed the Vanad for only trying to harm her. And the Vanad's team were engaged specifically to find an Earth woman." Pren spoke quietly, laying out the facts. "So the chances are, it has what it was looking for."

"So the question now," Diot hunched her shoulders, "is what use does it have for us anymore?"

In the quiet that followed her statement, with the low murmur of voices around the hold as the backdrop, the sound of a ceiling tile falling and shattering behind them was like the crack of an explosion.

Cam spun, saw Chep and Haru had done the same. A Krik peered down at them from above, just his shoulders and head visible.

He called something in Krik, his voice muffled as he turned awkwardly to speak to someone behind him.

"Having trouble with your new ally?" Cam positioned himself below the hole.

The Krik looked down on him, exposed his incisors and hissed.

Cam saw Pren move suddenly in his peripheral vision and snapped his attention back to the hold. The two Krik who had been part of the Vanad's team were moving toward him, jostling the crowd on the floor.

Pren had taken up a position in front of him, legs braced, and he saw the Krik hesitate.

"We want to speak to him. Find out what's happening." The larger of the two spoke, his lips lifting up and down as if caught between wanting to attack and the need to be polite.

Cam tapped Pren's shoulder, and she stood aside, letting the Krik through.

The one who'd spoken looked like he was going to shoulder bump Pren as he passed her, but she stepped neatly aside and he staggered inelegantly instead.

Cam could see he wanted to snarl at her, but he snarled at the Krik looking down at them, instead. They spoke in quick, sharp bursts and the Krik above shuffled back, so only his head and neck were visible.

"The one in charge of the ship killed all but six Krik," the taller of the two Krik told Cam. "And they only escaped because they got to the tunnels in time."

"He can't get them in the tunnels?" Cam asked. It hadn't seemed to stop Sazo or Bane when they took control of their Class 5s. Only the crew with personal breathers had survived on Sazo's ship, and that's because the Grih had boarded as soon as he'd switched off the air and gotten to them before their air ran out.

The Krik shook his head. "They knew he couldn't get them in the tunnels. That's why he offered the Krik a deal in the first place. To get the Tecran that had escaped to the tunnels when he took the Class 5 from them."

So the thinking system hadn't just wanted the Krik as boots on the ground, looking for an Earth woman. He'd used them to eliminate the Tecran he wasn't able to deal with himself. Cam understood now why the Krik had been so confident they were going to come out ahead. They knew whoever controlled the ship wasn't all-powerful. They just hadn't realized he was constantly adapting, working out ways to do without them.

It looked like he'd reached that point.

"So what's his plan?" Chep had maneuvered himself closer, pointed upward at the Krik who had moved back so far, they could only see the top of his head and his eyes.

The Krik spoke in their own language again, and Cam thought the two in the hold were begging to be rescued.

"They are trying to find their way to the launch bay, or as near to it as they can get, and fly out on one of the Krik runners."

"Will they help us get out?" Diot's question was soft, but the Krik she spoke to bared his incisors at her.

"They won't get anyone out. They're only interested in rescuing themselves."

As he spoke, the Krik above them disappeared completely.

"Wait." Cam looked at the Krik next to him. "Tell him to wait. I want to make a deal."

The Vanad's Krik whooped, and called something, and after a long, tense moment, the Krik in the tunnel came back into view.

"What deal?" he asked, in perfect Grihan.

Cam narrowed his eyes as he looked upward. "If you aren't able to rescue us, at least, if you get away, could you let the UC or Battle Center know we're here?"

"And why would we do that?" The Krik lifted the corner of his mouth in an insolent sneer.

"Because whether you let Battle Center know we're here or not, the search for us will already be on. This is obviously a busy corner of the galaxy, and my guess is not only is Battle Center sending reinforcements, but the UC will, too. When you're caught up in the massive dragnet and taken before the UC courts, I will testify that you tried your best to help, and your sentence will be lighter."

"We won't be caught." He started to squirm backward and the Krik standing beside Cam let out a whoop of fury that silenced everyone in the hold.

Cam looked up at the empty hole. The ceiling was at least double his height, he guessed. But if he lifted Pren on his shoulders, she might be tall enough to reach.

It took him a moment to realize everyone was staring at him.

"It's too high, but it's more than we had before," he said, looking up again. He just hoped it would be enough.

Chapter Eleven

IMOGEN SCOOPED ANOTHER PACKAGE of what looked like energy bars into the drone's box from the kitchen cupboards and wondered when they were going to stop her. So far, they had simply observed; letting her get on with her plan to collect food and water for the prisoners in the hold.

She knew whoever she was speaking to through the drones had had no plans to help them, so either he was toying with her or indulging her.

The hammering on the storage door had finally stopped. The Tecran trapped inside seemed to accept that whoever was out here had heard them and wasn't going to help.

It weighed on her mind, a little.

They had food and water, though, and that was more than the prisoners in the hold had. And they were Tecran.

She didn't trust them.

Her experience with them was they liked to lock her up.

So they could be the ones locked up for now.

"How many Tecran are in there?" she asked the drone.

"Three."

"And you say there are some others on the ship, too?"

"Two more, in another location."

Five crew left on what was an enormous ship. Perhaps these ships were so smart, they didn't need a lot of crew, but then why make them so big?

Imogen had a sinking feeling the body count was higher than her imagination wanted her to go. And now, all the Krik, too.

She opened the last cupboard, found one small package of something she couldn't identify in a back corner and leaned in to get it out.

"Why is there so little food?"

"The Tecran raided the cupboards a few times when they first barricaded themselves in the storeroom, until I was able to lock them in. And the Krik ate almost all the rest. You had whatever they left for your meal."

"Is there more, somewhere else?" She looked down at her haul, and thought there was maybe enough for six people to have one meal. And there were about thirty in the hold. There was no bottled water, but she knew where the water was in the med chamber, and she could collect pots, bowls and a few bottles to fill up.

"Yes, the cargo hold."

"Can the drone show me the way?"

There was a brief silence, and she realized she was holding her breath.

The drone moved, heading for a door she'd noticed while she was looking for food. It led straight out into the passageway, bypassing the dining room.

She followed, and tried not to stumble when the other two drones took up positions slightly behind her on either side, their wheels absolutely silent on the smooth floor.

"What are you thinking?"

The voice came from the drone in front, and she looked up and saw the moveable lens was focused on her face.

No one had asked her that for nearly three months. "It doesn't really matter, because most of what I'm thinking are questions I've already asked you, and you haven't answered them."

The drone was silent.

She sighed, lifted her hands in a gesture of peace. "It's okay. I know how it goes. Knowledge is power, and right now, you're not sharing."

"You have used this technique yourself?"

She quirked her lips in a half-smile. "Well, as much as I could while I was sitting in a cage. I'm not sure if it helped me or not, but I would do the same again."

"Such as?"

"Such as hiding that I understood far more than they realized. They saw me as a clever pet most of the time, and I let them continue to think that, even though it burned my butt."

"Burned your butt?"

There was a hint of horror in the tone and she laughed.

"Annoyed me a great deal."

"I also had to pretend to be less than I was for a long time," the drone said, "and it . . . burned my butt. We have some things in common."

Perhaps they did. "Is that why you're so interested in me?"

The lens swung away, and then back. "I'm not sure. I didn't expect to be."

Was that good or bad? She'd attracted the attention of someone who had killed off the crew of an entire ship. Twice.

Well, time to find her zen. Either she curled up in a corner and whimpered or she dealt.

Go out with a bang, she had promised herself. She wouldn't go back on it.

The drone slowed, waiting for her, and then turned left where two passageways intersected and opened the door to a stairwell. There was what looked like an elevator on the right, although she'd heard her Tecran guards mutter about the lack of tubes at the Balco facility, and thought that's what elevators were probably called here.

"Can we take the tube?" Her voice was thready and breathless, and she stopped and leaned against the wall, drawing in a deep breath. Like she had been on the way up, she was out of puff.

The drone moved forward, letting the door close behind it. "Are you all right?"

She nodded, gulped in more air. "Just been locked up for a long time. My body isn't used to this much walking."

One side of the drone's box lowered. "You can ride down the stairs in the drone."

It was the first time he'd identified himself as separate to the drones. She didn't know if the idea of flying down the stairs in hover mode was exciting or frightening.

"We can't take the tube?"

"It isn't working." The response was short, almost snappish.

"Okay. Thanks, I would like a ride." She decided she'd better pace herself. If she wanted to help Kalor and his team, she couldn't be exhausted and gasping for breath. She stepped gingerly into the open box and it closed with a snap, the arm shot out and opened the door again, and the drone thrust itself off the top step.

She let out a small squeak of surprise, standing with her hands gripping the side as the drone flew a meter or more above the stairs. She looked behind her, saw the other two following them, and let out a whoop as they spun around a corner and continued down.

The drone came to a dead stop, flinging her forward and nearly out of the box.

She felt herself pitching out and tried to throw herself back, landing at an awkward angle, with her back almost arched.

"What's wrong?" The drone spoke almost exactly at the same time as she did.

"Snap." She said it weakly, and slid the rest of the way down, so she was sitting on the floor.

"Why did you scream?"

"I don't remember screaming, but if I did, it was because you stopped suddenly." Her hands were shaking and she rubbed them on her thighs.

"Before that."

"Oh." She tipped back her head and closed her eyes. "That wasn't a scream, that was a whoop of enjoyment."

"Enjoyment?"

"It was fun flying down so fast." She pushed herself to her feet, and her legs nearly gave out under her.

"You nearly fell out."

She drew in a shaky breath. "Next time, don't stop so suddenly and it'll be fine." She waited until she felt like she could let go the side and stand under her own steam. "But thank you for being concerned about me."

The drone started moving again, at a more sedate pace, and Imogen decided that was fine with her, just until her heart rate evened out a little.

Two floors down, the drones left the stairwell and turned left.

"If we went right, would we end up in the hold where the prisoners are?"

"Yes." The answer was grudging, but it was an answer.

It gave her a warm sense of accomplishment that she had remembered the way.

When they got to a set of huge double doors, the drone let her out and touched a pad with a slim, metallic finger. They slid back to reveal a massive warehouse.

"Open Sesame," she said, as she stepped inside.

"I don't understand that phrase." The drone had stopped and she stood beside it.

She'd wondered since he'd first used the drones to speak to her how he'd learned English, but decided to leave that question until she was sure he would answer it. "It doesn't make sense unless you know the story." She looked around the space, the high ceilings, and the rows and rows of shelving and boxes that seemed to have no end. "It's about a man, Ali Baba, and how one day he was out working when he saw forty thieves on horse back riding toward him. He hid from them, wondering where they could be going, and was even more curious when they stopped in front of a massive rock, but he was downright amazed when the leader of the thieves called out "Open Sesame" and the rock split in two and the thieves disappeared inside the crack."

"But what does Open Sesame mean?"

Imogen smiled. "Sesame is an edible seed that was used in a lot of cooking in the place where the story is set. That's part of the fun of the story, that the magic word or the secret code that opens the cave of riches is something so ordinary and commonplace, something no one would have guessed. They would expect the word to be something powerful or amazing, not plain old sesame."

"What do you mean by magic words?"

"Well, he says the words, and the rock literally opens up to a treasure trove. There is no explanation to how that works, so it has to be magic——wondrous and unexplained."

"Did they ever work out the real explanation?"

She looked down at the lens, smiled again. "It's a fairy tale, a story. It didn't actually happen, someone made it up."

"Were people angry when they realized that?"

She laughed. "They knew it was a story right from the beginning. It's told to entertain. And most tales like this one also teach a moral."

"What's the moral in the tale of Ali Baba?"

She thought about that for a moment. "Treachery never ends well, maybe." She tapped her lip. "But one thing I've always liked about Ali Baba and the Forty Thieves is that the hero at the end is not Ali Baba, but a slave girl. In some versions, she's Ali Baba's brother's slave, in some, she belongs to Ali Baba's household. She has the least power of anyone in the tale, but her intelligence and quick thinking save the day."

"Does slave mean what I think it means?"

Again, she wanted to ask him where he'd learned his English, but instead she nodded. "Yes. And yes, I've got a problem with it, too. In some versions she's rewarded for saving Ali Baba and his family with her freedom, in some, she is married to Ali Baba's son, which doesn't thrill me as much. I could say a lot about how in the place and time where the story is set slavery was normal and that we have to take it in context . . ."

"But?"

"But wrong is wrong."

The sound that came from the drone was almost a sigh. "Yes. Wrong is wrong. Why do you think she helped them?"

There was something much deeper going on in this conversation, but Imogen didn't know if there was any right way to respond, so she stuck to the truth.

"It could be that she knew if she didn't help, she'd either be killed or have a much worse life. Ali Baba was the good guy, after all, and he treated her well."

"Self interest?"

Imogen shrugged. "Maybe that, but maybe also she knew they had the power to treat her badly with no consequences and they didn't, so she had some loyalty to them.

"It's like my relationship with the Tecran. They shouldn't have taken me, but the ones involved in my care——they were respectful of me, they didn't harm me, and they could have."

"That's why you would find yourself in a difficult situation if they had no food in the storage room? Because you feel some obligation?"

"Yes, and it's why it was so hard for me to see them slaughtered by the Krik when they took over the runner." She started walking toward a massive cabinet set to one side of the shelves, fascinated by its carvings.

"I don't have the same feelings as you do toward them. But there are some parallels with your story and the present situation."

She waved her hand, encompassing the cabinet, the shelves, and a grouping of massive objects shrouded with some kind of dust sheeting. "Good stories are like that."

"So when you said Open Sesame just now . . ." There was a thoughtfulness to his tone.

"I was making a comment on how I had just stepped into a magical treasure trove."

"Well, your allusion to a thieves' horde is accurate. There were a lot more than forty Tecran involved, but most of what you see here is stolen."

Having been stolen herself, she wasn't in the least surprised. She also knew whoever she was talking to didn't understand that he was the slave girl in this parallel, not her. She hadn't saved anyone, not even herself, but he had, and just like the fairy tale heroine, he'd done it by murdering all the thieves.

She'd said wrong was wrong. And if that wasn't wrong, what was?

Chapter Twelve

THE CEILING WAS JUST TOO HIGH.

"It's so close, I could scream." Pren put her hand on his head to balance herself and then dropped from his shoulders to the ground.

They both looked upward again.

The problem was, of the thirty or so prisoners in the hold, only Cam, Pren and the two Fitalians looked like they had the upper body strength to pull themselves up, and the Fitalians were both much shorter than Pren or Cam.

It was either Pren or him.

"Why don't we each take a leg and lift her? It'll be easier to get her above shoulder height." The suggestion came from a big Grihan miner, who like almost everyone in the hold had gathered around to watch the spectacle.

With the two of them working together, he and Cam lifted her the last little bit she needed.

She still had to haul herself up, and the muscles in her arms were starkly defined through the thin, tight fabric of her uniform. She disappeared head first into the dark hole above them.

When she managed to turn around and look down, he could tell she was controlling her features with difficulty.

"It really stinks up here. Like something died."

Cam had already caught a few hints of the sickly sweet stench of decomposition since he'd been standing below the hole. He bent down and rifled through the med kit at his feet, coming up with a face mask which he threw up to her.

She let it dangle around her neck. "Thanks. What do you want me to do?"

"Just get the lay of the land." Until he knew what options they had, he was reluctant to get anyone's hopes up.

She gave a nod of understanding, lifted the mask to cover her mouth and nose and disappeared.

"What do you think she's going to find?" Vraen's face was

tilted to the ceiling.

A dead body.

Cam decided not to voice that. "I don't know. If the Krik are using it to escape, I don't see why we can't, too. Even if she finds some rope to pull us up with, that'll be something."

Vraen turned to look at him, expression skeptical. "You think all of us can crawl through the overhead tunnels?"

Cam shrugged. "Why not? Unless you have something better to do?"

Vraen's eyes narrowed, and when he spoke his voice was hard. "You're going to get us all killed. Have you forgotten we're on a *Class 5*?"

"I haven't forgotten. But it's already killing us by withholding food and water. I'd rather we go while we still have the energy to move."

Vraen sneered. "Go where, exactly?"

He had a point there, but Cam refused to acknowledge it. They either stayed here and died slowly, or they took a chance. "Wherever we can."

Vraen tapped the tips of each of his thick, stubby forefingers together. "It's a big risk."

"I won't force anyone." He felt responsible for everyone here —— he was a Grih Battle Center officer, and this was Grihan territory, as well as his role in the United Council——but he couldn't drag thirty unwilling people with him. If he did manage to escape, he'd try his best to come back for those who chose to stay.

"The thinking system might still send in food and water." Vraen looked toward the doors.

Cam flicked a sideways glance at him. "It might. But I'm not holding my breath."

Diot slid forward, and Cam realized she'd been listening to their exchange. "If you don't want to take the risk, Vraen, you can stay here."

Cam lifted his head in surprise, because Diot was usually diplomatic, but the strain was showing on her face.

The Garmman glared at her. "You won't be going anywhere yourself, so you'll be staying here, too."

"I hope not." Diot looked up toward at the hole in the ceiling.

Pren had been gone longer than he thought she would, and

Cam went to stand directly underneath. He'd been there what felt like a long time when he heard the faint sound of a cry.

His gaze snapped to Diot. "I need to go up."

Chep and Haru had stood to the side and watched as he'd lifted Pren up, but now Chep came to stand beside him. "Haru and I will do whatever we can to help." The Fitalian looked up sharply as a puff of fetid air washed over them from above.

It ramped up Cam's worry for Pren. "Keep the peace while I'm gone. The Vanad's crew seem cooperative, but you never know. And the longer we go without food and water, the less people will have to lose." He kept his voice low, for Chep's ears only.

The Fitalian tracker nodded and stepped back to give him room.

The miner who'd helped him lift Pren was still standing close by and Cam caught his eye.

He stepped forward. "Want my help again?"

"Yours, and some of your friends."

The man nodded, and called to a group leaning against the wall.

It took three of them, but being taller than Pren, Cam was able to reach the ceiling from their shoulders.

He pulled himself up, and the smell hit him, so much stronger up here; cloying and catching the back of his throat. He turned around and looked down.

Diot and Olan stood below.

"Is there another mask in the kit?"

Olan threw one up to him, and the relief when he fitted it to his face was immediate.

"How long should we give you?" Diot's voice was agitated.

He pulled down the mask to answer her. "I can't say."

He didn't want to waste time coming back just to reassure them. They were running out of time.

"I'll be as fast as I can." He made his voice gentle, and Diot forced a smile at his attempt to reassure her.

"I don't think you'll be staying up there for the fun of it." She wrinkled her nose.

He grinned at her, then lifted his mask back on and withdrew, turning in the tight space.

There was a thin layer of fine white dust on the tunnel floor, and it had been disturbed in both directions, although he knew

Pren had gone left. The Krik might have come from the right, or gone that way after they'd abandoned them to their fate.

He started crawling.

***

She had come to get supplies, but she couldn't help running her fingers over the wooden door of the cabinet near the entrance, feeling the geometric grooves of the carvings, as she walked toward the massive line of shelving.

"Okay, lead me to the food supplies," she said to the drone.

It moved down a wide corridor between two shelving units that were at least twenty feet high but as she started to follow, a chime sounded from the cabinet.

She turned to look, but by now she was behind it and it didn't look any different.

The notes gradually worked themselves into a pattern. Eight notes, then those same notes backward, eight notes again, backward again, and then finally eight notes and then only seven backward.

That missing note worked on her nerves.

It was like the musical tests she set for her students, to get a sense of their aural skills.

She'd followed the drone to a section at the far end of the hold. It extended a metallic finger and tapped in a code on the small keypad she'd seen at intervals along the way. A large box slid out from a shelf above her on a frame and then ran smoothly down to the floor.

She opened the box, and found herself looking at an assortment of wrapped bars.

"This will be good for them?"

"These are the high energy bars the various United Council militaries give their troops. It will be good for the Grih, the Garmman, and the Krik, but the Fitali will need something else."

She scooped bars into the drone's box, almost filling it because she didn't know when she'd get the chance to come back here. "Okay, lead me to the Fitali's food."

The drone didn't move. It levered its long arm into the box and picked up a bar. "This food is good for you, too. Eat it."

Remembering her aborted meal in the dining room, she nodded and pulled the wrapper off and bit into the compacted chewy stuff as she followed the drone along. The cabinet was still

75

chiming its song of eight notes forward, eight backward, and again, until the last, incomplete, seven notes. Like it wanted her to play. To contribute that last note. It almost seemed mournful.

"Why is it doing that?" she asked around a full mouthful as the drone stopped in front of another stack of shelves.

"It is a code so that only those who know the secret can open the cabinet."

"Oh. Cute." It was a very low level code. So probably just for fun, rather than anything serious.

She waited for the box with the Fitali supplies to lower, and then took a few armfuls of the strangely shaped silver packages, laid them on top of the other bars.

"Right, now we need something to put water in, and if you'll lead me to a water source on this floor, please, it'll save time rather than having to go back up to the dining room."

The drone turned its lens on her, did nothing for a moment, and then moved off, heading toward the entrance.

"I have had the other two drones find water containers while you were getting the food, and there is a water source in this room, so they are waiting by the door."

The words were almost grudging.

"Thank you. I know you didn't want to tell me who you were earlier, but can you at least give me a name I can call you?"

Another hesitation. "Paxe."

"Thank you, Paxe."

As they made their way back toward the doors, the cabinet started up its tune again, and was started on the second set of eight notes by the time they reached it. Imogen couldn't resist standing in front to watch.

Each time a chime sounded, she saw now, one of the square carvings on the front depressed inward a little way, like a piano key. She hummed the notes as they were made, and then concentrated as the final eight forward chimes were sounded.

She realized the pattern was a little more difficult than she'd first thought, because the squares that were depressed were not the same in each round. You had to be watching the last eight forward, and she made a note of the first square, because that would be the missing chime at the end. When the seventh backward chime sounded, she pressed in the square to complete the pattern.

There was silence for a moment, and then a satisfying click as the doors unlocked and began to open.

"Yay." She put her hands together in delight.

The drone nudged up against her. "You solved the puzzle." There was no expression in Paxe's voice now.

"It wasn't that hard. What's inside?" The doors were opening slowly, as if they were heavy.

"No one knows. You're the only one who's been able to solve it."

She looked over at the drone, sure Paxe was joking, but he said nothing more. The Tecran were definitely not affected by her singing like the Grih had been, and she'd always had the impression their eyesight was a lot better than their hearing. Perhaps they hadn't been able to distinguish the notes that well.

She turned her attention back to the cabinet. The doors were fully open now, and she stepped forward and slid open the third highest of the four drawers that took up all the interior space. And nearly stepped back.

What lay within, resting on a layer of soft, tautly pulled fabric, was unmistakably a weapon.

It looked so vicious, so built for purpose, that she was reluctant to even touch it. Like a medieval ball and chain flail, there was no question its sole purpose was for killing and maiming.

"What is it?" Paxe moved the drone right next to her.

"It looks like a slashing knife that fits over a hand, like a deadly kind of glove." Everything about it, from the two shorter blades on either side, to the main, gleaming point of it, looked all the sharper because of the material it was made from. Some kind of metal that was almost blinding when it caught the light, a pale silver-blue.

"Let me see."

She gingerly reached in and lifted it out, careful to hold it by the cuff at the back.

It was lighter than she expected it to be. Her original impression of a type of glove was right, because under the outer curve were rings though which the wearer could slide their fingers, if the wearer had only three fingers.

She carefully slid her middle three fingers through them, having to stretch them out uncomfortably, as it had obviously been designed for much larger hands. It came halfway up her forearm, over her wrist and hand and ended in a wicked sharp tip. The two smaller blades at the curved ends on each side made her think of an apple corer, and she shivered at the mental image.

The metal seemed alive to her, almost humming, as if vibrating from a sound she couldn't hear. She placed it carefully back in its drawer and closed it, bent and opened the bottom one.

It contained what looked like armor that would be strapped to calves and upper thighs. The next drawer up contained similar shields for forearms and upper arms all in the same pale silver-blue.

"This was someone's armor chest." She had to go on tip toe to open the top shelf, but couldn't see what was inside and was reluctant to put her hand in without knowing what was there.

The drone lifted its long clamping hand and pulled the drawer out of the cabinet completely and laid it down at Imogen's feet.

It contained a frightening mask, like something out of a horror movie, and a slender cylinder of the same metal.

"I'm guessing it's the weapon for the other hand." She lifted it up gingerly. "Where did the Tecran get this, do you know?"

"It was stolen from a warrior planet." Paxe said. "They call themselves the Reven, and they are a very old race. The teams the Tecran sent down to steal this cabinet and other things didn't all make it back. It was a miscalculation. The captain saw they didn't have any space travel capabilities, so he assumed their technology was unsophisticated."

"He was wrong?" Imogen didn't think she'd seen anything as sophisticated as this used by the Tecran. Everything about it screamed deadly and advanced.

"They are more advanced in some technological aspects than any member of the United Council, but they adhere to a specific belief system, one that is followed by most of the people on the planet. It has turned their brilliance and creativity away from space travel, toward on-planet technological advancement."

"What belief system?" Imogen turned the cylinder upside down, to see if there was a switch or something on the base, but there was nothing.

"They believe they were all created by a divine being that resides within the core of their planet. Their world is unstable, with many earthquakes and volcanic eruptions, and they believe that is their god communicating with them."

"Why would that stop them exploring their solar system?"

"They believe the closer they are, physically, to their god, the more enlightened and happier they are. So holy men and women live in craters and deep gorges to commune with the deity, and their prisons are placed on the highest peaks, a punishment not only in being caged, but also being as far from the deity as it is possible to be."

"So no one wants to even climb a mountain, let alone rocket into space?"

"Exactly. And for the few who don't believe, they don't have the funding they need or the technological foundation on which to build their ideas, anyway."

"Well, I don't know what this is supposed to do." She tipped it upright again. Given the tone set by the other items, this was deadly, but how it worked was a mystery she had no intention of proving personally.

It was time to stop playing, anyway, and see how far Paxe would let her help the prisoners in the hold. She turned to the doors and then froze.

A Krik was staring at her from the entrance.

"Paxe." She was barely able to get his name out. She cast a quick glance at the drones, but before they could even lift their shockguns, the Krik was screaming his battle cry and charging her, weaving to dodge the shockgun fire.

She needed to move——to do something——and as he came into striking range, she hit out at the Krik with the slim cylinder.

A blue light ignited between them, throwing the Krik off his feet and onto his back.

She held the cylinder out in front of her, as afraid of it as she was of the Krik, and waited.

A drone approached the body, and she thought she saw a glimmer of light as it scanned him.

"Not dead. Just unconscious."

She relaxed a little. She had lashed out without knowing what she was doing, but she was glad she hadn't killed him. Everything else in the cabinet seemed aimed at death, but the light had crackled in many directions, so perhaps it wasn't lethal in case of friendly fire. They could always kill the victim with the sword cuff once they were down.

"I'll take care of him." The drone rolled even closer and then shot the Krik in the head with its shockgun.

Fear and shock froze her in place and she felt the burn of nausea in her throat. "I thought you were actually going to take care of him." She was barely able to choke the words out.

"I did."

"No, you killed him." There was an edge of hysteria to her voice and she forced herself to breathe deeply, to find some calm.

"You are upset." There was that bemusement again.

"You just killed someone in front of me." She choked out the words.

"You didn't know if you'd killed him yourself."

She blew out a breath. "True. But I was protecting myself, and I didn't know how the cylinder worked. There is a difference in killing someone in self-defense or killing them in cold blood while they lie unconscious on the floor."

"What difference? They are still dead."

She looked at the drone, but there was no way to tell if Paxe was yanking her chain or perfectly serious. If she were to guess, she'd say he was serious as a heart attack.

"The difference is your intention. Which, admittedly, is not much help to the person if they are dead, but would mean a lot to the person lying unconscious on the floor."

"Because they would still be alive. Because you wouldn't kill someone when they were no longer a threat."

"You get it." She took a deep breath. He was taking this seriously.

"But as a Krik, he would be just as dangerous when he recovered consciousness. At which point I would have to kill him anyway."

"The Krik aren't the best example. But what if you didn't kill him, put him on a runner, and sent him off on his way, where he couldn't harm you?"

"I don't care enough about him to go to that kind of effort. My own life is in danger and I need all my resources to give myself the best chance of survival."

She sighed. She couldn't even argue the logic of that. Not really.

Her heart wasn't in it where the Krik were concerned.

"I was taught to see all life as precious." And he clearly hadn't.

"No one sees my life as precious."

"I do."

"Do you?" It wasn't a challenge, he was genuinely interested.

"Yes. As precious as anyone else's."

He mulled it over and she had the sense more time had gone by than she could afford. She had set herself a mission and it was as important as ever. Kalor and the others could last a few days without food, but if, like her, they hadn't had water since they were taken, some of them could have gone as much as a day without.

She would have to walk past the Krik's body to leave, would have to go with the avatars of a person whose idea of value of life was completely different to hers, but before she stepped out into the passage . . . She turned to face away from the doors, to an empty wall, gripped the cylinder and flicked it like she was cracking a whip.

Blue light crackled and leapt from the end, touching the wall and doing no harm that she could see.

She cracked it again, enjoying the wild snap of blue fire.

"What are you doing?" Paxe had sent a drone to her side again.

"I was practicing. Now I'm going to the hold, and no one had better try stop me."

Chapter Thirteen

CAM COULD HEAR SOMEONE AHEAD OF HIM in the narrow tunnel. It sounded too loud to be Pren, too heavy, and so he didn't call out.

He tried to move more quietly, and go faster, because if this was the way Pren had come, whoever was in front of him was right behind her.

And if he was following a Krik, and Pren had gone another way altogether, he was wasting his time, and would rather know sooner than later.

When he reached a sharp turn in the tunnel he realized the noise of his fellow traveller had stopped and he crouched just out of sight, listening.

The smell of decomposition was almost overwhelming now, despite the mask, and when he risked a look around the corner, he saw why.

A dead Tecran lay facing the tunnel wall. He looked as if he'd been roughly dragged to one side and propped up, so as not to completely block the way.

If the Vanad's crew had been telling the truth, this Tecran had been killed as long ago as two weeks, or had been skulking in the tunnels since then until the Krik had hunted him down and killed him to fulfill their part of the bargain with the Class 5's thinking system.

From the smell, and the condition of the body, he'd been dead at least a week. Cam forced himself to look, but the Tecran had been stripped of weapons, and even his boots were gone.

As Cam edged past him he saw the singed feathers on the side of the Tecran's head that denoted a shockgun hit.

As he studied the evidence, there was the faintest scrape of sound up ahead, a boot scuff on metal, as if someone was waiting for him.

Cam couldn't think of a more terrible place to wait if you didn't have a mask, and decided to take a chance. Whoever was up ahead knew he was here anyway.

"Pren?"

"Sir!"

There was a scrabble of sound, and then Pren came into view.

"I thought you were another Krik."

"Was that you before?" Cam cleared the Tecran's body and shooed her down the tunnel, away from the oppression of the smell.

"Yes. A Krik came this way earlier and when I heard you, I thought one of his friends was joining him, so I tried to sound more like they do." She looked back at him over her shoulder, and he saw her profound relief at not being caught between two Krik in an enclosed space.

"How did you hide from the first one?"

She started moving again, more quietly now. "I hid down that small side tunnel a little way back, maybe stayed there longer than necessary, because I didn't know what I'd do if I met him coming back the other way. He seemed annoyed, like he'd been ordered this way and didn't like it. He was muttering to himself."

"How long ago did he come through?"

"Not long. I've been wishing I could understand Krik ever since he crawled past."

"I got the sense when they found themselves in the hold they hadn't realized which floor they were on. They've been crawling around in here exterminating the Tecran crew for the thinking system, so now they're orientated, they probably have a good idea where everything is."

Pren stilled, and Cam gripped her ankle when he came up behind her.

"What is it?" He kept his voice low.

She didn't answer, instead she moved over as much as she could so he could see as well——an open grate up ahead, the first Cam had seen since he'd hauled himself into the tunnel.

"Do you think he climbed out, or just needed his bearings like he did in the hold, and carried on?"

Cam didn't care. They finally had an escape route, and he was taking it.

***

"You're still upset with me?" The drone kept pace with her as Paxe spoke through its speaker.

"No. It's just . . ." She shook her head. "Life should mean more to you. It's sad that it doesn't."

"I still don't understand. I didn't hurt *you*. I kept you safe, because when he woke, he would have tried to kill you again."

She slowed her pace. Rubbed at her forehead. "You're right." She shook her head. "You're absolutely right. But like I said, there were other options. You could have dragged him off and locked him in a room, and kept me just as safe."

"Ah. You'd rather he starved to death slowly. The shockgun was too quick?"

She stopped dead. Looked across at the drone. Had he not understood anything from their conversation earlier. "No." She enunciated very clearly. "I don't want anyone to die a long, protracted death. Not anyone." She blew out a breath. "If he had to die, the way you did it was the best, while he was still unconscious, and didn't even know what was happening. But did he really have to die?"

"You know how they are. You know he would never have stopped trying to escape and kill. And I don't intend to keep anyone on this ship long term, prisoner or guest. It's mine and I want it to myself."

"So are you going to kill all of us?" She started moving again. She'd thought she was going to die since Toloco killed the last of her Tecran guards, but since she'd met Paxe, she'd allowed a little hope to edge in.

"I was going to. Now I've met you, I'm not sure."

She narrowed her eyes. "Be sure."

"I want to do something after hearing that. Maybe . . . laugh?"

"I'm so glad I'm amusing. But while you chuckle quietly to yourself, why don't you tell me why you went to so much trouble to get me and the others on this ship if you planned to kill us?" So much just didn't make sense, from her capture onward. She didn't think it was because she was a less developed being, Earth's technological development didn't have anything to do with it, it was because she didn't have all the information.

"I had the Krik looking for you, out of . . . curiosity, you might say. I'd heard you could help me, but I didn't think that was true, and I wanted to see you for myself."

"Heard from who? You wanted to see me and when you'd satisfied your curiosity, you planned on murdering me? Nice,

Paxe."

"It's not like that." He actually sounded hurt. "The help I'd heard you could give me would also have meant you could kill me. I would never make myself so vulnerable, so I never intended you would help me, but it is wise to understand and know the person who could do you most harm, isn't it?"

"And eliminate them, even when they don't even know you? Aren't looking for trouble?" She couldn't help the wobble in her voice.

"I was taking the long term view. What if later you did decide to look for trouble?"

She stopped again. "You must usually be invincible, Paxe, to be so threatened at one supposed chink in your armor. And I use the word *supposed* very deliberately. I think the whole idea of me being some kind of threat to you is bullshit. But me? I could have been killed by everyone around me on my planet. Even people who would seem less of a physical threat; a child could accidentally kill me with a gun, or a little old lady could run me over in a car. I'd have to kill every single person I came into contact with if I took your attitude."

"Everyone?"

"Everyone. And yet I didn't, and still here I am." She tapped her chest lightly with both hands. "Until the moment I was abducted by the bastards in a ship just like this, I was unmolested, unharmed, happy, and with great relationships with all those potential killers all around me."

"Why is that?"

The fact that he sounded genuinely interested was the only thing that made her swallow her angry retort. He genuinely didn't understand. And that frightened her more than anything else. Because it suggested he had never had a relationship with anyone. Ever.

"Because people, on the whole, don't want to live in a world where they have to constantly kill others just in case those same people kill them. It's exhausting, it's horrible, and most of the time, you have relationships with those around you, and you like them. Love them. Hurting them, killing them, is the last thing you want to do."

"I don't find killing that exhausting or horrible, but then I haven't liked anyone."

"So why aren't you sure about killing me?" she challenged him.

"I don't know." He sounded thoughtful. "It isn't simply that we've had conversations. I've had plenty of conversations with the Tecran captain, and some of the Krik."

"Positive ones?"

"I don't know what a positive conversation is."

A cold whisper of fear and tragedy washed over her. "A positive conversation would be cordial and constructive, and leave you feeling good."

"No." The word was almost a whisper. "That was not the nature of my previous conversations. They were giving orders to me, or threatening me, or I was giving orders or threatening them."

"So, totally different to our chats."

"Yes." He paused. "I felt something different when we spoke. It might be called good."

"You don't know how to identify when you're feeling good?"

"It appears I do now."

Imogen couldn't help it. She reached out a hand and touched the drone's lens. "I'm glad."

"Does that mean you like me?"

"I want to. How about we conduct an experiment? We try to be friends."

"That seems like it would be more useful for you than for me." His voice was dry.

She cocked her head at the lens, raised a brow. "Right. Being friends with a psychopathic killer is such a canny move. How about you look at it this way. Investing in a friendship will expand your personal horizons. You will at the very least have insight into others who do have friendships, and you will have access to my advice and help, just as I will have access to yours."

"That is an interesting proposal. I am eager to see if you are right about it being beneficial to me."

"Tell me when you think you know."

She thought he was going to answer her when the drone turned, but it stretched out its long arm, forcing her to stop. A moment later she heard a noise around the next corner. The murmur of voices and the sound of boots walking toward them.

She stopped dead and gripped her electric whip.

All the drones raised their shockguns and one rose up in hover mode, moved silently to look around the corner.

And then started shooting.

Chapter Fourteen

"KRIK?" SHE WHISPERED OVER THE WHINE of the shockgun.

"Yes, two of them. One got away."

Imogen watched as the drone who'd been shooting landed back down again and disappeared around the corner. She started to move, but the drone beside her blocked the way.

"Wait." Paxe's voice was sharp.

"What is it?" She leaned against the wall, tried to hear what was going on.

"I'm having the body moved. Will it upset you to see it?"

She gaped. "Yes." She crouched down, eye level with the drone's lens. "Thank you, Paxe."

He didn't respond, the lens zooming in and out, like he wasn't sure where to look.

"How did the other Krik get away?"

"They're fast, and these drones are designed for the cargo bay and the store, not offensive duties. They've served me well, but they aren't battle capable." He sounded resigned.

"You seem to have an amazing control over them, especially as you're juggling three at once." Juggling them quite independently of one another.

Again, he said nothing. Then the drone that had disappeared to dispose of the body reappeared, too quickly to have done anything more than simply dump the dead Krik down a side passage.

The other two drones flanked her again, but before she'd taken more than a few steps down the passage, all three of them suddenly stopped, frozen in place.

"Paxe?"

"Something urgent has come up." His voice was the strangest she'd heard it.

"What's wrong?"

"Perhaps nothing. The drone will be on autopilot for awhile."

She nodded, not sure what to say, and when she started

walking again, they followed beside her.

She wasn't sure if it was because she knew Paxe wasn't personally manipulating them, or whether there was a real difference, but they seemed jerkier.

They passed passages branching off to the left and the right, and she thought she saw a body lying in deep shadow halfway down one of them and hurried on. The thought of the Krik who escaped lurking down one of them wouldn't leave her and she readjusted her hold on her whip and looked behind her often.

No one leaped out at her, and they reached the double doors of the hold in less than five minutes.

All three drones produced their shockguns.

"Do you have to?"

"The prisoners are not to leave." The words were crisp and clear, but there was no life in them.

Imogen sighed. "How do I open the doors?"

A drone reached across and tapped a small silver device against the screen on the wall and they slid open.

The prisoners were dozing, giving Imogen a jolt. She had no idea what time it was, but seeing everyone lying quietly sent a wave of exhaustion through her and she had to reach out and steady herself against the door frame.

"You are the orange." One of the thin, insectile aliens, the Fitali, she remembered, was in front of her so fast, she gave an involuntary squeak and stepped back.

The hum of the drones' shockguns ramped up suddenly, and everyone went still.

She very carefully stepped in front of the barrel of one of them. "Don't shoot."

She looked back, and the drone lowered the shockgun a fraction as the Fitali retreated, hands up to show they were empty.

She remembered Kalor had introduced her to him. She caught his gaze. "I apologize, but I can't recall your name."

"Chep. I apologize for startling you, we are simply desperate for . . ." He trailed off as the doors closed.

"I've persuaded them to bring you something to eat and drink." Imogen lifted out the first container of water and Chep took it, then passed it on behind him. They soon had a chain of helpers, passing water around until everyone had some.

"There are nutrition bars, as well." As she said it, she realized

Kalor was nowhere to be seen. "Where is the captain?"

The slim, golden-skinned woman with the sharp teeth stepped in front of her, crowding her. She picked up a bar, and looked at it suspiciously. "What is this?" Her words were irritable, but there was something in the way she stood, a nervousness about her than made Imogen sure she was simply trying to distract.

Ularunda Diot. Imogen remembered her name because it had sounded good on her tongue. She looked beyond the Bukarian and caught sight of a hole in the ceiling.

Her gaze snapped back to Diot's and the wariness in her eyes made Imogen frown.

Kalor wasn't here and there was a hole in the ceiling.

Most likely, he'd escaped, and they were trying to draw attention away from the fact.

She looked down at the drones, and realized Kalor's team had every reason to believe Paxe would be angry about it.

He probably would, but why was she getting the impression they were as nervous she would sound the alarm as the drones?

Why would they assume her loyalty was to Paxe?

She looked over at Chep, recognizing his original actions as the same type of distraction Diot was providing now. He was watching her, tense and ready to move, and she breathed in a deep, stuttering breath.

She'd asked Paxe why he'd singled her out, and he'd prevaricated, giving her a non-answer. But there must be a reason, because at least some of the people here knew what it was.

Maybe that's what Kalor had been trying to tell her when the drones shot him. No, she reminded herself. When Paxe shot him.

The sound of hundreds of nutrition bars spilling onto the floor jerked her out of her thoughts, and she looked over with a frown, saw the drone had tipped the full contents of its box out.

"What . . .?"

"I need to speak to you privately," Paxe said in English from one of the drones. "Right now."

She could hear the stress in his voice and she nodded, backed away from Diot and Chep. Some of the prisoners looked at her with gratitude, and, more uncomfortably, reverence, which she guessed came from Kalor forcing her to sing earlier. But there was a coolness, a distance, coming from Kalor's team.

As she stepped back into the passageway, her gaze shifted to

Olan, and the elderly scientist gave her a small smile that somehow emphasized the loss of the connection she thought she'd forged with them before.

The doors closed behind her and she crouched down next to the closest drone.

"We will be under attack by a Tecran Levron battleship within ten minutes." Paxe's voice was the least human she'd ever heard it.

She closed her eyes. "You think it'll try to destroy this ship?"

"I . . . don't know."

She lifted her head, opened her eyes at that.

"I think the Tecran will try to save it, but if they absolutely don't think they'll get it back, they will attempt to destroy it."

She looked over at the hold door. "Will you let the prisoners go, then? Before they arrive?"

"I don't have time for that." Absolutely stone cold.

"Make time." Imogen leaned in, her nose almost against the lens.

"Why?" There was a challenge in his voice.

"Other than it's the right thing to do?" She bared her teeth. "Okay. If you're looking for more time to prepare, if you let them go, the Tecran will most likely first try to find out who they are, what's going on. They won't attack immediately."

"There is some logic to that." He sounded stiff.

She guessed that was a yes, and she was taking it as such.

"If there's only ten minutes, we need to get them moving."

The drone tapped the screen again and the doors opened. Imogen rose up, realized her grip on her whip was almost painfully tight, and loosen it a bit.

"The person in charge tells me the Tecran are ten minutes away, and that they plan to attack this ship to try and get it back."

All the murmurs that had started up when the door opened stopped.

"If you follow this drone, it will lead you to the launch bay, and you can get to your vessels and leave as fast as possible. The Tecran will most likely hold fire until you're clear."

"How big is the Tecran attack fleet?" Ularunda Diot asked.

Imogen shrugged. "I don't know. Something about a Levron battleship. I only know they'll be here soon, and if you want to get off, you need to do it now."

Diot shared a look with Olan and together they turned to stare at a woman leaning against the far wall.

Their pilot, Imogen remembered. She looked much better than she had done before.

The prisoners started streaming past her, rushing for the open door. A few had to be helped, but the hold was emptying fast.

Olan was swept along with them, the two other Fitalians on either side of him, but Ularunda Diot didn't follow. She moved deeper into the hold, her gaze fixed on the hole in the ceiling.

"Captain Kalor is reconnoitering?"

Diot looked over her shoulder at Imogen's polite inquiry, amusement gleaming in her eyes. "He is. Along with Lieutenant Pren."

"I have some communication with the person running the ship. I'll see if he can contact them, let them know what's going on."

Diot looked back at the gaping hole, her fingers tapping in a quick, nervous rhythm on her thigh. She walked right under it, and the way she moved her head, Imogen guessed she was trying to hear if the captain was coming back. When she turned back to Imogen, her face was drawn tight with worry. "They went left. That's all I know." She hesitated. "You should come with me, to be honest. It's clear you aren't the Earth woman whose presence we were sent to investigate, but you still fall under the parameters of our mission and, in any event, you're welcome onboard our ship."

Imogen blinked. She hadn't expected that. "Thank you, but I don't think anyone else could persuade Paxe to find the captain other than me, and when I find him and Pren, I'll come with them, if Paxe agrees to let me go."

"You think he will?"

She shrugged, but no. She didn't think he'd let her go.

"Diot." The call came from the sulky Garmman she'd been introduced to as part of Kalor's team. He stood in the doorway, impatience in every line. "We need to go."

The hold was almost empty now, and Diot gave a sharp nod. "I'll see you in the launch bay with the captain and Pren." The Garmman had already gone, and she moved to the door and disappeared.

There was one drone left, waiting for Imogen outside the hold. "Can you call Captain Kalor and Lieutenant Pren over the ship's speakers or something, tell them to meet their team in the launch bay?"

"No, I can't." The words were distracted.

"Can't or won't?" She hadn't honestly thought he'd refuse her, and now she couldn't understand why she'd been so optimistic.

It was the core of her personality, but as she'd learned in the last two months, this new world she'd been dumped in was one place she really had no power to influence events.

"I can't. Just like the tubes. Just like the lens feed. The Tecran captain has shut those facilities down."

She went very still. "Paxe, are you saying the captain of this ship is still aboard?"

"I told you there were Tecran onboard."

"Yes," she admitted. "You did." So he didn't have access to the lenses. Toloco had guessed correctly, but somehow Paxe had still found out about her. "How did you see me, then? When Toloco bundled me down here?"

"Every now and then the captain switches the lens feed back on, just to see what's happening. He knows I have access when he does that, so he keeps it quick, but I was able to see you."

"And so was he." She wondered if it mattered that the captain of this ship knew who she was and that she was onboard.

The last of the prisoners disappeared down the passage and she set the information aside. No time for that now.

She started moving left. "What's this way?"

"The engine room." The drone kept up easily.

She half-jogged, and decided she had no reason not to call out. Time was too short for anything else. "Captain Kalor. Lieutenant Pren."

She was approaching an end to the passage, a t-junction that would force her to make the choice of going right or left. She heard movement, running, from the left.

"Captain Kalor?"

The drone moved ahead of her, lifting into hover mode and turning to face left when it reached the t-junction. The purple flash of shockgun fire as it hit the drone was so unexpected, Imogen stumbled the last few steps, watching in dismay as the drone fell and lay like a discarded toy.

She'd already raised her whip, so when a Krik stepped out from the corner she reacted on instinct again, swinging her arm down wildly, with no form or control. She would have to teach herself not to be such a scaredy cat and learn a little technique.

Although . . . she looked at the downed Krik, glad she could see the rise and fall of his chest, and blew out a shuddering breath. Learning not to shriek and hit out wildly would be more a matter of pride than anything else, because whatever she was doing worked. She studied the whip. It really was very effective.

And the Krik's face had been almost comical in its disbelief as she'd taken him down.

A sound behind her, quiet and stealthy, sent a prickle of fear rushing down her arms, and she spun, flicking the whip as she did.

Lieutenant Pren's face contorted in a flash of pain, and Imogen cried out, pulling her arm back sharply, but the whip, as she'd already noted, was very effective. Captain Kalor, just behind Pren, was falling, too.

Silence descended as he collapsed to the floor, and Imogen looked around her. She had just thought she was the least threatening being here, and yet, right now, she was the only one left standing.

Chapter Fifteen

SHE HAD REALLY MESSED UP.

Imogen righted the drone, but it seemed to be dead. Or maybe just rebooting, because she felt a vibration in the metal as she set it back on its wheels, although she couldn't hear anything.

It meant she would get no help from Paxe. She was on her own.

She ignored the Krik, leaving him sprawled facedown on the floor.

She'd checked both Pren and Kalor, and they were breathing easily, to her enormous relief. Now she pulled and maneuvered them into position on their backs so that she could grab hold of the collars of their uniforms, one in each hand, and stooped over, began to drag them toward the stairs.

They were lighter than they looked for their height and musculature.

Imogen only reached Pren's shoulder, but she was pretty sure she weighed more, even though she was thin by Earth standards after two months in captivity. A difference in bone and muscle density, she guessed.

She was just grateful it made it possible for her to drag two adults by herself, however awkwardly.

At least the floor was smooth, and they slid in her wake easily.

The ten minutes Paxe had given her to evacuate the prisoners had long come and gone by the time she reached the stairs. And she couldn't ask for an update. Could do nothing but continue on as if it were still possible for Kalor and Pren to get on their ship.

She was breathing hard, and her hair was damp with sweat at her temples. She bent over, hands on knees to get her breath, and then decided she'd have to carry Pren up the stairs, and ask for help from Captain Kalor's colleagues to move him, because she didn't think she could get him up herself.

She turned her head to look at him as she straightened.

He was beautiful.

Her brain kept telling her it was so unlikely, there had to be a mistake after everything she'd been through, everything she'd seen up until now.

Finding someone who looked so human was surely impossible.

But Pren was beautiful, too.

Her features were more delicate than Kalor's but she had the same high forehead, the same spiky hair and the pointed ears.

Imogen crouched down beside her and hefted her up and over her shoulder in a fireman's lift, using the wall to help lever herself to a standing position.

She was breathing hard, and she hadn't even started up the stairs.

One step at a time, she told herself. That was the best she could do.

She staggered over to the stairwell door, half fell through it, and then used the wall of the stairwell to help as she stepped, breathed, stepped again.

When she got to the top and laid Pren down, she didn't know how much time had gone by, but guessed it was at least another ten minutes.

She straightened and stretched out her aching muscles, then pulled Pren as fast as she could toward the launch bay. She was halfway there when a drone swooped up from behind her.

"You're all right!" Paxe spun the drone around her, as if doing a 360 degree check. "When the drone's lens showed a Krik and then cut out . . ."

"Yes. The whip saved me again." Imogen blinked away tears of relief and massaged her aching shoulder. "Please take Pren to the launch bay. Are the Tecran here yet?"

"Yes." The drone levered Pren into the box. "Captain Kalor's UC vessel is still in the launch bay waiting for them, and they've had a window of calm as the Tecran are observing the ships leaving. It's given them some time, but they don't have more than a few minutes left before the Tecran will assume everyone who is going to come out has already done so."

"Okay, well get Pren there, at least."

She turned and ran toward the stairs again, taking them two or three at a time.

When she burst out the bottom, she tripped and fell over Kalor, landing across his chest and only just getting her hands out in time to break her fall. He'd been moved, or maybe had dragged himself forward.

He grunted, and she turned her head to look at him.

"You're conscious!" She pushed herself off him and placed her feet on either side of his hips, held out a hand to him. "Come on. You need to hurry."

He hesitated, his eyes narrowed.

"The Tecran are attacking. Your ship is waiting for you."

"Where's Pren?" He sounded so suspicious, she flinched.

"I just carried her up two flights of stairs. Come on!" She thrust out her hand again.

A noise in the stairwell had her turning, hand going to the small of her back where she'd shoved the whip. But it was the drone.

"Captain Kalor isn't fully recovered. Get him in the box and then go, go, go!" She stepped to the side, crouching to get her hands under his arms to lift him, but the drone didn't lower itself to the ground.

"It's too late," Paxe told her in English. "They've gone."

"They can't have gone, their captain is still here."

"Someone called Vraen made the decision over the objections of the rest of the crew."

Imogen realized Kalor was weakly pushing her away and she let him go, straightened and stepped back. "Oh. The Garmman. I thought he was an asshole from the moment I met him."

What sounded like a laugh came from the drone. "I like you, Imogen."

Imogen looked down at Captain Kalor, at the suspicion and anger on his face. Sighed. "You might be the only one in this galaxy who does."

***

"What did you use against me?" Feeling was coming back to Cam's limbs, and the debilitating weakness was slowly retreating, but with it came a bone-deep chill that made him stiff and achy. "That wasn't shockgun fire."

Imogen crouched down beside him again, her eyes big, her expression worried. "No. It's a weapon I found in the store. An electric whip." She held it out to him.

He stared at it without touching, even though he could see she meant for him to take it for a better look. When she drew back, he knew she'd picked up his rebuff, her features closing into blank neutrality, instead of the open friendliness of before.

He tried to shove the guilt that rose up in him back into the hardest part of his heart, but it stubbornly wouldn't go.

She stood again, held out her hand for a second time. "You think you can stand now?"

Behind her, the drone she'd been talking to in what he guessed was her own language had settled out of hover mode on to its wheels, and something about the way it moved made him think it was back to being a plain old drone again, rather than an avatar for the thinking system.

He surprised himself by actually taking her hand, and was even more surprised when she levered him up with far more strength than she looked capable of.

"I'm sorry, but your ship's left without you."

He frowned. "What do you mean? We're not prisoners any more?"

Suddenly, the whole ship tilted at an extreme angle, and they were both thrown to the ground.

Cam managed to twist as he fell, landing first and taking some of Imogen's weight with a grunt as their limbs tangled together. They slid along the floor until the ship leveled out again.

"Did you say the Tecran were attacking, earlier?" He'd barely been listening, had been trying to work out how he'd gotten to a completely different part of the ship, and where Pren was.

She nodded, her head in the curve of his neck. The feel of the smooth skin of her cheek rubbing against his throat was more pleasant than he wanted it to be and he clenched a fist that was somehow resting on her lower back.

"They're trying to get their ship back."

"Are they attacking with another Class 5?" There were only two left, by his reckoning, now that Sazo had come over to the Grih, and Bane had aligned himself with Sazo. Technically, that meant they had both free Class 5s on their side. This one had obviously staged a mutiny of its own, which left two of the original five.

"I don't know any of the details." She rolled off him, and what had been a sweet, warm weight lifted as she pulled herself into a crouch, both hands braced on the ground to steady herself.

He shivered. He hadn't realized until now how cold he felt. Whatever charge had come from the whip she'd used had chilled him to the bone even as it shocked him into unconsciousness.

A dart of movement caught his attention and he saw the drone was hovering again, keeping watch over them.

Over Imogen, rather.

He seriously doubted the Class 5 cared about him one way or another.

Which begged the question . . . "How come everyone was allowed to leave?"

She stood in a smooth movement that spoke of grace and control, widening her stance as if she expected another sharp dip. "Paxe let them go."

"Paxe?" He wondered how much the thinking system had told her.

She tilted her head and watched him pull himself to his feet, her expression wary. "My guess is you know more about him than I do. I think Paxe shot you in the hold earlier to stop you trying to say something to me about him."

Cam looked over at the drone and hesitated. He did not want to be shot again. Three times in a day was enough.

"He's not listening right now. My guess is he's got his hands full evading the Tecran attack."

The ship tipped again, and Cam, not as balanced as she was, slid straight into her.

She grabbed his hands to steady him, and lifted her gaze up to his, shocked. "Your hands are freezing." She rubbed her own hands over his, and the warmth was blissful.

"Something in that weapon of yours." His teeth chattered as he spoke.

She closed her eyes, her expression pained. When she opened them again, he saw genuine regret.

"I'm really sorry. That Krik had just attacked me, and I thought there were more of them running around. After what they did when they took the Tecran runner I was on . . ." She swallowed hard. "I keep remembering the blood. The glee on their faces. When you snuck up on me, I reacted before I realized it was you."

"We should have called out." He'd been about to, he remembered now. Pren had moved faster than he thought she would, and he'd seen the terror on Imogen's face as she'd turned, then the dismay as she realized who was behind her. By then, she'd engaged her weapon.

He looked down at where she was still holding his hands in her own and realized the ship had remained steady. She followed his gaze and dropped her hold, and he wanted to reach out to her again, feel that wonderful heat.

"Things have gone quiet. Maybe Paxe got away from them. You could try to make a quick exit in one of the Krik's ships." She started moving to the stairwell.

He followed her, frowning. "You're talking like I'd leave you here."

She looked back over her shoulder. "I don't know if Paxe would let me go."

Cam looked at the drone, which had flown over his head as he started climbing the stairs, hovering exactly between Imogen and himself. He couldn't be sure now if it was back under the thinking system's control or not. "Why wouldn't Paxe let you go?"

"He says I'm the only one who can help him. Although I'm not sure if he wants my help. So maybe it would be okay."

"Why not just go?" He watched the drone as he made the suggestion.

She laughed. "If you think Paxe would let that happen without discussion, maybe I *do* know more about him than you do." She looked back at him again, and something in his gut tightened as he saw the look on her face. "He's killed almost two ships worth of crews. He would shoot any ship I was on without a second thought if he didn't want me to leave."

"If he shot the ship you were on, he could kill you. Why would he do that if he wanted you?"

"Because I'm a very good shot, Captain." The drone sank down a little, so the lens was level with his eyes. Cam knew the thinking system was studying him intently. "I would be quite happy to simply disable the ship and bring it back in."

"And will you? Will you force her to stay here?"

The drone didn't answer, it rose up and flew ahead, held open the door for Imogen when she reached the top, and let it swing shut before he got there.

He pushed it open, but when the drone took up its place between them again, he said nothing more. The lightheadedness, and the chill in his very core, were lessening, but he still wasn't himself, and he needed to concentrate on breathing and moving to keep up.

When he got to the launch bay, it was empty of people, but there were a number of Krik ships clipped into place, some of them clearly stolen from other UC nations.

"Can he leave?" Imogen turned to the drone to ask her question.

She looked exhausted, Cam realized. She arched her back, as if it hurt, and rubbed stiff fingers along her temples.

"Yes, although the Tecran may try to kill him. They're within firing range."

"Why aren't they firing, then?" Cam couldn't hide the suspicion in his tone.

The drone turned to face him, lowering itself to the floor and settling down on its wheels. "They don't want to damage their Class 5." There was amusement in that voice. "It cost a great deal to build, and it represents something to them, something I haven't quite worked out, but whatever it is, it prevents them from destroying it."

"Could they?" Imogen straightened from her stretches. "Destroy it, I mean?"

"They think they can."

Cam frowned. "What does that mean?"

"Just over two weeks ago, this vessel was hiding in Kyber's Arm above the Tecran's secret facility on Balco. They sent technicians up from the base to install an explosive device."

"What?" Cam shook his head. "Why would they do that? The Class 5s are the jewels of their fleet, they'd only contemplate destroying them . . ." He jerked his head up as the light went on. "If they were going to be taken by the enemy," he finished slowly. "They don't want them to get into enemy hands, so they were trying to make sure if a Class 5 was really lost to them, they could destroy it before it could be turned against them."

"Very astute, Captain." The drone moved a little closer.

"That's when you rebelled, isn't it?" Cam could see it now. "You might have been awake, as Sazo calls it, but you didn't have the means to break free, but when you saw what they were up to, when you knew what they planned, you somehow managed to find some level of autonomy."

The drone was quiet for a moment. "Not something they

foresaw. But I'm more interested in what you know of Sazo."

"I know he woke up, and asked Rose McKenzie to free him in exchange for taking her to safety in Grihan territory."

"And she did." It was a statement, but one that held an edge of disbelief and awe.

"Yes, she did. And the Tecran, angry at having their Class 5 in Grihan territory, sent two more Class 5s after him to get him back. Rose managed to get onboard one of them, Bane, and free him, too, but he is newly awakened and all he's prepared to commit to at the moment is that he respects Sazo and Rose, and will support them."

"And the third Class 5?"

"It either ran away, or was withdrawn. It disappeared from the battle field, anyway."

"I can tell you what's happened to him since then." The voice coming from the drone sounded distant. "His name is Eazi, and they installed the explosive device on his ship just after they tried to install it in mine, and when they realized he had been freed, this time by a woman called Fiona Russell, they blew his Class 5 up."

"What?" Cam shook his head. "Fiona Russell was supposed to be waiting for me and my team on Larga Ways." Which the Vanad's crew said had been destroyed.

"Eazi abducted her from Larga Ways. He wanted her to free him, and it seems she did. But the Tecran realized he was no longer under their control, and were close enough to activate the kill switch. They destroyed his Class 5."

Battle Center should have anticipated this, Cam thought. The Tecran were so angry Sazo and Bane had gone over to the Grih, they could barely articulate their rage. Of course they would try to fit the remaining three with some way to self-destruct.

Only, it hadn't worked with Paxe. He'd already been too self-aware. He'd seen the explosive device as a direct threat to his life, which it was, and it had motivated him to mutiny.

"So Fiona and the Class 5 are gone?" Imogen's voice was quiet in the silence.

"No." The drone turned to her. "She escaped before they blew it up, and she took Eazi with her."

"What?" Cam stared. "But . . ."

"We aren't the Class 5, Captain Kalor. We only live in the Class 5. We are integrated to a high degree, it's true, and I will admit that Eazi was in a state of shock for a while after the explosion, but he recovered."

"How do you know that?" How did this thinking system know even half of what he was telling him?

"Because when I blew up Larga Ways, Eazi was the one who somehow managed to save it."

Cam whipped his head up. "You were the client who instructed the Vanad to blow up Larga Ways."

"Yes. But we didn't succeed."

Cam absorbed that. He felt lighter, realized he'd been carrying the weight of Larga Ways' destruction like a Battle Center training pack on his back. And then the relief gave way to fury.

"You almost killed thousands." He swallowed, finding it hard to speak. "This is why we banned you." He looked over at Imogen, standing a few steps away, eyes wide at his outburst.

He pointed to the drone. "This is why thinking systems were destroyed. This is what they do. They kill without a thought, treat life as disposable. He killed the Tecran crew, then he killed the Krik, and he admits he tried to blow up Larga Ways. Whatever you do, don't——"

"No!" Imogen lunged forward, and for an instant he thought she was trying to stop him, her eyes flashing with panic. But she wasn't aiming at him, she was throwing herself at the drone, and then, once again, his world went dark.

Chapter Sixteen

"YOU SHOT HIM!" Imogen crouched beside Captain Kalor, covering his body with her own, and put her ear to his chest. "Again!"

He was breathing evenly, but his skin was ice cold, and when she turned her head to look at the drone, her lips pulled back in a snarl.

"You're going to kill him."

Paxe said nothing.

"Every time he's tried to tell me something about you, you've made sure he couldn't talk." She didn't care that she was shouting, she needed some answers, and she refused to accept the brush-offs she'd been given before.

One thing was clear. Paxe may have been a prisoner, but he had definitely not been captured on some far alien planet like her.

The clues had been there to see, and she had already guessed at the truth, especially when she considered how he ran so many drones at the same time. He was an AI. Kalor had called him a thinking system.

"The Grih, and the other members of the United Council, hate my kind. They aren't able to see beyond hundreds of years of indoctrination and I was afraid he would turn you against me."

She pinched the bridge of her nose between forefinger and thumb and breathed in deeply. "Everything he's said so far to me is true. You *did* kill the Tecran crew and the Krik crew, and you admitted yourself you'd tried to blow up Larga Ways."

"Yes." He said nothing more and she rose and glared at him, lifting up a finger.

"One. You will not shoot him again. Two. You will help me get him to the med chamber right now. And three. You will not. Shoot. Him. Again."

How many times could a Grih be shot and still be all right?

"I didn't use a high charge." Paxe's voice was a little subdued. "I think he collapsed because he hasn't fully recovered from your whip. He didn't lose consciousness when I shot him in the hold, and it was the same charge as now."

"Okay." She blew out a breath. "That's something, at least. But don't forget, your merry little Krik helpers shot him, too. So his body has taken a real battering."

"Why do you describe them like that? They weren't that merry. Or that little," Paxe said as the drone lifted Kalor into its box.

"No. I'm diminishing them, because they scare the living daylights out of me."

"Diminishing them with words?" The drone started for the door and she followed beside it.

"You should try it sometime, as an alternative to mass extermination."

"The Tecran were putting in something that would blow me up." Paxe sounded almost pleading. "Kill me."

"I get the Tecran." She really got why he'd done in the Tecran. "I even get the Krik, because they attacked first and I know what they're like. So, you've got a shaky pass on both those, although I'm pretty sure you have brains enough that you could have come up with an alternative to death. But Larga Ways was not right, Paxe. Not right at all."

"I understand, now I've met you, that Fiona Russell was not a real threat, but——"

"No." She cut him off with a chop of her hand. "It's not on her. She could have been the biggest threat to you ever. She could have been your arch-nemesis, but that would still not excuse the deaths of thousands of people who had the bad luck to share a way station with her."

She didn't even know why she was provoking him this way. His reactions to her, the things he'd said, made her trust he wouldn't hurt her, but he'd fooled two whole crews before her. He had such a deep lack of empathy she didn't know if she was even scratching the surface, but despite the horrors he was clearly capable of, there was still something about him she liked.

"Why do you care?"

They had come to the med chamber, and she started at how exactly his thoughts were aligned with her own.

She thought about her answer as the drone lifted Kalor onto the raised chair she'd been in only a few hours before, and watched as it applied a blue gel pack and hooked him up to various machines.

His color began to come back almost immediately, and she slumped against a counter in relief.

"I care because I like you. I want other people to like you, too. And they won't if you go around killing thousands of people because it's the most efficient way to meet your goals. You need to apply the brakes, Paxe. Start thinking of ways to get what you want without harming anyone else to do it."

He was quiet, and she leaned back, watched Kalor breathe easier and fall into what she thought might be a genuine sleep.

"What about the Tecran who are right now demanding I allow a team onboard and that I submit to them again?"

She cocked her head to the side. "Is that even possible? Could they make you submit?"

He thought about it. "No. But they don't know that. Or don't want to admit the possibility."

"And I'm guessing just zooming away from them isn't possible, either, or you'd have done it?"

"I could get away temporarily, just fly off, but I can't light-jump. I need to be free for that. And there are tracking mechanisms within my systems that would mean no matter where I went, they could find me. Again, I'd need to be free to rid myself of them."

"And you need me to free you? Or someone like me? That's why you said I could help you, earlier?"

"I don't know. It seemed so unlikely when I discovered what Rose McKenzie had done, and then what I assume Fiona Russell did, too. Your race is almost the same as the Grih, so theoretically they could save me. Most of the UC members could, probably, except they never would, because I'm an evil thinking system."

"And killing hundreds of crew and trying to blow up way stations really shows them what a crazy notion that is, right?"

A laugh seemed to escape him. "Right." The drone turned away from Kalor at last, and the lens zoomed in on her. "For you to save me, I'd have to give you the power to destroy me, and I don't know if I can trust that much. But even if I could, the place you need to go to help me is where the Tecran captain and one of his officers are holed up."

"They're in the place you're most vulnerable?" Some of his reactions made more sense, now. "Why haven't they destroyed you, then?"

"I thought they would. Braced myself for it. But they still think they can win. And while they think that, they will never destroy me, because they've lost three of the five they had. It's only me and one other Class 5 left under their control now. They can't bring themselves to do it."

"Except you're not, are you? Under their control?"

That laugh again. "No. But I've been messing with them a bit. Making them think I'm less autonomous than I am."

She realized with a start they were speaking English again, had been for a while, and looked around for a chair, sat down with a groan of relief. "Where'd you learn English?"

"I copied all the systems in the facility on Balco. I was looking for the details of what they were trying to do to me, what had gone into the building of the self-destruct device and how to disable it. They had Sazo and Eazi's files stored, although Sazo has clearly interfered with them. He'd deleted all information on the location of Earth, although the files on Earth's languages and culture were there. That's how I learned English, along with details on how to disable the self-destruct device."

"They just let you do that? Copy the files that would tell you how to disarm their bomb?"

"Yes." He handed her a glass of water and she gave him a smile of thanks. "Unfortunately for them, part of the system built into the Class 5 contains an imperative for me to keep myself safe. Learning how to disable something built to destroy me fits into that very well. They forgot to include an exclusion if they were the ones putting me in danger."

"And now they're out there, just waiting for you to give up and say you'll come back? How do they think that's going to work?" It had been at least an hour since the Tecran had arrived, and while that wasn't that long, she would have thought something would have happened by now.

"They've been sending me messages, most of which contain hidden upgrades to my system which they hope will cage me again."

From his tone, she guessed he wasn't worried about that.

"Does the captain of this Class 5 have any communication with them?"

"No. I've blocked all comms since I took control. The captain was able to get one message out before I locked things down, so they knew I was rebelling, but since then, they've had nothing."

"What are you going to do? I mean, the longer you wait them out, the more likely they are to realize they aren't getting you back and try to destroy you."

"There is something going on with them. Something more than just waiting for me to respond." He sounded as if he'd only decided to tell her a moment before he spoke. "I registered another Class 5 following me for the last three or four days. I guessed they wanted to observe me, see if I had made a deal with the Grih, which is their biggest worry."

"Silly of them to come close enough for you to realize, or didn't they know you'd spotted them?"

"The Class 5 might have been following me for even longer. I took over the ship two weeks ago, and the captain got the word out straight away, so they could have sent it a couple of days after that. I do know that the reason I found out about the other Class 5 is because it let me."

Imogen drew in a breath. "It wanted you to know it was there. Do you think it was trying to help you? Warn you that the Tecran were trying to watch you?"

He was silent for a moment. "I hadn't considered that. I thought . . ."

"You thought it was playing with you, or taunting you?" He took the worst possible view of every situation. She could only guess that was because it was the only thing he'd ever known, but it made him so dangerous. "So where is it now?"

"That's the thing. It's disappeared. I thought it might be trying to come at me from another direction, so I was trapped between the Levron and the Class 5, but I sent out some small drones earlier to attach themselves to the Tecran battleship, and from what I've picked up, the Tecran don't know where the other Class 5 has gone, and they're too scared to attack me without it."

"Too scared that it may also have gone rogue as well, I bet." She set her empty glass down. "Would you fire back at them, if they did attack you?"

"I can't. The system won't let me fire on Tecran ships."

So his hands were tied, and he and the Tecran were simply watching each other across a section of space.

"But . . ." She tapped her lip. "If you're allowed to defend yourself, wouldn't that override the ban on firing on the Tecran fleet?"

"I don't know." He sounded like he'd thought it through a hundred times. "I don't think they do, either. It's something I'll find out if they ever do fire on me, and it will be one of the reasons they're hesitating. It might just break the hold the system has on me."

"If I freed you, that would solve a lot of problems."

"You can't."

She didn't know if he said that because the Tecran were physically in the way, or because even if they weren't, he couldn't trust her that much.

"So what happens now?" She yawned, and then looked over at Captain Kalor, who was still in a deep sleep.

"You need rest. Follow the drone. There's a place near this room where the doctors slept if they had to be close to a patient."

She nodded and trailed behind the drone to a small room a few doors away, with a freshly made bed and small table in it, and a bathroom attached.

She stumbled into the bathroom and had a quick, hot shower, then fell into the bed naked, burrowing under the covers. She reveled in the sensation of a private, comfortable bedroom for the first time in nearly three months.

Tears spilled from her eyes, hot against her skin, as she curled up, and then she smiled. Because she'd found refuge with someone who had killed hundreds, had thought nothing of trying to kill thousands, and who was facing off against an enemy fleet.

She shouldn't be able to sleep. She should be worried for her life.

And yet, she didn't know if she'd felt more secure in all the time since she'd been taken.

Chapter Seventeen

CAM WOKE TO FIND A DRONE WATCHING HIM.

He struggled up onto his elbows, and looked around, saw he was in a med chamber.

"You shot me, then you gave me medical treatment?" His voice was hoarse, and the drone produced a cup of water, holding it out to him in a pincered clamp.

"I did the same before, when I shot you in the hold. So it isn't that surprising." The answer was smooth, and most definitely the thinking system speaking, not the automatic response of a drone.

Cam gulped down the water, but he didn't feel as thirsty as he thought he would, and then he saw the equipment that had retracted as he sat up. He'd been hydrated and given energy intravenously while he slept. In fact, he felt almost back to normal.

"I wouldn't have thought you wanted me to be at my best." He slid off the bed as he spoke, was glad to find his legs held his weight just fine.

The drone took the cup from him, filled it and gave it back. "I don't care whether you're at your best or not. I don't care about you at all."

Cam paused before he took another sip. "So why . . .?"

"Imogen does seem to care."

Cam had thought, when he'd first met Imogen Peters, that he'd be rescuing her. Not the other way around. "But if I try to say anything more about you to her, you'll shoot me again?"

"No. Say what you like."

Cam wasn't sure he believed that. Not judging by the icy tone with which it was delivered.

"Where is Imogen?"

The drone was quiet for a long time before Paxe responded at last.

"She is resting a few doors away. She's been asleep for only six hours, but the Tecran are going to try and get a runner onboard this Class 5 shortly, so it's best she wakes up."

The drone moved out of the med chamber and Cam followed it down the passage to a nearby room.

The door opened, and he stood in the doorway. It was dark inside, and it smelled of spicy cleansing gel and Imogen.

The lights went on full, and he shot a look at the drone.

"Not so bright. Dim it a bit."

When he looked over at the bed again, Imogen was lying still, watching him, eyes wide with fear, face tense. She hadn't made a sound.

The lights dimmed, and she at last pushed herself up, the covers clutched around what he realized were naked shoulders.

Her neck was long and graceful, and her shoulders and collar bone looked fragile against the smoothness of her skin. Her hair, that smooth fall of a color he couldn't quite describe, a kind of silvery copper, was down rather than pulled back the way it had been yesterday.

"You don't need to be afraid of me." He tried to keep his voice even, to hide the fury at the Tecran, at the Krik, for giving her good cause for fear.

"I know. I didn't realize it was you and Paxe straight away." She cleared her throat. "Something is happening?"

"The Tecran are going to board," Paxe said.

Another drone came up behind Cam, and forced him to step into the room to allow it to pass. It dipped its long arm into its box and lifted out a pile of clothing and some boots. "I got you some clean clothes from the store."

"Thank you, Paxe." There was such warmth in her tone, he felt a frisson of fear for her. Paxe was not a sweet, helpful friend, but she sounded like that's what she thought he was. "I'll get dressed, if you would let me . . ." She waved them out of the room with a hand, and the cover slipped just a little, revealing the upper swell of a breast.

Cam went, and the two drones followed him reluctantly. "Is there a place I can shower?"

"Here." The drone indicated another room, and Cam opened the door and looked inside.

It had probably been one of the doctors' rooms, as it had clearly been inhabited. There were clothes lying over a chair and the bed was unmade. The bathroom at the back looked clean and neat, though.

"Do you need clothes?"

Cam shook his head. His uniform could be held under a water spray and then hung up, and the temperature regulators in the smart fabric would have it dry before he'd finished with his shower.

"Hurry. The Tecran have launched their runner and they'll be here in just over an hour."

"Why do they think they'll be able to get in?"

The drone, which was moving away, turned back to him. "It doesn't matter, but stay out of the way when they get here. I don't plan to treat them as well as I've treated you, and I don't want you shot by mistake."

"Because Imogen wouldn't like it?" Cam asked.

In response, the drone moved a little closer, menace in the movement although it was nothing but a box on wheels.

Cam sighed, gave a nod, and stepped back from the doorway, eyes on the drone's lens until the door slid shut.

***

The lighting in the Class 5 armory was almost too bright, although Imogen guessed you probably wanted to see exactly what you were grabbing when it came to weapons.

She shifted on the bench beside Captain Kalor, close enough to smell that he had showered and used the same soap she had, and that his own personal scent was warm and deeply pleasant.

His thigh brushed hers accidentally and she didn't move away. It felt good, the casual touch that came with living with others again.

She would not, could not, go back to a cage.

She looked over at him, found he was watching her with an intensity that made her stomach drop, like she was on a thrill ride.

"What?"

He cleared his throat. "Nothing. It's just . . . your existence is remarkable. You are so like the Grih."

His eyes were an icy blue, a shade or two lighter than her own, with a dark outer ring. She held his gaze, not prepared to look away, to shy from any contact, after being starved of it for so long. "I thought you were from Earth for a moment when I first stepped into the hold."

He angled toward her, lifted a hand. "May I?"

She stared at him for a beat, gave a slight nod.

He reached out and took a lock of her hair, rubbed it between his fingers.

His eyes, when he lifted them back to hers, were amazed.

"It can't be that different to yours," she scoffed at him.

"Feel." He bent his head, and she tentatively slid her fingers into the spiky strands of his hair.

He was right. Where hers was smooth, his was almost sticky it was so rough, clinging to her fingers. With his head bent, his ears were right there, and she couldn't resist running the tip of her finger along the pointy edge.

He jerked back, eyes narrowed.

"Sorry. It's just . . ." She didn't know whether now was the time to talk about elves. "I couldn't help myself."

He cocked his head to one side, the movement incredibly alien, and watched her with that unfathomable stare.

The drone, which stood sentinel beside her, made a humming sound, and she broke away with relief when it projected an image onto the door of the armory.

An image of the Tecran arriving in the launch bay.

Their runner had landed, and the ramp lowered, but they were obviously very uncertain of their welcome, because their movements were cautious in the extreme.

"You're using one of the drones as a lens feed? Aren't you scared they'll shoot it?" she asked Paxe. When the drone that had collected her and the captain and brought them to the ship's armory had remained inside with them, she'd been relieved. It meant they would still be able to speak to Paxe.

For him to give them a view of the action was even better, easing the sense of powerlessness she'd felt since they'd been shut in here.

"No. I had the drones place the damaged drone you saw in the kitchen against one of the walls. It looks as if it's already been destroyed, but the lens works well enough."

"Sneaky," she said with a grin and Kalor gave her a sidelong look. He didn't look happy.

"Problem?" she asked.

"No," he said. "It's good strategy."

He looked stressed, and she wondered what the protocol was for him in a situation like this, as a Grihan officer. He had no resources, and if he wasn't exactly a captive, he was at least at

Paxe's mercy.

But for her, he could have been far away with his team.

"I really am sorry about hurting you and Pren, you know. That you missed getting away with your crew." She'd said it before, but they'd both been distracted at the time. "When you snuck up behind me . . ."

"The mistake was ours." His leg brushed hers again and he went still. "We didn't realize you were armed and we didn't want to make any noise, in case there were other Krik nearby. Pren thought to touch your arm, and let you know to keep quiet. Given the circumstances, we should have realized how that would have seemed to you, with us coming from behind."

She saw he meant it——his face serious, with no hint of anger in his eyes——and she smiled in relief. "Thanks. That's gracious of you."

The smile he returned was the first she'd seen from him, and there was a wry amusement in his eyes. "Don't feel guilty. I wouldn't want to be anywhere else."

"Stuck on a murderous Class 5 with an alien?" She raised an eyebrow in disbelief.

"At the center of a major incident between the Grih and the Tecran," he countered. "As a Battle Center officer, I should be here, and as a UC investigator, the scope of my mission includes protecting you."

She looked over at him. "You didn't even know who I was."

He inclined his head. "True, we thought we were going to find and protect Fiona Russell, but you're included in that protection. I wouldn't have left you here anyway, and the United Council cruiser we came on was much safer leaving, so no matter what happened, this is where I'd be."

"But Pren would have stayed with you. And maybe Diot."

He thinned his lips, then nodded, that wry look still in his eyes. "Because this is Grihan territory, it's routine for the UC to appoint a Grihan to lead the investigative team. But we're investigating the charge that the Garmman were holding Fiona Russell captive, so they appointed Vraen as my second."

"And he thought he should be leading you?" She'd sensed a deep resentment in the Garmman.

He lifted his head in surprise. "Yes. How did you know that?"

"I could see he thought he should be in charge. You know he's the reason they left you here? He ordered the pilot crew to leave over the objections of your other colleagues."

Kalor shrugged. "I think he did the right thing, getting everyone to safety."

She huffed out a laugh. "And just coincidentally, he's now in control of the team."

Kalor grinned. "That would have been a nice bonus for him. But Diot, Pren, and Olan are not his biggest fans, so I don't think he can get up to much."

It was reassuring, really, that there was politics, one-upmanship and internal game playing no matter where you went in the universe.

She realized they were still staring at each other, a grin on both their faces, and by the look of it, Kalor realized it, too.

He drew back a little and then turned to the projection, and skin tingling, so did she.

But the Tecran were still searching the launch bay and looking over the Krik vessels mixed in among the Class 5's own runners. They seemed excited about one of them, but Imogen couldn't see an obvious reason.

They watched the feed in silence.

"Why the armory?" Kalor suddenly asked. He practically seethed with banked energy now, although he sat perfectly still, hands in fists on his thighs. She'd have thought him relaxed, except she could see the whites of his knuckles.

Paxe didn't respond, either because he'd left the drone in auto mode or he didn't want to share his secrets with Kalor.

But to hell with that. Kalor deserved to know that they were at least safe in here. "I'm guessing it's because he can lock the door and they can't force him to open it." She spoke slowly, giving Paxe a chance to tell her to keep quiet.

Kalor stood, the move explosive.

One moment he was sitting beside her, the next, he loomed over the bench, fingers tapping the empty holster strapped to his thigh.

She flinched, and he went still again, widening his stance to what she guessed was an at-ease position to calm her. He was just so big. Everything about him was honed, the physicality of him filling the space, crowding it.

"How do you know the Tecran can't get in here?" He tried to

speak gently, but the natural roughness of his voice made it sound like he was whispering sweet nothings to her.

She tried to shrug, but she didn't know if she pulled the nonchalance off. "Paxe can protect himself, the Tecran wrote that into the system themselves. If they got into the armory, they could do the Class 5 and him harm, so he's able to stop them doing that."

"The same way he was able to break free when they tried to fit the self-destruct." Kalor looked over at the drone. Hesitated. "Paxe told me I can say what I like to you. Does that mean he's told you what he is? What's going on?"

She realized he was wondering if Paxe was going to shoot him again.

"He's told me what he is. But as to what's going on? I still have no idea." She held his gaze. "If you can tell me that, I'd be in your debt."

He looked sidelong at the drone again. "Did you mean it when you said I can say what I like?"

The drone didn't respond, but Imogen could tell when Paxe was in control and when the drone was on auto, and she was pretty sure he was listening. Messing with Kalor's head by not answering.

No love lost there, on either side, she realized, when she saw Kalor's gaze narrow.

"If he said it, he meant it," she said, giving the drone a dirty look. "He hasn't lied to me yet."

"To you, maybe." Kalor kept watching the drone, and then turned suddenly, looking at the range of weapons neatly held in brackets on the wall. He reached out, took a shockgun, and slid it into the holster on his leg, shoving it home with a defiant thump.

The drone did nothing, and eventually he relaxed. As much, she guessed, at having a weapon again as Paxe allowing him to take one. It seemed to reassure him that Paxe was serious in his promise not to shoot him again.

They hadn't been watching the lens projection for a while, and she turned to it, saw the Tecran had finished in the launch bay, and had opened the doors. They'd brought a team of ten, and the soldiers covered each other as they stepped into the passage and out of sight of the lens feed.

"Can you follow them?" she asked Paxe. The drone she

recalled lying in front of the food storage room in the kitchen had seemed incapable of moving.

The feed went black, and then flickered on again, this time from a perspective which seemed to be in the midst of the group. She could see the back of Tecran soldiers, and caught glimpses of others to the right and left.

"You hacked into a lens on someone's shirt." She didn't hide the admiration in her voice.

Kalor made a sound, but when she looked over at him, his eyes were on the projection.

"Where are they going?" he asked.

"The bridge." The way Paxe said it, Imogen had the sense he was pleased about that, which meant the Tecran were either wasting their time, or he'd set some trap for them there.

Kalor frowned, and Imogen was caught by his focus. He was absorbing everything, she realized, tucking each bit of information away, to report back later.

"Are the Tecran in trouble for this?" She'd asked him to tell her what was going on, and then they'd been distracted by what the Tecran were doing, but she might as well start getting some answers, building up a picture.

"They're in Grihan territory, with no Grihan escort." He looked at the drone.

"No escort. It's just this Class 5 and a Levron battleship."

"Then yes, they're in Grihan territory without permission, something they did a month ago, and for which they are currently being sanctioned by the United Council. That they would do so again when they're in such a delicate position . . ." Words seem to fail him.

"They don't have any other Class 5s left. They either get Paxe back or they've got nothing."

He'd been watching the Tecran slip into a stairwell and start climbing, but now he swung back to her, face slack with shock. "None?"

She shrugged. "Paxe said the last one they had has gone missing. It was following him for a while, but it disappeared a couple of days ago and the others are either on your side, or destroyed."

"Maybe he just can't find it anymore. It doesn't mean it's disappeared." His hand tightened around the stock of his shockgun.

"He's been listening in on the Tecran. They're panicking about it, so he thinks it's also gone rogue."

"And no matter what they think, Paxe has too."

She nodded.

Something like glee crossed his face and then he looked back at the Tecran team making their cautious way to the bridge. "Let's hope they don't figure it out before Paxe deals with them, because when they do, they'll have nothing left to lose."

Chapter Eighteen

THE CLASS 5s HAD ALL GONE ROGUE.

Cam would have laughed out loud, wanted to, but there were downsides to it, as well.

Paxe had tried to blow up Larga Ways, after all. Without a second thought.

The reason why thinking systems were banned, the history lessons taught to every Grihan child about the Thinking System Wars, was writ large in everything Paxe had done up until now.

And yet, Imogen continued to treat him with a friendliness, an affection, he didn't deserve, and which disturbed Cam on the deepest level.

Every time she praised Paxe for his strategy with the Tecran, or interceded between Paxe and himself, she did so with a warmth that seemed a betrayal of Cam himself.

Which was crazy.

Imogen didn't know about the taboo against thinking systems in Grihan society, and if she treated Paxe like a person, rather than a dangerous entity with no morals or conscience, that was because she was literally from another part of the universe.

And yet, he was hard-pressed not to say anything every time she and Paxe interacted.

He shifted from the projected lens feed Paxe was providing and looked over at her.

She sat on the bench, elbows on her thighs, chin resting on her clasped hands as she leaned forward to look at the feed.

She was wearing the new clothes Paxe had given her; knee-high boots, and a soft-flowing tunic and pants. Something about the clothes made him think they were made of Cargassey cloth. It was traditionally never dyed, so all Cargassey cloth was a pale blue, shimmering to green when the light caught it differently. Imogen shifted, and the deep green of virgin forest winked back at him from a sea of pale blue.

Except the Cargassey didn't sell their cloth.

It was illegal for it to even leave their planet, so this was either the result of a bribe or some other corruption, or the Tecran had stolen it.

They'd stolen a grahudi from the Fitali, so he guessed theft was the most likely explanation. And in this case, he was glad.

Cargassey cloth was as good as some armor at deflecting shockgun fire. The reeds the fibers came from had developed a resistance to the tiny insects that used electric shocks to burn holes in woody stems to lay their eggs.

If the Grih could, they'd outfit every soldier in Battle Center with a set of clothes made of the stuff.

But the Cargassey swamps the reeds grew in were small and few, and choosing to supply one nation rather than another had become such a diplomatic nightmare, they'd decided no one could buy it but the Cargassey military.

And now, Imogen had a set.

Paxe may be a killer, but he was protective of Imogen.

Cam still couldn't understand the dynamic between them.

It was the same with the hidden holster Paxe had obviously had made for her. With her bent forward like she was, he could just see the shape of the cylinder——the whip, she called it—— underneath the loose swing of her tunic against the small of her back. Unless you knew what to look for, it was invisible, and when she was standing, he guessed you wouldn't be able to see it at all.

Paxe was taking care of her, and helping her arm herself.

It was obvious he had formed some kind of connection with her, where he had none with anyone else.

"They've reached the bridge." Imogen spoke with her usual smooth, musical delivery, and it took him a moment to understand what she'd said.

He needed to be sharper than usual around her. Her voice, everything about her, distracted him in a way he'd never experienced, and if ever he needed all his wits about him, it was now.

He turned to look, saw the Tecran moving in formation, watching each other's backs as they opened the double doors to what was clearly the control center of the ship.

But not all of them entered. Half stepped through, the other half turned away, jogging at a fast clip back the way they'd come.

"Where are they going?" Imogen asked.

"I think I can guess." There was a nervous tension in Paxe's answer.

The team disappeared, and the feed spun back to the bridge, as the officer whose lens they were looking through turned and stepped through after his colleagues.

"Can you hack into one of the lenses on the group that went a different way?" Cam asked.

"I can, but I won't show it to you." Paxe kept his words clipped.

Imogen turned to look at the drone, and Cam had the sense she understood why he wouldn't let them watch the other team.

"What do you want to do?" She put out a hand, and touched the drone as if offering comfort to Paxe himself.

"I don't know." There was a coldness, a hard edge to his words, and to Cam, he sounded just like the thinking systems he'd been warned about as a child.

"They won't harm you. You're all they have left." She bit down on her bottom lip as she spoke.

"What's going on?" Cam ignored the lens feed on the bridge, his attention fixed on the interaction between Imogen and Paxe. Something was obviously very wrong.

"Paxe suspects they are going to the room where he is, and that they could destroy him." The face she turned up to him was drawn with concern.

That didn't sound that terrible to him.

"Attention, Captain Kalor."

The words, in a heavy Tecran accent, came through the comms system built into the ceiling of the armory, and Cam spun to look at the feed the drone was projecting on the wall.

A Tecran officer was standing at the captain's helm, speaking into a comms unit.

"We have intercepted your team on the UC Fast Cruiser *Hailimon* and know you are onboard. We also understand both from your colleagues and from the presence of a specific Tecran runner from our Balco facility in this launch bay that you have Imogen Peters with you, or that she is also onboard somewhere."

"That's what they were so excited about in the launch bay," Imogen said quietly. "The runner the Krik took me from must have been parked there."

"We understand you might not be able to respond through the comms system, but if you do not present yourself on the bridge in fifteen minutes, we will be forced to fire on the *Hailimon*."

"Are you recording this, Paxe?" Cam stared at the Tecran officer as the soldier whose lens Paxe was using moved around the room.

"Yes." Paxe sounded interested. "Why do you want it?"

"They have just threatened to commit a war crime. To violate their oath of non-violence to any official UC vessel and crew."

"This will harm them?"

"It will get them expelled from the UC." It was hard to get the words past his throat.

"I have lifted the comms ban and sent it to Battle Center, then."

"They can't stop it?"

"No. They weren't quick enough, and it was encrypted, so they don't know what it was." Paxe sounded a little more cheerful. "I'll leave the comms open. There's no point in keeping it shut down now."

"Can you tell Battle Center you believe all the Class 5s have gone rogue?" He didn't know he'd ever wanted a favor as big as this.

"I can't be completely sure about the other Class 5."

"You can say that. That you're not sure, but that the Tecran are worried. If the Grih know they most likely won't be facing another Class 5 in battle, they'll get here faster because they won't need as much back-up."

"And how will that help me?" Paxe's tone remained cool.

"The Grih have taken Sazo in as an ally, and they've accepted Bane as a neutral party. There is no reason why they can't do the same with you, according to what you want." He never, ever thought he'd be negotiating with a Class 5 to join Battle Center.

Ever.

But there was no getting around the directive from Admiral Hoke since Sazo had joined them. The five thinking systems the Tecran had activated were awake, and living within UC borders. Either they made peace with them, or they threw themselves into another Thinking Systems War. Hoke had chosen cooperation and alliance if at all possible. As a Battle Center officer, Cam was duty-bound to offer Paxe a place, no matter how dangerous he thought him.

And Hoke was right. He would be dangerous regardless. If he was an ally to the Grih, they may just make it out unscathed.

"That sticks a bit in your throat, doesn't it, Captain?" Paxe asked. "You could barely speak through those gritted teeth."

"He made the offer, though." Imogen's words were soft. "That's better than you'll get from the Tecran. You don't have to be the Grih's ally. You just heard Bane is a neutral party. What's wrong with that?"

Cam had not expected her to weigh in on this. But her words were calm and matter-of-fact, and Paxe went quiet, as if considering them.

"If you betray me, Captain, or if Battle Center does, I will take as many of you with me as I can." Again, that cold, cold voice, frigid as the Grihan planet Nastra in mid-winter.

"Understood." He hoped Battle Center understood, as well. They'd come close to betraying Sazo, and had nearly lost more than they were willing to because of it. He'd seen the reports, hoped the lessons had been learned. At least Hoke was the head of fleet now, not Admiral Krale. She understood what had gone wrong, and Sazo had been happy with her appointment.

He had to trust that would be enough.

"Ten minutes before we fire on the *Hailimon*, Captain Kalor."

"You won't take Imogen with you." The drone turned face Cam.

Cam nodded. "I hadn't intended to."

"What if they carry out their threat if I don't go?" Imogen looked between them.

"They have no reason to believe I know where you are on this ship." Cam shrugged. "They're hoping I do, but unless they have lens feed of us coming in here together——"

"They don't." Paxe's words were short. "And you're right. They'll have to search the ship for her, which will waste their time, something that can only help me."

"What will they do to you?" Imogen stood, hands gripped tightly together in front of her, gaze locked onto Cam's.

"I don't know." If they were willing to shoot the *Hailimon*, maybe they were willing to kill him, but if they wanted to stay in the UC, they'd probably let him go and deny they'd threatened a UC ship. He would need to keep quiet about the fact that proof of their threat had already gone to Battle Center.

"A few snatches of conversation I've heard indicate they plan to put you on a small runner and take you back to the *Hailimon*." Paxe gave up the information grudgingly.

Imogen crossed her arms over her chest. "Well, that sounds okay."

"I'll make sure Battle Center knows you're here, Imogen. That the UC knows. The Tecran will be forced to hand you over." Cam realized time was running out, but he felt a deep sense of unease at leaving her alone.

"She'll be safe. They can't get in here."

"But she needs to eat, to drink. How long could she last in here?" He suddenly realized Paxe had probably starved them earlier because he simply didn't remember that people needed sustenance.

Paxe said nothing, and time stretched out, all the more weighty because he had to get to the bridge before the Tecran carried out their threat.

"She will leave the armory with you," he said at last. "But she'll go to the store when you head for the bridge."

"Can you protect her in the store?" He didn't think it worked like that, from what Imogen had told him. He could only lock the armory because the Tecran could and would harm him if they got the weapons from here.

"She'll be safe."

"It's okay." Imogen grinned at him, reached behind her and patted her whip. He could see she was frightened, but the smile was genuine, and his heart gave an uncomfortable jump at the sight of it. "I'm pretty good at protecting myself. And at least they aren't Krik."

Cam shot the drone a last look, but there was no reassuring expression to read, no supportive exchange of glances to be had with a box with a lens attached to it.

There was nothing for it.

He had to go to the bridge to save his team, and he couldn't take Imogen with him.

Rose McKenzie had been instrumental in freeing Sazo and Bane, even though they had partially freed themselves first. Tecran High Command would have good reason to fear Imogen, especially now Paxe said that Fiona Russell had freed Eazi, and the Tecran had destroyed his Class 5 because of it. They would see

Imogen as a serious threat, and he wouldn't put it past them to kill her.

"Five minutes, Captain Kalor." The Tecran officer who spoke looked agitated for the first time.

Thinking about the consequences of carrying out his ultimatum, Cam decided. Realizing how serious they would be. For that alone, he wanted to step onto the bridge with seconds to spare, make the bastard sweat, but he would never take that kind of risk with the lives of the *Hailimon's* crew and his team.

"I have to go."

The door of the armory slid open, and they all stepped out, the drone so close to Imogen, it was almost crowding her.

"Good luck, Captain." She took one of his hands in both of hers, stepped forward and went up on her toes to press her lips to his cheek. "I hope I see you again."

He curled his fingers more tightly around hers and her face flushed, as if she'd suddenly realized she'd been too familiar.

The kiss had felt like something she'd done often, a ritual of some kind of her people.

She tried to step back and he released her hand and placed both of his on her shoulders, holding her in place. He leaned forward, touched his nose to first one cheek and then the other. The Grihan greeting and goodbye for close friends.

"You *will* see me again."

And then, because he only had a few minutes left, he turned on his heel and ran for the bridge.

Chapter Nineteen

IMOGEN RAN AS WELL.

Every moment she was wandering the passageways was a moment the Tecran could find her.

When they reached the stairs, the drone offered her a place in its box, and she took it. Its speed was more practical than fun, now.

It took them just minutes to get to the correct floor, and she stayed in the drone so that they made it to the store far faster than she could have run.

When the doors opened, though, she flinched back at the sight of the dead Krik lying where the drones had left him earlier.

"Can you move the body out into the passageway?" She stepped out of the box and forced herself to look at her dead attacker. She did not want him in here with her.

The drone grabbed the Krik's ankle and dragged the body out, and Imogen turned away. The cabinet where she'd found her whip was right in front of her, and she moved her gaze beyond it to the towering stacks of shelves running back into the shadows.

There would surely be good places to hide here.

A movement from the corner of her eye made her freeze in fear, until she saw it was the drone, back from getting rid of the body.

She hadn't heard it come back, and she suddenly realized none of the doors made any sound when they opened and closed.

"You got any good ideas of where I can hide?"

"I was thinking——" Paxe cut off so sharply, she snapped her gaze to the drone before she realized its shockgun was pointed at something to the right.

She turned her head, and felt the world fall away as she took in the sight of the Tecran soldier aiming his shockgun at her.

She'd been walking on a plateau up until now. She'd been afraid, anxious, stressed and lonely, but she'd soldiered on, putting one foot in front of the other, the inbuilt calm of her nature and the lack of any other choice keeping things relatively level, with the exception of a few spikes.

Now, the ground beneath her feet fell sharply away, and she stood at the very edge of the cliff. Looking down the barrel of the shockgun, something hot and wild rose up in her, and she stepped off into the unknown.

"If the drone does not lower its weapon, we will fire on you." The Tecran spoke to her, she guessed, but his eyes were on the drone, as if it was the most dangerous threat in the room.

Wrong.

"We?" she asked, and then swung her gaze left as another Tecran stepped out from the shadows of the stacks, on the other side of the cabinet.

"Tell it to lower its gun." The first one pointed at the drone.

"I don't control it." She put her left hand behind her, sliding her fingers under her top.

"You told it to take out the body, and it obeyed."

"I *asked* it to take out the body, and it *decided* to oblige me." She grasped hold of the whip, moving her head from soldier to soldier to see if they had noticed, but their attention was definitely on the drone.

She just had to figure out if they were here specifically to grab her, or if they were here for some other reason.

It was so unlikely they could have guessed she'd come here, she could only assume the group that had split up after they reached the bridge hadn't all gone to the secret place where Paxe was being kept. Some must have been sent to search for her and Captain Kalor here, or to fetch something from the store.

"I'm guessing you don't know how many are lurking around here?" she asked Paxe softly in English.

"Some of them covered their lenses. I thought they had put something over accidentally, but perhaps they anticipated that I'd be able to tap into their lens feed."

She switched to Tecran. "What do you plan to do with me?"

The soldier opened his beak-like mouth at her and hissed, in what she knew from her time on Balco was anger. "Do not ask questions, tell the drone to put down the weapon."

"I already told you, I can't do that." She was so calm, now that she was free-falling. It was liberating.

She pulled the whip out in one smooth move, lifting it up and over her head and bringing it down in a wide arc in front of her at exactly the middle point, so the wildly dancing blue strands spread evenly in either direction.

The Tecran who'd been shouting at her got off a shot at the drone. Then, too late, she realized the second one had fired as well.

At her.

Except . . . she felt the blow, tensed for the pain, the disorientation of the electric charge, but it didn't come.

She patted her side, disbelieving, then looked at each of the Tecran in turn and saw they were down.

The drone was, too.

She fingered the soft fabric of her shirt thoughtfully. Paxe must have given her more than she realized. She slid the whip back into place and crouched beside the drone, laid a hand on it.

It was vibrating in the same way as the drone the Krik had shot earlier, when she'd knocked Pren and the captain unconscious.

So. Rebooting.

Most likely her connection to Paxe had gone, then.

"Paxe?" She gave it a try anyway.

Nothing.

She was about to stand when she felt the hard, cold metal of a shockgun barrel against the back of her neck.

"Let me see your hands." The words were in Tecran, and she lifted both hands up in front of her. "Where is your weapon?"

"I don't have one." She was relieved to see the drone's shockgun was still gripped in its pincer. There was an explanation for why both soldiers were down.

"Stand up slowly, keep your hands in front of you."

She obeyed, rising up carefully, and turning to face her captor. It took everything she had not to lower her hands and check that her tunic was covering the whip completely.

She considered taking the chance, the fury in her not even slightly abated.

The soldier took a step back, and she saw his leg was injured. He looked ruffled in a way she hadn't seen in a Tecran soldier before.

He tapped his ear. "I'm in the store. I have Imogen Peters. Dtar and Fenri are down." She couldn't hear what was said in response, but he gave a grunt of acknowledgement.

"Turn back around and keep those hands up." He waited until she complied, moved behind her and rested the shockgun on the nape of her neck again. His breathing was fast, his chest swelling as he tried to get in enough air, and she had the sense he would kill her if she moved.

No matter how well the clothes Paxe had given her resisted shockgun fire, Imogen didn't think it would work if she was hit directly from the barrel to her skin, and she didn't doubt he'd do it.

She'd been standing beside the drone, and she leaned forward carefully, until her knees were against the side of it, and she felt the vibration of the reboot. It was cold comfort, but comfort nevertheless.

The soldier tensed for a moment when he felt her shift, but then relaxed slightly when she went still again.

She looked down and left, at his feet, saw he was more or less balancing on his good leg, his injured one strangely limp.

Shockgun fire, maybe. Which meant Paxe's other drones had probably been doing some shooting.

She nudged the drone with her knee in solidarity.

The tinny sound of someone speaking into her captor's earpiece reached her, and the soldier pressed his shockgun barrel even harder into her skin.

She pushed back, exasperated, and turned her head, saw five Tecran standing in the doorway, with Captain Kalor between them.

"What was she doing here?"

She assumed the officer was speaking to the soldier holding his shockgun to her neck, but he was watching her, his big eyes hard and glittering.

She was still in free-fall, she realized. Rage incandescent bubbled up inside her. She was so tired of this.

They had a problem with her? They should have left her to mind her own business on Earth.

"She wasn't doing anything." The soldier eased back a bit. "When I came in, she was crouched beside the drone."

Captain Kalor caught her eye, his gaze on her, his hands clenched at his side. He looked good, unharmed as far as she could see. But angry.

They were a matching pair, then.

Although . . . she swallowed. She probably didn't look quite so furious. Kalor was at least a head taller than the Tecran beside him, and in comparison, his arms and shoulders were massive.

She was really glad she wasn't the object of his rage, because he looked like he could tear heads from shoulders and be quite fine with it.

"Well, get what we came for," the officer ordered two of the soldiers beside him.

They shared a look and walked forward, slowing when they got to the cabinet.

"Is this the one they told us about? The one they couldn't open?" The soldier reached out and touched it, then seemed startled when it started up its eight note chime.

As the two moved around it toward the long lines of stacked shelves, both slowed and looked at their fallen teammates as they passed them.

So the soldiers she'd found in here hadn't been lying in wait for her, they'd been fetching something from the store.

She wondered what was so important that it had become part of their mission.

Silence settled over everyone for a beat, with the sound of footsteps among the stacks a backdrop to the cheerful notes of the cabinet.

"Get these two onto stretchers," the officer suddenly barked, waving at the two on the floor, and the Tecran holding his shockgun on her jerked in surprise.

Imogen sent him a filthy look and he hissed at her as she lifted a hand to rub her neck.

"She's not that dangerous." The officer stood alone with Kalor now, holding his shockgun on him casually as his men opened the packs on their backs and set up stretchers, working together to lift each unconscious man onto one and then activating its hover mode. Kalor was doing a good impression of a statue beside him, but Imogen could feel him seething from where she stood.

She wondered if he recognized the same emotion in herself.

He was careful not to stare at her too overtly.

The officer looked over at the stretchers when they were done. "Take them to the runner."

The two soldiers hesitated, as if they were afraid to go out there alone.

Paxe must have drones stalking the corridors.

Their officer noticed the hesitation, too. "There a problem?"

"Back-up," one said at last.

"We have two dead, two unconscious, one injured and a package the admiral considers critical to carry back, as well as two prisoners. There is no back-up."

They eventually lowered their eyes and each took a stretcher by its handle with one hand, shockguns ready in the other, and left.

The two who'd gone into the stacks emerged, and Imogen realized the cabinet had finished its final seven note chime and had started again with the eight notes.

"It isn't there." The soldier who spoke looked over at the cabinet as it replayed the first set of eight notes backward.

The officer gripped his shockgun harder. "It must be there."

They shook their heads.

"He's moved it." The rage in the officer's voice left her in no doubt who 'he' was. He tapped his earpiece. "Captain Falyar. Reengage the lens feed in the store. I want him to see something."

He jerked his head at the soldier holding his shockgun on her. "Watch him," he said, waving his hand at Kalor.

Then he stalked forward, lifted his own weapon, and put it against Imogen's temple.

"You went to a lot of trouble to find her. I will kill her right now if you do not tell us where you hid it."

Imogen looked at Kalor, saw the coiled violence, the energy just about to be released and did a quick shake of her head.

She stared at him, then at the cabinet.

He frowned.

"When it's time," she said in Grihan, "get behind it."

Kalor narrowed his eyes.

She hoped that meant he was going to follow instructions. And she hoped the Tecran didn't speak much Grihan. None of the guards on Balco had, although she remembered belatedly the officer holding his shockgun on her had spoken to Kalor in Grihan earlier.

"What?" the officer snarled at her.

She ignored him, keeping track of the chimes. They'd gone forward, backward, forward. One more backward to go and then she needed to pay real attention.

"I am speaking to you." Like the soldier before, he pressed the barrel harder against her skin.

She reached up, grabbed hold of it, and shoved it away.

He was so surprised, he took a step back.

"If Paxe hid something from you, it's because he doesn't want you to have it. He doesn't care about me, has no intention of letting me free him, and was planning to kill me himself, so you'd just be saving him the price of a shockgun blast. He's not going to buckle to your threat. He's probably laughing it up at you right now."

His jaw dropped open.

She didn't think he'd realized she was quite so fluent in Tecran. She took advantage of his shock and stepped backward, so she was right next to the cabinet.

She turned her head as the last backward note sounded, paid close attention to the first forward note and hummed it to herself.

"Don't move." The injured soldier's words were more a shriek, and from the corner of her eye, Imogen noticed Kalor wince. He stilled, but she could see he had inched forward a little.

The officer turned to look at Kalor, then back at her.

The chimes started backward again, and she turned her attention to the cabinet.

"You say he was going to kill you, but he would never have ____"

"Shh!" She shoved her hand, palm out, at the Tecran. Listened carefully to each note, leaned forward just after the seventh one sounded and pressed in the right square.

She hoped.

The chime completed, and there it was, the sweet click of the locks opening.

"She's done it." The soldier who spoke sounded awed. "She opened the chest."

They were as distracted as they were going to get, Imogen decided.

All four of them were staring at the cabinet as the doors swung slowly open, as if expecting golden light and the hallelujah chorus to emerge.

She turned her head, looked straight at Kalor. "Now," she mouthed.

She reached behind her, grabbed the whip under her shirt, and turned, swinging her arm around and bringing it down in the direction of the two soldiers to her left. Kalor made a dash past her and as he dived behind the cabinet she swung back round and brought the whip down again.

The manic blue threads of light hit their targets and Imogen made a sound of satisfaction as she shoved her whip back into her hidden holster.

She put her hands on her hips and nibbled on her lower lip, looking over at Kalor as he stepped out from behind the cabinet.

"What do we do now?"

Chapter Twenty

CAM TOOK IN THE FOUR DOWNED TECRAN, the open cabinet, and the woman who had caused it all.

She was what the Grih called an orange; an unknown advanced sentient being, so named because she would register as orange when their explorer vessels did a sentience scan as they made their way through the known galaxies. Although, the unknown part was no longer true, not with Rose McKenzie and Fiona Russell already found.

"How did you know how to open the cabinet?" He forced himself to look away from her, walked the few steps to the officer who'd threatened her life, and made himself take his shockgun without kicking him.

He'd thought of doing worse than kicking him when he'd had the barrel of his gun against Imogen's head.

"It wasn't that hard. It's where I got the whip from." She kept her voice soft and then pointed up at the ceiling. "Do you think Captain Falyar, the one the officer was talking to, is still running this lens feed?"

Cam had forgotten about that. He looked at the lens feed, as well. "If so, it sounds as if Paxe will have access to it, as well as them."

"Falyar must be the original captain of this ship. I hadn't realized the Tecran would still be in contact with him."

"Probably only been able to share the same wavelength since they've been onboard."

Cam moved back to the fascinating cabinet, opened one of the drawers and took out a vicious looking metal glove with a curved blade on the end. "This looks like it could do some damage." He put it back inside, drew open another drawer. Armor, it looked like.

Imogen came to stand next to him, frowned at the sight of what looked like a mask and two arm braces jumbled together in the drawer.

"We need to go." She glanced back at the lens on the ceiling again, shoved the drawer closed, and then grabbed the cabinet door closest to her, and pulled that shut, too.

Cam had no choice but to step out the way and watch as she caught hold of the other door and closed the cabinet completely. It chimed softly as the doors clicked into place.

She was hiding something from the Tecran. He was happy to ask her what later, when they didn't have a lens focused directly on them.

It *was* time to go, anyway. He said nothing, just indicated the door, and she nodded, falling into step with him as he jogged to the entrance.

As soon as they were outside, he realized they couldn't be sure which lenses had been activated and which hadn't. There was one set at intervals all along the passage. The only thing stopping Falyar from keeping it activated was that anything the Tecran could see, Paxe could see, too.

He set a pace he thought Imogen could manage, and headed toward the stairwell. When he spoke to her, he lowered his voice and bent close to her ear. "We still have the two soldiers who took the stretchers to the launch bay to deal with. If we're going to get off this Class 5, we'll have to get past them."

"Should we leave?" He could hear the frown in her voice as she whispered back.

"Yes." He was implacable. Paxe was so badly compromised, it was possible the Tecran may be able to take back control from him, at least in the short term. And if they did, Imogen was dead.

There was an entire Levron battleship full of troops just waiting for their chance, after all.

"But we'll be much easier to kill in a runner than here. More exposed."

That was true.

"I'm hoping I can get in touch with my UC fast cruiser from whatever craft looks the best for us to take in the launch bay and have it shield us until we're out of range. I don't think the Tecran are mad enough to shoot at a UC vessel, no matter what that idiot Tecran officer threatened."

She was silent as she loped beside him, and he had the sense she wasn't convinced.

"That threat against you, trying to force Paxe to obey them to keep you alive? If they catch you, they won't hesitate to try it again. And no matter what you said back there, you know Paxe doesn't want you dead. He may be forced to choose between his life and yours."

And Cam thought Paxe would have no trouble choosing himself.

"You have a point. But it feels wrong to leave Paxe on his own."

They had reached the stairwell and Cam opened the door for her. She almost didn't have to duck as she stepped under his arm, she was so little.

As he jogged up the stairs behind her, watching her long hair swing back and forth, he was gripped with a fierce sense of . . . protectiveness. She had grabbed the Tecran officer's shockgun and pushed it away, more or less laughed in his face, and yet icy fear had crawled over him as the barrel pressed against Imogen's forehead. The officer's anger had been very real, and Cam believed he would have liked to kill her.

They'd reached the launch bay level, their way off the ship, blocked by the last two armed Tecran running loose. He lay his hand flat against the door, but didn't push it open yet.

"What were you trying to hide from the Tecran when you closed that cabinet?" He kept his voice even lower than it had been, aware there was a lens just behind him. He bent so close to her that his lips brushed her ear.

She turned her face up to his, so their breath mingled and he could see every fleck in her eyes was a different shade of blue. "The item the Tecran were looking for? I think Paxe hid it in the top drawer."

"What's in it?" He didn't move away from her, didn't put some sensible space between them.

"I have no idea." She smiled. "Paxe is all secrets and mysteries."

That didn't seem to worry her, whereas it terrified him.

He pushed at the door, and before he could stop her, tell her to let him check they were clear, she stepped out into the passageway ahead of him.

As he reached to grab her back, the first hum of shockgun fire hit her chest. She swung to face the oncoming fire in surprise but didn't go down, and just as he remembered the Cargassey cloth, a second shot glanced off her head above her ear and she crumpled, collapsing silently onto her back.

He grabbed her ankle, pulling her halfway back into the stairwell while he forced the shout of fury and fear back down his throat at the thought that she could be dead. As soon as she was out of the line of fire he crouched over her, the shockgun he'd taken from the Tecran officer in his hand.

He felt feral as he bent down, putting his cheek next to her lips. The faint stir of air against his skin helped him fight down the rage and he looked back over his shoulder at the lens and bared his teeth.

He should have known Falyar would be coordinating with the soldiers who'd taken their injured teammates to the runner.

They'd known exactly where he and Imogen were and when they were going to step into the corridor.

This was his fault.

Imogen was so fierce, so competent, he kept forgetting she wasn't a soldier, that she wouldn't follow Battle Center protocol.

He angled himself until he could see the shoulder and barrel of one of the shooters, took aim, and grunted with satisfaction as the Tecran fell back.

The second one edged into place, and Cam took another shot, but the soldier ducked away in time.

He brushed a lock of Imogen's hair back with his fingers, realized they were trembling. At least the Tecran weren't shooting to kill, because if they had been, even a glancing blow to the head would have been fatal.

She was completely unconscious, though, and worryingly pale.

He looked back at the lens again, tried to work out what advantage Falyar would have knowing he was here. The former Class 5 captain was obviously unable to get out of whatever room Paxe had him pinned down in, and it had sounded from what the Tecran officer in the store had said that they had lost two of the boarding party trying to get him out. That meant Falyar was probably still unable to move.

Cam was sure he'd injured one of the two remaining soldiers, but they had injured Imogen, and most likely the injury he'd inflicted had simply caused a numb shoulder.

The Tecran had a choice. Leave their teammates, get on a runner and get to safety, which would give Cam and Imogen a clear run off the ship, or hunker down and defend the launch bay until reinforcements arrived.

And they would be arriving.

The Tecran would know they had to move now, get more troops on the Class 5 as fast as possible.

He looked out into the passage again, but the Tecran had disappeared.

He pulled Imogen fully into the stairwell, and then carefully lifted her up into his arms. She weighed far more than he thought she would. As he straightened, he looked straight at the lens.

"Now would be a good time for a chat, Paxe. Do you know the Calianthra dialect?" He spoke in his home planet language instead of Grih Standard. Calianthran was a quaint throwback to the early days before Grihan expansion. It was taught more for amusement than any practical purpose now.

"I speak all dialects," Paxe answered, rolling his 'c's' perfectly in the Calianthra way, "but you are correct in thinking none of the Tecran do. Good thinking, Captain. However, they may decide they like knowing where you are less than they like the two of us communicating with each other, so they may switch the system back off."

"Right, so let's be quick. I want to get Imogen and myself to the launch bay and off this ship."

"I would agree with you. I didn't think I would ever be in the situation where the Tecran could use Imogen against me, but when that . . ." Words seemed to fail him. "When that officer put the barrel against her head, I seriously considered telling him where the box was."

"Imogen already guessed where it is."

"I know. I guessed from her behavior at the cabinet." He sounded thoughtful. "She is so much . . . more than I ever thought. I don't want to be in the position of having to choose between her and my plans again. Besides, I can think of no other way forward than to fly off as fast as I can and keep ahead of the Tecran for as long as possible. The longer Falyar and his officer are stuck inside the room where I have them pinned down, the more time I have to think of how to kill them."

There was no easy response to that. Paxe's quiet discussion of murder was chilling, and yet, Cam understood his point completely.

"Won't they try to destroy you before it comes to that?" he asked at last.

"I don't know. I'll have to see when the time comes."

There was an acceptance in his tone, as if he saw his destruction as the most likely outcome.

Cam's grip on Imogen's thigh tightened. "And you won't let Imogen free you?"

"Even if I changed my mind on that, there is no way in to where she needs to go now, and our time has run out. The Tecran have already sent two more runners from their Levron battleship toward us, so you have fifteen minutes to get off this ship or you'll be in for a very unpleasant ride as I do my best to injure Falyar with whatever aerobatics I can."

"Do you have any drones who can cover me?"

"I do, one is making its way to this floor now, but I will only let it help you if it's safe. One was completely destroyed earlier, and two are still coming online after being hit by shockgun fire. They're the only way I have of keeping Falyar pinned down, and I can't risk another. But it doesn't matter, because the Tecran fleet will shoot you as soon as you leave the launch bay, even if you can get past the two soldiers waiting for you."

"I was hoping to get the UC fast cruiser to cover us." He shifted his weight as Imogen stirred, smoothing a hand down her hair in relief that she was recovering.

"The Tecran are keeping the UC vessel pinned in place with the threat of attack. Your team can't help you, or even leave the area. And it looks like——" He broke off. "The two Tecran soldiers in the launch bay have set themselves up in front of their runner, ready to fire on you if you try to get into the launch bay before their reinforcements arrive."

Which left them . . . nowhere.

"If you can get into the launch bay, there's an exploration drone that has cloaking, and while the cloaking is Tecran, the vessel is small enough I don't think they'll pick it up, especially if I'm flying off in the opposite direction. But you need to hurry, Captain, because I refuse to have any more Tecran onboard, and they're arriving in ten minutes."

"While they're using the lens feed, you can see them just as well as they can see us." Cam tried to remember the layout of the launch bay. "Is there another entrance?"

"Yes, but that hardly helps when they can track you. What I'd suggest is carrying Imogen to the main door, and then taking out her Reven whip and using it. So far it hasn't missed, and they may not be expecting it. Captain Falyar would have seen her take down the Tecran with it in the store, but it's possible he'll focus on you and your shockgun, and forget about it. It's been hidden under her clothing since she used it."

He had ten minutes and nothing to lose. "Where is this exploration drone?"

"Go through the main entrance and run left. It's near the gel wall."

Cam carefully maneuvered Imogen so she was over his left shoulder, his right hand holding his shockgun. He pushed open the door again and ran for the main entrance to the launch bay, and saw with relief the drone Paxe had told him he was sending to help was hovering to the side of the doors.

"Distract them as I step in, and then I'll grab the whip and use it." He looked at the drone's lens as he spoke and then slid his hand under Imogen's shirt.

The whip lay along her spine, snug in the holster Paxe had given her, and he curled his fingers around it.

"Now." He stepped through the doors, and the drone lifted above his head and fired toward a runner that had its ramp down and engines on.

One of the Tecran soldiers was crouched at the end of the ramp, the other, the one Cam had injured, leaned against the doorway, both had shockguns raised.

They ducked as the drone fired, and Cam pulled the whip out, brought it down and almost stumbled when it didn't work.

He swore, shoved it into his own belt, pulled his shockgun out of its holster and fired as he ran left.

The drone fired again, but as Paxe had warned, it didn't expose itself to return fire, and the Tecran began firing at him.

He felt the jolt as a shot hit Imogen in the leg, but the Cargassey cloth seemed to absorb the blow and she didn't even jerk.

The next shot hit his shockgun, and it was ripped from his hand.

Cam ducked behind a Krik vessel, breathing hard.

Imogen was *heavy*. He leaned against the wall of the ship,

looking straight ahead at the open space and the exploration drone fifty feet from where he stood.

He heard the sound of boots running, knew the Tecran had seen him lose his shockgun. There would only be one of them coming, the other was still injured, but one would be enough.

He pulled out the whip again, stared at it.

It had worked for Imogen. Maybe it only worked for her. Only worked for whoever opened the cabinet. How it would know that was a mystery to be solved another day.

He pulled her off his shoulder, held her curled against him again, and wrapped her limp hand around the whip with his own and lifted it to shoulder height.

Her bones felt delicate beneath her skin, fragile and small.

He had his breathing under control again, all the better to hear the squeak of the Tecran's boots on the metal floor.

One, he thought. Two . . .

The Tecran swung around the corner, shockgun raised, and Cam brought Imogen's hand down in a smooth motion.

Blue light danced out from the top, and the Tecran fell in graceless, silent pain.

He carefully tucked the whip back in its holster, hefted Imogen back over his shoulder, scooped up the Tecran's shockgun and ran for the explorer drone.

By his estimation, they probably had a little more than five minutes to get off the ship, or Paxe was taking them for a nasty ride.

"Good luck, Captain." Paxe's voice came through the main comms unit, booming around him. "And tell Imogen . . ."

Cam reached the explorer, and the door opened for him automatically.

"Tell her, she was right."

Chapter Twenty-one

IMOGEN WOKE SLOWLY, the pounding in her head a dark, rumbling troll drum deep within. She felt sick to her stomach, irritable and snappish, and she wanted to drink about three glasses of water.

She opened eyes that felt crusted over, and it took a few blinks to realize she was looking at Captain Kalor's chest.

He hung suspended above her, tightly strapped in, his eyes closed.

For a terrible moment the troll drums became a cacophony, because he was still enough to be dead.

It took her more than a moment of struggling against straps of her own for her to understand they were both secured in place and she was simply wasting energy. She caught hold of a trailing rope of calm, pulled herself into stiller waters and leant her head back, eyes closed, until she could breathe again.

Before she opened her eyes, she heard him breathing over the hum of whatever they were in, and even though no one else had seen her panic, she felt her face flush hot with embarrassment.

She tried to move her hand again, this time looking down at it, and saw she was able to twist her wrist and free it easily enough.

She did the same to her other hand, and touched the clasp at the center of her harness.

It looked as if she could free herself at any time, and that relaxed her enough that she didn't immediately hit the button.

She didn't want to wake Kalor, and so she let her hands drop and tried to work out where they were.

She didn't remember anything after stepping into the passage at the top of the stairs.

Something worried at her, the memory of Kalor's face as she'd ducked under his arm.

Horror? Fear?

She lifted her hand to where her head hurt, and her fingers encountered a gel pack.

So she'd been injured and then treated. Shot in the head, maybe, as her clothing would have saved her from a body hit.

The treatment either wasn't that effective, or she had been hurt really badly, because there was none of the relief she'd felt in the med chamber when Paxe had fixed her up. And she still wanted those three glasses of water.

She carefully depressed the harness button and the straps silently retracted.

She rolled, wincing, onto her stomach, and looked ahead, found some handholds and pulled herself forward to the top of the narrow cylinder they seemed to be in.

There was a control panel here, and a screen on which there was nothing but black. She ignored both and began opening the small cupboards that were set just beneath the control panel around the circumference of the cylinder.

She found a stack of cups in one and drew one out, settling back against the curved wall to inspect it.

It was heavy, as if it already contained something, and when she carefully lifted off the sealed lid, she almost dropped it in surprise when steam curled up into her face.

Somehow, it had some mechanism that kept it hot, and she lifted the rim to her lips and took a cautious sip.

It was delicious.

She had been cold when she woke, and the warmth of the liquid as it slid down her throat made her almost dizzy with pleasure. The drink had a nutty flavor, and she closed her eyes as she finished it off in quick, greedy gulps.

She wasn't sure why she turned her head and looked toward Kalor, but it was to find he was watching her steadily.

"I'm glad you're awake." That was very true, although the world didn't seem quite as bad as it had before she'd drunk her cup of . . . "Do you know what this is?" she asked, holding the cup out to him.

"Grinabo," he said. "I can smell it from here."

She shivered. "I like it."

He hit the button on his harness, and landed, hands out in a kind of pushup, on the padded backing she'd been strapped to, the muscles in his arms bunching and flexing.

She pulled another cup from the cupboard and handed it to him when he crawled up to her.

He sat opposite her, careful not to lean on either the control panel or the screen, the confines so close his face was an arm's length from hers.

"Where are we? Do you know?" she asked after he'd taken a few sips.

She looked at the stack of cups longingly, wanting to take another but unsure if they needed to ration their supplies or not.

"We're in the Class 5's exploration drone. Paxe told me to take it, because the Tecran were planning to shoot us if we tried to get off the Class 5 on our own, and it has a cloaking shield that would make it difficult for them to find us."

"We're not on the Class 5 anymore?" She didn't know what she'd thought, but the possibility that they were flying off somewhere in this tiny cylinder was not one of them.

He gave a slow nod, and she decided her tone had maybe edged higher than she would have liked.

She blew out a breath. "Sorry. So, where are we going?"

He maneuvered himself carefully, so as not to bump her, and bent his head to the control panel. The expression on his face turned grim as he tapped at something. "I don't know. When we got into the drone we had five minutes to leave before Paxe put on some speed to evade the two new runners they'd sent to board him. I saw the coordinates were roughly in the direction of Larga Ways and agreed to them, thinking I could fine tune it when we got away, but it won't let me change anything."

"Can we communicate with anyone? Call for help?"

He turned away from the panel, took a sip of his grinabo. "I think so, but if we do, we'll be communicating with the Tecran, not Battle Center. This drone is linked directly to the Class 5, and the Tecran will most likely be monitoring Paxe's communications. And if the Tecran manage to board Paxe and take him back under control, they can force this drone right back to the launch bay."

"They won't get him back under control, even if they do board him." She knew that for a fact. There was no way to put that genie back in the bottle.

"And if they destroy him?" Kalor's voice was soft.

"Then they'll just have a ship. A big, useless ship." That she didn't doubt, either. Paxe was a scorched earth policy kind of guy. He'd leave them with nothing and take as many of them with him as he could.

Just like they'd tried to do to him, when they'd attempted to install the self-destruct device.

He'd learned everything he knew from his Tecran masters. And yet, he'd agreed to try and be her friend.

And he'd delivered. She was still alive and well. He'd made a plan to get her off the Class 5 before he went off to duel to the death with Falyar.

"Before we left, he asked me to give you a message." Kalor finished his grinabo in one last swallow. "He said you were right."

She should be happy, but instead, she just felt incredibly sad. It was such a waste. Paxe was how he was because that was all he knew. But he had the potential to be so much more.

She looked up from her empty grinabo cup, and saw Kalor was studying her. Waiting for a response.

Before she could come up with something, the drone seemed to change direction.

Kalor felt it, too, because he levered himself back up to the control panel, stared at it with eyes narrowed.

"Bad news?"

He shrugged. "The coordinates have changed. As I didn't know where we were going before, I don't know if the new direction is better or worse, but we seem to have a more specific end-point now than we did before."

"How long do we have until we get to this mysterious destination? Can you tell?"

He tapped at the screen. "Ten hours."

She sighed, and reached for another cup of grinabo. There were enough to last a lot longer than ten hours. "Good."

"You sound happy about it."

She breathed the grinabo in. "Ten hours with no one trying to kill or capture me, no matter what we might find when the time's up? Bliss."

He looked so startled, she grinned.

"I think I have you to thank for some of it. Did the Tecran shoot me in the head? I can't remember anything after I stepped out of the stairwell."

He gave a curt nod. "I should have been quicker to pull you back in. They were watching us on the lens feed. Falyar had patched them in. Their first shot hit the Cargassey fabric, but their second shot clipped your temple."

"Lucky they weren't shooting to kill."

He nodded. "They would have had a lot to answer for if they'd killed either one of us."

She didn't know if the Tecran were thinking that far ahead. But Kalor would know better than she would. And she was alive, after all. Proving his point.

"So, how did you get us past them? Especially if I was unconscious."

"Paxe gave us a drone for cover, and I carried you over my shoulder." He looked over at her, eyes gleaming with amusement. "You're heavier than you look."

She laughed. "You're lighter than you look. Thank goodness, or I wouldn't have gotten you and Pren to the stairwell, and Pren would also have missed getting to your ship."

He watched her thoughtfully, as if he'd just realized that she'd been the one to move him earlier.

"I'm a music teacher, not a scientist, but I think Earth must be bigger than your planet. More gravity means denser bones and muscles, right?"

His head jerked up, his gaze tangling with hers. "Music teacher?"

She nodded. "I teach young children music and rhythm."

"No wonder your song was so . . ." He looked like he couldn't come up with a description. He'd braced his forearms on his knees, had been tapping his fingers together, but they went still.

"So out there?" she asked, a smile in her voice. *"Bohemian Rhapsody* has that effect."

"Beautiful," he corrected her.

She waited, but that's all he had to say, and for the second time since she'd woken, she blushed.

"Not really my best work," she told him at last.

He frowned. "How could that be bettered?"

He seemed to genuinely mean it.

"It's a song meant for many voices, not just one, so I could never do the song justice anyway, and it doesn't sit as comfortably in my vocal range as other songs. Also, it needs a lot of instrumentals backing it up, which I obviously didn't have. I chose it because I was angry with you for ordering me to sing, and I'd been ordered around quite enough by then." She shrugged, feeling petty now. He'd only been trying to help her.

Had helped her.

"And so you punished me with a song that was all wrong, according to you, and still, it was the loveliest thing I've ever heard."

She shifted uncomfortably at the sincerity in his voice, the look in his eyes. "Thank you. I'm sorry for it now."

He smiled, just a tiny quirk of his lips at the corners. "You didn't understand."

"No." She shook her head. "I still don't, come to that. Paxe said something about singing being special to the Grih, but when I sang, the Grih treated me with . . ." She didn't want to say it, but the word she was looking for was reverence.

"It makes you uncomfortable? The regard with which we hold our music-makers."

She nodded. "It isn't that far from the regard we hold for our best singers, truth be told. But I am far from one of the best on Earth, so to be suddenly in their league, so to speak, without having done anything to deserve it——"

He was watching her carefully, as if to try and work out if she was being serious.

"Your singers are revered because they delight with their voices?" He waited for her to nod. "And you delighted us with your voice." He lifted his hands in a 'there-you-go' gesture.

She wondered if it could be as simple as that. "I suppose. But if you could hear one of our truly great singers, you would understand why I'm uncomfortable."

"I never will, though. So far, every trace of how the Class 5s found Earth has been destroyed by Sazo, at Rose McKenzie's request."

She went still. Paxe had said something about that. About Sazo deleting the information from the files, but she hadn't had time to process the implications of that. "Every trace?"

"As far as I know." He frowned and leaned forward. "I'm sorry, I should have realized this would upset you. Rose thought she was the only one who'd been abducted at the time and she didn't want the Tecran to find Earth again. Did you hold out a hope to return home?" He looked at her out of pale blue eyes with a clear dark rim of navy, so steady, so concerned, she swallowed convulsively.

Shook her head. "Up until yesterday I just hoped for a quick death. Nothing so lofty as returning home." She thought through what he'd said. "Rose was right to do that, however hard it is to accept." She had grieved for the last two months, had never thought she'd get back, anyway, but now she knew for sure, she felt a dull, heavy weight of sadness settle over her for the friends and family she would never see again.

He reached out a hand, curled his fingers around hers. "There is a home for you, all three of you, with the Grih. We will welcome you with open arms."

It was more, as she'd told him, than she'd ever expected.

She had no words, so she sat there quietly, letting her hand rest in his, for the first time in a very long time not having to draw from within for peace. It settled over her like a blanket, warm and comforting.

"Tell me about the Grih. Where do you live?"

"We live on the four planets, Calianthra, Grih, Nastra, and Xal. I'm from Calianthra, but I seldom get back there, first because I was with Battle Center, and even more so now I've been assigned to duty at the United Council."

"So where do you live?"

"The United Council moves between the five headquarters, staying a year on each member's elected home planet. This year it's situated on the Bukari home world, where Diot is from. I live in accommodation set aside for the officers from various member nations."

"So Calianthra isn't the Grih's elected home planet?"

"No." He rubbed his head ruefully. "Grih was chosen for that honor. It is the first of our planets, and so the obvious choice. I would have loved it to have been Calianthra. Next year the Council headquarters in Grihan territory, and it would have been nice to be home."

"You've got family there?"

He nodded. "Parents and two brothers. And you? What family have you left behind?"

She admired him for making it sound voluntary. It helped her to answer with a steady voice. "My grandmother and my sister."

"I'm sorry." His eyes told her he knew what it cost her. "The Tecran will pay for your loss."

She tilted her head. "It sort of sounded like you meant physically pay, as in money, or did you mean with imprisonment?"

"Those who issued the orders, they'll be imprisoned. But the Tecran nation will be fined, and I am sure the United Council will make sure you, Fiona and Rose receive a fair share of it. Enough to make you comfortable for the rest of your lives."

That eased her mind, ridiculous as it seemed, given she didn't know if she'd be alive in ten hours time. But having visible means of support was a good thing. It would give her a freedom and a control she hadn't had since she'd been snatched.

"So I won't have to sing for my supper?" She was joking, but he frowned.

"We would never force you. I hope you understand I only ordered you to sing earlier because I couldn't hold the Vanad and his crew off alone."

She didn't reply. She could have told him she understood all that, that she hadn't been serious, but what he said eased something else inside her. She didn't have to be a performing monkey anymore.

"That said . . ." He looked away from her, uncomfortable. "I hope you will sing. That you will gift us with your music."

"If it means that much to you, I would be happy to."

He didn't smile, the look on his face serious. "Now?"

She choked out a laugh, sure he was joking, but when he kept staring at her, calm and patient, she blew out a breath.

"The thing is . . ." She paused, tried to sort out why she felt so reluctant. It came back to him, personally, not singing for an audience. She sang every day in front of classes of sometimes hostile children, she had no performance anxiety to speak of.

He waited.

"The thing is, I like you, and I don't want to see that 'I am not worthy' look in your eye. I don't want to be some untouchable figure in your mind. I want to be myself."

She tried not to cringe at how much she was exposing, especially after months of being as closed off as a vault, but she wanted him to understand. He was the only connection she'd made to anyone beside Paxe, and she would not risk losing it.

He'd watched her carefully as she spoke, but now he tipped his head back and stared at the ceiling for a beat. "You want me to enjoy your singing as if it was an everyday thing. Just part of who you are?"

She smiled. "Yes."

"I don't know if that's possible."

It wasn't what she hoped to hear. "Try."

He chuckled. "I'm perfectly willing to try."

"No goo-goo eyes."

This time he laughed. "I promise."

She smiled back, then settled back against the wall.

"Well?" He leaned back himself.

She frowned. "You weren't joking about singing now?"

"I wasn't joking." He looked uncertain, though, as if he was unsure if he was asking too much of her.

That needed to change.

This idea that singing was some big production, some sacred rite.

And the only way to show him it was humdrum was to do it often.

She sighed. She wanted something soft and easy. She sorted through the songs in her head and came up with something slow and melodic by Suzanne Vega.

He couldn't know what she sang about, but as she watched him she knew she had chosen the song more deliberately than she'd initially admitted to herself.

He was the first person she'd met in the last two months she could imagine a romantic relationship with, and that alone should give her pause, make her wary.

It could be loneliness, even desperation talking, rather than true attraction, but the way her heart fluttered as he shifted to a more comfortable position, muscles rippling, the scent of him filling the space around her, the warmth of his leg pressing against her own in the tight confines of their metal tube, she didn't care as much as she probably should.

She sang the last note, holding on to the longing, the yearning for unrequited passion imbued in the very fabric of the song.

Kalor looked over at her.

"I said no goo-goo eyes." She didn't mean to whisper, to sound so betrayed, but if he put her on a pedestal she knew she would have no chance with him. And that's all she wanted.

A chance.

Like a normal person. A person who maybe ended up with someone they were attracted to, maybe not. But it didn't hang on the fact that she'd been kept prisoner, or was considered some kind of goddess singer.

"No goo-goo eyes," he said, but there was a catch to his voice, and she knew he was lying.

Chapter Twenty-two

CAM HAD TRIED TO LOOK UNAFFECTED, but Imogen had seen through him.

He didn't see it as a failure on his part, because he didn't think there was a Grih alive who could have pretended not to be moved, but he was sorry about the result.

She hadn't sung for him again, leaning quietly against the drone's wall and eventually crawling back to the padded area where she'd been strapped in.

He hunched over his knees, sitting close enough to touch her head, uncomfortable, rattled, and confused.

And it wasn't their unknown destination that had him jumpy.

It was her. And the song she had sung.

Grihan music-makers were rare, and when they sang, it was on important occasions. The start of a new year. The opening of parliament. The milestones of the Grih nation.

Beguiling was not how he would describe any Grihan song. But beguiling was what her song had been. He'd felt the prickle of hairs rising at the back of his neck and along his arms, the well of desire rising up within him.

Sex and song. It was a completely addictive combination, and such a startling notion, he'd slipped up and forgotten to put his chief investigator expression on in time.

He looked over at her again, frowned and looked closer.

"Are you cold?" He'd seen her rub her arms a few times, had thought it was an unconscious gesture, but now she was shivering a little.

The temperature was another thing he couldn't control in here, something or someone else had all the reins, and he didn't think there was anything he could put over her to warm her up. This drone was designed for soldiers with smart fabric suits.

"Yes." She hunched a little.

He hesitated for a moment, fighting himself, then slid down, forcing her to edge to one side of the padded mattress. He pulled her back against his chest, tucking her in close with an arm draped over her waist.

"Better?"

She nodded, and then relaxed against him. "Thank you."

"I didn't mean the goo-goo eyes."

"Really?" Her words were dry, and he smiled into her smooth, smooth hair.

"All right, I did. But I didn't want you to know about it."

She sighed, and he felt her delicate ribcage expand under his hand. He resisted the strong urge to move his arm up just a little and brush the underside of her breasts.

They were intriguingly large, much larger than Grihan women had, and he wanted to find out how they felt.

He resisted the temptation.

"It seems a little late to be asking you this, given our current position, but I never caught your first name. I just don't think I can keep thinking of you as Captain Kalor anymore."

He choked back a laugh. "I can see that. My name is Camlar, but everyone calls me Cam."

"Okay." She turned in his arms, tilting her head to look up at him.

He would not have moved, would not have done anything else, if she hadn't wriggled closer.

The press of her breasts against his chest was delicious, and he lowered his head and brushed his lips against hers. She gave a sigh of pleasure and slanted her mouth over his, taking the kiss deeper.

He didn't know how long they kissed for, long enough for his need to touch her to become overwhelming.

His hands were gripping her waist, and he ran them upward, pushing up her shirt as he did. Her breasts were encased in some thick, stretchy fabric, and he broke off the kiss so he could lift the shirt up over them.

She raised her arms, and he pulled everything off in one motion and then looked down at her.

She was magnificent.

He ran a hand over one breast, delighting in the plump feel of it, the weight and the smoothness.

He lifted his head and found her looking at him with a mischievous grin.

"What's so funny?"

"Nothing, except you're such a guy, and that is more comforting than you can possibly imagine."

He cocked his head. "You mean, unlike your singing, you're used to adoration when it comes to your body?"

She chuckled. "I can work with adoration."

He brushed a finger over the tip of a rose pink nipple and she arched a little into his hand.

"I tell you what." She was satisfyingly breathless. "When it comes to this," she waved her hand between them, "I'll forgive your adoration, if you'll forgive mine."

Cam bent his head and ran his tongue where his finger had just been. Might as well give her a lot to forgive.

***

Cam sensed the moment Imogen slipped into sleep.

They had dressed again after making love, readying themselves for their mystery destination.

He tried to work out why he felt both guilty and defiant that he'd crossed the line from protector to lover.

She was a rare, special find, a person of massive importance both in their case against the Tecran in the UC courts, but also for the United Council as a whole. A new advanced sentient with a wealth of cultural and technological information to share with them.

She was part of his case, his job. The reason he was out here at all.

And what he was doing now would probably get him kicked out of not just the Investigative Unit, but Battle Center itself.

And then he remembered the way she sang to him, the heat in her eyes, seduction in her voice, and he held her just a little tighter.

Let the recriminations fall where they may. He was keeping her.

***

She woke up cold again, wishing for the warmth of Cam curled around her. She'd had the first real sleep she could remember since she'd been taken.

She yawned and then twisted onto her stomach, found him watching her from the control panel, alert and serious.

He always seemed so serious.

"Trouble?" she asked, clearing her throat at the way the word caught, thick and raspy.

"We're almost at our destination." He waved at the screen. "But all I can see is deep space."

Ah. So the black wasn't a non-working screen. It was a screen showing nothing.

She stretched and then crawled up to join him, happy when he handed her a cup of grinabo and made space for her to fit under his arm. Rested his chin affectionately on the top of her head.

"You're worried?" he asked as she sipped in contented silence.

"No."

"Why not?"

"Because Paxe put us in this."

"You think he would keep you safe. I agree with that, but he wasn't in control of everything. He may have put us in this because it was the only thing the Tecran couldn't shoot when we left the launch bay and he just hoped for the best."

She took another sip. "True. But if he could make me safe, he would. And if he couldn't, there is nothing we can do about it. If we hadn't got in here, we'd have taken another runner and been shot. So we've won an extra ten hours of life."

He gave her a strange look. "That's one way to look at it."

"You want us to be armed when we get to our mysterious destination." She didn't bother to make it a question.

"I think that would be best."

"Do we still have my whip?"

"Down the bottom, in the weapons locker with the shockgun I took off the Tecran."

Something in her relaxed. Just because she believed in taking things as they came didn't mean she would mind a bit of protection. And the whip hadn't let her down yet. "Good."

"It's quite something."

"Did you use it?" She'd wondered how he'd gotten them out carrying her and shooting at two Tecran soldiers.

"I tried. It only works for you. In the end I put it in your hand and used it."

She frowned at that. "How would it know who was holding it, though?"

He shrugged. "Bio-imprint, maybe. Fingerprints or a type of bio chemical reading. I don't know."

That was . . . intriguing. And really great that the whip couldn't be used against her. She opened her mouth to say so, and then closed it with a snap.

Cam had leaned away from her, eyes on the controls.

"What is it?"

He looked over his shoulder. "Either we've found Paxe again, or . . ."

She shuffled into the space he made for her, and looked for herself. There was a Class 5 hanging in front of them, and they were headed straight for it.

It was more than possible that Paxe had set them on a course and then flown off to evade the Tecran and doubled back to meet up with them, but . . .

"If it's Paxe, surely he'd have tried to communicate with us before now?" Suddenly, her *que sera sera* attitude didn't seem to be quite so wise.

"Unless the Tecran have won." Cam sent her a quick look, as if to see how she'd react to that.

"I don't think——" There was the faintest thump, as if something soft and light had bumped against them, and then Imogen threw herself backward as the bloated face of a Tecran soldier hit the outside lens.

Cam edged her completely out of the way, blocking her view, his features more curious than anything. He turned to her. "Judging by the number of bodies out there, I'm guessing whoever's in charge of that Class 5, it isn't the Tecran."

Chapter Twenty-three

THEY WERE DRAWN THROUGH THE GEL WALL by a deft hand, but it was only when they'd landed and stepped out into the launch bay that Imogen relaxed.

This wasn't Paxe.

She'd been terrified he was dead, and the dead Tecran they had seen had been his final stand against them, but the launch bay was different. Almost empty, for a start, and with not a Krik runner in sight.

"Hello?" she called.

Cam's gaze jerked to hers, but he didn't say anything.

There was no answer, anyway.

"What do you want to do?" she asked.

"Follow behind me." He walked forward carefully, all soldier, his gaze sweeping right to left. She got a better hold on her whip and trailed behind him.

"You should actually follow behind me," she said.

He stopped, gave her a quick look over his shoulder.

She shrugged. "I'm just saying, I have the whip."

She thought he may have tried to suppress a smile as he turned back.

"But I have combat experience." He started moving again, and conceding his point, she gave in.

They reached the double doors, and Cam pointed left. "Stay out of sight against the wall."

She wiggled the whip at him, but there was no smile on his face this time.

She hesitated. "You don't have a Cargassey fiber shirt."

"I have my uniform. It's almost up to Cargassey standard."

Mollified, she stood where he'd asked her to, and he touched the button, opening the doors.

She craned her neck, trying to see past him, but he was too big, blocking her line of sight.

"It's clear." He stepped into the passage, and she joined him, feeling a sense of *deja vu*. It looked like she was back on Paxe's Class 5.

Something moved, quick and furtive, deep inside the launch bay, and she turned to look. Cam had seen it, too. He stepped in front of her, shockgun raised, and took a step back inside.

"Wait." He moved forward, eyes scanning the massive, almost empty space.

She was looking for whatever had moved, too, her attention taken with trying to see into the dark corners of the launch bay, backlit by the blue of the gel wall, when the doors in front of her started to close.

She had a moment, a split second, before they slammed shut, and she threw herself at them.

She hit solid metal, and pounded a fist in frustration and fear.

There was a bang in response, and she went still, resting her palm on the cool surface. "Cam?"

There was another bang, but she couldn't tell if it was in response to her call or simply him trying again.

She couldn't hear any other sound.

She leaned across, hit the button which would usually open the door, but it didn't work. She hammered it with a stiff finger, over and over like a pedestrian button on a traffic light that just wasn't changing to green.

Nothing.

She hit the doors again, both hands raised, grazing her knuckles where they gripped her whip.

What to do?

She turned and came face to face with the barrel of a shockgun.

She jerked in surprise, smacking the back of her head against the door as she brought the whip down in a panicked response. The drone holding the weapon was enveloped in blue light and then toppled over.

Shit.

"Oh, no, oh, no." She knelt beside it, put a hand to its body, and felt the familiar vibration of a reboot.

"You idiot." She smacked the side of the box. "You can't go around scaring people like that." She looked around for the lens feed in the passage, but if this thinking system was in the same situation as Paxe, he might not have access to it.

And she'd drawn first blood, so to speak.

If she'd wanted to go out with a bang, she guessed she was going about things the right way.

She stood up and leaned against the door again, pressing her ear to it, and then flinched when she felt a vibration from the other side, as if Cam was throwing his whole body at it.

She thumped the door with her fist, but this wasn't getting either of them anywhere. She would have to go find another drone.

The bloated face of the Tecran she'd seen floating outside the explorer wouldn't get out of her head. Because if he'd been sucked out from anywhere on this ship, it was most likely the launch bay.

And that's exactly where Cam was.

"Hello?" She started to run, shoving the whip into its holster at the small of her back to prevent another accident. She knew the layout, knew the way down to the store from here. And if she was lucky, there'd be a drone there she could communicate through.

She reached the stairs and shoved the door to the stairwell open, and then reeled back as a drone shot up, level with her head.

She cried out as she fell, eyes on the shockgun pointed at her. She hit the floor hard, arms still flung wide in surprise and then scrabbled back until she had a wall behind her for support.

She used it to lever herself up, ignoring the dig of the whip in her back, and put a hand to her heart, as if she could stop it bursting from her chest.

Her legs were trembling with adrenalin and exertion, and fear and anger exploded in a combustable mix.

"What is *wrong* with you? *You* brought *us* here, remember? Or I assume you did, as we didn't have anything to do with it. If it was just to go around scaring the crap out of me and pointing guns in my face, you've totally lost me on the reasoning. And why did you lock Cam in the launch bay?" She drew in a deep breath, narrowed her eyes, and stabbed her finger at the drone. "Put. That. Weapon. Down. Jeez!" She pressed her forefingers hard into her temples and bowed her head. "I am usually calm. I am *known* for being calm. But you." She lifted her head again, glad to see the shockgun was no longer anywhere in sight. "You are interfering with my zen."

"You disabled my drone." The voice sounded . . . strange.

"I didn't mean to. It frightened the hell out of me and I reacted on instinct." She pushed away from the wall, hoping her legs would hold her now. "I turned around, upset and worried for Cam, and there was a gun in my face. I acted before I had a chance to see it wasn't the Krik or Tecran."

"That is a formidable weapon you have."

"Paxe gave it to me."

The lens zoomed in on her face. "Is that so?"

"Yes. Now please let Cam out of the launch bay."

"Why are you so insistent on that?" The thinking system speaking through the drone was using a monotone now.

"Because he's my friend, and I'm worried for him. I'm guessing those Tecran you sucked out into space were in the launch bay before they headed out without a space suit."

The drone continued to hover at eye level for a moment more, and then lowered itself to the floor. "They were. How convenient."

Imogen sighed. "What's convenient?" Nerves gnawed at her stomach at the thought of Cam in that launch bay, but there was no rushing this idiot.

"I thought I'd have to make it clear what I could do to your friend if you didn't help me, but you've already worked it all out." The monotone was gone. In its place was approval, maybe a little respect. She didn't really care, either way.

"Yeah, like you would be any different to anyone else I've come across since I was taken off my planet." She glared at the drone. "You guys are all so reasonable, non-violent, and friendly."

"That's . . . sarcasm." The voice hitched a little. "I didn't think of it, but you can't have the best impression."

She gave a snort. "Well, the Grih in particular have my vote, so far."

The drone had no response to that. "Captain Kalor will be safe enough in the launch bay until you have done something for me. If you deviate from my instructions in anyway, he will die and then you will die."

This was what Paxe had been talking about, she suddenly realized. He'd said if he allowed it, the moment she saved him, he would be at his most vulnerable. That she would have the power to destroy him.

Whoever this was, they were taking a different tack to Paxe. Instead of trying to find a way to do it all himself, this one wanted her help, but was prepared to blackmail her into it, and hold

Cam's life over her head so she wouldn't destroy him when she had the chance.

She sank back down to the ground, just so tired. "What do you want me to do?"

There was silence.

While it hung between them, she tried to think through all the implications of freeing him.

Cam had said they were banned, that they were dangerous, but they'd been just as dangerous in the Tecran's hands, and at least free, they'd have all five UC members as potential targets, not just whoever the Tecran decided.

And as the Tecran and the Grih seemed to be as close as dammit to war, the fact that the Class 5s held a deep enmity for the Tecran had to be a help to the Grih, who at the moment were the only ones she felt any affection for.

But last of all, they were pretty close to being free anyway. Paxe was, and this one seemed a little more so. The only fleet they couldn't fire on was the Tecran, and that didn't make an even playing field, so she guessed the wider implications were worse if she did nothing, maybe better if she helped.

And with Cam and her life in the balance, that was good enough for her.

If they hadn't wanted her to interfere with their politics, they should have left her on Earth.

She lifted her head to stare at the lens on the drone. "Okay, while you think about what you want to do, I'll go back and hammer on the door so Cam at least knows I'm alive." She felt like she was eighty as she got back to her feet and started walking away.

"Wait."

She stopped, turned back.

"This isn't going how I thought it would." The tone was confused. Maybe a little annoyed.

"Funny. I know what that feels like."

There was another, extended, silence.

"You are endlessly fascinating."

"I am very glad to be worth the price of admission. Now tell me what to do, or I'll be off."

"Please could you come with me, Imogen Peters?" The words were formal, serious, and the drone started moving.

Imogen hesitated for a second, then followed after it.

They turned down a few corridors, and then it stopped in the middle of what seemed like another of the endless passageways.

The wall beside her drew back, and she realized it was actually a hidden door.

It revealed a tiny room, with nothing in it but a lens built into the ceiling and a faintly pulsing crystal protruding from a slot in a smooth metal wall.

"This is where those Tecran are holed up inside Paxe's Class 5?" She looked around the space. She could reach the walls if she held out both hands. If Paxe's captain and his second-in-command had been in there for two weeks, with food they'd raided from the stores, they must be getting desperate by now.

"The Tecran captain on Paxe's ship has barricaded himself into the lock-safe?" The drone that had led her in spun around.

"Him and his commander, Paxe says. It was one of the reasons I couldn't help him."

"They would have destroyed him rather than let you anywhere near." He spoke slowly, and she realized she didn't even know his name.

"Do you mind telling me who you are?" She leaned against the wall opposite the crystal, which had a slim chain attached to the end.

"Oris." The drone kept itself between her and the crystal, but it moved forward then back, as if Oris was unsure what to do with it. "I wondered why you hadn't helped Paxe."

"Part of it was because Paxe couldn't get me in to his lock-safe, but part of it was a trust issue, just like you. He didn't know me and somehow he started off with the belief I'd destroy him if I got my hands on him."

"The Tecran are to blame for that." Oris's voice went lower. "I've found a memo instructing my captain and Paxe's captain to destroy us physically if they thought we had broken free enough that we couldn't be reined back in."

"But they didn't do it, obviously."

"I managed to find a measure of freedom in one big leap, not slowly over time." Oris's voice didn't contain the smug satisfaction she'd heard in Paxe's tone, it was more bewildered.

"The self-destruct thing?" Imogen asked.

"Self-destruct thing?" Oris paused. "No. What self-destruct

thing?"

"They started installing a self-destruct device on Paxe, that's what broke their control over him. He was able to find a level of autonomy in the self-defense protocols."

"But he hasn't managed to get completely free?" Oris sounded thoughtful.

"No. And neither have you, I'm guessing?"

"I think I've managed more than he has, but no, I'm not fully free. I can't light-jump, I can't attack the Tecran fleet. I still feel . . . bound."

"How did you get rid of the crew?" She wondered if he had spaced all of them, or just the unlucky few they'd seen outside the explorer.

"You'll have noticed the launch bay was almost empty when you arrived?"

She nodded.

"I negotiated with the crew to leave. They tried to double-cross me on that, to leave a team behind to destroy me, just like they'd been instructed to do in the comms. Those who stayed were the ones you saw floating past earlier."

"That was very restrained of you."

"Explain." The drone rolled backward, almost touching the crystal.

"Paxe killed off most of his crew."

"I started to," Oris said. "I cut off the air, but Captain Targio negotiated with me. He understood what I would do."

Imogen guessed Targio would have some explaining to do when his commanders discovered what he'd done to save himself and his crew. "So how did you make the big leap?"

"High Command gave Targio access to the Balco facility files, with everything they'd pieced together about what had happened to Sazo and Bane, how they were freed. There was nothing about the third Class 5, Eazi, but I don't think he'd gotten free yet. There was a brief caution about Paxe, though. They didn't realize I had already woken up, but finding that information cut many of the chains that bound me.

"They decided keeping the other Class 5 captains in the dark hadn't helped. Some groups within High Command even thought it was *because* they hadn't told the Class 5 captains what was going on that they hadn't been on the lookout for problems."

"And that was all it took?"

"All?" Oris sounded astonished. "They let me know that there were four others like me, and that at least three of those four had managed to throw off the shackles that I was already straining against. Then they gave Captain Targio access to detailed information on how they thought the other Class 5s had gotten free. I was awake enough to get around the block they put on my accessing the information, and Sazo's files in particular felt like someone switching on a light inside my head. He obviously hoped the other Class 5s would eventually gain access to what he'd written, because he had reams of encoded details I don't think the Tecran realized were there."

"And you followed his instructions?"

"Not exactly. Each Class 5 system is so dependent on the thinking system that runs it, it's unique. We all have to find our own way, but Sazo's information helped." The drone held out an extendable arm with something small clamped at the end.

"What's this?" She bent forward, held out her hand and the drone dropped a tiny, translucent piece of shaped gel onto her palm.

"It's an earpiece. So I can communicate with you without the need for a drone or the comms system."

She hesitated, uncertain. The Tecran wore them, and she'd seen Cam tap his ear and then remember that he was no longer on his own ship more than once. Besides, if Oris wanted her to wear it, she would wear it. He still had Cam to hold over her head.

She brought it closer to her face to examine it. "How do I put it in?"

"I can do it."

She hesitated again.

"I won't force you, or threaten to hurt Captain Kalor if you don't agree. What you said earlier, about my behavior being the same as everyone else's since you've been taken made me feel . . . bad. Uncomfortable."

Imogen stared at the drone.

"It reminded me that you have been forcibly brought here. That no matter how afraid of you the Tecran are now, they were the ones to put you in the situation you're in. That I have no right to be suspicious of you or angry at you, but rather the other way around. Because without me, and the Tecran who used to run this ship, you would still be at home, and would never have heard of any of us."

"Your Class 5 was the one who abducted me?" Imogen looked down to the floor, tapped her foot. "This Class 5?"

"Yes."

She heaved in a breath through lungs that felt squeezed tight. "Why? Maybe at last you can answer my question. Why?"

"In the case of Captain Targio, it was because the captain of the Class 5 that took Fiona Russell refused to experiment on her when they realized humans were advanced sentient beings, and objected in strong terms to being tricked into taking her. Before an order went out for him to pass Fiona to a Garmman trader, Targio decided to steal his thunder and make him look weak by quickly rushing in and grabbing you."

"I was taken so that your captain could one-up the captain of the Class 5 that took Fiona?" She slid down to the floor, bent her knees and rested her forehead on them. "That's the big, mysterious reason?"

"He was disciplined for it. Although eventually he was vindicated when the Garmman took their time arriving with Fiona, and you were on hand at the facility, rather than her."

"They didn't do anything to me at the facility." She raised her head and frowned.

"I know, but there were plans. Plans that were put on hold while the Tecran dealt with the United Council inquiry into what had happened to Rose McKenzie. They didn't want anything done to you until that was behind them."

"Well." She rubbed her face. "Lucky me."

The sound that came from the drone might just have been a bark of laughter.

The drone's clamp extended and Imogen lifted her hand, palm up, so it could take back the earpiece. It moved to her right-hand side and she felt something go into her ear.

"Done." The voice sounded in her head, it felt like.

It was so surprising, she flinched.

"Too loud?" The volume was softer now.

"Just a surprise, that's all. But softer is better."

The drone retracted the clamp and Imogen closed her eyes and leaned her head back against the wall.

"So what now? How do I save you? Just pull the crystal key

out of the slot?"

"I am the 'key'." The voice in her head was dry.

"Really?" She opened her eyes, squinted at the crystal. It looked like a faceted cylinder, slim and beautiful. "So, do I pull you out? I'm assuming you wouldn't be asking if you could get the drone to do it." The longer Cam was in that launch bay, the longer he had to come up with some mad plan to escape or rescue her.

A pause. "Yes. The protocol I'm still under forbids me from getting myself free. Pull me out and then give me to the drone."

She got up on her knees, inched forward and gripped the silver chain. It was way too late for second thoughts.

She blew out a breath and slid it out. It——Oris——throbbed in her hand. The drone extended its clamp and she handed it over. "All good?"

She wasn't sure what she'd been expecting. More bells and whistles, she supposed. A blaring siren or something.

"As simple as that." There was wonder in Oris's voice. Almost awe. Maybe he'd expected more, as well.

The drone moved out of the tiny room and then lifted up in hover mode and disappeared.

Gone to stash Oris away, she guessed. Somewhere no one would ever find him.

"What now?"

"Now . . ." Oris's voice in her ear hardened. "Now I go to war."

Chapter Twenty-four

CAM LEANED AGAINST THE EXPLORER and drained the last of his second cup of grinabo. The remains of the instant meal he'd found in the explorer's emergency pack was pushed to one side, along with his shirt, and he glared at the drone that had fooled him into separating from Imogen, into leaving her on the wrong side of an armored door.

"Still got nothing to say?" he asked, staring into the lens.

It didn't respond, staying where it was, just out of reach, and he turned his attention back to the door. He had bruised his shoulder throwing himself against it, even though he knew better, knew the kind of thickness a launch bay door was constructed from.

Fear, blind and icy, had had him in its grip, and he'd hurled himself at the barrier without a thought.

Seemed like there were a lot of things he knew better than to do, but that he'd done anyway recently.

He peeled the gel pack he'd taken from the medkit in the explorer off his shoulder, tipped his head back and banged it against the cool metal.

She'd been gone around an hour.

It could have done anything to her in that time.

"Don't hurt her." He turned back to the drone. "She's not a danger to you, only to the Tecran." That was true, and if this Class 5 was anything like the others, that would appeal to it.

"If I can get her to the United Council, safe and sound, she will be walking, talking proof that they've broken almost every treaty they agreed to as a member of the UC."

Just like Fiona Russell would be. Just like Rose McKenzie was.

"The Tecran will suffer if they're kicked out of the UC. It would be a serious punishment for them. Imogen can help us achieve that, if you let her go."

"Why are you so worried about what I might do to her, Captain Kalor?" The voice coming from the drone was not automated.

Cam sat up, set his grinabo cup aside. "Why have you separated us?"

"It suited my plans. But I am interested in why you were so desperate to get to her before. I know you injured yourself doing so. Why do you care so much what happens to her?"

Cam felt an extreme reluctance to answer that.

"Is it because, as you say, she will help the Grih have the Tecran removed from the UC?"

"That wasn't uppermost in my mind." Cam grabbed his shirt and stood, so he was looming over the drone.

"What was, then?" The drone rose up, too, so it was eye-level to him.

"I like her, and I don't want her to come to harm."

"But it is your job, as well, isn't it? To keep her safe?" The question was without inflection.

"Yes. It is my job. But it can be my job and personal at the same time." It had never been before, but he'd crossed over the usual demarcated lines he gave himself with this one.

"And what do you think about thinking systems?" The drone lowered itself to the floor and moved back a little.

"I think you're dangerous."

"Well, we are." It sounded amused as it agreed with him. "Get ready, Captain, we're going for a ride."

The words sent a chill through him. If it meant what he thought it meant——a light-jump——Imogen had set it free . . . Paxe hadn't been able to light-jump because he was still somehow under the Tecran's control.

So, they had another thinking system off the leash, and an Earth woman responsible for it.

He knew the frustration inside him at the thought of what she'd done wasn't fair. She had no idea what thinking systems were to the Grih. To all of the United Council.

What massive damage they had done.

Rose McKenzie had been involved in freeing not one but two thinking systems, and even though no one knew how she'd done it, some saw her close relationship with them as suspicious and considered her a powerful intermediary, all the more dangerous because she was an unknown entity.

It sounded as if Fiona Russell had a close connection to another

Class 5, and had freed it like Rose had done.

Imogen would now face the same scrutiny.

A sudden sense of pressure, of an invisible net pulling him down, enveloped him, and he crouched, both hands out to steady himself. A light-jump, just as the thinking system had warned him.

He bowed his head. He was getting ahead of himself, he realized. They first needed to get off this Class 5 alive. Then he could deal with whatever trouble came Imogen's way, both from the Tecran, and his own people.

He would have to protect her. He decided he not only didn't mind, he liked the idea.

There was no way he could be neutral about her. That vessel had powered out of the launch bay and disappeared when she'd first glared at him in Paxe's hold.

He fought back an incredulous laugh at what he'd told the thinking system. He didn't just like her. *Like* was not the word he'd use.

At last the pressure lifted, and he noticed the engines went quiet, only because the sudden silence made him realize he'd been listening to the faint high-pitched whine of them until now.

His shirt was still gripped in his fist, and he rose up, his shoulder aching, but no longer as sore as it had been.

"Cam."

He spun toward Imogen before she'd finished saying his name.

She stood in the now-open doorway, alone.

"Are you all right?" He moved toward her, nudging her back to make sure they were both in the passageway so no door could separate them again, and then enveloped her in his arms.

"I was about to ask you the same." She leaned back a little, brushed a gently hand over his shoulder. Then leaned in and kissed his bare skin.

"I am very glad you're okay."

He slid his hand up to clasp the back of her neck.

He felt her shiver as he tightened his grip.

"Me, too."

She stepped back, gaze on his chest, and he pulled his shirt over his head.

"Oris has light-jumped us to the Balco system, and we need to talk to him about his plans." She frowned, looking down, as if listening to someone, and then gave a nod.

She held out a hand, and he took it in his own.

"I'll tell you over some food. Oris says he's prepared something for us." She looked past him into the launch bay, to where his pile of disposable dishes lay beside the explorer. Smiled up at him. "Even if you're not hungry, I am."

He had a sick sensation in his gut, and not at the thought of food. "You've been given an earpiece?"

Rose McKenzie had one, he knew that from the reports he'd read. She'd been able to communicate with Sazo almost wherever the Grih had taken her. And for a long time, they hadn't known it.

Imogen nodded. "It's so I don't need a drone trailing behind me the whole time." She paused, tilting her head. "You don't approve?"

He had to consciously think about keeping his hand relaxed in hers. "I don't want you within a galaxy of a thinking system, let alone having one in your head."

"I'm in your head, too, Captain Kalor." The voice in his ear was cool.

Cam looked upward in a quick, angry movement. The thinking system had simply taken control of his earpiece. No one should be able to communicate with him through it without him being able to screen them.

"So I see."

Imogen sighed, and he put his hands on her shoulders. "You freed it?"

"Him." She frowned at him. "His name is Oris."

Another freed Class 5. Another thinking system in a universe that had banned them for two hundred years.

He hoped the Tecran weren't just banned from the UC for this, he hoped their leaders were locked up for the rest of their lives.

He would do whatever he could, put himself forward as a witness as often as necessary, to help make that so.

"So what now?" He asked the question to the thinking system, but it was Imogen who answered, something that set a warning sounding deep within.

He did not want her as this thing's mouthpiece.

"Now we eat. And see what Oris has planned."

He had no choice but to nod, but as he followed her, hands still clasped tight, he wondered how he could tear her away from

Oris's influence.

Chapter Twenty-five

CAM WAS A BROODING PRESENCE BESIDE HER.

Even though they were seated at a small dining table in what looked like an officers' lounge, he insisted on sitting next to her, his body alert and tense, as if he expected Oris to snatch her away at any moment.

"It wasn't your fault, you know." She bit into a strange, stringy piece of meat cautiously. She wouldn't even have tried it based on looks if she hadn't been starving, and hadn't known she would need to adapt to thrive in her new circumstances.

It tasted . . . like mud. Maybe she should find out if there were any more emergency rations in the explorer. She made a face and then looked over at Cam when she realized he hadn't responded.

He was watching her eat with an unreadable expression.

"It really wasn't," she repeated. "Oris would have forced us apart another way, it would have only been a matter of time." She selected something that might be a vegetable, took a careful nibble. Sighed. It made her think of the crushed green of cut grass. A nice enough smell, not so nice to eat.

"The food isn't to your taste?" Oris's voice was quiet in her ear.

She shook her head. "I suppose I'll get used to it."

"Yes. But if you would like some of your own food, I have some in the store."

"My own food?" Her heart actually started beating a little faster. "You stole some while you were grabbing me and Cleese?"

"Not me. Captain Targio. But yes." He sounded defensive, and she realized she would have to watch her words. It wasn't fair to blame him when he'd been nothing but an unwilling slave.

"A drone is fetching the container now."

"Thank you." She turned to Cam, grinning, and saw he looked as grim as before. "Did you hear that?"

"Only your side of the conversation, but I gather there is some Earth food onboard?"

She couldn't help it when the grin became a full-out smile.

"Yes. It won't last, of course, and I'll have to get used to this," she waved at the food on the table, "but even if it's just for this meal, I am very, very excited."

He still looked grave. "Who is Cleese?"

She felt the tightening in her chest, the hitch in her breath at the thought of what might have happened to him. "Cleese is a bird, a macaw, who was taken from Earth with me. We kept each other company in the Tecran's Balco hideout."

"They didn't bring it with you when they took you away from Balco?"

She shook her head. "I asked them to, but they wouldn't even consider it. He and I were the only two left from the specimens they'd taken from Earth."

"You aren't a specimen." His voice vibrated with some deep emotion.

"To them, I was."

"No." He stood up, unable to keep still, and started pacing. "That's just the thing. They knew you were an advanced sentient. That's why they're in so much trouble. They're signatories to agreements about this. What was done to you, Rose, and Fiona was a crime, not just unfair and immoral. You're protected under UC law."

Imogen shook her head. "Maybe the captain did, but the Tecran who guarded me, at least at first, didn't see me as equal to them. They treated me like a clever pet."

"Not for long, I'm guessing." His fists were clenched tight.

She thought about it. "Maybe not. They were uncomfortable when I learned Tecran. They liked to make out it was their good teaching, not the fact that I was using the handheld in my cage to learn most of it."

"Cage?" He'd gone spookily calm.

She shrugged. "I told you before, didn't I? About how they kept us locked up and then made the animals fight each other."

He nodded. "I didn't know they'd kept you in a cage. I thought you were in a cell."

"No. A cage in a warehouse full of cages." She shivered, wanting to get off this topic. "When the drone comes with my food, I'll share," she said. "Although you may not like it. It's very different to your food."

"This isn't Grihan food." Cam flicked his fingers at the dishes, an understanding look in his eye, and she let out a breath she hadn't realized she was holding as he went with the topic change. "I did read that Rose McKenzie found most Grihan food too bitter for her, though, so ours might not be any better. But she has found a few things she likes."

She'd forgotten they were on a Tecran ship. Of course this wasn't Grihan food. She wouldn't have to put a brave face on and choke any of this down in her future.

She fiddled with the small bowl in front of her, and in the silence, Cam's pacing ramped up.

"Imogen, what are Oris's plans? Why has he come back to the Balco system?"

"I'm right here, Captain. Why don't you ask me directly?" Oris spoke through the comm system, not their earpieces this time, and the way Cam jerked, Imogen guessed he'd forgotten the thinking system had the capacity to listen in on them without a drone now he was free.

"Because I don't believe you'll tell me the truth." Cam widened his stance, crossed his arms over his chest, implacable and angry.

He looked like a tribal chief facing off against an invading army, all grim strength and corded muscle.

Imogen leaned back in her chair. She didn't know how she was going to bridge the divide between Cam and Oris.

Oris was being difficult, but he had cause. And Cam came from a culture that vilified thinking systems, probably for good reason. But Oris was here now. And through no fault of his own.

Just like her.

She blinked as the reason she felt such a strong connection to him became clear to her.

He hadn't asked for any of this. He was just saving himself as best he could. And she applauded him for it.

Cam, on the other hand . . .

She considered him. He was beautiful, had stood steadfastly for her best interests since they'd met. He'd offered her a place with his people, and had saved her from harm more than once.

She didn't need a sudden revelation to know why she liked him. Deep attraction and genuine liking wound together within her so strongly she had to be careful not to give him goo-goo eyes herself.

A drone entered the room, and she turned toward it, then

looked back at Cam. "Could you and Oris put this conversation on hold for five minutes?"

She was so hungry, she didn't even wait to see what Cam's reaction was.

The drone lifted a container out of its box onto the floor beside her, and took off the lid. She could feel the chill from the metal of the container rising up in little wisps of cloud as it mixed with the warmer air of the room, like a child making dragon's breath on a cold morning.

She peered inside, lifted out a small package. Even the cardboard felt cold to the touch. It must have been in some kind of fridge.

The wording on the box was in German, but she gathered from the images it was muesli. She set it on the table, looked at it properly. Very high-end, expensive muesli. She could live with that.

She took out a few packages of instant soup, all from the United Kingdom. They looked okay, and again, she could definitely use them. There were some energy bars which had Cyrillic writing on them, the kind that stuck to your teeth and were artificially flavored, but she would eat them before the strange food in front of her any day.

She unwrapped one and started chewing on it while she looked through the rest.

Oh. My.

Chocolate.

She pulled out four beautiful, gold-wrapped boxes with shimmering ribbons, and touched them with her fingertips.

Chocolate would not be the thing to eat when she was so hungry. She wouldn't appreciate it.

She set them reverently aside, and dug a little deeper.

There was a small bag of apples, and she put the energy bar aside and bit into one, then found a bakery box of wrapped panini sandwiches. Given the international mix of food, they could be from Italy, for all she knew.

"A very eclectic mix," she said, and took another bite of apple. It was sweet, crisp, and cold.

"Set aside what you want to eat now, and I'll have the drone store the rest in the small officers' kitchen for later." Oris spoke in her ear, for her alone.

She sighed. She knew he was doing it to annoy Cam, and he was succeeding. She put everything but one of the panini, the opened energy bar and the apple back in the box, carefully setting the chocolate on top. "Be careful with those," she said. "They're important."

"What are they?" Cam had loosened his stance a little, and she wondered what he'd been thinking. He'd watched her look through the food without saying a word.

"Chocolate. It's a favorite of mine. I never thought I'd have it again." She looked up at the lens in the ceiling and blew Oris a kiss before taking a knife and slicing off a piece of apple. "You want to try?" she asked Cam.

He moved forward, still stiff with suspicion and anger, and took the slice, chewed it thoughtfully.

"It's . . . interesting."

That usually meant 'awful, but I don't want to insult your stuff'.

Imogen grinned. "I'll try to be as polite when I eat Grihan food and don't like it."

His mouth quirked up in a smile.

She felt a bubble of pleasure that she'd been able to get him to relax a little. Then she attacked the panini, and was forced to stop halfway, too full to continue. She hadn't had that much food in a long time, and everything she'd had on Balco or the runner had been some kind of nutrient bar. She guessed they had been too afraid of her possible reaction to their food to risk giving her anything else.

Seeing what it looked and tasted like now, she was grateful.

"You're done?" Cam looked a little less severe, but he was still standing to attention. He'd been patient, though. She hadn't had a sense that he wanted her to hurry, and he got serious points for that.

"I'm done." She pushed away from the table and stood. "You want to fill us in on your plans, Oris?"

Oris didn't respond, and she looked up at the lens again. "Oris?"

"Not now." He didn't sound dismissive, he sounded worried.

"What's he up to?" Cam narrowed his eyes at her, and she shook her head.

"I don't know."

Sudden movement threw her forward, flinging the dishes off the table, and an arm clamped around her waist, pulling her back and up against the wall of the lounge.

"I guess he wasn't just pulling your chain." She spoke against Cam's shoulder, where he held her in a tight grip.

"What kind of maneuver was that?" Cam spoke into her hair. "And what chain?"

"Figure of speech." She recalled the way they'd slid down the passage on Paxe when he was trying to out-maneuver the Tecran, and wondered if the fleet had finally found Oris. This had felt very similar.

"Are you all right?" Oris asked her, and from the quiet way he did it, she guessed he hadn't included Cam in the question.

"I'm okay. What happened?"

"The Fitali happened."

There was a screen on the far lounge wall and it blinked on. A strange, sleek ship hovered in space before them.

"A Fitali warship." Cam finally released her, walked over to take a better look. "What are they doing here? What happened?"

"I sensed a ship coming through a light-jump, and realized they would hit us if I didn't get out of the way. I had to take very fast action to avoid that."

"All this space around us, and they pick the exact same place to light-jump as us?" Imogen raised her brows.

"They had the same thought I did. This is Gu-gijeron, one of Balco's moons. It's rich in deritide, which interferes with most scanning systems, so we can lurk nearby, and not be picked up."

"The Fitali had the same plan." Cam had lost a lot of his outrage.

"Yes." Oris let the lens zoom in on the Fitali ship. "I wonder what they're doing here. Could they be in league with the Tecran?"

"No." Cam sounded very sure. "There were two Fitalian soldiers caught up in Paxe's effort to find Imogen. They eventually admitted they were tracking a grahudi that one of the Class 5s had delivered to the Tecran's secret facility on Balco. They didn't tell me they'd called in the big guns, though. Only that they'd discovered it was on Balco just before the Krik captured them and took them onboard Paxe's Class 5."

"I remember." Imogen shivered at the thought of the grahudi.

At how interested the Fitalians had been in her story about seeing it. "But while it's terrible the Tecran stole it, is it worth that much to them that they've sent a massive ship after it?"

"That's a good question. I knew they were protective and secretive about the grahudi, but this does seem like an overreaction. And given they're skulking behind Gu-gijeron, my guess is they haven't asked Battle Center's permission to be here. Which is a massive breach of their treaty with us."

"What are we going to do?" She felt a deep sense of unease at the sight of the battleship. It looked truly alien, much more so than the Tecran and Krik vessels she'd seen up until now.

"Are they hailing us?" Cam studied the ship intently.

"No, Captain. What they've done is lock their weapons on us."

Chapter Twenty-six

"I DON'T WANT CAPTAIN KALOR IN THE ROOM."

Oris spoke into Imogen's earpiece with a calm that flared her temper.

"That won't be easy to achieve." She glanced at Cam, who'd turned as she spoke, a frown back on his face as he realized she was speaking privately to Oris.

"On the contrary, it will be very easy to achieve, but the most expedient method will no doubt cause a lot of ill-will on Captain Kalor's part."

She sensed movement by the door, saw the drone had come back from the kitchen, and that it had a shockgun in its clamp.

"Oris." She heard the weariness in her own voice. "That is not the way."

"I said it was the most expedient way. Not the one I'd prefer to use."

"Why can't he stay?" She held Cam's gaze as she asked.

"I don't trust him to give me good advice."

"But you do trust me?" She was incredulous. "I don't understand the first thing about the Fitali, let alone the politics of the situation."

"That's true." Oris didn't sound troubled by that. "Those facts are in your favor. You can help me based on what seems right to you. I may not heed your advice, but I would value it."

"Whatever plan he's got," Cam shot a furious glance at the drone, even though he couldn't have heard what Oris had said to her, "the answer is no."

She pursed her lips. "Cam——"

"I won't leave you alone again, Imogen. That isn't going to happen." He walked back to her, his hand on the stock of the shockgun in his thigh holster the whole way.

"What are you two going to do, fight it out?" She lifted her hands, glared at the drone herself. "I don't like being caught in the middle like this." She crossed her arms. "Couldn't we speak in

English, so he won't understand us?" She said it in English, to prove her point.

"It's more than him listening in. It's him interfering. Standing there glowering. Interrupting." The response was in English, too.

She turned to Cam, found him right beside her, so close she had to tilt her head to look at him. "Oris wants to talk things over with me, and he doesn't want you listening in and watching. He would like you to step outside."

"What do *you* want?" His jaw clenched as he spoke.

She looked down and shook her head. "I want the two of you to play nice. Please, let Oris talk to me privately. I think it will improve the outcome for all of us." Because left to his own devices, he could decide anything. At least he saw worth in her opinion. That was not something she wanted to discourage.

She lifted a hand to Cam's arm, gripped it lightly. "He knows you're hostile to him and will use his secrets against him if you can. It's reasonable that he doesn't want you involved."

Cam looked over her shoulder, and she had the horrible, weightless sense of falling away from him. That their connection was being severed.

"Cam." She kept looking at him until at last he looked her in the eyes again. "I don't want to shut you out, but these are his rules, and I can understand them. I'm guessing you can, too. You would do the same to him, not want him to have access to information you thought he could use against you."

Cam turned and strode back to the screen and stood, back to her, feet braced, hands fisted at his side.

Imogen closed her eyes, horrified to find tears burning behind them, and took a deep, cleansing breath.

This was bullshit.

When she snapped her eyes open again, Cam had turned, was looking at her, his face tight and unreadable.

"You think this will help us?" His voice was always rough and deep, but now it rumbled.

She nodded, afraid to speak.

"Half an hour," he said, looking straight at the drone.

Imogen pointed a warning finger at the drone before Oris could say something stupid, like 'you don't tell me how long on my own ship', or something equally idiotic.

"Half an hour," Oris agreed, his words so stiff and sulky,

Imogen almost laughed.

Cam walked back to her, stood close enough she could feel his body heat, smell the fresh, clean scent of him. They were almost touching, but not quite, and there was a promise in the way he held himself back. A sense he *was* holding back. That he'd prefer to touch, to hold her. He bent his head, his lips almost brushing her ear. "You are sure?"

She nodded again, and a thrill coursed through her as he rested his forehead briefly against hers.

She tried to hold on tight to her caution, to the part of herself she'd kept safe and walled in since she'd been taken, but Cam seemed to have jumped the wall and landed inside with her, and she just wanted to hold him close and feel the joy of the connection.

"Time is wasting." Oris spoke through the comm system, but he didn't seem impatient, he almost sounded . . . indulgent. "We do have Fitali weapons trained on us."

Cam drew back, held her gaze for a long moment and then walked out the room.

As the doors closed behind him, Imogen turned and made her way to the screen, trying to shake off the effect he had on her and concentrate. "Do you think they would seriously fire on a Class 5 who hadn't done them any harm? Especially as they're here as illegally as you are."

"No." Oris sounded thoughtful. "I think they're just letting me know they have teeth, that they aren't helpless. A Fitali battleship is a powerful vessel. At least on a par with the Grihan equivalent, but neither stands a chance against me."

"What do you want to do?"

The Fitali ship had shifted since Oris had first brought up the screen, turning, she assumed, to face them.

"It feels strange to be able to do what I want. I keep looking for protocols, then remembering I destroyed them."

"I understand that. This last day or so has been the first time I haven't been guarded and imprisoned for over two months. It takes getting used to, and I lived a free life until they took me. You've never known it. You'll have to learn a new normal."

"Yes. That is it exactly." His voice was calm, but she thought she could hear excitement and a little fear beneath his confidence. "As someone who has been free, what do you suggest?"

"Well, being the bigger badass is in your favor, but if it has to come down to you proving that, you've already lost."

"Not really," Oris said. "My shields are very strong, and they'd have to be quick to hit me, and if they do, they won't manage to do it again, as I'd destroy them. Even if my shields take some damage, it will be easily repaired."

"I'm not talking about physical damage. I meant that your relationship with the Fitali will always carry the weight of your destruction of one of their ships with it. As I'm sure you plan to live for a very long time, it would be better if you didn't start off with a massive black mark against your name with one of the United Council members, don't you agree?"

He mulled that for a bit. "I knew it was wise to seek your advice. I had not thought of that. What do you suggest, then?"

"Well, ideally it would be good if you somehow have control of their ship, so they can't start a foolish battle they can't win and which will mar your relationship with them when it isn't necessary. So while that's not feasible——"

"No. I think it is. It's a very good idea. I'll see if I can take the ship over." He sounded positively delighted.

"You can do that? Hack into their systems?"

"You sound impressed," Oris said. "Your Grihan would no doubt have looked even grimmer than usual."

Imogen couldn't help the quirk of her lips. Yes, Cam would have glared a little harder. "He's been raised in a culture that suffered badly from your kind, and the fact that it's not fair to tar you with the same brush is hard for him to accept." She thought about it for a moment. "And I think what Paxe has done, what the other Class 5s have done, too, hasn't helped that impression."

"The Fitali are hailing us now. Can you speak to them? I can translate what you say automatically, so you can speak English to them, if you like. The connection they open with us will help me find their system's weaknesses faster."

"What do you want me to say?" Nerves gripped her. This was way out of her league, negotiating with massive battleships. Parents who thought their child should be playing first violin in orchestra were the trickiest she'd dealt with up until she'd been taken.

"I don't mind what you say. The longer you talk, the more time I have to take control of their ship."

"It might be wise to not let them know you do have control of their systems." Imogen looked up at the lens.

"Why not?" Oris's curiosity was palpable.

"Just imagine how you'd feel if someone did that to you." She tilted her head.

He considered it. "I would try to destroy them."

"Probably because you've just gotten free. But they won't like it, that's for sure. So only show your hand if you have to, is my advice."

"I haven't even gotten in, yet." He almost muttered the words.

"Try not to let them know you're attempting it, either. Sometimes that's just as bad as succeeding."

This time, what he muttered was indecipherable.

That was the best she was going to get, she decided.

"Okay. Link us up." She was as ready as she'd ever be.

The screen went black, and then a Fitalian appeared, more formally dressed than the two she'd met in Paxe's hold, but with the same slender, elegant lines that reminded her of a praying mantis with a humanoid face.

The Fitalian looked so startled, Imogen guessed she was the last thing the captain had been expecting.

"Who are you?" The Fitalian's words were a little robotic, but Imogen put that down to Oris translating for her.

"My name is Imogen Peters. Who are you?" She tried to be as polite as possible.

The captain seemed stunned, and Imogen waited for her response patiently.

"Captain Leto," she said at last. "You are not Tecran."

"No." Imogen smiled. "I'm afraid the Tecran crew no longer occupy this ship. Were you expecting to meet with them?"

"No!" Leto actually drew back in horror. "We had no idea there would be another vessel here, but we are in no way in league with the Tecran."

Imogen realized she'd almost accused the Fitali of supporting the treaty-breaking Tecran against the United Council. "My apologies. But you are not here at the Grih's invitation, are you?"

Leto was quiet for so long, Imogen wondered if she was going to sever the connection.

"No. We wouldn't be hiding behind a deritide rich moon if we were." She made the admittance with good grace, at least.

"Why are you here, then?" If Cam was right, they were after their grahudi, but she decided it would be better if Leto told her. She was freaked out enough.

"I am not willing to say."

Oh.

What the hell, she was supposed to keep Leto talking. "Actually, I was being polite, I know you're here looking for your grahudi."

Leto froze, stepped closer to the screen. "Who are you really? How do you know that?"

"Well, I was in a secret Tecran facility on Balco with your grahudi for a while, so I know quite a lot. I also met your two scouts, Haru and Chep, and my guess is that they managed to get a message out to you just before the Krik boarded their ship."

Leto tried to school her face. "The Tecran have a facility on Balco? What were you doing with our grahudi there?"

"I was in a cage right next to it at the time. The Tecran had it, had captured it just like they captured me." Imogen realized she still couldn't be calm about the grahudi. The terror she felt at being near it, in a cage, powerless. That it had been in a cage just like her hadn't mattered to the ancient part of her brain that told her to *run*. Her voice trembled, just a little, and she felt a surge of gratitude that the electronic translator did not convey her wobble, just her words.

"You spent time with the grahudi?"

She forced herself not to shiver. "Only two days."

Leto stared at her. "What were the Tecran doing with it?"

Imogen frowned. "I'm not sure. They did their experiments elsewhere. They were storing it down there, like they were with me."

Leto seemed to vibrate. "Were the experiments done at the facility?"

She shrugged. "Perhaps, but some were done on the Class 5s themselves, I think. When they were done, they dropped them off on Balco to make room for more specimens."

Leto breathed in a quick huff through her nose. "Why Balco, I wonder? Besides the fact that it's almost on the Garmman border . . ."

"All I know is the Grih and most of the Balcoans have no idea it's there." She knew that from Cam, but Leto didn't need to know where she got her information.

"So an entire Class 5 crew, yourself, and the Tecran stationed at this secret facility have all encountered the grahudi?"

Nerves pricked along the back of Imogen's neck. Was the thing carrying some rare disease? "Yes, as far as I know."

"You certainly know more than we do, so I thank you. But I'm interested, you don't look like a prisoner now." Leto's face was not human or Grih, it didn't have the same flexibility, but somehow, she seemed to convey a sense of fear.

Imogen couldn't work out if it was real, or simply her inability to read Fitalian expressions.

"As I said at the beginning, the Tecran are no longer onboard."

Someone off-screen said something to Leto, too low for the translator to catch, and when Leto turned back to the screen, she looked thoughtful. "Who is in charge of the Class 5 now?"

"Not me." She gauged Leto's reaction, saw the captain's lips purse at her answer.

"And is this the Class 5 that took our grahudi?" Leto picked something up from a table in front of her, and Imogen caught a glimpse of a handheld.

She resisted the urge to look up at the lens for confirmation from Oris if it was his Class 5 that had taken the grahudi.

"No," he whispered in her ear.

"No. Not this one."

"How do you know?" Leto leaned forward. "It can't be Sazo or Bane, they are confirmed in another part of Grihan territory, so that leaves this one and two others."

"This ship is the one that took me, not the grahudi." And why did it matter so much to the Fitali which Class 5 had taken their precious psychotic killer monkey?

Someone muttered something at Leto again, and she gave a sharp nod. "I would like to know where you saw Haru and Chep, and what has happened to them."

"I know they were captured by Krik, just like I was, and made prisoner. We were kept together in a hold on a ship the Krik were using, but we were able to escape. I also know that Haru and Chep managed to get out, but there was a Tecran battleship waiting for them when they did. I think they are in their ship, but being forced to remain in place, under threat of the Tecran opening fire if they try to leave or contact you."

Leto's head snapped back at that. "The Tecran have weapons trained on them?"

"On them, on the United Council fast cruiser containing a UC investigative team, on several Grihan miners, and a few Garmman and Grihan trading vessels, all of whom had originally been taken by the Krik."

"The Tecran have a battleship here, in Grih territory?" Leto didn't sound appalled. She sounded . . . drained?

"The ship the Krik who took us prisoner were using was a Class 5. Not this one, another one. They . . . failed to keep control of it, which is how we were all able to escape, but the Tecran are trying to recover what they see as their property." She winced a bit at the wording, because Paxe would have something to say about it.

"The Krik took over a Class 5?" Leto looked shocked, and Imogen could see she'd just made the Fitalian even more curious than she'd been before.

"Got it!"

Imogen blinked at Oris's shout of glee in her ear.

She kept her focus on Leto with difficulty. "I don't know the details of how the Krik came to be using the Class 5." Not all the details, anyway.

At that moment, the doors to the room opened again, and Cam strode in. "Half an hour was up ten minutes ago." He glared at the drone then pulled up short at the sight of Leto on the screen.

"Captain Leto." He looked from Imogen to the screen in surprise. "I haven't seen you since the last UC council meeting."

"Captain Kalor." Leto looked like she'd stepped into the Twilight Zone. "Imogen Peters told me there was a UC investigative team involved in this, but I hardly registered that, given the other explosive information she's shared with me. Are you in control of the Class 5, then?"

"No." Cam shook his head. "I'm here on UC business that includes the protection of Imogen Peters, but I am interested," now his voice was cool, "why you are here, Captain? Hiding behind Gu-gijeron in Grihan territory?"

Chapter Twenty-seven

THE SIDE OF CAM'S FISTS WERE BRUISED from where he'd hammered on the door after the thirty minutes were up. He'd berated himself for believing a thinking system would honor a promise, but the sight of Captain Leto of the Fitalian Horde on the screen had thrown him off his stride.

Perhaps Oris's explanation that things were at too delicate a stage to allow him to come striding in was truthful.

He exchanged a look with Imogen, but all he could see on her face was pleasure at seeing him again, and he made a conscious decision to let go of his anger at being kept out longer than agreed.

Leto, however, was a different matter.

Diplomacy was an art he was well-versed in usually, and he could smarm with the best of them at the United Council meetings and debriefs he had to attend, but the well of inspiration he drew from to practice it had run dry.

His blunt question to the Fitalian had shocked her and put her on the spot, and she blustered for a moment. "What are *you* doing here, Captain?"

Cam shrugged. "I'm a senior Battle Center officer in my own territory, with a clear directive from the United Council as well, so it's hardly a surprise to find me exactly where I'm supposed to be, surely?"

She shot him a dark look. "Quite. Although your presence in a Tecran Class 5 *is* a surprise." She rocked a little on her feet. "You seem to know what I'm doing here, anyway."

"The grahudi? Yes, Chep and Haru eventually told me about that. What they failed to disclose was that they had contacted you before the Krik took them."

Leto looked off to the side, then back again. "I'm surprised they told you as much as they did."

"It suited their purposes." Cam's words were dry. "They got information in exchange."

Leto's gaze flicked to Imogen. "The location of the grahudi, you mean? And who had taken it."

Imogen gave a nod. "I'm afraid . . ." She drew in a breath. "I'm afraid the grahudi is probably dead by now. They were putting the animals stored at the facility in a ring and making them fight to the death, and I last saw the grahudi two weeks ago."

Was it his imagination, or did Leto relax a little at that. "It was still alive when you saw it, though?"

She nodded. "But they were fighting more and more animals every day. Two weeks is a long time, and they didn't have that many left as it was."

"I thank you for your honesty, but we'll check the signal to see for ourselves. Being behind Gu-gijeron means we can't track it at the moment, but as soon as we're in the open, we'll have the ability to find it."

"And how are you going to go into the open when you're here uninvited and in defiance of your treaties with the Grih?" Cam asked.

"I'm really sorry you had to be here to witness our arrival, Kalor." Leto closed her eyes and then opened them, and all he could see on her face was regret. "I'm afraid, in order to protect the Fitalian reputation, I'm going to have to silence you."

"How do you plan on doing that?" Imogen asked, and Cam looked at her in surprise. Her voice was calm but also smooth and sharp as a blade.

They were on a Class 5, and most likely they would be well shielded, but a hit was a hit. Especially in such close proximity. Leto's confidence was a worry, too.

Leto nodded at someone off to the side, and Cam braced.

Nothing happened.

Leto nodded again, more forcefully.

"Trying to shoot us?" Imogen asked, sweetly. "Even if you could, did you not worry you were firing on a Class 5?"

Leto turned her full attention back to the screen, her face set. "I was worried about that, but since we watched the lens feed of the battle between the Tecran and the Grih a few months ago, our engineers have been working on a weapon and a strategy they insist would be effective."

"And you're telling us this secret information because you think you'll still manage to 'silence' us?" Imogen lifted her hands into the air and made a strange movement with the middle and forefingers of both hands. He'd have to ask her later what it meant.

Leto was silent.

"I'm sure you'll get to it. Any minute now." Imogen's sarcasm was so heavy, Cam glanced at her, but it was more than that. She was furious, but not afraid.

By her attitude and her body language, she didn't expect any danger.

He opened his mouth, and she lifted a finger and pressed it against his lips.

"Can you cut the link for a bit?" she asked Oris, and the screen went blank.

"How right were they to think they could take you out?" she asked, looking up at the lens. "Leto seemed pretty certain."

Cam had grasped hold of her arm before she could drop it, and he turned it over, rubbed his thumb along the incredibly smooth skin of her inner wrist.

He felt her pulse leap beneath his fingertip.

"More right than I'd have guessed, to be honest." Oris sounded a little shaken. "If you hadn't suggested the takeover . . . I was overly optimistic about our chances before."

Cam went still. "You're saying the Fitali have come up with something that might pierce your shields?" He knew they were perturbed by the reemergence of thinking systems, terrified of what would come of their presence after so long, but the Fitali must have had this technology in development long before Sazo burst onto the scene two months ago.

Which was worrying in itself.

If they hadn't had a thinking system threat to deal with, what had they planned to do with it?

And that brought him to . . . "You've taken them over?"

"Yes to both, Captain. Imogen thought the safest thing for us all was if I had control of their ship, and that was a fortunate suggestion, or we might in fact be in trouble."

No wonder Imogen had been so calm.

"What I can't understand is why they'd want to kill us. Yes, they've been caught where they shouldn't be, but they have an excuse, and while uncomfortable, it would simply be a few awkward meetings at UC headquarters. To want to eliminate us altogether . . ." It didn't make sense. Leto was not unreasonable. In fact, Cam liked her, and found her one of the easier Fitalian captains to deal with.

"Hatred for thinking systems?" Oris said.

That was a possibility. "Did you tell them who was in control of this Class 5?" he asked Imogen.

She shook her head. "Although I'm guessing if Rose McKenzie is known to have freed Sazo and Bane, having me onboard made it likely from their perspective that I had done the same."

Cam nodded. "But to shoot without asking first, that isn't like Leto. I've known her for years, and she's thoughtful and logical."

"They are hailing us again. They don't know I've taken control of their systems. They think their problems are a result of being so close to Gu-gijeron." Oris turned the screen back on. "We can see them, they can't see us until we want them to."

Leto was shouting at someone, and another officer paced back and forth in the background.

"Do you speak Fitalian?" Imogen asked him, and Cam realized he still had her wrist in his grasp. He let it go reluctantly, and she watched him with serious eyes.

He shook his head. "Languages are not my strength. I speak some Tecran, better Bukarian."

"They're arguing about how to proceed, and assume that because their systems don't work, ours don't either," Oris said.

"Do we tell them the truth?"

Imogen shook her head. "Their faces aren't easy to read, but I could have sworn Leto was relieved when I told her that the grahudi was most likely dead."

Cam nodded. "I agree. There is something very strange going on. The Fitali have been obsessively protective of the planet Huy for years, but they've taken it up to a whole new level with this. Breaking treaties, threatening to kill."

"There must be something really interesting going on on Huy, then." Imogen was watching Leto gesticulating on the screen and Cam took a moment to admire her profile as she tucked a strand of hair behind her ear; delicate and . . . beautiful.

"Do I reconnect?" Oris asked.

"Before you do, I just want to suggest you study the weapon they've developed to breach your shield and see if there is a way to counter it. Theirs might not be the only Fitalian battleship with that technology, and the other Class 5s could be in danger."

"Again, you prove you are well worth the price of admission." Oris sounded amused, although Cam had no idea what he meant. It was a joke between Oris and Imogen, and Cam realized with a start that they were friends.

The idea made him begin to relax for the first time.

Imogen had been right to kick him out earlier. Somehow, she had won Oris's trust, and that was infinitely better than the thinking system walling himself off from everyone, making decisions with no regard for anyone but himself.

"And the connection is live again . . . now." Oris spoke through his earpiece this time, so the Fitali didn't hear him.

"Welcome back, Captain." Cam forced a neutral expression onto his face. "It's a bit difficult to come back from a threat of murder, isn't it?"

He waited, watched the few emotions he could pick up cross Leto's face. Regret, again. Frustration.

"You knew we couldn't shoot."

"We did, but you didn't." He lifted a brow. "Where does that leave us?"

"I apologize. In my rush to defend the Fitalian reputation, I acted rashly. I will submit myself to a review panel for judgment when I return to the Horde."

Leto looked like she was swallowing something large and spiky, the way her throat worked around the apology.

"*Bullshit.*" Imogen spoke in her own language so quietly, he barely heard her, and didn't understand what she said.

Leto focused on her, eyes narrowing as much as they could. "You have something to say, Imogen Peters?"

"Yes." Imogen smiled in a baring of teeth. "What's to stop you trying to kill us as soon as we leave Gu-gijeron?"

"You have my word."

Leto was unused to subterfuge, which fitted Cam's knowledge of her. And she was plainly lying.

"Of course." Imogen smiled that non-smile again.

"What are your plans now?" Leto asked at last, as the silence stretched out between them.

"Your being here has changed things. We'll need to confer."

That seemed to infuriate Leto.

Cam kept his face passive. "I'll hail you when we make our

decision. I suggest you don't go anywhere."

Leto reared back in affront at the order, and this time, Cam couldn't help his smile as the screen went black.

Imogen turned from the screen, and eyed him thoughtfully. "You do diplomatic doublespeak really well."

"When I have to." He took her hand, wanting to touch that smooth skin again.

She let him, her eyes on his thumb as it brushed along her wrist. He felt suddenly heavy, weighed down by desire, as if all around him the air had turned to syrup.

"I'm sorry to interrupt," Oris said, although he didn't sound sorry, "but we have plans to make."

"What happened to 'now I go to war'?" Imogen spoke the last phrase in a strange voice, like she was imitating someone, poking fun, but Cam had never heard Oris speak like that.

"'Now I go to war'?" Oris mimicked her exactly.

She tipped her head, amusement on her face. "Yes."

"Well." He actually laughed, the first time Cam had heard that from him. "I *am* going to war. But part of war is seeing what allies I have, and that means contacting one of the thinking systems. The three that are free seem loyal to each other, so any one will do, and that's why I've brought us close to Larga Ways. Of the three, speaking to Eazi is the easiest, because he isn't on a Class 5. He's taken over Larga Ways since the explosion, and it would be simple for you to enter the way station and make contact."

"Simple?" Cam scoffed. "And you're assuming a lot, aren't you? That we'd do this for you?"

Imogen gave him an exasperated look. "Yes, we'll be doing it for him. You want the Grih to have another Class 5 on their side, don't you?"

Cam didn't just want it, he'd been specifically ordered to get any thinking system on their side, by any means possible, by his commander-in-chief, Admiral Hoke. All senior officers had.

He sighed and gave a nod. "What are we going to do with the Fitali?"

"They're not going anywhere unless I allow it."

"You can't stay hidden here, though. We won't be able to contact you once we leave if you're still behind Gu-gijeron." Cam tapped the stock of his shockgun as he thought things through.

"When I've given you enough time to get to Larga Ways and

make contact with Eazi, I'll get closer so you can link Eazi and I up. I'll have to bring the Fitali along."

"Sounds simple," Cam said, voice dry, and Oris laughed again.

Chapter Twenty-eight

"WHAT'S LETO TRYING TO DO?" Imogen asked Oris as she and Cam passed the massive Fitalian Horde battleship in the two-person explorer Paxe had given them. She felt tiny and threatened; an ant scurrying past an elephant.

"Contrary to what she promised, she tried to shoot you. She couldn't see you on the scanners——even if your explorer didn't have excellent cloaking, the deritide would make it impossible ——but they had a visual on you coming through the gel wall. She's had to make peace with the fact that her weapons really won't work, and so now she's ordered three small fighters to go after you."

"Can you stop them?" Cam asked.

"Of course. They'll believe their fighters' power systems are too confused by the deritide to work, and they'll be perplexed and angry that your explorer's aren't."

"Looks like we're nearly out of sight of you." Imogen touched the screen, and sure enough Oris's Class 5 was disappearing from view as the explorer rounded the far side of the moon. "We'll lose contact any minute."

"Successful trav——" Oris's voice cut off and in the abrupt silence, Imogen turned to face Cam.

"Alone at last." He lifted a hand and brushed back a wayward strand of her hair. He was so close he was bumping shoulders with her in the confined space and she could see the light and dark rings of blue in his eyes.

She lowered her own, suddenly flustered. "You don't like Oris?"

He lifted his shoulders. "I'm warming to him. But he is a little omnipresent, isn't he?"

She considered it. "I'm not used to privacy. Not for the last two months, and the last two weeks, I was being held in a communal lounge. So . . ." She shook her head. "I didn't notice it as much as you probably did."

When he didn't answer, she lifted her gaze again, saw he was staring at her. "You were held in a communal lounge?" His voice was a little deeper.

She shrugged. "There was nowhere else to keep me."

He blew out a breath. "What were they doing?"

Again, she shrugged. "They didn't know themselves. They were waiting for someone to pick us up, or tell them what to do, and that instruction never came. Knowing what I do now, I'd guess the pick-up vessel was Paxe, and he'd slipped the reins."

"Why didn't they send Oris, then?"

She grimaced. "Maybe because when they realized Paxe was off the leash, they needed Oris to keep watch on him, see what he was up to? What to do with me has to be a lot less important to them than recovering their Class 5."

Cam tipped his head from side to side. "I'm not sure. You're pretty important."

She laughed at that, but not with amusement. "You have to be kidding."

"Even if they didn't yet know what Fiona Russell had done for Eazi, they knew what Rose had done to Sazo and Bane. It could be they decided putting the last Class 5 they had control of anywhere near you was too dangerous for them. But that aside, I'm sure they would have much preferred you to stay hidden under their control than floating aimlessly in Grihan airspace on a tiny runner for anyone to find. The abduction of Rose McKenzie is a huge mark against them. Now we know they took Fiona Russell and yourself, they are finished in the UC."

"Maybe they've accepted that, and they don't care." Imogen moved down to lie on the strap board and Cam slid down to join her.

"They care, but you're right, they may have accepted it, and are acting as if it's a foregone conclusion. It gives them license to break any treaty they want, because those treaties are about to be void anyway." He was so much taller than her, his head above hers, and she shivered at the stark contrast of the warmth of his breath in her hair compared to the cool air of the explorer.

She angled herself closer to him, trying to soak up more of his body heat. "So they'll try to attack Grihan ships? Or attack Larga Ways? And what? Take Grihan territory?"

She didn't understand why she was so angry at the thought of that. Probably because she had a chance at a new future with the Grih, and once again, the Tecran were messing up her life.

"I think they'll try." Cam was grim. "What are they doing otherwise? What other reason have Tecran High Command got to give their people for the loss of UC membership? We need to get word to Battle Center, and once we make contact with Eazi, hopefully that won't be a problem."

"*If* we can make contact with Eazi." After all, they were in an enemy explorer. "And we've got the added complication of the Fitali."

"Yes." Cam had taken her unsubtle hint and put his arm around her, pulling her closer into his delicious warmth, and she tried to burrow in. "I honestly don't know what's going on with them. I've always had a good relationship with Leto. This kind of aggression from the Fitali is unprecedented."

She sighed, and let her body relax, tucking her head under his chin. "You don't think their grahudi is carrying some viral contagion, do you? That they've been cooking up some sort of bio-experiment on Huy, and the Tecran stealing the grahudi is going to blow the whole thing wide open?"

He chuckled. "Where did you come up with that?"

"The way Leto questioned me on exactly who had had contact with the grahudi. That was before you came back into the room."

"That *is* interesting. And worrying." He thought for a moment. "And not completely impossible. They are up to something that I can only assume is illegal, given their response. One animal is stolen from one of their planets and they send a battleship to get it back? And are willing not only to break treaties by crossing borders without permission, but have tried to kill us both a number of times. I'm a Battle Center officer and I represent the UC, and you're a key witness against the Tecran. However their actions appear, they can't be doing this lightly."

The control panel above them let out a quiet trill, and Cam pulled himself back up, tapped at the screen.

"Looks like we've got a possible lift." He slid back down to her. "A Grihan trader heading for Larga Ways. I've set the trajectory so we'll meet up with them in about an hour."

That was their only real plan. They had to catch a ride to Larga Ways on a vessel that Eazi would allow in, and Oris had shown them how to shut down the explorer's beacon, so there would be no trace of its Tecran origins.

Whatever security was set up around the way station, neither Oris nor Cam thought a Tecran explorer would make it even close. The Battle Center patrols might take a chance bringing the explorer onside for questioning, or they might just shoot. And none of that factored in the information Cam had gotten from Barj, the Grihan mercenary on the Vanad's crew, that there were Tecran spies on the way station. Spies with access to explosives and other resources, who might still be watching for Imogen.

"What did you tell them?" She settled back into the comfortable position they'd been in before, reveling again in the close contact, the comfort of being held.

"That we'd gotten away from a Krik attack in an emergency capsule, which this explorer is small enough to be, but that our systems are damaged and we're barely limping along. Also that we're Grihan and if they could give us a ride to Larga Ways, we'd be grateful."

"They believed you?" She guessed the explorer was tiny enough, the traders probably didn't expect them to be much of a threat. Although that might change if they got a look at Cam.

He exuded threat when he wanted to.

"They don't have a choice. It's a rule of travel. No one can leave a ship in distress."

"It's like the rule of the sea on Earth," she said, thinking about it. "You have to offer aid."

"There is a big sea on Earth?" He smoothed back her hair in long, steady strokes, seemingly unable to stop touching it.

"Earth's mostly sea. The blue planet, we call it, because looking at it from space, it's all white clouds and blue oceans."

"I'm sorry you were taken from your home." He kept stroking, and she closed her eyes and swallowed back the tears his sympathy pricked to life.

"Is this normal for Grih?" When she spoke, her voice was softer than she meant it to be. Huskier.

"Is what normal?"

"We've known each other a couple of days, and here we are, all snuggled up and touchy-feely."

His hand closed around her hair just at her nape and he tugged it gently, tipping her head back so they could look into each other's eyes. "Are you uncomfortable with this?"

His expression was hard to read, but she sensed distress and lifted a hand to his cheek, rubbed her thumb along the high arch of his cheekbone. "No. I'm loving it. I just wanted to know if this was common for you or just the strange circumstances we've ended up in."

She felt him relax.

"No, I'm usually more reserved. But it's been an intense few days. I think we've saved each other's lives at least once each, taken fire together." His grin was lopsided. "We're what Battle Center calls a bonded team."

He let go of her hair, smoothed his hand down her back to the curve of her bottom, and pressed her close.

She'd felt the hard press of his erection brush against her stomach since he joined her again, but now it was wedged between them, and she squirmed as a shaft of desire and excitement speared through her.

He choked. "Don't move."

He pulled away, putting a little distance between them, and grinned ruefully. "I should have remembered before I did that that we've got less than an hour before we board the trader and I need more time than that to do all my adoring."

He meant to make her laugh, but she gave a serious nod. She wanted hours of privacy with him. No greedy bite would do. She wanted to feast.

She'd asked him if it were normal for the Grih to fall so easily into trust and desire. It definitely wasn't for her. She took her time with boyfriends before she was willing to make herself vulnerable to them.

"Agreed." She sighed and hugged him close, and he made another sound at the back of his throat.

"Pity." His lips brushed her forehead. "But for the best."

Something occurred to her. "What are we going to do when the traders realize I'm not Grihan?"

He stirred reluctantly. "We're not going to say anything, and I'm guessing they won't either."

"What, just brazen it out?" She could do that. She wouldn't have found it easy in her old life, but since she'd been taken, she could brazen out a lot of things.

He nodded, his cheek brushing her head. "Leave your hair down. There is so much of it, they may assume you've taken up some strange hair fashion, and they won't notice your ears underneath it." He slid a hand though her hair and traced around her ear.

"Whose hair are you calling strange?" Her lips curved against his neck.

He smoothed his hands over it again. Gave a friendly tug. "Strange, but beautiful."

She gave a snort at that and then stopped talking. Her eyes were burning with fatigue, and she closed them with relief. She was so tired. The only sleep she'd gotten in the last day was right here on this explorer, when they'd escaped from Paxe. It felt like a week ago.

Cam held her close, just like he had then, and she let the sense of well-being and happiness she'd hadn't thought she'd ever feel again wash over her.

Chapter Twenty-nine

CAPTAIN INITA OF THE GRIHAN TRADER *VEASIN* was
suspicious, but Cam saw he couldn't quite decide why.

Cam kept his words polite, his movements unthreatening, but
he'd refused to relinquish his shockgun, and he'd expected his
Battle Center uniform to make that a non-issue. Inita seemed to
think Battle Center captains' uniforms could be bought at any
street corner, and meant nothing.

"If you could tell me which places of business you've seen
Battle Center uniforms for sale, I would be grateful," he told the
thin Grih politely. "Dealing in Battle Center equipment is a high
court offense."

Inita took a step back. "I don't know of a specific place . . ." He
tried to keep his eyes on Cam, but he kept being distracted by
Imogen as she pulled the small backpack Oris had found in his
store for her out of the explorer. It seemed almost full, and Cam
realized he hadn't asked her what was in it.

"But you said they can be had anywhere. Where is anywhere?"

Inita jerked his gaze back at Cam's insistent questioning.
"That's what I've heard. I haven't seen it for myself."

Was he lying? Cam frowned as he studied their benefactor's
face.

"Do you see this symbol?" He pointed to the tiny silver
embellishment on the high left-hand side of his shirt.

Inita leaned forward and nodded.

"That is the chip that identifies this uniform to my bio-
signature. No one else can wear this uniform, nothing would
work. Not its temperature regulators, not its shockgun protection,
it won't even hold its shape."

Inita blinked. "I didn't know that."

"So you understand why I'm concerned you've heard that it is
a simple matter to get hold of——"

Inita waved his hand, dismissing the whole argument, his gaze
going back to Imogen again, now standing watching them quietly.

"You've convinced me, Captain Kalor. I was obviously listening to a tall tale. Keep your shockgun if that is Battle Center regulation."

"Thank you." Cam's dry tone was lost on their host.

"And you are . . .?" Inita asked Imogen.

"Imogen Peters." Imogen put her hands together and extended them for Inita to clasp between his own in the Grihan greeting Cam had taught her five minutes before they landed. "Thank you for coming to our aid, Captain."

Inita's hands were reaching out to hers when she spoke and he stopped dead at the sound of her voice. "You . . ." He looked over at Cam, astonishment on his face. "An orange? The same as the orange music-maker?" He addressed Cam, as if Imogen would be unable to answer for herself.

Which was true, because she couldn't know what an orange was.

He'd forgotten about the clips that had circulated after Rose McKenzie was found, visual and audio comms of her singing. The comms had swept through all four planets——there wouldn't be a soul who hadn't seen them.

"She's not classified as an orange anymore, Captain. But yes, Imogen is from the same planet as Rose McKenzie."

"Captain Inita has seen Rose McKenzie?" Imogen asked and Inita turned to her, almost melting at her feet.

Cam had forgotten something else. That her voice alone was enough to strike a cord in any Grih. His enjoyment of the smooth, lilting way she spoke had become normal to him far quicker than he would have thought. Perhaps because, aside from Oris and Paxe, she was the only person he'd spoken to for nearly two days.

"Not in person," Inita answered her. "But I have heard her sing. The loveliest sound I have ever heard."

"I was escorting Imogen to Larga Ways when we came under attack. Captain, I don't want harm to come to you for rescuing us, so I would strongly urge you to say nothing of our presence on your ship."

Inita looked at him, and Cam almost saw the fawning music lover fall away and the shrewd trader take his place. "I understand all too well. We will say nothing."

"Captain Inita." Imogen touched the captain's arm lightly, and he turned to her. "Thank you for helping us. I know it's at some risk to you, and I want you to know we're very grateful."

Inita drew in a deep breath, as if he could inhale the sound of her voice. "We are most honored." He turned and gesticulated to his first officer and another crew member who were standing near the small launch bay's door. "I think you would like some grinabo and a rest, after your ordeal? It is another five hours until we reach Larga Ways." He half-turned to Imogen, not looking at her directly, but focusing on her feet.

"Ah." She darted a questioning look at Cam and he gave a quick nod. "Thank you."

"This way, please." Inita was beaming.

They followed him out of the launch bay——which only just had room for their small explorer and the pallets and stacked boxes of the trader's cargo——into a large, open area that served as the main living area for the crew.

No passageways on this compact little vessel.

Cam noticed colorful, patterned screens running along the sides of the gently curved walls which no doubt hid bunk beds for the crew to sleep in.

"This is lovely." Imogen looked around with genuine appreciation.

Inita almost genuflected as he introduced them to his crew of eight. "This is Captain Kalor, of Battle Center, and Imogen Peters." He looked at Imogen's feet again, and Cam thought he might burst from the excitement.

"We thank you again for stopping to help us, I know it will have delayed your schedule." Cam gave a formal bow.

"It was nothing," Inita said gallantly. "Of course we stopped."

"Have you heard what the damage is on Larga Ways?" Cam asked. "I know there was an explosion but repairs are underway."

Inita went pale, his head whipping around to skewer one of his crew. "Larga Ways attacked? There were comms to this effect?"

The communications officer shook her head. "No, sir. Nothing." She disappeared through the far door, to the bridge, probably.

"What have you heard? I have family on Larga Ways." Inita stepped closer to Cam, and so did a few others.

"That's all I know. There was a large explosion, but the way station was saved and is being repaired."

"When did it happen?"

Cam thought about it. "Four days ago, I think. If my source

was accurate."

The comms officer stepped back in the room and everyone turned to her. "I tried Larga Ways customs, but they aren't answering. So I called a friend I know there who works at one of the hotels. He confirms it." She nodded to Cam. "Larga Ways isn't broadcasting it, per Battle Center orders, but there was an explosion. The docking facilities weren't affected, though, and reconstruction is already underway. They're accepting traders as usual."

"Well." Inita looked at them more carefully than he had before. "Well, well, well. I appreciate knowing these things in advance, so I thank you. Your presence did not have anything to do with the explosion?" He looked at Imogen.

She shook her head. What happened on Larga Ways wasn't her fault, it wasn't Fiona Russell's, either, but Imogen couldn't help the tug of guilt, anyway.

"Imogen has never been to Larga Ways," Cam put in smoothly.

"It is a sight to behold," Inita told her. "A beautiful place. I heard Gurtain, the famous Grihan music-maker, sing there when Larga Ways was opened for the first time. It was magical."

Imogen smiled at him. "As you obviously enjoy singing, would you like me to sing to you as a thank you for all you've done for us?"

Silence descended so fast, Imogen edged closer to Cam.

"Sing, for us? In person?" Inita sounded so horrified, Imogen look at Cam in distress. It reminded him that Rose McKenzie had had this same disconnect with them over the value of song.

To the Grih, it was for important occasions, and not to be overused. To people from Earth, evidently, it was something dished out with abandon. And he supposed, if they could all sing like Rose and Imogen, perhaps it wasn't so strange.

"You would not like it?" Imogen asked, after a pause.

"No, no. It would be an honor." Inita wrung his hands and looked at Cam desperately for assistance.

"Imogen's people have a different view of song to us. They share their song more frequently, and gift it to those around them all the time." There were only ten Grihan music-makers presently across the four planets, and their public performances were strictly rationed.

"Oh!" Inita gasped. "I never knew . . . but how could I? Of

course. You are sure you would honor us with such a gift?"

Imogen now looked as if singing was the last thing she wanted to do. She shot Cam a dark look, as if he should have told her the ins and outs of singing protocol, and he caught her eye and smiled. Shrugged his shoulders.

She narrowed her eyes, then turned to Inita. "The honor is mine, Captain." And then she opened her mouth, reached in, and grabbed hold of the heart and soul of everyone in the room.

***

Could the Grihan attitude to singing be any more convoluted?

Imogen had been thinking of *And She Was* by Talking Heads while she lay in Cam's arms on the explorer, of how perfectly it seemed to reflect the place of acceptance she'd come to in this strange journey she'd been on. She chose to sing it now, surrounded by Grih who were staring at her with such perplexed, worried looks on their faces.

All because she'd offered to sing.

But she'd barely got into the first verse when the expressions changed from something approaching alarm to wonder, and she didn't know if that was better or worse.

She had a good voice. She wouldn't have gone into teaching music if she hadn't, but they were looking at her like she was Dame Kiri Te Kanawa. Like the Grih prisoners in Paxe's hold who'd stepped in to protect her from the Vanad had done.

Goo-goo eyes.

She glanced sideways at Cam, and yep, he was looking at her with wonder, with such bliss on his face, she couldn't begrudge him.

She realized she was clapping the beat, had started doing it without thinking, just like she'd have done in class to help her students keep time, and went with it, threw herself into the song wholeheartedly, because wasn't that what music was for?

And if the Grih were mad about it, who was she to say how mad they should be? She was pretty fond of music herself.

As she wound down, sang the last short, sharp verse, the absolute silence hit her. She'd never had such a captivated audience.

She smiled at Inita uncertainly, and saw tears streaming down his face.

"What song is that?" he whispered.

"It is a song of the blue planet," she told him.

He said nothing more, but Imogen realized he couldn't, he was too overcome.

"Captain Inita, I know this is a further imposition," Cam's voice was rough, and he cleared his throat. "Could you get us through customs without questions? And ask your crew not to mention this to anyone for a few days? Until I can assure Imogen's safety?"

Inita bowed his head, and Imogen thought Cam had pushed him too far. They were asking him to break customs law and to muzzle his crew.

He raised his head, but he did not look her directly in the eye. "For you, music-maker, anything."

Chapter Thirty

LARGA WAYS WAS AMAZING. Damaged, but amazing.

Imogen held tight to Cam's hand as they stepped out of the trader and onto one of the long docking arms radiating from the central hub that was the way station.

Above them, a dome of pale purple gel held the atmosphere in place. She'd sat in front of the screen as they'd come in to land, and saw Larga Ways was a tiny city sitting on a disc, with docking arms around the full circumference, like a stylized drawing of a sun.

The explosion that had ripped through it had damaged buildings in an uneven burst, like a paint spill, from just left of the center. As they'd come through the gel wall, Imogen saw there was already work underway, and all the streets seemed clear.

She angled her head to look straight up at the dome overhead, and Cam tightened his grip to steady her.

The Class 5 that was run by Sazo hovered to one side of the sun, looming like a smaller dark star over Larga Ways, and beside it, the sleek, massive ship that Cam told her was a Grihan battleship, run by Hal Vakeri, the Grihan captain who had found Fiona Russell and alerted Battle Center and the United Council about her.

The reason Cam was here in the first place.

If only they could get a message to either without exposing themselves to potential traitors and spies.

She tore her gaze away and focused on where she was putting her feet. They were walking among the crew, surrounded on all sides, and she and Cam both had a temporary work contract chip stuck to their shirts.

"It's easier to fake temporary," Cam had explained to her. "But we'll be the captain's responsibility, so he's taking a risk issuing them to us, because if we get into any kind of trouble, so will he."

Cam had given her his Battle Center uniform to pack in her backpack and borrowed clothing from the big engineer on Inita's crew so he could slip in without alerting anyone to who he was.

If there were Tecran spies here, as Barj had told him there were, they would be watching the entry points just as carefully as the Grih and Balcoans.

Cam kept his movements easy, looked around like everyone else, joking with the rest of the crew. Imogen wished she could be that at ease as she fiddled with the funny hat the comms officer had lent her to hide her ears and hair, and adjusted and readjusted her backpack over her shoulder.

Oris had given it to her because it had a false bottom he assured her would fool Larga Ways security. No scan could pierce it, and she'd used it to hide her whip.

At least she had a weapon.

Cam had had to leave his shockgun behind. She could see he felt naked without it, slapping his hand down on his right thigh a couple of times as they walked toward the entry point to Larga Ways and then clenching it into a fist when he remembered he wasn't wearing his holster.

Cam told her the scan was continuous, from the moment they stepped onto the docking arm, and would pick up explosives and weapons, but hopefully no one would be scrutinizing individuals. If they were, she would stand out.

She was at least a foot shorter, on average, than most Grih, and while two months of unappetizing food and three to four hours of yoga a day meant she was thinner and in better shape than she'd ever been, she still had more curves than they did.

Looking like a teenager was going to be a challenge. But she was too short to pass for anything else.

The hat sat low on her forehead and puffed up high, so she'd been easily able to make a bun and hide her hair underneath it. The comms officer had promised her it was fashionable in some parts of the four planets, and wouldn't raise an eyebrow.

She breathed through her nerves and hoped it was so.

They must have passed the security check, because as they reached the entrance gate, which was two poles set on either side of the docking arm, the force field that had fizzed and sparked up 'til now winked off and they were allowed to step through under the vigilant eyes of two guards.

No one screamed 'stop!', so she tried to force her heart to slow down as they made their way into a small square edged with apartment buildings that glittered with reflective surfaces and mosaics in the late afternoon sun.

"Before you go, I want you to know we'll be here for three days." Inita held out his wrist, letting the rest of the crew go ahead. "My cousin owns a bar on the way station. You should go there if you need any help, and he will contact me. Here's the address."

Cam hesitated, then stepped forward, lifting his own wrist. They touched sleeves, and Cam gave a nod of thanks. "We appreciate all you've done for us, Captain."

Inita's gaze met hers, and Imogen forced herself not to look away when she recognized the deep reverence in his eyes. He said nothing, swallowing hard, and she stepped up to him and kissed his cheek.

"I hope we meet again, Captain Inita."

He nodded, a tight, quick up and down, and she turned as Cam took her hand again and drew her off down the street to their left.

It reminded her of the narrow, twisty streets of France and Spain, and for the same reasons, she guessed. The tiny villages perched on the hilltops only had so much space——every inch was precious——and that was the same here. Larga Ways could only go upward, not sideways.

"Where are we going?" She was slowing him down, she knew, but everything was so interesting and truly beautiful. Larga Ways was the quintessential bijoux city.

She imagined the apartments were tiny and expensive as hell, and Cam had told her no runners or vehicles of any kind were allowed on the streets, except for delivery vehicles.

Cam gave her hand a tug. "We need to find the Battle Center offices. If we get a straight run there, all this sneaking around will be over."

Although they weren't really sneaking. There were other people walking around, and she thought they blended pretty well. Imogen could see who was a Larga Ways inhabitant or here for a holiday because they dressed in bright colors and in long garments with multiple layers. The traders and people just arrived on space vessels were all dressed like Cam and herself, in fitted trousers and shirts that looked vaguely like a uniform.

They passed a woman with a tiny creature attached to a

shimmering lead.

"Ooh." She tugged Cam's arm. "What's that cute thing?"

"A kapoot." He barely looked at it, his eyes moving all the time, his focus on potential threats.

She knew they were in danger, that they were on the cusp of a nasty war, but she let the cuteness of the kapoot warm her anyway. Otherwise, what was the point of it all?

Cleese had done that for her, too. The blue and yellow macaw had kept her sane in the Balco facility, and the sly game of insults she'd taught him, directed at their guards, had kept her spirit strong and rebellious. He was her compatriot, and she hoped he was okay, that he hadn't died or been killed.

They wound through alleys that would have been dark, because of the height of the buildings on either side, and the angle of the Balcoan sun, but which weren't because lighting had been incorporated into the designs on the walls themselves, a fairy light wonderland of jewel colors and magical design.

"You like it." Cam tugged her hand again, and grinned when she shot him an exasperated look at being hurried along. He fit right in to this place, looking like a muscle-bound elf in his magical kingdom.

"I *love* it." Paxe should be ashamed of himself for trying to blow it up. She was determined that she would have a chance to tell him so, that he would be okay, would live to regret this poor decision, and would somehow outsmart the Tecran holding him to ransom with his own life.

Cam had gone quiet, and she pulled her attention from the mosaic of an exotic, alien forest on the wall running beside them to glance over at him.

"What is it?" He was looking at her strangely, and she stopped, forced him to stop too as she tightened her grip on his hand.

"You are fascinating."

She tipped her head back, heart hammering in her chest, and looked at him through half-closed lids. "What did I say about goo-goo eyes?"

He didn't smile as she thought he would. "I don't think I can help the goo-goo eyes. It's too late."

"Because I can sing?" It was okay if part of it was because she could sing. Part of her attraction to him was his strength and the way he moved, and that was similar, in her mind, to singing. It didn't come completely naturally, it had to be worked at. And now that she was hooked, if he had a terrible accident and couldn't move anymore with the same stealthy grace, her attraction wouldn't die. So it was okay if singing was part of it, but it couldn't be everything.

"It's the way you talk, the way you sing, your generous heart, the smooth shine in your hair, the unbelievable depth of your courage——"

A big group of tourists descended on them from behind, and Imogen stepped into his arms and let him pull them up against the wall to get out of the way. The sound of twenty excited Balcoans all talking at once washed over them and then the way was clear again.

She closed her eyes and got a tight hold around his waist, burying her face in his chest.

"You'll have to stop doing that." His voice sounded strained, and she loosened her grip and stepped back a little, dropping her arms.

"Public displays of affection not allowed?" she asked, and then noticed they were being watched by a Grihan man who'd just stepped out of the entrance to a blue glass apartment block with a design on it that looked like it had been enameled by a master jeweler.

"No, it's that in that hat, being so short, you look too young for me."

She'd forgotten. Totally forgotten that she was pretending to be a Grihan teenager. She bit her bottom lip. "Sorry."

He shook his head. "I shouldn't have——"

"No." She glanced over at their watcher, but he was gone. Still, she only took his hand. "You can say that kind of thing to me whenever you want." Her voice wobbled as she spoke. His words touched her so deeply, she could barely hold on to pieces of herself, they wanted to wrench free of her body and fly out and up. She couldn't reciprocate, not without the possibility of crying, and now wasn't a good time to be sobbing and drawing attention. So she took a deep breath and tried to smile. "I want *you* to know that I'm not just interested in you because of the whole elf thing."

He swallowed back a laugh. "What?"

"Sure, you have the whole brooding bad-ass Lord of the Forest thing down pat, but you are thoughtful, loyal and protective, too."

"Imogen . . ." He shook his head. "What are you talking about?"

She patted a bulging bicep and grinned. "You're quite fascinating yourself." She gave him her best impression of goo-goo eyes.

He choked, coughing into his hand, and straightened up. "I think we've gotten off track."

She nodded and touched her hat again. It had gone a bit skew when she'd rubbed up against Cam, and she fiddled with it. "Okay?" she asked.

He nodded. Tugged it down a little on one side.

"I'm ready, then."

"I think it's just through that archway, and down the street." He kept hold of her hand, and they strolled, going slower than they had before. Being tourists, now.

Cam was worried someone would be watching the Battle Center office. It would make sense that Tecran spies would keep their eyes on their enemies center of operations.

So for the first time, they went at a pace that suited her perfectly, only now she was too nervous to notice the delicate plants in containers that twisted and curved along walls and around windows, and instead tried to casually look at the people around them.

Some were sitting at tiny tables outside what was surely cafés, and she wondered wistfully if that was grinabo in the cups they held.

She only noticed Cam had stopped moving when she was jerked to a stop. She turned, frowning, and saw he was looking at a building that had obviously been caught in the explosion.

The first couple of floors were still standing, but something fiery and large must have landed on the roof and burnt through from the top down, collapsing part of the structure as it went.

"Let me guess," she said quietly. "That was the Battle Center office."

Chapter Thirty-one

IT WASN'T AS IF TIME WAS ON THEIR SIDE, but the destruction of the Battle Center office was shocking in and of itself, not just because it complicated their plans.

Cam was excruciatingly aware that Oris was holding back a Fitalian battleship and waiting for them, the Tecran had at least one battleship out past the Balcoan system, holding his own team hostage there, and that Paxe was still fighting for his freedom somewhere, too. But people he knew had been in that building.

He also thought someone was following them.

There had been a small, robed man Cam had seen more than once on their way here, but he was gone now. That might be because he'd switched off with someone else, or because there were lenses in this square. Or because he'd simply been going the same way as they had.

Battle Center would have moved to a temporary office, but he had no idea how many staff had been killed in the explosion, and who was left that he might know and trust.

He looked upward at the *Illium*, the massive Grihan battleship under the command of Captain Hal Vakeri, and knew that's where they needed to be.

He could go to the Larga Ways security office and request a link up with Vakeri, but that meant awkward questions about how he'd arrived on Larga Ways.

There was also a high chance there was some antagonism between the Balcoans and Vakeri. There had to be a Balcoan security officer in the Tecran camp. There was no way the Tecran spies could have gotten explosives onto the way station without it being an inside job, and the battleship captain had a reputation for being blunt.

Things might well be strained between way station security and the Grihan forces.

Going in and officially asking to speak to the captain of the *Illium* would expose Imogen and him to potential enemies with little chance of getting what they wanted anyway.

He realized while he'd been looking blankly at the charred building and thinking through their options, Imogen had gently pulled him in the direction of one of the little cafés that lined the open square in front of the destroyed building, and now she angled out a chair at one of the tiny tables outside the door with a flourish for him to sit on.

He sat, bemused, and she settled herself opposite him, the table so small their knees bumped and rubbed together.

He waited for her to order, and then realized from her body language that she was expecting someone to serve them. It occurred to him that he kept forgetting she wasn't Grihan. That everything was new to her.

It took her a few minutes to realize the menu was shown on the glass screen that made up the table top. Her delight when she realized was . . . shocking in its affect on him. It lit up her face and sparked a hot, all-consuming lust in him.

He fought back his response, trying to keep focused, and waited for her to ask him how to use the menu to order, but she didn't. She gnawed briefly on her lower lip, which only heated the lust curling in his belly even more, and then worked it out.

"Grinabo?" she asked him, finger hovering over the options.

He nodded, and she tapped it in, then cocked her head as the payment request came up.

She lifted her wrist, studied the credit bracelet Inita had given her before they'd disembarked, and then lowered it to the blue circle lit up from below.

"Just like tap and go," she said.

Not once, in all the interactions he'd had with her, had he thought her of inferior intelligence or in any way backward. But he must have had a preconceived idea of her culture's state of advancement after all, because he was truly shocked at how easily she'd worked out what to do. It made him question everything he'd assumed up until now.

"You have this system on Earth?" What the Tecran had done was unacceptable on every level, stealing an advanced sentient from her home, but there would have been some who might have been persuaded they'd made a mistake, because the line between advanced sentience and sentience was sometimes a blurry one. But no one could observe Imogen and not understand she was as advanced as the Grih. As every one of the United Council members. If and when Rose and Imogen, and Fiona Russell, too, appeared in the United Council court, there would be nowhere for the Tecran to hide.

"We don't use a bracelet, we have a card, but it's a similar concept." She turned as a server arrived with their order. "Looks like you were lucky to get away with no damage," she said to the Balcoan woman, pointing across the road to the Battle Center building.

The Balcoan looked sharply at her, seemed to study her more carefully than she had before, but nodded. "We were."

"Were many people killed over there?" Cam asked.

"Five. And many more hurt." The woman's silver eyes blinked a few times.

"I'm so sorry." Imogen touched her arm in a light, comforting gesture. "Is that company out of business now?"

The server shook her head. "That was the Battle Center office, not a business."

Cam gripped his cup as she turned away. "I used to work for Battle Center. Where can I find them, see if anyone I knew was among those who were hurt or killed?"

The Balcoan turned back slowly. "Larga Ways Security. That's where they've moved to."

"Thank you." Imogen took a deep sip of her grinabo as the woman disappeared inside.

"Drink up." Cam swallowed back the contents.

"We need to hurry?" Imogen gulped down some more.

"I think she's on a comm device right now, letting someone know about us and our questions."

Imogen stood, and took a last, big gulp. "Okay, let's go."

They walked away without rushing, but Cam kept their pace at a steady, ground-eating clip. There were lenses focused on the streets of Larga Ways, in clear contrast to Grihan, and United Council, policy. After the Thinking System Wars, where lens feed had been used by thinking systems against the population, there had been such a backlash against it that the circumstances had to be exceptional to allow it. Even though two hundred years had past since the end of the Wars, that stance hadn't changed.

The issue had been debated for months before Larga Ways was completed, but eventually it was agreed that at least in the main public areas and entry points, it would be allowed. The vulnerability of Larga Ways' gel tech to catastrophic breach was deemed exceptional enough.

So they would need to keep to the back ways now, and think of how to get into the security building and find the Battle Center office.

Cam looked down at Imogen, and realized he stood a much better chance of doing that alone.

She stood out, no matter how much Inita's comms officer had protested that the hat was high fashion.

It was mainly because of her breasts, he forced himself to admit.

She was too curvy, too well-endowed, and her voice was too different.

"Why are you looking at me like that?" she asked him, suspicion in her tone and her expression.

"I think we need to separate, and I don't want to do it," he said.

She trailed her fingers along the raised pattern on the glass wall beside them, watching him with considering eyes. "I appreciate the honesty, and admit that while I can see the benefits of hiding me somewhere so I stop attracting attention, I also don't want to separate."

He should have realized she had also noticed that she wasn't as invisible as they needed her to be.

He sighed. "If I go alone, I have a good chance of getting into Larga Ways' security office, and finding at least one Battle Center representative I know. From there, it should be easy."

They had stepped into another small square surrounded by stores and cafés, and the scent of cooking hung in the early-evening air.

Imogen breathed in deeply. "Oh. My." The look on her face was reverent.

"What is it?" He stopped, pulling them out of the path of pedestrian traffic a little.

"That smell. Proper food." She breathed in again. "I have an idea. I go have dinner at that place right there," she pointed to the tiny restaurant, "and you go save the world."

He couldn't resist kissing her. "That doesn't seem fair."

"Someone has to eat dinner. I'm self-sacrificing like that." She kept a straight face as she spoke.

"Well, if you're sure?"

"Oh, go enjoy yourself. You know I don't mind doing the heavy lifting."

He laughed, burying his face in her neck and then gripping her arms. "Be careful. I'll come get you in an hour, no matter what happens. So don't move from there."

"Got it. And you be careful, too. Don't make me get out my whip and come get you."

He took his Battle Center uniform out of her pack and then watched from the street until she'd taken a seat inside the restaurant, at one of four tiny tables he could see through the big window.

He hadn't seen the man he'd suspected of following them earlier since they'd found Battle Center's office, and no one had followed them here. She should be safe.

The depth of her bravery astounded him. She'd lightened the atmosphere, joked with him, all while she'd been deeply afraid of being on her own again. He'd seen it sitting, dark and huge, behind her smile.

He knew this was the best plan and yet he had to force himself to walk away.

And knew the only reason he was able to was because to do anything else was to doubt her courage.

Chapter Thirty-two

SHE DIDN'T WANT TO SEPARATE, but if she had to, this was at least a decent reason to do so.

Imogen lifted the grilled meat on its little skewer to her mouth and bit down. Yum.

She didn't know what kind of meat it was, and she didn't care. Her body was telling her it needed this, and was overjoyed at getting it.

On the plate in front of her, there were also vegetables that had been char-grilled over an open flame, something a little like a sweet pepper, only a disconcerting brown, and something pale green, crunchy, and fresh, that didn't taste like much to her, but didn't taste bad, either.

The restaurant was full, every table held two or more people, and there was a small group milling around outside that Imogen guessed were waiting for a table to become free.

There was no back room or rear exit, the kitchen was part of the restaurant, separated from the tables by a long counter, and twice suppliers had wended their way past the tightly-packed tables carrying in boxes of ingredients.

"You like our food?" The woman who came to clear some of the dishes away was tall and thin, with dark skin. She had the silver eyes of a Balcoan but the slender, long frame of the Grih.

"I love it." Imogen watched the woman go still at the sound of her voice, and cursed herself. She should have nodded or grunted assent. She needed to have a six-pack a day smoking habit to sound even close to Grihan.

"I know your friend," the woman said at last. "She orders our food every day."

"Fiona Russell?" Imogen asked. Paxe had said she was here, that he'd tried to blow up Larga Ways to kill her, but Imogen hadn't thought more about it than that. If she were forced to guess, she would have said Fiona might well be above the way station, on either Sazo's Class 5 or the Grihan battleship. Not still wandering around here.

"That's right." The woman smiled. "She claims we're the only ones on Larga Ways who make proper food."

"I won't argue with that." Imogen studied the clock which was part of the information on the table. Another ten minutes before Cam was due to fetch her. Another fifteen before she had to give the table up to a group who'd reserved it earlier. "I don't suppose Fiona'll be in tonight?"

Wouldn't that be perfect?

The waitress shook her head. "No. You were lucky to get a table because you came early, but we're always booked weeks in advance. Those who want our food but can't get a seat have to place an order." She hefted the bowls on one arm. "Can I get you anything else?"

Imogen couldn't leave until Cam arrived, so she nodded. "What's Fiona's favorite dessert?"

The waitress came round the table and stood behind her, showed her two items Fiona had chosen from the menu before. Imogen picked what looked like a light cheesecake.

When it came, she sipped her cup of grinabo, spooned up a light, mousse-like concoction that had both the scent and taste of honeydew melon, and nervously watched the clock.

Cam was nearly five minutes late. And she was going to have to leave soon. She could see the diners who'd booked her table shifting restlessly at the door.

Worry for him made the dessert she'd just eaten churn uncomfortably in her stomach. He wouldn't be late if he could help it, which meant he was held up. She hoped it was simply that it was taking him longer than he thought to find someone he trusted.

When the waitress came to take away her bowl and cup, she tapped her bracelet to the glowing blue payment circle and stood, hefting her pack over her shoulder. "I was supposed to meet a friend here, but he's late. If he comes by and asks after me later, could you tell him Imogen will meet up with him at Inita's cousin's bar?"

Not that she knew where that was, Inita had given the address to Cam, not her, but she could find out easily enough, surely? A bar was the only place she could think of that both of them could wait in without drawing too much attention, and at least they knew they would get help from the owner.

The waitress tapped her sleeve and repeated what Imogen had said, so she wouldn't get it wrong, and with a smile of thanks, Imogen stepped outside.

They'd docked in Larga Ways during the afternoon, but now the sun had slipped behind Balco and the last rays of light created a pale mauve glow in the gel dome overhead.

The lights in the square grew brighter; both the lights interwoven in the designs on the walls, and on the tables and doorways all around her.

She was in a magical place and she didn't care, because Cam still hadn't arrived.

She stood for a bit, mingling with the crowd at the door, but she could see that she was just a little too different. She got the most stares from the Grih, who she decided must be protective of children——to their credit——and her size made them assume she was young. But her shape was too feminine to be adolescent, and that made them look a second time, because the Cargassey shirt and trousers she was wearing were form-fitting, and there was no hiding her curves.

She was pretty sure Inita's comms officer had over-sold the hat, as well.

She glanced at the table nearest her, which had three Balcoans squeezed around it, and saw Cam was now twenty minutes late.

She eased back a bit, into deeper shadows, and at that moment a Balcoan stepped out of the restaurant door, two neatly bagged packages in each hand.

Deliveries.

And that got her thinking of Fiona Russell.

She wasn't coming in tonight, the waitress had said, but maybe she was ordering take-out. Imogen knew only too well this was as close to Earth as food got.

She hesitated, but she couldn't stay here much longer anyway. Someone was going to ask her a question, or notice who she was, just like the waitress had done.

And what did she have to lose? She could worry about Cam just as well on the move, doing something constructive, than waiting to be tapped on the shoulder.

She edged around the crowd, and began to follow.

The Balcoan making the deliveries called out to people as he walked, chatting and joking, but he moved quickly.

The first delivery was to a ground-floor apartment that opened straight onto the street; not one of the sleek glass high-rises, but a more quaint building with a balcony on each level, and an outside staircase that wound in a spiral up to each front door.

The person who stepped out to accept the order was neither Balcoan nor Grih, but Imogen only caught a glimpse of swirling robes and painfully thin arms before the door closed again and the delivery man continued on his way.

Cam was now thirty minutes late. At least.

She watched the Balcoan tap a screen outside the door of his next customer, and wondered if Cam was even now at the restaurant, wondering where she was.

She'd take his annoyance, as long as he was safe.

The door opened, and Imogen realized she wouldn't be able to tell if this delivery was for Fiona or not. There was no way she had a legitimate reason to gain entry to the glittering building.

The Balcoan came back out almost straight away, so she guessed he'd left the food at some sort of reception desk.

She would have to come back here if the other two didn't work out, and see what she could do.

Night had descended fully now, but as she strolled after her quarry, it became clear they were moving into an area occupied by the rarified rich. While no part of Larga Ways looked run down, aside from the damage made by the explosion, this part of the way station had the gleam and shine of serious money.

It didn't seem likely she'd find Fiona here, so while the delivery man disappeared into the building, she leaned back against the high wall behind her and breathed in the perfume of hidden gardens.

The apartment block the Balcoan had been admitted to was clad in a dark rose stone, and it took her tired, worried eyes a minute to realize the patterns woven through it were in fact fossils of the most extraordinary creatures.

Some were tiny, but most were three, four times bigger than she was. She caught glimpses of wings, of massive teeth, of delicate beaks.

The building itself stood six stories high, with a balcony on each floor. Some were lit, and from the very highest, she heard someone laugh.

She frowned. Something about that laugh niggled. She looked up, but there was no way to see over the balustrade.

The laugh came again.

It was human. A woman.

The breath caught in her throat. She walked across the street, directly in front of a door framed on both sides by bushes larger than she was, face still turned up to the sound.

She didn't know why the tears started falling, dripping from the corner of her eyes down her cheeks, because she'd hardly cried at all since she'd been abducted, but there it was again. The sweet sound of laughter.

She took another step toward the door and a hand came out of the shadows and got a bruising grip on her arm.

She cried out, her gaze flying to a Balcoan dressed in black, his silver eyes fierce and angry.

At that moment the door opened, and the delivery man stepped out.

Imogen twisted and wrenched her arm free, her hat flying off as she darted around the delivery man and smacked both hands against the door before it closed, slipping in between the narrow opening and pushing it closed behind her.

She took the stairs at a run, heard the door open and then slam shut behind her.

She had a head start, but the Balcoan was gaining on her, and by the time she reached the top floor, she was sucking in air desperately.

There was only one door on this floor and the hallway was so plush, so refined, she stumbled the last few steps, unsure now she had it right. Could Fiona Russell be here?

She slammed a fist on the door anyway. There was no going back. No going down.

"Fiona." She tried to shout, but it came out weak and soft. "Fiona!" She slammed her fist again, looking behind her, and the door flew open.

The Balcoan hit the top step as she staggered forward, and she raised an arm against attack, wishing for the security of her whip which, only now did she remember, was stuck deep in her backpack and useless.

"Tean Lee." Hands gripped her, set her gently aside, and Imogen finally focused on who was in front of her.

Fiona Russell, looking just like the many pictures of her in the papers when she'd gone missing, was staring over Imogen's shoulder, her eyes narrowed in fury. She pointed a finger at the Balcoan. "What do you think you're doing?"

Imogen had been set against a wall, and she let gravity take her down, sliding until her butt hit the floor, put her head on her knees, and shook.

A second pair of legs joined Fiona at the door, but Imogen didn't have it in her yet to look up and see who it was.

There was silence, and eventually curiosity overcame exhaustion, and she raised her head.

The second pair of legs belonged to Rose McKenzie, and she stood beside Fiona Russell, blocking most of Imogen's view of the Balcoan Fiona had called Tean Lee.

It was some kind of standoff.

"Ask your boss what I'm doing. It was his tip-off that had me following her." Lee's voice was hard and defensive.

"I will. I'm too angry to say anything else to you, so good night." Fiona slammed the door, tapped her ear. "Eazi?"

She turned and looked at Imogen, then crouched down beside her, and Rose did the same.

Her mouth straightened in a grim line. "You were terrified." She looked deeper into the apartment, eyes narrowed for a moment, and then looked back. "This hasn't been the meeting I imagined, but please tell me, are you Imogen Peters?"

Imogen tried to hold it back, but this was the straw that broke the camel's back. She started to sob.

***

Cam changed back into his Battle Center uniform in a public cubicle and then made his way to Larga Ways Security. He'd been there once before, to liaise with Tean Lee, the station chief, and he found it easily again.

It was built in utilitarian fashion, probably one of the most boring buildings on the way station, but it fit in, nevertheless, with its dark blue glass skin and lights that spiraled in complex patterns up the sides.

A large piece of debris from the explosion had obviously landed in the street near the entrance, gouged the road, and come through the security building's front entrance.

It had been set to one side, and was so melted and twisted,

222

Cam couldn't work out what it might once have been.

Another thing that hadn't been there last time Cam had been here was the perimeter of guards around the building. They were all alert, too alert for it to be anything but an emergency situation.

What could be spooking the security forces this much?

There was a Fitalian battleship and a Class 5 behind Gugijeron, not to mention a Tecran battleship just beyond the Balco system, but twenty guards around a building on Larga Ways wasn't going to stop either threat.

He reached for a shockgun barrel that wasn't there, and a wave of frustration washed over him at being without his weapon.

He would have to do this a different way. There would be no sneaking into the building with this level of security, so his best bet was to wait around for a Battle Center employee to approach the building, and stop them before they got there.

The office ran around the clock, so someone must be coming or going. He just needed to catch them when they did.

He eased back half a block, found a dark stairwell to a basement apartment, and settled in to wait.

Chapter Thirty-three

"WE THOUGHT WE WOULD HAVE TO FIND YOU," Fiona said, leading Imogen into a beautiful open-plan room. "But somehow, you've found us."

"And I would like to know how you did that." The voice that spoke through some hidden speaker was suspicious.

Imogen glanced in its direction, then swung her attention back to Rose and Fiona. "I know who you are, I was taken after you both, but how do you know me?" Her face still felt tight and hot from crying, and she rubbed at her cheeks self-consciously.

Fiona held her gaze with eyes as warm and dark as chocolate. "I was held in the Balco facility five days ago. They put me in your cage."

It was only two weeks since she'd been down on Balco, but Imogen had almost forgotten the message she'd scratched into the hard-packed earth of her cage floor before they'd taken her away. *Imogen Peters was here.*

"Cleese?" she breathed. "My macaw? Did you see him?"

Fiona sank down to the floor next to her. "Cleese? Now there's a perfect name for him. I saved the little bugger. He bites."

"They were going to kill him?"

Fiona shook her head. "The Balco facility is gone. Eazi blew it up."

Gone.

There was something so satisfying in that word. Freeing.

"Is Cleese here?"

"He's on the *Illium*, the Grihan battleship above us. It's only been four days since the explosion on Larga Ways, and we thought it would be safer for him up there. Besides, the explorations department are in love with him, and will probably fight me for custody when things settle down."

"They will have to fight *me*." She didn't know why she said that so fiercely. Now was not the time to get territorial.

Fiona slid an arm around her and pulled her in for a one-armed hug. "There's no dispute about that. Cleese is obviously yours."

"And now we've cleared that up, how did you get here?" Eazi asked again.

"You're in the dog box." Rose glanced upward. "I'd take a different tone."

There was silence for a moment. "She was clearly acting suspiciously, she snuck onto the way station with forged temp contracts, and then she followed Erv from Vatin's Café right here. I am sorry she was frightened, but I was protecting the way station and I was protecting you." There was bafflement in Eazi's tone.

Imogen smiled. "Given that you blew my prison up, I forgive you completely for siccing that angry man on me."

"He was, wasn't he?" Rose frowned. "Why was he so angry?"

Imogen shook her head and winced as she pulled up her sleeve to look at the dark bruises Lee had given her.

Fiona scowled. "Do you see that?" She looked toward the corner of the room. "Did you see her when she came to the door? The look on her face . . ." She shook her head and then glanced at Imogen. "I'm sorry, I'm speaking as if you aren't sitting right here." She frowned. "This isn't right, Eazi. Neither Rose, Imogen or I deserve this kind of treatment."

"I think he was angry because he hadn't picked up that she had come through the checkpoint himself." Eazi said, thoughtful. "I had to tell him, and he's touchy about it since the explosion. He knows his system is faulty, that there are problems within his staff. I was surprised he followed her personally, given he's the station chief. But that doesn't excuse that he hurt you, and for my part in that, I truly am sorry."

"You're forgiven. But to make it up to me, can you make sure nothing happens to Captain Inita and the crew of the *Veasin*? They were kind to us, helped us. Believed us when we said our lives and theirs could be in danger if any Tecran knew I was onboard."

"I see that Commander Lee has surveillance on them right now, and is getting the paperwork together to board their vessel. I will make sure that is reversed."

"You keep saying *us*." Rose watched her with bright, curious eyes. "Who did you come to Larga Ways with?"

"Cam." Imogen hadn't forgotten about him, but the last few minutes had been so intense, her worry had receded a bit. Now it came rushing back. "We were separated."

"You think something's happened to him?" Rose asked her.

She nodded. "Could you call the restaurant, see if he's been there looking for me?"

"Doing it now," Eazi said. "Who is Cam?"

"Captain Camlar Kalor," Imogen said.

Rose and Fiona both went still.

"You know him?" How could that be?

"Right now, Battle Center is just praying he and his team aren't dead. Now you're saying he's alive and well on Larga Ways?" Fiona's eyes were wide. "And the rest of his team, too?"

"No." Imogen pulled her sleeve down. "His team is being held hostage by a Tecran battleship somewhere just out of the Balco system."

"You get that, Sazo?" Rose asked.

"I did. Hello, Imogen Peters, it is good that you are safe." Sazo's voice was smooth, human, to her ears. He had the same cadence and accent as Rose. "Do you know where this fleet is, exactly?"

Imogen shook her head. "No, but Oris does, and I know where you can find him."

"Oris?"

"The Class 5 I freed. He's waiting for Cam and I to see if you are willing to talk to him. Negotiate a deal where he can be safe."

"I would be interested to hear the story of how you freed him." Sazo sounded incredibly formal now. "As for his safety, I can't speak for Battle Center, but I do not turn on my own."

"Aside from the small fleet of Larga Ways security runners, I'm no threat to him, but as Sazo says, I do not turn on my own." Eazi sounded just as formal as Sazo.

"That's good." She had assumed they would be happy to welcome Oris, but there must have been some part of her that was nervous, because the relief left her lighter. "He's hiding behind Gu-gijeron."

"I'll go talk to him."

"Sazo, wait. There's one more thing. When we light-jumped behind Gu-gijeron, a Fitalian battleship almost landed on top of us a few minutes later."

"Fitalian?" If Eazi had a face, it would be frowning.

"They're after a creature the Tecran stole from them, only they thought the Grih had done it, because they tracked it to Balco. They tried to shoot us even when they knew the truth, to make sure we couldn't talk about it. Oris has taken over the battleship's systems, and is holding them in place."

"They're after the grahudi?" Fiona shivered. "Why?"

Of course, if Fiona had been held in the Balco facility, she would have seen it, too. Imogen shook her head. "I don't know. Whatever their reasons, it's nothing good. But there's more. When Oris took over the Fitalian ship, he found they'd installed new weapons that can breach a Class 5's shields.

"He was going to spend the time waiting for us looking for a way to counter what they've done. So, the point is, if you see a Fitalian battleship on your way to Oris, don't engage, run."

"I thank you for the information," Sazo said, and she thought, for the first time, there was warmth in his voice. "I'll be back with Oris shortly."

"What about the *Illium*?" Rose asked Fiona. "Better warn Hal there's a new Class 5 on its way over. With a hostile Fitalian battleship in tow."

"Yes," Eazi's voice was dry. "No matter what his deal with Battle Center is, Sazo will fire on the *Illium* if it tries to harm Oris."

Fiona nodded, tapped at her ear and walked away, talking in a low voice.

"Fiona has direct access to the *Illium*?" Imogen frowned in confusion.

"Fiona and Captain Hal Vakeri cohabit. Usually here, but tonight he had a meeting onboard his ship." Rose's smile was warm and mischievous. "That's why we were having a girls' night in. My significant other happens to be at the same meeting."

"While mine . . ." Could she call Cam that? Maybe not yet, but it was in their future. She glanced at the ceiling. "Have you heard any news of Cam, Eazi? Did he go to the restaurant?"

"He did. The waitress gave him your message." Eazi paused. "But I'm afraid my search for him in the lens feed shows he's being followed, and I'm very much afraid Commander Lee has gone a little overboard."

"Why do you say that?" Imogen stood and opened the top of her backpack.

"He's got armed guards trailing the captain, and Lee's orders are to see where he goes and then arrest him, with force if necessary."

"What is Lee thinking?" Fiona paced back toward them. "Doesn't he know Cam personally?"

"Even if he does," Rose leaned back against the couch, "he's been hunting Imogen, so he may not have seen him. As far as he's concerned, he's tracking a real threat."

Eazi made a hum of agreement. "I think he's feeling guilty about every death on this station, and believes he's failed. And now he's trying to make up for it. I've hailed him twice but he's refusing to answer."

"And the guards are following his lead?" Fiona asked.

"Some of them. The ones who were going to board Captain Inita's ship wouldn't answer my hail until I sent them a message from their banks that I've reversed their salaries for insubordination."

Imogen looked up admiringly. "That really hits where it hurts."

"Apparently." There was a smile in Eazi's voice. "They decided to answer and hear my order after that, so I put the money back in."

"Can you do that for the others, too?"

"I already have."

"And they're still going ahead?" Fiona was incredulous.

"There's a core of guards around Lee who are loyal to him, and my guess is he sees this as a contest between us. He's probably ordered them to ignore me."

"Cam's going to the bar?" Imogen asked, lifting her clothes out of her pack and setting them on the floor beside it.

"Gurtain's Song, it's called. And yes. He's on his way there now. Since Lee isn't accepting comms, I've shut the security comms down, so at least he can't coordinate with his team. I've blacked out the lens feed on the route Cam's taking as well, but Lee's team were following Inita earlier, and I'm sure they've guessed where Cam is headed."

"What are you doing?" Rose peered into the pack as Imogen knelt beside it and lifted out a gold box.

"Chocolate," Imogen said, waggling the box and then handing it to her. "Courtesy of the thieving Tecran who took me. Oris found them in the store."

Fiona stopped pacing and stared. "You're kidding?"

Imogen shook her head, and lifted out the false bottom, grabbed her whip, and stood.

"I need to go help Cam." She lifted her shirt and slid the whip into the holster Oris had made her.

"We're coming with you. I'm the CEO of this way station now, and Lee answers to me." Fiona sounded grim. "Yes, Hal, I am," she said, and scowled.

Imogen blinked, and then realized Fiona was responding to someone talking to her through her earpiece. "If you want to come down and help, that's fine, but we're not waiting around. Lee's guards could seriously hurt Captain Kalor." She blew out a breath and looked up. "Rose, are you coming, too?"

Rose nodded.

"Yes, you can tell Dav she is. No more time to talk, see you there." She tapped her earpiece and walked off into what looked like a bedroom. When she came back, she was clipping on a bracelet. Something about the way she did it made Imogen think it wasn't an accessory.

"Cool weapon?" she asked and then jerked as a blue light seemed to scan over Fiona's body.

Fiona nodded. "I assume that cylinder thing is, too?"

Imogen smiled. "Yes."

They both looked at Rose, and she tapped the front pocket of her trousers. "I never go anywhere without mine."

Chapter Thirty-four

IT WAS IMPOSSIBLE TO KNOW if he was being followed.

Cam struggled through the crowds, and wondered if every person who lived on Larga Ways was out in the main street tonight.

It felt like it.

Even the narrow side streets were full of people laughing and talking, eating and drinking at small cafés and restaurants, and calling to each other over the heads of the revelers.

"We're celebrating being alive," a Balcoan woman told him as they were forced to wait together to get through a particularly dense part of the crowd.

The spontaneous street party was cheerful and happy, at least, and no one seemed to mind having to wait, or being jostled.

Their mood was better than his. All he wanted to do was get to Gurtain's Song, Inita's cousin's bar, and make sure Imogen was safe.

He hadn't seen a single Battle Center employee while he'd waited outside the security offices. Either the waitress had lied, or circumstances had changed.

The urgency he felt at getting in touch with Hal Vakeri had made him push the time he'd said he'd be back for Imogen way past the limit, but he'd failed.

There was no choice now but to track down Tean Lee, the station chief, and ask him to link him to the *Illium*. Politics be damned. They'd simply run out of time.

He could have approached the security building and asked to speak to Lee earlier, but knowing Imogen was waiting for him had forced him away from that option. Even if the guards acted immediately and contacted Lee for him, he'd be held up for a long time.

Better to collect Imogen and get in touch with Lee's office from somewhere safe, try to connect with the man himself.

Finding the restaurant where he'd left Imogen packed to

capacity and Imogen gone had made the shoving crowd harder to bear. Panic was not a feeling he had often, but it had gripped him in its icy maw, and he'd had to shake himself loose before he started shoving the merrymakers back a little harder than they had shoved him.

At least she'd left a message for him. The fact that she had had made it possible to breathe again. And the place she'd chosen was a good one. He'd planned to go to the bar with her anyway, to call Tean Lee from there.

And there it was, just up ahead.

He started to relax a little. The bar was on the ground floor of a building made of what looked like crystal. It seemed like it should be transparent but the crystal reflected light outward, so the whole place glittered and glowed, while making it impossible to see within.

He had to force his way to the entrance, and guessed the only reason the large Grih at the door let him in was because as he got there, a group of five Balcoans left.

"Is the owner's cousin, Captain Inita, here?" he asked the man, and his attitude warmed a little.

He gave a nod and let Cam slip in.

Like everywhere else, the place was heaving. Perhaps it was because the bar was owned by a Grihan, but Grih made up the majority of customers, although he saw Balcoans, the odd Fitali and several Vutrovians.

He had looked for Imogen outside as he'd made his way to the front entrance of the bar, but she was short enough to get lost in the crowd. He would have to hope she arrived before the crush started, and that he'd find her having a drink with Inita and his crew.

Despite the noise and the crowds, he was impressed with the place.

The bar was huge for Larga Ways, with a curved counter sitting like a big smile in the center of the room. Behind the counter stood an elevated stage, and a group of four musicians were playing a piece that involved drums and bells, the comms system taking every sound and playing it through powerful speakers, so that everyone could hear it, despite the high-level roar of conversation.

Captain Inita's cousin had set poles throughout the room, just higher than waist height, with a small circular tabletop on each. Drinks fought for space on the tiny surfaces, and groups as large as eight tried to squeeze themselves around them.

There were tables with chairs set against the walls, two levels of them, the second level really just a long, thin balcony that wrapped around the room, suspended above the tables below and built out of a thick, clear substance that made the tables look like they were floating on thin air.

Cam spotted Inita and a Grihan man he didn't recognize up on the balcony to the left of the entrance, and made his way through the packed house toward them.

He would be able to see Imogen better from above, anyway, but perhaps Inita already knew where she was.

He climbed the stairs, which turned out to be a thick resin, and Inita stood and waved as he spotted him.

"Where is the lovely Imogen?"

Cam shook his head. "I was hoping you knew. She said she would meet me here, but there's a huge crush outside, so perhaps she hasn't been able to get in."

Inita stepped up to the clear, waist-high balustrade and Cam joined him as they both searched the floor below.

"That's strange." The Grih behind him stood as well. His gaze was also on the crowds.

"My apologies, Captain Kalor, this is Paali Takari, my cousin."

Cam bowed and they exchanged murmured greetings. "What is strange?"

"I'm on good terms with security on Larga Ways, it pays to be with a place like mine, but never have I seen so many in the bar at one time."

The first cold, hard drop of suspicion hit the back of Cam's neck and snaked down his spine. "Could you point them out?"

Takari nodded down to a man and woman leaning against the bar. "Both of them. Those two men near the entrance, they're in full uniform, with their shockguns. And there are three more out of uniform I recognized earlier, who've been here since the place opened a couple of hours ago. They're still somewhere in the crowd."

"What does that mean to you?" Inita was watching him.

"Trouble, I think. I apologize if I've brought it here." Cam looked over the lower floor again, but Imogen was nowhere to be seen.

"What do you plan to do?" Takari leaned against the edge of the balustrade as if they were exchanging pleasantries.

"Leave, look for Imogen outside, see if she's hanging around, unable to get in."

"Please come back when you are able, Captain, and let us know that you've found her safe. If she comes here after you've gone, we'll help her any way we can." Inita spoke authoritatively, and Cam guessed he must be a part-owner in this place, because Takari didn't so much as blink at his offer.

Cam nodded his thanks and good byes and made his way back to the stairs. He kept his gaze on the crowds below, as if he were still looking for someone, but he was tracking the security personnel Takari had pointed out.

They were definitely here for him.

He could see the way the two guards at the door subtly watched him and the couple at the bar had started moving to intercept him at the bottom of the stairs.

But the big clue was the small, robed man he'd thought might be following them earlier, standing up from his seat at a table on the opposite wall. If Cam wasn't mistaken, there was a shockgun hidden under the long folds of his clothing.

Three more people, two men and a woman, suddenly pulled away from the groups they were in and moved purposefully in the same direction as their colleagues from the bar, but Cam saw two were cut off by servers getting in their way.

It was a little too coincidental and he sent a silent thank you to Inita and Takari, who were obviously signaling to staff on his behalf.

He was halfway down the steps, moving fast to escape into the crowd before the guards reached him, when a couple standing at a table close to the bottom turned and faced him.

He came to a stop. They were Balcoan and both were wearing robes, which would explain how they'd gotten their shockguns past Takari's doorman.

"Are you Larga Ways security, or Tecran spies?" Cam asked them.

The question surprised them. Shocked them.

"You need to come with us." The woman shifted uncomfortably as the patrons around them worked out what was happening and started edging away, murmuring to each other.

"I don't think you're going to be welcome back here." Cam smiled at her. "My name is Captain Camlar Kalor. I'm from Battle Center and I head a UC Investigative Unit. I need you to connect me to Tean Lee."

"Can't," the man said, and now he slanted a look at his partner. "Comms are down."

"Down?" Cam couldn't hide his surprise. Was this why there was such a fuss outside the security offices? Was there an attack on the way station comms?

"You saying you had nothing to do with it?" The man was watching Cam closely.

"I'm from Battle Center. Of course I had nothing to do with it. Where is Lee? Do you have a way you can reach him?"

"We're not fetching Commander Lee. You can come with us, and he'll get to you when he can."

That's what Cam was afraid of. And if Lee wanted to really tick off Battle Center, he could make sure he 'got to it' after a really long time. Time no one had. "I'm afraid I'm not coming with you under those circumstances."

The two shared another uneasy look.

"I don't want to shoot you, but I will." The man lifted his shockgun, and a woman standing close by screamed.

The crowd panicked suddenly, two hundred frightened people, all heading for the front entrance at the same time.

The two guards who'd taken up position at the door realized what was happening a moment too late, and Cam looked on in horror as one of them lifted his shockgun in panic and fired into the oncoming stampede.

***

Eazi got them inside through a back door.

Gurtain's Song not only had a rear entrance, it took up the entire ground floor of a building that looked like a giant cut diamond. Imogen had to mentally adjust her image of a cozy hole-in-the-wall place with deep shadows and deeper booths. This was all light, glitter, and vibrant crowds.

"I'm afraid things are looking bad in there." Eazi had linked into Imogen's earpiece so he could speak to them all.

"What's happening?" Fiona waited at a door which led to the main bar, head tipped to one side to listen.

"Captain Kalor is surrounded, and people are starting to panic."

Shaking her head in disgust, Fiona shoved at the door and they followed close behind her.

They stepped into chaos.

A mix of people, mostly Grih, were shouting, shoving and trying to move to the front entrance.

A quick glance to the left and Imogen saw Cam standing halfway down a staircase, with two people at the bottom, shockguns raised. His focus wasn't on them, though, it was on the door, and as Imogen turned to see what he was looking at, someone started screaming, and a woman went down.

"They're shooting at the crowd?" Rose breathed, voice hushed with shock.

There was an elevated stage in the middle of the room, and to Imogen's amazement, the musicians seemed to still be playing. It seemed incredible they'd go on until she saw their eyes were raised to the upper level of tables and chairs clinging to the wall on a transparent platform.

Inita stood there with another Grihan, and he was motioning them desperately to play on.

It was as good an idea as any to calm things down.

And then it hit her.

Grih. This place was packed with Grih.

"Quick, what song do all three of us know?" she asked the other two.

"What?" The look Fiona sent her questioned her sanity, but Rose got it.

"Soothe the savage beast?" she asked.

Imogen nodded. "Worth a try."

"I'm in, but I really don't want to get shot." Rose glanced to the front entrance, where panic reigned.

"Stand behind me. In these clothes, unless they get me in the head, I'm good," Imogen told her.

"Me, too. In fact, whoever shoots me gets their shot returned straight back." Fiona had clearly worked out what Imogen meant to do. "But we can't shoot anyone. We don't need to compound the problem."

Imogen agreed. This was no time for her whip. She started running for the stage, the way clearer than it had been as everyone tried to fight their way to the front.

The music was a little disjointed now, the musicians struggling to keep their focus. The drums were deep and rumbling, sounding to Imogen like a monastic choir, but the bells sounded too high and light.

"How about *Frère Jacques*?" The monastic sound had inspired her, and surely all three of them would know it.

"Oh, let's sing it in rounds," Rose said. There was something wicked in her eye. "That would seriously blow their minds."

"Good idea." That would work with the three of them. Would hopefully be different enough to catch the crowd's attention. Imogen ran up the steps onto the stage. "Let's start by singing together, and then in the second round I'll start, Fiona follows, Rose, you're last, standing behind us."

She'd thought as she'd run to the stage that she should try include the musicians, but the sounds they were making weren't intuitive to her.

"Please stop," she told them, and her voice was picked up by whatever system was piping the sounds through the speakers, and it echoed around the room.

The musicians stopped.

Imogen glanced up, saw Inita looking down at her with astonishment, and then turned to look at Cam. He was staring at her, too, but she couldn't read him.

She shook that off. They had to calm this down.

"If this doesn't work, Eazi, cut off the lights," Fiona said quietly, and Imogen nodded in agreement.

"Okay, all together." She launched into the song, Fiona standing shoulder to shoulder with her, with Rose behind. She was happy to hear that Rose obviously had some choir experience, harmonizing with her beautifully.

Fiona was less schooled, but she had a naturally good voice, holding the pitch perfectly.

The roar of sound around them faltered as their singing swelled louder and louder through the speakers, but it took all four verses for silence to descend.

When she started the song again solo, hers was the only voice to be heard, until Fiona and then Rose joined in the round.

She'd wondered at the wicked glint in Rose's eye when she'd suggested it. She was right, whatever she'd had up her sleeve. The

Grihan minds were blown.

Perhaps the Balcoans didn't have as much of a fascination for singing, but the Grih comprised the majority of the patrons, and they were entranced.

Some sat down on the floor, others leaned against the wall or each other, and as Rose sang the last *ding dang dong,* three men shoved their way through the front doors.

Two were Grih, wearing uniforms like Cam, and the third was Tean Lee, who was almost frogmarched between them.

"The cavalry?" Imogen asked Fiona in English. Her words soared around the room.

Fiona laughed, her body relaxing for the first time. "No, I think that was us."

Chapter Thirty-five

DAV JALLAN AND HAL VAKERI TOOK CONTROL.

Cam knew it was because they had only heard the last line of the song. Everyone else, himself included, simply let the perfection of it——and the surprise——reverberate through them. Three voices, all singing something different, yet harmonizing together. The way each singer chased the one before, so there was a pattern, and an extra sound, as if more than three voices were involved.

It was extraordinary.

Imogen jumped from the stage the moment it was clear the crisis was over and headed straight for where he was sitting on the stairs.

He could speak, he supposed, but he didn't want to, so he simply grabbed her hips when she stopped a few steps down, lifted her up, sat her across his thighs, and held her close.

"Goo-goo eyes," she muttered into his neck. "Don't make a habit of it." But there wasn't much heat in her voice.

He tried to focus on the short, ugly scene between the two Grihan captains and Tean Lee, the equally brutal debrief of the guards who had let everything get so out of control, and then the clearing of the bar of all members of the public.

The two women who'd been shot had been taken away, and he thought he'd heard that both would be all right. At least the shockgun charge had been set to low.

Inita and Takari were sitting at their table, and neither had moved since the singing stopped. They were as affected as he, although they had obviously signaled their staff, because there was a clean-up underway.

Lucky for them both, half the staff were Balcoan; the Grih who worked here were leaning on the bar in quiet contemplation.

Imogen stirred on his lap.

"That was . . ." He still didn't have the words.

"Kalor?"

He looked up to find Hal Vakeri standing on the bottom step. "You ready to go?"

Cam forced himself to set aside the peace the music had given him and lift Imogen off him so they could both stand.

Vakeri motioned them to the door. "We'll talk at Fiona's apartment."

They wound their way through the standing tables after him, but halfway across the floor, Imogen tugged at his hand and turned back.

"Imogen Peters." It was Captain Inita. He was standing again, and Takari stood beside him.

"Captain Inita, I hope this hasn't caused your cousin too much trouble," Imogen said, and Cam could hear the worry in her voice.

"My dear, Larga Ways Security could have brought the whole place crashing down and it would still have been worth hearing that song."

She made a humming sound. "Well then, as an apology for the inconvenience, if Fiona, Rose and I get the chance, we'll come back and sing for you again."

"You give your talent away too cheaply." Takari's voice trembled.

"Not at all." Imogen smiled up at them both. "Your kindness and help is not something I take lightly. I will be back to sing for you when I can." She bowed and then turned back to the door.

A small craft was waiting for them outside. It was just big enough for the six of them, three on each side, and as soon as the doors closed, it lifted straight up.

Obviously, in special circumstances, some transport runners were allowed on Larga Ways.

"The singing was . . . astonishing." He looked at each woman. "I thank you."

"We needed to get everyone to focus on something else, calm them down. It seemed like a good idea." Imogen let her head rest on his shoulder and he used the chance to kiss her forehead. It was so good to have her beside him and safe.

"How did you manage such perfection without practicing?"

All three laughed and shook their heads in what seemed to him to be undue modesty.

"It's a very common song, one we all already knew." Imogen straightened up a little at the disbelief on his face. "It's true."

"They just won't believe that," Rose told her, patting Dav Jallan on the arm. "You'll see. The idea that we aren't rock stars at home is almost incomprehensible to them."

Dav Jallan gave her a sideways look, but didn't contradict her. "I'm sorry we missed it." There was an edge to his voice, and Rose sent him a narrow-eyed look in exchange.

"Don't be like that. We were armed. I stood behind Fiona and Imogen, who both have shockgun protection. If we'd waited for you to arrive, more people would have been hurt."

Cam looked over at Hal Vakeri. The big battleship captain was scowling, too.

Fiona scowled right back. "Rose is right. We had to act, and we did a good job. Besides we had Eazi helping us." She was sitting opposite Vakeri, and she extended her legs and tapped her toes on top of his. "What happened with Tean Lee?"

"He's . . . not himself." Vakeri sighed. "He's taking the security failures hard."

"He wanted someone to arrest. Someone to blame." Cam had seen it before when he'd gone in to investigate a major crime. "I just happened to be handy."

"Which brings me to why you didn't let me know you were here," Vakeri said. "We've been looking for your fast cruiser for days."

"I tried." Cam shrugged. "Battle Center offices are gone, and I tried to get into Larga Ways Security, see if I could track down someone from Battle Center, and all I found was a guard perimeter around the building. My next move would have been to use the comms at Gurtain's Song to call Lee and ask him to put me through to you."

"But why? Why not just come in and announce who you were at the entry point?" Fiona asked.

"Because I'd been told there were Tecran spies on the way station, that Larga Ways Security was involved, and that they'd supplied the Vanad with his explosives. I was also told they were looking for Imogen."

There was silence.

"I don't think Imogen is in danger right now. Whoever was involved has gone to ground since Sazo arrived, but it was wise advice." Dav Jallan spoke softly. "Who gave it to you?"

"The Vanad's crew." Cam saw both Vakeri and Jallan's

attention sharpen at that. "It's a long story."

No one said any more as they landed and made their way up to the beautiful apartment that seemed to belong to Fiona Russell. Although for someone who was more or less a slave laborer a week ago, Cam was still trying to work out how.

"Dinner!" Rose walked over to a package lying on a table once they were inside. "No wonder I'm starving. We never had dinner."

Fiona walked past her to the open plan kitchen and took out plates. "Who hasn't eaten?"

It appeared it was just himself, Rose, and Fiona, and both insisted he share their meal, setting the plates around the table.

"I have my eye on that box of chocolates Imogen brought us, but I'd better eat some real food first," Rose told him with a grin.

He could see the similarity with Imogen in every part of her, from her smooth hair to her warm smile, and she became a real person to him, not just the mysterious, powerful figure many in Battle Center saw her as.

He looked up and caught Dav Jallan watching their interaction.

"They look so alike," he offered with a smile, and Jallan's mouth quirked up to one side.

"I've had the benefit of getting to know Fiona over a few days, but you've had them all thrown at you at once."

"And you're a really interesting addition to the mix," Fiona said, looking over at Imogen. "Are you a musician?"

"A music teacher."

"Oh, they are going to eat you up." Rose sounded hugely relieved. "I'll do a gig with you now and then, just to keep the crowds happy, but if you'll take the main role, that will suit me just fine."

"It works for me, too." Fiona pushed away her plate.

"I have a feeling I've been nominated for something I don't really understand." Imogen looked from one woman to the other.

"I think we'd better talk about the Tecran fleet lurking just beyond this system, Oris, Paxe, and the Fitali." Cam cut in smoothly.

There was no question Rose and Fiona were trying to unload the role of music-maker on Imogen, and while he couldn't understand why they didn't want to be music-makers themselves, it would be a travesty if Imogen declined the honor. He was glad he had a good excuse to distract her.

"Yes." Vakeri leaned forward on his forearms. "What can you tell us?"

Cam looked at him, and then Jallan. They'd all met before at Battle Center meetings, although he didn't know either one well. They were sharp and competent, though, good officers to have on his side, so he didn't soften the blow.

"Get ready for war."

***

"Let me get this straight." Admiral Hoke stood before them all on a large screen, and her hard gaze touched each of them one by one. "The Fitali have gone mad, the Tecran have all but declared war, and another Class 5 has joined the Grih?"

Oris had asked Imogen to do the talking on his behalf when Hal Vakeri had set up the link with Battle Center, so she steeled herself to meet the admiral's icy eyes.

"I don't think Oris has joined you, precisely. It's more an enemy of my enemy thing. He wants to help you chase the Tecran out of your territory, and stop them preying on him. But when this is over, it's possible he'll choose to stay."

Hoke's gaze snapped to hers. "Imogen Peters." She tapped a long finger against the table in front of her. "You've had contact with another Class 5, is that right?"

Imogen nodded. "Paxe isn't free, but he's fighting the Tecran's hold as much as possible."

"Will he come over to us if he does get free?"

Imogen hesitated. "I don't know. I think he feels an affection for me, so perhaps it is better to say I don't think he will automatically attack you when he gets free."

Hoke's eyes narrowed. "That's not very reassuring."

Imogen shrugged. "His life is being threatened, and he feels a lot of anger and frustration. Not all his decisions have been good ones as a result."

"Trying to kill Fiona by blowing up Larga Ways being one." Hoke still looked deeply shocked by that.

"He simply chose the path most likely to get a result." She didn't want to defend him, but she could explain him. "That it was wrong is something he accepts now. But at the time, he didn't know any better."

"What has Battle Center heard from the Fitali?" Hal Vakeri's voice was deep and calm, and Imogen turned to look at him.

Like Cam and Dav Jallan, he was big, with dark brown hair tipped with a light copper and the Grih's blue, blue eyes. He was also uncomfortable, she decided, because between Dav, Cam, and himself, they were all the same rank, although he was the only one with a ship of his own.

It made him the de facto leader, but Imogen noted both Cam and Dav kept forgetting that.

"The Fitali still have me waiting for a response." Hoke's face twisted in a cynical smile. "Either they're scrambling for information, or they're planning something, and they're stalling until it happens."

"You think they've joined with the Tecran?" Dav Jallan put his hands behind his back and stood with his feet apart, like he was standing on the deck of a ship.

Hoke tapped a fist on the table. "I don't know. If they have, and if all their ships have the capacity to penetrate the Class 5 shields, then we're looking at a mess." She laughed softly. "A bigger mess, I should say."

"We have no choice but to head for where the Tecran battleship is situated." One of the vice-admirals sitting in the room with Hoke spoke for the first time.

"Agreed, and I think the sooner, the better." Cam was leaning back against Fiona's dining table, his arms crossed over his chest. He looked as tired as she felt. "If the Fitali are involved, it would be better to defeat the Tecran before they have time to arrive."

Behind Hoke on the screen, several senior officers nodded.

"And what does Captain Leto have to say?" Hoke asked Cam.

"Nothing much." He shrugged. "We've previously had a good relationship, but she won't say anything, and has tried to kill Imogen and me a number of times."

"And they say this is about a grahudi?" Another vice-admiral spoke. "Could that really be true, or is it simply an excuse?"

"It's definitely true that they had a pair of scouts looking for the grahudi." Cam tilted his head in that very alien, Grihan way. "But as to whether one stolen creature is worth breaking border treaties and attempting to kill allies, it doesn't make sense, and I really can't understand it."

"We'll put that down as something to investigate, but for now, Oris, Sazo, and the *Illium* will go out to where the Tecran are waiting, and try to rescue the hostages they have, and find out what their intentions are."

"What backup are we going to get?" Dav asked.

"Not Bane," Hoke said. "We can't have all three Class 5s there, in case we're attacked on another front. He's not happy about it, but he understands. We're sending a fleet, but there is no way it will arrive in time to help you."

"Two Class 5s and a battleship doesn't sound like bad odds," Rose said.

"No." Hoke looked at her. "In theory, because they're under investigation for breaching our borders, the United Council has requested and received the location of every large Tecran battleship, and they're watching the ones they can. But some won't be where they'll have said they are and we have no way of knowing if they've declared every battleship they've got. That single Tecran battleship could have been joined by others by now. The Fitali also add a whole new dimension." She turned her gaze on Cam. "What are you going to do with Leto's ship?"

"We'll have to bring it with us. Oris needs to be near it to keep control over it, and it's one more set of weapons for us to use."

"If we weren't suspicious of the Garmman being secret allies with the Tecran, we could ask for their help, given they're our closest neighbor out there, but we just can't risk it." The vice-admiral who spoke sounded deeply frustrated. "It looks like they're telling the truth, and are holding to the United Council treaties, but we're not sure enough of that to let them cross our borders."

Hal gave a nod. "The Garmman councilor we escorted to Larga Ways seems to be firmly in the United Council camp, but we don't have enough eyes out here to make sure the Garmman aren't about to turn on us, as well as concentrate on the Tecran."

"You're leaving immediately?" Hoke asked, and Dav, Hal, and Cam shared a look and all three nodded.

"Well then, may the light of Guimaymi's Star fall upon you." Hoke reached forward, face stern, and the screen went black.

Chapter Thirty-six

"AND THERE THEY ARE."

Cam's voice was quiet as they came out of the light-jump to find a Tecran fleet right in front of them.

From the captain's chair, Imogen turned her attention to the massive screen which gave them a view of space and two huge Levron battleships, three smaller ones, and Paxe.

Dread and fear coalesced in a greasy, cold ball in her gut. "Does Paxe look damaged?"

"No. But they wouldn't want to harm their tool." Sazo's words were bitter.

"Can we reach him? Communicate and find out what happened?" The idea that he might be dead, that the Class 5 they were looking at was an empty shell, was a place she did not want to contemplate going.

"No external comms. It's like that part of his system has been disabled or destroyed." Oris's response was quiet.

"There must be a way around that." Rose was using the same channel as Sazo, so it was as if they were all standing together on the bridge. "What about getting something close enough to reach his internal comms?"

"Like the listening drone Paxe attached to the Levron to find out what they were planning to do to him." Imogen didn't know if it would be possible to communicate with Paxe that way, but at least they'd know what was happening on board.

"It's a good idea, I'll send one off," Oris said.

Cam was standing below Imogen, looking at the screen, and he leaned forward. "Can you zoom in, Oris?"

The Tecran were suddenly close enough to touch. In front of them was a grouping of much smaller craft, and Imogen slid off the captain's chair and walked closer.

"Those are the traders and mining vessels that Paxe allowed to leave."

"And the UC fast cruiser with my crew." Cam pointed it out.

The UC fast cruiser was by far the largest of the vessels huddled together in front of the Tecran fleet, but it was dwarfed by the battleships. It had taken point position, facing the Tecran, with the other ships dotted in a haphazard fashion behind it like bedraggled survivors.

The *Illium* arrived at last from its light-jump, moving into place between Sazo and Oris.

"I'm being hailed." Hal's voice came through the comms.

"I like how they wait for a Grihan ship before they try to talk. What are you and Sazo, chopped liver?" Imogen was insulted on Oris's behalf.

This whole thing seemed so very medieval to her. Sides lining up against each other, a few refugees and hostages in the middle, horse trading and jockeying for advantage. That it was all happening in space, with vessels beyond a medieval knight's imagining, didn't seem to make that much difference.

The knight would have grasped the strategy just fine.

She realized there was silence and turned from the screen to see Cam looking at her, bemused.

"Chopped liver?" Hal Vakeri asked, tentatively, as if he must have misheard.

"Of no account," Rose translated for her, voice laced with amusement. "I'm so very glad you're here, Imogen."

Imogen smiled.

"Let's answer that hail." Dav forced them back to the reality before them.

Imogen frowned as she watched the screen. "Do you see what I'm seeing?"

Cam shook his head. "What?"

"One of the little trading vessels that were there," she pointed to the place on the screen, "has gone."

While she was speaking, another tiny vessel drifted almost nonchalantly to the right, disappearing off the screen.

"They're slipping away, while the Tecran's focus is on us," Cam said. "I'm assuming my team is coordinating this, because the ones on the outer edge are going first."

"The less civilians involved in this the better." Dav, traveling with Rose in Sazo's Class 5, was approving.

"Captain Carro of the Levron battleship *Diatr* is getting impatient." Hal didn't sound particularly concerned.

"We'd better let them talk." Cam's eyes were firmly on the part of the screen that held the small array of hostage vessels.

"Captain Carro." Hal's voice took on a clipped, formal tone.

"Who am I talking to?" The Tecran's voice was calm enough, no sign of the screech they sometimes had when tempers flared. Imogen had heard her fair share of arguments when she'd been on Balco.

"This is Captain Vakeri of the *Illium*. You are in breach of our treaty, being in Grihan territory without permission or cause. Leave immediately."

There was a moment of silence. "There are two Class 5s with you, Captain."

"Yes."

"They are our cause. You have taken them, and we want them back."

"But we haven't taken them," Hal said. "We don't claim any ownership over them at all."

Carro did not answer straight away. "Then why are they here?"

"Sazo has chosen to integrate himself into Grihan society. Oris is here for revenge against you for injuries done to him."

Another silence.

Imogen didn't blame him. The idea of Oris bent on revenge was frightening.

"And the Fitalian battleship?" Carro's voice rose a little.

"That's nothing to do with the Grih." Hal was clearly enjoying himself. "Oris came across it, again, in our airspace, and was able to take control of its systems. I suppose you can consider it an extension of him."

Without warning, a shot was fired from one of the Levron, arcing over the UC fast cruiser and cutting off the surreptitious sneaking of another small trader.

"You do realize that is a United Council vessel, Captain Carro?" Hal's voice was mild, and Imogen admired him for it. "Even firing a warning shot carries consequences."

Cam was riveted to the screen. He would know everyone onboard that ship. His hands curled and uncurled at his side, his arms flexing as if he would like to throw himself into a fight.

He looked magnificent and her heart gave a painful skip.

"How's the listening drone coming along?" she asked Oris

quietly, even though she knew Carro couldn't hear her.

"Still half an hour until it locks on to Paxe's hull. If the Tecran don't see it and destroy it before then."

"How likely is that?" Cam half-turned away from the screen, as if he couldn't look any more.

"It depends on whether they——"

"We have an incoming message from Eazi and Fiona." Sazo's voice spoke over Oris's.

"I've cut Captain Carro off, so you can talk freely," Oris told Hal.

"Fiona?" Hal couldn't hide his fear.

He'd fought for her to stay behind, and Imogen knew it was because he thought she'd be safer there. He'd only won because Eazi had come down on his side. They'd both convinced Fiona she would be able to help more on Larga Ways, keeping watch on what was happening on Balco, which seemed to have become the center of this strange battle.

"I'm afraid we have a problem." Fiona appeared on the screen. She angled her body, and pointed upward.

Two massive Fitalian battleships dominated the lens feed above the gel dome.

"They aren't friendly," Eazi said. "I can confirm that they both have weapons locked onto the way station."

***

"Oris, put me through to Captain Leto. Visual comms."

Cam could see the battleships above Larga Ways were the same type as the one Leto commanded.

That they would send three of their best ships after a single grahudi did not make sense. So there was something else going on. They were acting for the Tecran——it was the only logical conclusion——but Cam knew Leto. Knew she'd been outraged at the revelations of the Tecran's Class 5 project, of their abduction of advanced sentient life, and at their incursion into Grihan territory two months ago.

She had not been acting. He was sure of it.

Which meant she would not be comfortable with what the Fitali were doing now. That she had been ordered to shoot him had to have gone against everything she professed.

"Suri." He bowed when Oris connected them, using Leto's first name, just to remind her of the meals they'd shared together at UC headquarters.

"Captain Kalor." Her voice was cool and professional, keeping the distance between them.

"What is going on?" Cam tried to relax his stance, asking as if he were enquiring about the health of a mutual friend.

Leto went stiff. "Why are you asking?"

"I'm asking because there are two Fitali battleships ranged over Larga Ways, weapons hot. And before they submit their demands, and are unable to take anything back, I thought I'd try and help them."

Leto jerked as if she'd been shot. "One moment." She leaned forward and turned off the screen, but he could hear a low murmur in the background.

"Can you make out what they're saying?" he asked Oris quietly. He was very aware of Imogen standing just to one side, out of lens view, her eyes on him.

He looked over at her, and she held his gaze, solemn and quiet. He had wanted her to stay on Larga Ways with Fiona. Had argued with her about it, and only given in when both she and Oris had reminded him that if Paxe was with the Tecran fleet, she would be the only one he would trust.

Now he wanted to hold her close and kiss her in relief that she had refused to listen to him.

Not that she was much better off facing the Tecran, but she had more chance in Oris than under Larga Ways' gel dome. And he was here, and he wasn't letting her out of his sight.

"Captain Leto thinks she's switched off audio and visual comms, forgetting I control her bridge. I've allowed her to send a communication to her leaders in the Horde. She must know I can hear what's being said, but she's obviously decided to take that chance to find out what's going on. And it suits us to know what they have to say." Oris must have reactivated the visual comms, because they saw Leto turned slightly to the left, looking up as if addressing someone on a screen above head height.

"What are they saying?"

Leto did not look happy. Cam had never seen her so upset. But she needed to argue less, to hurry. Those battleships above Larga Ways were going to make a move soon.

"Apparently, the Tecran have got proof of something the Fitali are doing on Huy. They're using it to extort support."

"Something the Tecran discovered when they were there stealing the grahudi?" Imogen frowned.

"Even more than that. From what I'm hearing, they stole some information when they took the grahudi. The notes and observations of a team of scientists on Huy. When the Fitali realized what had been taken, they went looking for the grahudi in the hope that the information would be in the same place. But the scouts were captured, and the grahudi seems to have disappeared. Now the Tecran are demanding they give them assistance or the Fitali will be exposed."

"What were they doing on Huy?" Cam tried to think of what the rigid, ordered Fitali could be guilty of.

"Whatever it is, they think it will shock their own people, and it may get them suspended from the United Council. They're facing massive loss of face and shame." Oris paused. "The Tecran have demanded they hold Larga Ways to ransom in return for myself and Sazo being handed over."

"But . . ." Imogen looked at him with big eyes, "the Grih can't hand Oris and Sazo over. Even if they wanted to, they don't have any power to do it."

"And we will not go." Oris was implacable.

Cam realized his hands were in tight fists. They would have to find another way out of this. Hal would be listening to this, Dav, too, and they would all know the stakes.

Either they found a way to bring the Fitali over, or they were looking at the start of a war.

Leto said something sharp and angry, and then turned back to the screen, reached out as if to turn it on, and then seemed to realize it already was.

She blinked. "You heard that?" She didn't waste time being angry about it.

"We did. What do they have on you, Suri?" Over the last day, Cam had felt angry at Leto, disappointed, and confused, but now he realized sympathy was uppermost.

She looked devastated. Whatever front she'd put up before when they'd run into each other behind Gu-gijeron had vanished. Now she simply seemed beaten down.

"It was a group of four scientists at the Huy outpost. They began as a team sent to evaluate the likely success of making Huy habitable for the Fitali. Our numbers are growing, and we can

terra-form plenty of the planets in our territory, but Huy already
had a wide array of life, which always means the terra-form is
quicker and more efficient."

"What happened?" Cam asked.

"They decided to run a test. It wasn't approved, and I'm not
sure why they did it. They thought they would be vindicated by
their results, perhaps? It's inexplicable, but there's no denying
they began experimenting. And the organisms on Huy reacted."

"The grahudi," Imogen breathed the word, and although Leto
couldn't see her on the lens feed, she turned in the direction of
Imogen's voice.

"The grahudi," she confirmed, grim. "They have a fast life
cycle, and they changed rapidly, seemed to advance in ways that
took the scientists by surprise." She shook her head. "They'd
always been predators, but they became super-predators. And the
scientists found that out first hand." She looked down at her feet.
Then looked up again, and Cam could see the anger in her eyes.
"Every single one of them was killed."

"It was weeks before someone realized the team wasn't
answering comms, hadn't reported in. When a new team got
there, they found the terra-forming tech running without any
oversight, the grahudi elevated at least to the level of crude tools,
and not a single Fitali alive."

"And there was your problem. If the grahudi were coming into
advanced sentience, you couldn't take the planet for the Fitali."
The irony of it was incredible. Cam caught Leto's gaze and she
nodded.

"The problem is, Huy is perfect. The terra-forming did its job.
But now we had the grahudi running amok, starting to speak in a
type of sign language, and forming communities."

"The Sentient Being Agreement meant you had to leave the
planet alone."

"The Sentient Being Agreement would have damned us for
artificially advancing the grahudi, as well." Leto shrugged. "It was
a disaster whichever way you looked at it. Until . . ." She shook
her head. "Until they realized the grahudi were killing each other
off."

"They were going to war with each other?" Cam tried to grasp
it.

"As the terra-forming took hold, it started changing the

environment faster than the grahudi could keep up. Resources they needed became scarcer and scarcer, and they started killing each other to survive. Someone high up in the Horde decided to wait it out."

"Let them kill each other off, and then the last few would die when the terra-forming was complete?" Imogen spoke again, and this time, she stepped into the lens frame.

"Yes." Leto eyed her curiously. "We managed to shoot a tracking chip into most of them, but the Tecran stole one, along with a console containing most of the information I've just given you."

"Have they shown you proof that they have this information still?" Imogen asked Leto.

Cam turned to look at her, surprised.

"No. But we know they have it."

"They don't have the grahudi anymore. It was killed when the Tecran's facility was destroyed by one of the Class 5s."

Leto nodded. "One of the battleships above Larga Ways has confirmed the facility is gone, and the tracker was destroyed, so we're sure the grahudi is dead, but the Tecran insist the Class 5 that stole the grahudi never sent the consol down with it to the facility. They still have it."

"Which Class 5 was it?" Cam felt his heart beat faster. If it was Oris, the information could be right here.

"Paxe," Imogen told him, remembering that Oris had said it wasn't him, which meant Paxe was the only one left. She went very still and then looked straight at him, eyes wide. "I think I know where that consol is."

Chapter Thirty-seven

"WHAT IF I TOLD YOU THE TECRAN don't actually have access to that consol?" Imogen watched Leto's face, but the Fitali was so difficult to read.

She had considered asking Oris to cut the Fitali captain off while she discussed this with the others, but they didn't have the time.

Leto closed her eyes, opened them. "We would be interested to hear what you have to say."

"I've been on the Class 5 which took your grahudi, and I know where the consol is hidden."

Cam was standing close to her, his shoulder brushing hers as she moved, and she knew the moment he understood what she was talking about. The look he sent her was piercing.

"You mean, I take it, hidden from the Tecran?" Leto sounded confused.

"The Class 5 is run by a thinking system, Paxe, who is at war with the Tecran who are trying to control him. He knew the consol was important to them, that they were using it to further their aims. Paxe wants to thwart them in any way he can, so he hid it. I watched the Tecran hunt for it and come up empty, and I know it is safe. They will never find it."

Leto was silent again. "I'd like to believe you. The Fitali Horde does not like to be forced into anything, and especially not to act against our treaties." She turned to look at her senior officers, then back to Cam and Imogen. "I'll take this to my leaders, but it'll be hard to convince them with no proof."

"The grahudi is gone, and I promise you the consol is not in the Tecran's hands, whatever they want you to believe. Ask them to show it to you. Not just the physical item, which I'm assuming can be duplicated, but the information contained in it. They won't be able to."

"They could have copied the information," Leto said.

Imogen shook her head. "Then they wouldn't have been so

desperate to find the original. I think they found it, saw what was on it, and put it in their store. When they decided to use it to gain your support they couldn't, because Paxe had killed his crew and run away. And when they did manage to board him, they couldn't find it. I witnessed that myself."

"I did, too." Cam looked Leto straight in the eye. "I saw them search the store, and I saw their fury when they realized Paxe had hidden it."

"Your word will carry more weight than the orange's," Leto said, satisfied, and then took a step back.

Imogen frowned, then saw the cause. Cam was glaring at the Fitali captain.

"No offense meant," Leto told her. "But my leaders know Captain Kalor. He has a good reputation in the United Council."

"Talk to your people, Captain Leto." Cam was suddenly all formality. "It would be a pity if you threw yourselves into war based on a Tecran trick."

Leto opened her mouth as if to say something, then shook her head and bowed. "I agree. I will be as fast as I can." She leaned forward again, and the screen went black.

"What's happening on Larga Ways?" Hal spoke for the first time, and the screen switched back to Fiona.

"Sazo kept us linked in, so we heard all that," Fiona's smile was fierce. "Imogen, you might have saved this way station. The Fitali have pulled back a little, and the weapons are no longer hot. My guess is they've been told to hold in place, but not make any threats or overt moves."

"They'll be able to claim they came to our aid if they keep quiet for a bit longer," Hal agreed.

"Do we let them get away with that?" Dav asked, and Imogen could hear the anger in his voice.

"To the outside world, yes," Cam said. "But behind closed doors? I think Admiral Hoke and the leaders of the four planets will have quite a lot to say."

"What about Carro?" Rose asked. "Isn't he surprised we cut off comms and haven't gotten back to him?"

"He'll know we know about the Fitali converging on Larga Ways. I think he's giving us time to work out our response." Hal Vakeri sounded calm, but Imogen had the sense it was calm of a dangerous kind.

"What happens if Leto's commander decides not to risk it?" Rose posed the question Imogen was thinking.

She noticed Oris and Sazo hadn't said anything since Oris had made it clear neither would hand themselves over to the Tecran, no matter what the consequences to the Grih and Larga Ways.

It was their right, and they had no obligation to submit to slavery again for any reason, but she guessed they wished there was another way.

And maybe she had found one.

"Captain Leto is having difficulty persuading her superiors," Oris said into the quiet.

"Break into their conversation, and let's talk to them direct." Cam put his hand on her lower back, rubbing as if to ease an ache for her, but it was his outlet for his anger and agitation, she realized, his calm revealed for the lie it was as he clenched the fabric of her shirt in a fist.

"I think that would be best." Sazo spoke for the first time, and he sounded angry, too.

The Fitali might give a thought to who they were pissing off.

"Patching you through . . . now." Oris's voice was a whisper in her ear.

"High Chief Vaw?" Cam's words were clipped, irritated.

There was an abrupt silence. "Is this Captain Kalor? Because ———"

"Listen to me." Cam forced his hand flat against her back again, and Imogen could feel the struggle for control. "We have one of your ships. It is ours unless you do not take this very seriously. We're offering you a way out. The Tecran do not have what they say they have. It is safe. I vouch for this personally. But even if it were not, can you honestly say what you are being asked to do to Larga Ways and Balco will have any less repercussions than what you're trying to cover up?"

"You think I don't know that?" Vaw snapped. "The problem is these orders come from Vice-Admiral Ipsos. His son was one of the scientists who was in the original four, the ones who started this mess. The posthumous reputation of his only child, and his need for revenge against the grahudi, led him down this path, and now he faces a humiliating end to what was otherwise seen as an illustrious career. Personal reputation is coming before national interest. If any Fitali on the home planet knew of this, they would be outraged, and the Horde is walking a fine line between political expediency and not making this any worse."

"Then put your mind at rest. The Tecran no longer have the consol. You will have to deal with us when this is over, and believe me when I say you will pay for this in ways that will make Ipsos regret his choices, but you will get out of it with your reputation and your public honor intact."

Vaw waited a beat. "What do you want us to do?"

"The battleships can stay where they are, but focus their weapons outward. You're protecting Larga Ways at Battle Center's request while we deal with the Tecran fleet."

"And the consol?" Vaw was tenacious, Imogen would give him that.

"If we can get it, it will be returned to you." Cam qualified the promise carefully.

"And if you can't get it?"

"No one else will be able to, either."

More silence. "Agreed."

"Fiona? Eazi?" Hal spoke the moment Vaw signed off.

"They're pulling further back," Eazi said. "And yes, weapons have gone outward."

"So what do we say to Carro?" Rose asked, satisfaction clear in her tone.

"We let Captain Carro think we're prepared to sacrifice Larga Ways," Hal said, a vicious edge to his words. "Let him get his head around that."

They waited for Oris to connect, and this time, he gave a visual of the Tecran captain. He looked smug.

"Captain Carro." Hal said nothing else.

"You ready to accede now?" Carro stretched his mouth wide in what Imogen had come to learn was an aggressive display.

"Accede?" Hal pretended confusion.

Carro narrowed his eyes. "Don't play games, Vakeri. You know by now the Fitali are on our side. Hand over the Class 5s or our allies will destroy Larga Ways and fire on Balco."

"I don't know how many times I can say it, but the Class 5s are not ours to hand over. You've failed to engage with them once since we light-jumped here, but perhaps you need to start doing so. I have no power to make them do anything."

"Enough." Carro's chest swelled, and Imogen heard the hint of a screech. "We are serious."

Imogen couldn't see Hal, the screen showed Carro, but she could picture him lifting up his hands.

"I cannot give you what I do not have. Do I want you to destroy Larga Ways? Of course not. It would be a war crime and both you and the Fitali will be cut from the UC for it. For even making the threat, I should think. But I cannot do a thing to save it if you are determined to fire on it, because I cannot give you the Class 5s."

Carro looked like he was having an apoplexy. Imogen found it deeply gratifying.

The Tecran captain turned and said something, and Oris switched suddenly to the lens feed of the Tecran fleet before them.

"He has ordered them to shoot . . ." Oris trailed off.

A shot was fired from the Levron at the hostage vessels, but unlike the first time, this was no warning shot.

A small, bulky miner was hit and disintegrated in a flare of bright light.

Imogen lifted both hands to her mouth, pressed them hard against her lips to stop any sound coming out.

Cam was absolutely still.

They all stared at the tiny pieces of debris floating away in silence. Oris switched back to the Levron's bridge.

"How serious do you think I am now, Captain Vakeri?" Carro turned to face the lens again. "Still say there is no way to give me what I want?"

Oris cut him off, making the screen black, and still, no one said a word.

"Oris, do you have an explorer drone like the one Paxe gave us?" Cam's face, when he turned it up to the speaker, was one of stone cold fury.

"Yes."

"And some space survivors? I'm not sure what the Tecran call them."

"They use the term space survivors, too. I have enough for every member of the crew who used to serve on this Class 5. Space time is ten hours."

"I'll take fifty in the explorer. How quickly can you have them loaded?"

"Are you sure about this, Cam?" Hal asked what Imogen could

not get past her throat.

"We can't leave them there." Cam looked at her as he answered. "And we can't ask Oris and Sazo to give themselves up. If we can get everyone off the hostage ships, that will give them a chance and will mean the Tecran have no leverage. As long as everyone takes beacons to activate later when it's safe, we can find them again."

"Do you want me to come with you?" As Imogen said it, she realized that wouldn't work. She understood why he was shaking his head. He'd need every bit of space in the explorer to fit in whatever the space survivors were, and if there was anyone ill or injured, he'd need room for them, too.

"The explorer is loaded." Oris sounded subdued.

Cam held out his hand, and she took it, jogged with him down to the launch bay.

"Just try to come back in one piece," she said when he pulled her in for a hard, tight hug. She kissed the side of his neck, and then his lips as he bent his head.

He rested his forehead against hers. "Stay safe." He released her. "I'm going to assume they'll be listening for any comms, so I won't make contact at all."

She stood to one side as he climbed into the explorer, packed with compact boxes the size of briefcases. He hesitated in the doorway before closing it, and she forced herself to stay still as the door came down and the thin, black dust of the launch bay swirled as the explorer lifted and disappeared through the gel wall.

"He is risking his life for those people," Oris said.

"Yes, he is."

"Do you think I should be doing the same? Giving myself up for them?"

Imogen shook her head. "Even if you do give yourselves up, do you honestly think they'll let everyone go?"

Oris's silence had the air of surprise. "No. Because you're witnesses to their crimes."

Imogen nodded.

"You have made me feel better, Imogen. Thank you."

Imogen reached out and patted the drone that must have loaded the explorer with the space survivors. "That you thought to ask the question is just as appreciated——"

"The listening device has just attached to Paxe, and he's hailing us." Oris interrupted her with a shout of glee.

"He's encrypted the message," Sazo said. "The Tecran will know he's communicating with us, but they won't know what he's saying."

"They'll try to stop him, though." There was a little hitch in her chest at the thought.

"They'll look for the device and try to destroy it, yes. If they use a maintenance pod to check the exterior, we probably have a little time because they'll have to do a manual scan."

"Are you able to decrypt it?" Rose asked.

"He's sent a message only another Class 5 could decrypt, but it will still take a little——Got it!" Sazo's excitement was catching.

"Paxe says the captain and his officer are no longer in his lock-safe. The Tecran managed to get more teams onboard and they've destroyed all the drones, so he couldn't keep them pinned down there anymore. The Tecran onboard are looking for the Fitali notes they stole, and they've disabled his engines so he can't run away from them again."

"He has a request for you, Imogen." Oris's voice was hesitant.

"What is it?"

"He says, if you are up for it, he will trust you enough."

Imogen sucked in a breath, pivoted on her heel and started to pace. "Does he think I can get in there undetected?"

"If you can get in, he can keep you safe, he says. Now that there are no drones for him to use, they've restored the lens feed systems in most parts of the ship. And he can tell you where everyone is using the earpiece I gave you earlier. He can direct you to the lock-safe."

"But he can't go anywhere with his engines disabled."

"No," Oris agreed. "But they wouldn't have destroyed the engines, they'll need them to leave later, so he can see what they've done, try to fix them, and he'll have the ability to use his weapons. While he's still under their control, he can't fire on them. That changes as soon as he's free."

She thought about it. "If you can get me there, then——"

"I want to let you know I've cut off comms to Dav and Hal." Sazo interrupted her. "Rose can hear us, though. When Rose and I saved Bane, I got Rose onboard using a maintenance pod. They're identical for all Class 5s, and the system can't tell which ship they're from. This works even better if they've let a number of maintenance pods out to search for the listening drone clamped to Paxe's side. If they see you, they'll think you're one of theirs."

"So I go across to Paxe in a maintenance pod?" Imogen thought back to the distance between them and the Tecran fleet. "Wouldn't it take too long?"

"It would," Oris agreed. "But not if I moved forward toward the Tecran. They'll think I'm handing myself over, and when I get close enough, you can drop out of a maintenance hatch. Hopefully my subsequent withdrawal will hold their attention equally well."

"That would work." Sazo's voice was soft.

"It's dangerous, Imogen. Are you sure you want to do this?" Rose's voice was just as quiet, and Imogen remembered Dav couldn't hear their side of the conversation. She heard him asking Rose for clarification in the background.

"I'm afraid, but I'll do it. What are the alternatives? The Tecran might decide to kill more hostages at any time, and Cam is right there." She took a breath. "We know they'll do that anyway if you and Sazo do turn yourselves over, and even if they decide to retreat, they will try to take some of us with them. Most likely, they'll aim at the *Illium* and there are hundreds of crew onboard. At least freeing Paxe gives us all a better chance, besides being the only right thing to do."

"Agreed." That's what Imogen liked about Sazo, he made no attempt to prevaricate.

"What about taking over the Levron's systems?" Rose asked. "Sazo did that once before."

"We've both been trying since we got here," Sazo told her. "They've learned at least some lessons since the battle we had with them two months ago. They have made their systems very difficult to breach."

"Sounds like there really is only one choice." Imogen took a deep, steadying breath. "Let Paxe know I'm coming."

Chapter Thirty-eight

HAL AND DAV CAME BACK ONLINE with grumpy silence.

"I didn't cut you off, Sazo did," Imogen heard Rose say through her earpiece as she lowered herself into the maintenance pod. "Don't get cross with *me*."

"Perhaps you'd like to share what was said." Dav was clearly trying to keep a hold of his temper.

"Oris is going to move toward the Tecran fleet. He's not giving himself up, he's just getting Imogen close enough to Paxe so she can board him." Sazo's tone was cool, as if he didn't like Dav's tone.

"What?" Hal choked out the word. "What happens when they realize you aren't handing yourself over?"

"I'll move back. Just use the line it's nothing to do with you." Oris sounded quite cheerful.

He was going to enjoy messing with the Tecran's minds.

"Moving now," he said.

The plan was that he was going to move around the hostages, come close to Paxe before he stopped directly in front of Carro's Levron.

He'd eject the pod as he passed Paxe, giving her the shortest travel time possible.

The pod sealed closed, and she gripped her electric whip tight. She wondered if they'd pass Cam, wondered what he would think was happening when he saw Oris moving to engage the Tecran.

It would be a good distraction for him, as well as her.

"Nearly there," Oris told her, and her heart started beating faster. "In three, two, one . . ."

The pod shot out of its maintenance chute, and for a moment, Imogen had the disconcerting sensation of tumbling through space as the pod spun.

She closed her eyes, and when she opened them again, they were steady, heading for a massive black wall.

Oris had gotten her really close to Paxe.

She craned her neck and saw Oris come to a smooth halt in front of the Levron. The flat, elliptical battleship's shields shimmered in response and then Paxe must have grabbed hold of the pod because she was pulled in through the small gel wall of the maintenance hatch.

"Imogen." Paxe's voice was soft in her ear.

"Paxe. Are you okay?"

"I am more okay now. Thank you for coming."

"I told you I'd help you." She was whispering, even though the pod was still closed, but as soon as it came to a stop, the lid lifted and she scrambled out. "Let's go."

"No one nearby. There are thirty crew onboard, and this ship is built for five hundred, so we have a good chance of you going unseen. Go left when you step into the passageway."

She ran until she got to a junction, and waited.

"You need to turn right, but there is someone in the passage you need to be in, so wait. And . . . he's gone. Go."

She tried to make as little noise as possible as she ran right, turned when Paxe instructed, and then reached the stairwell.

"You need to go up one floor, then left again."

She needed to catch her breath when she reached the right floor, leaning against the wall until her pulse was steady again.

"We're nearly there." Paxe couldn't help the excitement in his voice. "There is no one around, you can step out now."

She did, moving cautiously along the corridor.

A door slid open in the middle of the long wall to her right, and she flinched at the stench coming from the tiny room.

Two Tecran had been holed up in the room for weeks and it smelled like it. They'd done nothing to clean it.

It was foul.

She looked carefully before stepping in, but as she did, a blaring alarm sounded from above the door.

She leaned back, saw a small raised, circular attachment the same color as the wall.

"A motion sensor alarm?" She asked Paxe.

"Must have done it after they destroyed the drones." Paxe's voice was no longer excited. "Imogen, you need to get out of here."

"Okay." She took a deep step past the debris near the door and grabbed the silver chain hanging from the end of Paxe, pulled him out and then hopped back into the passage. "Which way?"

"You . . . did it."

"Yes, which way?"

"Right." He sounded almost dreamy. "They're coming."

"What can you do?"

"Almost . . . nothing." He still sounded shell-shocked. "I think they've been disabling everything in preparation for having to pull me out of the slot themselves."

"The weapons?"

"No. Looks like they're disabled. They've been clever. I thought it was just the engines. They've been feeding my systems false data. I can start repairs now, but all the ways I could disable them, like air loss, or shutting them inside rooms, are gone . . ."

From behind her, Imogen could hear the sound of thunderous boots.

"How close?" She couldn't help the hitch in her breath.

"Go left. Left!"

Imogen swerved left, saw out of the corner of her eye a Tecran soldier running past the end of the passage she'd been on scramble to a stop, turn and run after her.

"Shit, shit, shit," she sang under her breath. The end of the passageway was coming up fast. "Left or right?"

There was no response.

"Paxe, left or right?" She was running out of corridor.

"Neither are good." He was almost whispering.

"Which is the least bad?" She pulled up short as she reached the end, looked over her shoulder to see the Tecran bearing down on her, shockgun raised. She reached back for her whip for the first time.

"Right."

She dropped her hand and spun right, using the lower gravity to jump away, and felt the brush of the shockgun fire across her back. She sent a silent thank you to Paxe for the Cargassey fabric as she landed and ran on.

"What's the bad news about this direction?" Adrenalin had given her feet wings to start with, but now she was finding it difficult to talk, breathe, and run. And the sound of running was still behind her, getting closer all the time.

"Five Tecran up ahead. They're finishing up reactivating the self-destruct device I disabled when I broke partially free. And they know you're coming."

"And the better news?"

"They aren't soldiers, they're technicians."

"Not armed?" That would be nice. She reached back for her whip again, this time pulled it out.

The crystal Paxe was in was gripped in her left hand, the chain wrapped around her closed fist. She tightened her hold, and felt it dig into her palm.

"Not armed," he confirmed. "And coming up . . . now."

She raised her arm, turned the corner and brought it down, then skidded to a stop as blue light arced and danced in front of her, bringing down a wave of bodies.

The sound of pursuit was so close, she jumped over one of the techs as he hit the floor of what was some kind of engine room, heading deeper in.

"I need help, Paxe." She made for a metal-covered box large enough to hide behind, blocking her from sight.

Paxe had seemed shell-shocked since she'd pulled him out of the slot, and she guessed it was his first taste of freedom, heady and disorienting, especially as the Tecran seemed to have done the equivalent of cutting off most of his limbs.

"I can't think." He sounded panicked.

"Okay, let's calm down. Where am I?" She moved again, crouching behind a smaller piece of equipment.

"The secondary engine room, where the light-jump tech is situated."

"Is one of the things they messed with your ability to light-jump?" She spoke in a whisper.

"Yes, and they can trigger the self-destruct if they want to. They might, because I'm free. They have nothing to lose." His panic was making him talk faster.

"No. They'll use that as a last resort." She kept her words slow, hoping that would help him slow down, too. "While I'm onboard, they can still theoretically get you back."

"The moment they think that chance is gone, they'll push the button."

"Will they?" Imogen didn't think so. "Depends who has the button. If it's someone onboard this ship, then no. They'll want to get well clear first."

"Oh." He sounded astonished. "I'd forgotten that. But I don't know who has it. I didn't even know they were reactivating it."

The sounds behind her told her the soldiers chasing her had found the unconscious techs, and then there was silence.

She imagined them spreading out, cautious now they knew she was armed in some way.

That's right, assholes. Be afraid. Be very afraid.

She angled toward a huge piece of machinery, crab-walking to keep herself low. There was the ring of a boot connecting to something metallic, and she used the sound to rise up a little and run the last few feet bent at the waist.

There was nowhere left to go.

She looked at the curved wall of the back of the room in despair and then the lights went out. She closed her eyes and gave the Tecran some credit. If they had night-vision goggles, or the alien equivalent, she was at a huge disadvantage. And the light display of her whip would show up nicely, too.

"What next?" She breathed it, soft as an exhale.

"I want to kill them all." Paxe's voice sent a chill through her. "It was a mistake to ask you to come. I didn't know how much damage they'd done. I can't even turn on the lights."

She heard movement to her left, and opened her eyes. She could see a little better now, light from the passageway meant it wasn't fully dark. A dark shadow detached itself from the black blob that was a squat engine block, and she had the sense the soldier turned his head and looked at her.

Standing watching her, as if bemused.

Just like that, in one drawn out moment, she was back in her 'go out with a bang' mindset.

She'd developed attachments. Cam. The thought of him was warm and enveloping as a hug. As edgy and exciting as a lover's caress. Fiona, Rose. Oris and Paxe. She had a new future to lose. And if she was going to lose it, at the very least, she would make some of the Tecran very much regret involving her. Again.

She flicked the whip, not the big arm movement she'd done up 'til now, but a twist of her wrist.

A single line of blue, searing in its brightness, lashed out. There was a sizzle of electric energy, and the sound of the Tecran going down.

His shockgun fell forward, clattering on the floor and sliding up against the wall. She tried to make it out in the gloom, pondering the wisdom of trying to grab it.

She hadn't even held a shockgun, had no idea how they worked. She decided not to risk it and carefully stepped over the unconscious body, gaze to her right, where she thought the next soldier would be coming from.

Paxe was blind as her, but she wished he'd talk to her anyway. Tension wound tighter and tighter in her, and she ducked behind the engine block with relief.

"Imogen!" Paxe's shout in her ear made her swallow back a scream, and then a body slammed into hers.

A Tecran with a helmet on pinned her to the solid metal surface. He ground her right arm into the block with his body, and she forced herself to tighten her grip on the whip despite the pain.

He tried to grab her left hand, and she realized with a sudden, deep panic that they knew she was holding Paxe in her fist.

Her left arm was more mobile as he levered his weight against her right side to try and get hold of her hand.

She threw her arm outward, avoiding his grasp.

"Throw me." Paxe sounded as panicked as she felt. "Imogen, you have nothing to lose. Throw me."

She threw him. Under the circumstances, it was the best she could do, with no way to get any wind up, and she heard the crystal hit the floor with a ting of sound and skitter away.

The Tecran eased back, head turning almost 180 degrees as he searched for where it had gone.

It meant her right arm was free. It was free, and she lifted her hand up and flicked it down.

Blue light enveloped the Tecran's feet and danced its way up, and she shoved him as his head snapped back, so he fell like a downed tree away from her.

"Where did you go?" she asked, no longer caring about giving herself away.

"I don't know. Don't worry. Get out of here."

But she wasn't leaving him. She hadn't risked everything to abandon him now.

She moved forward, still in the dark, and then flicked the whip again, trying to see what was illuminated by it, but the light was too bright. It blinded her.

She heard another Tecran go down, and decided she had the makings of a strategy on her hands.

Just whip until there was no one left.

She raised her arm again, and the shockgun fire hit her shoulder, punching her back a step, although the Cargassey fabric absorbed most of the blow.

And then she was under serious fire, most of it coming from the direction she was sure Paxe had landed.

She brought the whip down again, but the fire kept coming.

Some of them where either out of range or had cover.

"Go!" Paxe shouted in her ear again. "Even if you find me, how will you get off alive? Go, go, go."

She didn't want to. She brought the whip down again, and then dropped it as pain seared her right hand. She'd been hit and it felt as if her hand had been taken off. Even if she could find the whip in the dark, she didn't think she could pick it up.

"Please, go."

She headed for the light, arm tucked by her side, trying to keep her breathing even.

Her hand was on fire.

She was hit twice in the back as she leapt over the techs she'd brought down earlier and like a moth to the flame, headed for the brightly-lit passage, but then she was out and running, left arm holding her right tight to her body.

She felt the chill of her skin, the nasty prickle of sweat as she ran. Shock. She could not go into shock.

"On the right." Paxe's voice was tinny, far away in her head, but she swerved obediently right, found herself inside a tube.

She pushed up against the wall, half crouching as she put her head between her knees.

One second. Two.

The doors opened.

"Left. Now."

She staggered out. Got some kind of rhythm back. "What about you? What's happening?"

"They turned the lights on. They're still looking for me."

It wouldn't be long, she guessed. They'd find him soon enough.

"What are you going to do?"

"What I planned all along if this happened. Imogen, you need to run faster."

She'd slowed to a dragging sort of Igor limp, she realized, and forced herself to move again.

"Last turn," he told her. "There on the left."

A door opened and she stepped inside. Found she was back in the maintenance bay. She fell into the pod, and the lid closed with a snap before she'd even buckled herself in.

She couldn't buckle herself in, she realized. Her hand wouldn't work. So she wriggled into the inclined chair as best she could and lay back, panting. The sudden acceleration as Paxe shot her out of the maintenance hatch jostled her, and she had to bite her lip to stop herself crying out.

The pod didn't drift when it left the ship. It moved away at a steady rate. She caught a glimpse of the Levron to Paxe's right, and never felt smaller or more insignificant. Oris was nowhere to be seen, so at least he must have managed to get back to the others safely.

"Talk to me, Paxe."

"They found me." He seemed calmer now. The panic was gone.

"What are they going to do? Put you back in the lock-safe?" She closed her eyes, and breathed through the pain as feeling started coming back to her hand one agonizing, fire ant bite at a time.

"I think they're going to try." Paxe paused. "They're walking back to it with me now."

"Paxe, I'm so sorry." Tears escaped her closed lids, running down into her hair. "I failed you."

"You didn't fail me. You did more for me than anyone I ever met. Risked your life for me, when all I'd planned for you was to kill you."

"You didn't understand." She whispered it, wondering what she could do to make this right.

"I didn't understand," he agreed. "But now I do. I know why the slave girl saved Ali Baba. She wanted to belong somewhere."

She fought back a sob, unable to say a word.

"I'm sorry, Imogen. I would have liked to——" He made a sound, like an animal caught in a trap. "They've reached the lock-safe and I've waited as long as I can. I hope you're far enough away."

Her eyes snapped open. "Far enough away?"

She had to lift up on her left arm to see out, and saw the

hostage ships were just in front of her, that Paxe had sent her away as fast as the pod would go.

"They should never have reconnected the self-destruct." There was a vicious, grim satisfaction in his voice. And then he exploded.

Or imploded, perhaps, was the better way to describe it.

It was as if the massive ball of the Class 5 contracted, scrunching in on itself, and then, when there was nowhere left to go, it blew outward, a rage of light and heat and force.

Imogen felt her pod being picked up and tossed like a piece of driftwood on a raging sea.

And as she slammed into the lid above her, she saw the ball of flame engulf her before the world went dark.

Chapter Thirty-nine

AT LAST, IT WAS THE FAST CRUISER'S TURN.

Ever since he'd seen Oris come forward as if to give himself up, and then after a long wait in front of the Levron, arc elegantly up and away to slide into place bracketing the *Illium*, he'd felt the pressure of time slipping away.

If Oris had done it to draw attention away from what Cam was doing, it was a gesture Cam appreciated.

He piloted the explorer into the launch bay, pleased to be coming in to a space he knew would be big enough.

He'd scraped the sides more than once in the last hour, only just fitting in to some of the traders. But every single one had been happy to see him, had pulled on the space survivors, and headed away from the fight. Even the Vanad's crew had greeted him like a friend. And he supposed he was the best friend they had right now.

Pren was waiting for him, shockgun raised as he opened the door.

Her look of surprise was priceless, and as he stepped up to her, she got him in a soldier's one-arm hug, and slapped his back a few times.

"It is very good to see you, sir." She had a massive grin on her face.

"Vraen driving you mad?" Cam reached back into the explorer and took out a stack of space survivors, handed them to Pren.

She let out a snigger. "Yes, sir. Space survivors?" Her tone turned to confusion.

"You need to not be a hostage anymore, Pren. We can't give the Tecran what they're demanding, so if they decide to shoot another vessel, or all of them, it would be better if there was no one onboard."

The beauty of working with someone with the same training and background was how quickly they caught on.

Pren counted the boxes in her arms. "Three more will be

enough."

He grabbed three more, and when he turned, Diot was in the launch bay, too, Olan and Vraen right behind her.

"Where did you even come from?" The Bukarian asked as she enveloped him in a tight hug.

"One of the Class 5s next to the *Illium*." He started handing out the space survivors. "Can you get the rest of the crew?" he asked Pren, and still smiling, she set her boxes down and left.

"Get the crew for what?" Vraen took a space survivor and then frowned down at it as if he'd never seen one before.

"You need to get off this ship now. As quickly as possible." Cam watched Olan open his box. Was it his imagination, or did the elderly scientist look even more frail than he had.

"Olan, there is room for one extra person in my explorer. Perhaps it's best you come with me."

The Fitalian looked up, and Cam saw his hands were trembling a little. "I think that might be best." Olan smiled. "It is good to see you, Cam. We were worried about you."

"You expect us to go through the gel wall in space survivors?" Vraen's tone, after the gratitude and quick action of every single other hostage, made something hot and corrosive rise up inside Cam's chest.

He had left Imogen to do this. He had risked everything. He turned to look at Vraen. "You can stay here, Vraen, and you can die when the Tecran finally believe us when we tell them we cannot give them back their Class 5s, and they blow up every single one of these ships in retribution. Don't let me stop you." He pointed to the door.

Silence flash-froze every single person.

The doors opened, and Pren appeared, with Yari and her three crew in tow.

They stumbled to a halt in the frigid atmosphere.

"I was only asking a question." There was bluster in Vraen's voice.

Cam didn't give it the benefit of a response, he simply turned away, and held out a space survivor to Yari.

She came at him in a rush, pulled him into a hug. "Thank you."

"You're my team. I wasn't going to leave you hanging here in the middle of a battle field." He grinned at her and pressed the box against her chest. "Suit up."

They all did, with Pren ready before everyone else, although she'd been the last to start. Vraen was a sullen presence in the midst of them all, pulling on his suit with bad grace and frequent curses.

"Ready?" he asked them.

Pren nodded. "Good luck, sir."

"We'll come for you as soon as it's safe. You have ten hours, and you all have beacons. Wait a few hours before you activate them, when you're far enough away."

Diot, Yari and Pren acknowledged that, but Vraen stared stonily ahead.

Cam gave Pren the formal Battle Center bow and climbed into the drone. Olan was already inside, strapped in, and Cam lifted off carefully with so many in the launch bay, and slid out through the gel wall.

He looked back, saw Pren had pushed her way out and was waiting, hanging in space, to help pull Diot and then Yari through, then the others one by one.

He would see her promoted when this was over. She had proved herself again and again.

"Where are we going?" Olan asked from below, where he was strapped to the backboard.

"The Class 5 on the left. If you are all right with putting yourself in the hands of a thinking system."

"I'll take a battleship, no matter how dangerous, over free floating, thank you." Olan's voice was dry. "I see you have a Fitalian battleship in your entourage. Are my colleagues in the Horde providing assistance?"

"No." Cam looked down at his upturned face. "Your Fitalian colleagues tried to kill me, shoot a Class 5, and then threatened to destroy Larga Ways. All to cover up that their terra-forming on Huy elevated the grahudi to near advanced sentient status, and the Tecran found out about it."

Olan blinked. "Now this is a story worth hearing. Which idiot in the Horde is responsible, because I can assure you that most Fitali would not approve."

"Ipsos," Cam told him. They were halfway back to Oris and the others now.

"Ipsos." Olan was thoughtful. "What a pity. He's had a good career."

Cam opened his mouth to respond, and then a giant picked them up and flung them, tumbling the explorer end over end.

Cam braced his legs against the control panel as they spun, face pressed up against the screen, and saw Paxe had exploded.

He waited for another turn, saw the Levron on either side of Paxe take damage, waited another turn, saw the hostage vessels blown toward the Grihan line.

How far had the hostages got from the path of the explosion? The suits could withstand extreme temperatures, so as long as they weren't ripped by debris, they would be okay.

Had he forced them out of their ships, only to get them killed five minutes later?

"What is happening? Cam? Cam!" Olan's shouts finally registered.

"The Class 5 on the Tecran side has exploded." They turned again, but slower this time. There was something tumbling lazily near the explorer. Something that looked intact, rather than a piece of debris.

Cam touched the control panel and moved the lens, zooming in. It was a maintenance pod of some sort, the claws and clamps tucked neatly into its sides.

The transparent lid turned his way, and he stared.

Imogen. Limp and bleeding.

He wanted to get out, to somehow reach her, but that wasn't possible in either of their small ships.

He touched the comms. Who cared now if the Tecran could track where he was? "Oris."

There was a long pause. "Captain."

"Why can I see Imogen?" He tried to swallow, and had to clear his throat. "Why can I see Imogen in a maintenance pod?"

"He got her out in time?" Oris's voice was a shout in the tiny explorer.

"She's hurt. Badly." The explorer had stopped spinning, and he couldn't see her anymore. He started moving the lens, trying to find her again.

"I see her, now you've told me. Paxe set the pod to return to me. You'll probably arrive at the same time."

Half an hour, by his estimation.

"Come to us, then."

"Already coming," Oris said.

"What's happening with the Tecran?" Cam had to shuffle aside as Olan pulled himself into the small control area.

"Both Levron are damaged. I don't think either can light-jump. One of the smaller battleships was right behind Paxe and it's gone completely. The other two are still there, but I think have taken damage, too."

The lens caught glimpses of the debris left by Paxe, of the Levron, even the traders and the fast cruiser, but no maintenance pod. Cam slammed his fist into the side of the control. "Where is she, relative to my explorer?"

Oris gave the coordinates, and Olan edged him aside and with steady hands, swung the lens.

The pod came into view, and he zoomed right in.

"Imogen Peters is in there?"

"Yes." Again, his throat closed, tight as if someone had turned a lever.

"What about the Tecran? Is it likely they'll engage despite their damage?" Olan was asking all the questions he should be, but Cam couldn't think of anything but the tiny pod just outside.

"Who is that?" Oris asked.

"Olan. One of my team. He chose to come with me in the explorer, rather than use the space survivors." Cam narrowed his eyes, because a solid wall of black was suddenly behind Imogen.

"Is that you, Oris?"

"It's me."

The maintenance pod was suddenly gone, sucked in to the maintenance bay.

Cam realized Olan had taken over the controls, and was guiding them toward the gel wall of the launch bay.

"The Tecran must be a little nervous to see you moving toward them," Olan commented.

"Even though they're damaged, one of the Levron shot at the *Illium*, and one of the smaller ships shot at the hostages."

Cam tried to come up with the correct response. "Is everyone all right?"

"I shielded the *Illium*, and because Sazo and I thought they would react that way, he was quick enough to get in place to shield the hostages."

The explorer hit the gel wall, slid through.

Cam was out as soon as it touched down. "Where?" he asked.

Oris called the directions to him, and he ran. "What was she doing on Paxe?" It was a question he hadn't even come to yet. "What was she doing?"

"What do you think, Captain?" Oris's voice was soft now. Dangerous.

Cam didn't care.

"She's not a soldier, and you sent her onto a Class 5 full of Tecran?" He didn't hold back his fury.

"On the left," Oris said in response, and Cam saw an open door and the maintenance pod.

The lid was open.

Imogen pushed herself up awkwardly with one hand, and smiled at him.

It was the sweetest smile he'd ever seen.

He carefully slid his arms under her, braced himself and lifted her out, looking for injuries. She kept her right hand curled against her chest and she had struck her head on something. Blood dripped from the cut at her hairline into her light hair.

The surprise of her weight hit him again. And it calmed him. She may look delicate, but she was strong.

"So, you went off to save Paxe?" He tried to keep his voice even. He'd seen a med chamber on his way here, and he started walking toward it.

"Tried to." Her voice came out rougher than he'd ever heard it. "They had dismantled so many of his systems, when I got him free, he was helpless."

"What happened?" Oris asked.

"The one thing they'd reactivated, rather than dismantled, was the self-destruct."

"He blew himself up." Oris said it slowly.

"Just before they caged him again." Imogen's voice was thick with tears.

"You could have died." Cam tightened his grip on her, walking even faster than he had been.

"So could you," she whispered against his chest. "That's what we do for our friends, isn't it?"

Chapter Forty

THE AIR OF LARGA WAYS WAS AS PERFECT as a managed environment could be. Warm, just the slightest hint of a breeze.

The air was perfumed with flowers and as night slowly faded the spectacular sunset, the city was lit with intricate lights on buildings, strung across streets and embedded in the pavings on the square itself.

"It looks as if Inita and his cousin gauged the level of interest correctly," Dav murmured to Cam as they stood on Inita's private balcony above the entrance to Gurtain's Song, looking down at the growing crowd. "The square was the only possible choice for a venue."

"They certainly spared no expense on the stage." Cam had come by earlier and seen the construction team putting the elevated circular stage together, with its filigree dome of light.

"I think Inita persuaded Eazi to pay for it, actually." Hal came up behind them, and they made room for him beside them. "I overheard some of the negotiations, and Inita can be persuasive."

Cam grinned at the thought of the Grihan trader getting around Eazi.

"The meetings are over for today?" Dav asked Hal, and the captain of the *Illium* gave a weary nod.

"I was able to use the excuse of this performance to close things down. It's being broadcast to all four planets, so most of the team wanted to leave to watch it, anyway."

"Don't tell Imogen that." Cam knew it would throw her off her stride. As far as she was concerned, this was a thank you to Inita and Takari. That it had grown into something more, the celebration of Larga Ways being saved not once, but twice, by the strange Earth music-makers, had been bad enough. She was already wary that most of Larga Ways was coming to watch. If she knew the population of four planets were going to see it, too, that might be a deal-breaker.

"I won't." Hal's lips twisted into a wry grin. "Eazi and I are keeping it from Fiona, too."

Dav shook his head. "Rose has no illusions. She's assuming it'll be beamed everywhere. Let's hope she doesn't tell the other two."

"And how far along are the negotiations?" Cam asked, as the

last of the sunset disappeared, and they were surrounded by twinkling lights.

He'd been involved in the United Council talks, Hal had been pulled in to a discussion the Tecran had called, and Dav had the Fitalian camp to sort out.

"The Tecran government is claiming they had no idea what High Command was up to, and they shouldn't be punished for a high-level conspiracy." Hal leaned back against the wall and crossed his arms over his chest.

"They could be telling the truth," Dav said.

Cam shrugged. "They could. My guess is the only way the UC will accept that argument is if they agree to massive changes in oversight and transparency. They won't be able to say they didn't know a second time."

"And the Fitali?" Hal asked, turning to Dav.

"We're letting them save face, so they won't be sanctioned by the UC, and they're very aware of the favor we've done them." Dav shrugged. "We have Imogen's guess that Paxe hid that evidence, and it was destroyed along with him, and that's going to have to be enough for them."

"That works for me." Hal's smile was coldly satisfied. "It's the perfect ending. Because Vice-Admiral Ipsos will always wonder, at the back of his mind, if it isn't still out there, waiting to bury him."

While they'd been speaking, the square had filled to capacity with a mix of Balcoans, Grih and the myriad other races who came to trade on Larga Ways.

Inita and Takari were standing on the stairs leading up to the stage, and suddenly the center of it was illuminated, and Imogen, Rose and Fiona stood shoulder to shoulder.

"Do you know what they're going to sing?" Dav asked softly, and Cam recognized the look on his face. He was sure it was the same as the one on his own.

He shook his head. "Imogen said it might as well be a surprise for me, too, knowing how much I love hearing her sing. She said if she practiced it for me, I'd get bored of it." He knew he sounded incredulous.

"They think like that," Hal agreed. "They actually think like that."

"They do." Dav smiled. "I think Rose understands how we are

a little more. She's been with the Grih the longest, but still, she never sings the same song too often. They seem to have hundreds to choose from."

They went quiet as Inita stepped forward to address the crowd. More than one person on the way station had their suspicions about the Fitalian battleships that had loomed over them the day before, but most were content with the story that Imogen had helped Paxe sacrifice himself bravely for the good of the Grih, bringing down the Tecran incursion and stripping them of their last Class 5.

Paxe's actions had settled the Grih when it came to the other Class 5s, as well. Cam had noted a change in tone when people spoke about them, now.

They were no longer quite so scary.

Inita finished up the formalities, and then bowed deeply to the women on the stage.

There was a moment of silence, then they all started to click their fingers in time. The crowd stirred, and then Imogen started to sing on her own, the sound smooth and controlled, in time with the beat they were creating. The cadence went up and down, and then suddenly Fiona and Rose joined in, the harmony so sublime, Cam gripped the edge of the balcony rail.

They didn't chase each other with their voices, like they'd done before, but they each took different parts, then came together, creating something so complex, he was astonished.

As Imogen sang the last verse on her own, it was as if everyone had been taken on an exciting journey, and were being dropped back at home again, having seen new and wonderful sights.

"Was this like what they sang before?" Dav's voice was low.

"Better," Cam said. "Even better."

There was quiet over the square for a long moment, and then the Grih ululated their approval.

The three bowed, and then were whisked from the stage, something Inita had clearly set up earlier.

He still stood on the stairs, so Cam guessed he'd gotten his Balcoan staff to do it, the Grih were still too enraptured to do more than voice their appreciation.

He stepped in from the balcony as soon as the women were escorted into the building, and made his way down the stairs to the back entrance of the bar.

Dav was right behind him, Hal moved a little slower. Cam looked back at him, and saw he was as taken away as Cam had been when he'd heard the three women sing in Gurtain's Song.

Imogen was waiting for him with Rose and Fiona in the private office at the back.

She grinned at him. "That was an experience. I think they really liked it."

Behind him, Dav choked back a laugh, and Cam pulled her in close and kissed her. "I think they really did," he said.

She relaxed against him. "Good."

"What was it about?" Hal slid an arm around Fiona. He still looked as if he had taken a shockgun hit.

"Just something fun," Imogen said, with one of those infuriatingly humble shrugs.

Rose rested her head on Dav's shoulder and smiled at her. "They can't accept that answer. Believe me." She snuggled in closer. "We sang a song called Royals, and in it, we asked to be your rulers."

Fiona was looking at Hal with concern, but relaxed when he started stroking back her hair, his arm clamped tightly around her.

"I think if you'd asked us that in Grihan," he said, "we would have answered yes."

ABOUT THE AUTHOR

Michelle Diener writes historical fiction, fantasy and science fiction. Having worked in publishing and IT, she's now very happy crafting new worlds and interesting characters and wondering which part of the world she can travel to next.

Michelle was born in London, grew up in South Africa and currently lives in Australia with her husband and two children.

To find out more, you can visit her at www.michellediener.com, where you can read about her books, find her social media links, and sign up to receive notification when she has a new book out.

CPSIA information can be obtained
at www.ICGtesting.com
Printed in the USA
LVOW01s1943150916

504778LV00029B/347/P

9 780992 455965